STEPHANIE
DENNE

SANGUINE PROPHECY

3

BLACKTHORN
SAGA

Published in Canada by Amethyst Corvid Press, Ontario, Canada.

Sanguine Prophecy.
First Edition.
ISBN: 978-1-7387272-7-8
Stephanie Denne.

See more books by Stephanie Denne at https://stephaniedenneauthor.com
Editing by Kelly Schaub

Cover Design by Story Wrappers – storywrappers.com

"The plague of avarice affects us all.
Transcending reason, discriminating against neither age nor species,
it casts the hearts it infects into ruin."
—the Oracle

A Message from the Author

This book contains content that may be unsuitable for certain readers. To learn more about content warnings in the author's work, please visit her website: https://www.stephaniedenneauthor.com/content-warnings

Playlist

Breaking Benjamin – Close to Heaven
Digital Daggers – Bleed for Me
Breaking Benjamin – Without You
Breaking Benjamin – Angels Fall
Project Vela – I'm Sorry
Digital Daggers – Out of the Fire
Sleep Token – Alkaline
Lola Blanc – Angry Too

Instrumentals from YouTube (added exact title so they are searchable):

A Soundtrack for the Anti Hero – Music for Pure Vengeance
Rok Nardin – The Devil
Voces Perdidas – Subheim
Book of Maps
Abestoscape – Arctic
Abestoscape – Thursday
Silent Hill OST – Lisa's Theme
Fairy Lands | FANTASY MUSIC in a Magical Forest | Fantasy Ambience
I don't want to be part of this anymore | dark ambient playlist
you're studying in a haunted library with candles (dark academia playlist
The closer I got, the further I was from you
Tattle Tale – Glass Vase Cello Case
Circles – Ambient Dark Sexy Cinematic Instrumental (NSFW Video)
Invitation – Ambient Dark Sexy Instrumental

Blackthorn Academy Campus

It's easy to lose your way at the mysterious Blackthorn Academy. But with a little luck, and this handy map, I'm sure you'll do just fine… maybe.

1

ELIMINATION

W*itches… Magical bloodlines…*

The human's blood held more secrets than Angelo could have ever predicted.

He pinched the bridge of his nose as he sat in the darkened room. Candlelight flickered across the papers on his desk as he scanned the researcher's reports, his agitation growing with each passing second. How could they have been so foolish as to let a human join Blackthorn Academy? They should have destroyed her immediately upon the information reaching their ears that a Vasirian student saw his Korrena mark on a human, but they hadn't. They allowed the human girl to enroll in Blackthorn and even complete the claiming ritual to seal the pair bond.

Humans have no place in this world.

Angelo sat back in his wingback chair, the leather creaking in the room's silence. His ringed fingers curled tightly around a tumbler; the burn as the amber liquid slid down his throat did nothing to banish the thoughts in his mind.

Somehow, the small group of students who had become a thorn in his side found the human. They ruined not only his plans, but those of his daughter. He rubbed his eyes, taking another sip of his scotch. Clarissa had been beside herself. His daughter's fascination with Lukas Virtanen bordered on obsessive, but he couldn't deny his only girl her heart's desire—even if he would have preferred she walk amongst the elite at Blackthorn Institute in the United Kingdom. The school rivaled Oxford and Cambridge in its prestige. Blackthorn Institute made Blackthorn Academy look like a human technical college. His shoulders shook as a shudder of disgust passed through him. His daughter was better than such lowly places, better than the boy she set her sights on.

The folder at the edge of his desk taunted him with a photo on top featuring Lukas Virtanen sitting with his arm around the human girl. His grip tightened on the crystal in his hand.

Angelo considered eliminating the problem in the beginning. A swift accident, with enough damage to override the Vasirian ability to heal quickly. It would have been so easy to kill two birds with one stone. Had he followed his instinct and removed the Virtanen brat from this world, his daughter would have had to listen to him, and the human would have no reason to be here any longer.

Hindsight was a fickle friend.

With the human girl rescued, Angelo endured the tears, the anger, and the demands of his young child. In the end, Clarissa relented. In a couple of weeks, once the Christmas holiday passed, the Blackthorn Institute would house one additional brilliant mind with a name bearing the lineage of power. Everything turned out as it should.

The same could not be said for Vincent Brandt.

Angelo mildly regretted what befell the boy.

He set the crystal tumbler on his desk and picked up the report, leaning back in his chair, studying the typed summary of Vincent's condition.

Subject appears to be regaining a sense of self. Vitals have stabilized, and the skin has lost its pallor. Bodily functions have returned to normal—urine passage and bowel production are as expected of a twenty-two-year-old Vasirian male.

Involuntary muscle movements have ceased, and the subject appears to respond to academy-supplied blood packets once again.

Providing substitute stimuli to trigger the brain neurotransmitter dopamine is no longer necessary.

Sleep is still a point of concern. Subject frequently talks in his sleep, and wakes screaming. His violent outbursts upon waking have reduced, but we have taken precautions to reduce the number of injuries to both the subject and the guards at night. We hypothesized these fits in the night resulted from a lack of control. When the subject sleeps, he cannot keep the cravings for the esoteric blood at bay, and in the moment of sleep-wake, he is helpless to his mania.

Final Recommendations

It is safe to move subject Vincent Brandt to Cresbel Asylum to serve his sentence with the following precautions:

- *Increased blood consumption until dependency on preternatural blood is eliminated.*
- *Bi-weekly follow-ups with the health team.*
- *24/7 observation — with no contact or access to personnel during sleep hours.*
- *Guards to carry tranquilizers during sleep hours to control mania if necessary.*

Angelo propped his elbow on the armrest and rested his cheek on his palm. The scientists lacked the ability to say if the effects of drinking from the human girl would be permanent. Even with most of the withdrawal symptoms subsiding, thanks to the forced detox and supplemental stimulants they'd provided, the boy still craved.

Vincent had barely reached a point where he functioned enough to stand trial. Then, he went and did something so asinine as to lay claim to the human—declaring his love.

Angelo's nose wrinkled.

After listening to the recorded deposition made by the human about everything that transpired in the diplomat's wing, he was not surprised Vincent reached a point of truly believing the human belonged to him.

A knock against the wood of Angelo's office door echoed in the room.

"Enter."

Tobias moved into the room with the grace of a cat. Pressed slacks of the darkest black and a pair of polished Mocassino leather loafers with a slight heel made his long legs appear longer—his height more imposing. A wine-red button-down shirt hugged his lean body. The man had commissioned Versace to custom make the garment. The quality was to be expected of a man with such refined tastes—tastes that, while darker and more modern, rivaled his own need for the finer things.

Beneath his robes during the council meetings, and when they attended Blackthorn functions and events ordained by the Blackthorn Clan, Tobias looked no different from the rest of the Order. Only younger, with his artfully styled hair designed to look as if he'd just rolled out of bed, and features that made him appear no older than the students walking the academy grounds daily, despite being forty-seven. His refined style stayed tucked away beneath his robes. Unlike

Angelo, who wore rings with expensive gemstones, and whose robe differed from the rest of the council—as it should be; he was the leader, after all.

Tobias sat across from Angelo's desk, leaning back in the small, black leather chair, crossing his ankle over his thigh. "News?" Tobias looked like a wraith with his alabaster skin and pale blond hair glowing against the candlelight. His ethereal beauty even made Angelo pause to appreciate it, if only briefly.

Angelo passed the report he finished reading to Tobias and moved to the cabinet housing several expensive bottles of alcohol. "Drink?"

"You know the only liquid pleasure I partake in is of the red variety and much thicker."

Tobias never told him why, but he was against drinking alcohol. It still didn't stop Angelo from offering—it was what any reasonable host should do. It wasn't his fault Tobias lacked the cultured palette to appreciate the top shelf value of his liquor collection.

Tobias placed the paper back on Angelo's desk. "Didn't they transfer Vincent last night to Cresbel?"

Angelo poured another tumbler of scotch and strode back to his seat. "After King Blackthorn sent down the order, yes." He sat back in his wingback chair. "This report is a couple of days old."

"Do you think he'll recover?"

"As much as one can after feeding on a human with magical blood," Angelo said, expression flat as he took a sip from the crystal tumbler.

"Which means you have no clue."

"It's not like we have a baseline to draw conclusions from, Tobias. I can only speculate on the outcome as much as you. In the meantime, he'll remain locked away from the population where he will do the least harm."

Tobias breathed heavily out of his nose. "You honestly had nothing to do with this?"

Tobias Nilsson, ever the observant one. Too observant.

"If I did?"

Angelo didn't believe Tobias would say anything to the other Order members or even report him to King Blackthorn. No, Tobias was smart. It wasn't a matter of loyalty, but a matter of knowledge. If the Blackthorn Clan replaced Angelo with one of the other members of the Order—or worse yet, an entirely new member—Tobias would no longer be the right-hand man. He would lose the leniency that came with being closely connected to Angelo. Tobias would lose his meal ticket.

They stared at one another in silence, the candlelight playing on Tobias's stoic expression. He gave nothing away as he assessed Angelo, who lifted his brow in challenge.

"What of the human?"

Good boy. Smart boy.

Angelo spun the ring on his index finger, staring at the rubies inlaid in the gold band that matched the ruby cufflinks on his white Prada dress shirt. "As Maxwell so eloquently suggested, we need to harness the human's magic. Control it until we can understand it."

"Nathaniel thinks we should just kill the girl."

"Blaire Wilcox is a priceless commodity, a link to a lost time. I, for one, am intrigued."

"Of course you are."

Angelo didn't know if the Oracle spoke the truth when she revealed her knowledge of a history where humans and Vasirian connected in a way he only knew possible between two Vasirian. Yes, Vasirian and humans could lie with one another—partake in each other's physical pleasure—but bond as a Korrena pair? The idea seemed absurd.

Not more absurd than humans with magical blood.

He exhaled heavily and closed his eyes, resting his head against the soft leather of his chair.

"If she's a witch—"

"She's not," Angelo bit out between clenched teeth.

"*If* she has magical blood, and comes from a line of witches, do you think she poses a danger to the students of Blackthorn Academy?"

"As long as they don't drink her blood, I don't think so. She's been part of the academy for nine months. Aside from Vincent Brandt succumbing to whatever sickness overtook his mind—which resulted from his consumption of her blood—no one has reported anything out of the ordinary."

"And what of her Korrena, Lukas Virtanen?"

"Beyond the effects of the actual Korrena bond, consuming her blood hasn't changed him. I am loath to agree with Professor Velastra in saying his dramatics during the trial—while entertaining to watch—were a result of his separation from his Korrena pair."

Tobias rested his elbow on the arm of the chair and pinched his lower lip between his thumb and index finger in contemplation. "Detaining him was just for show," he finally said after a long silence stretched between them.

Angelo hated explaining himself, but keeping Tobias's natural need for information satiated provided a solid backing when parts began shifting out of his control.

"No." Angelo flopped a hand from left to right. "Yes. A bit of both." He smirked. "Our rules are clear, and we must abide by them. Taking Lukas in for his actions against Vincent Brandt was simply protocol. Had we not done that, it would set a precedent for future Korrena pairs. If they believe having the bond overrides Blackthorn rules and regulations, then we might have anarchy."

"I doubt it would be quite so dramatic."

Angelo waved a hand.

"No matter. It was a necessary action that served two purposes."

Tobias arched a brow, tilting his head.

"First, as I stated, it reinforces that despite the Korrena pair bond, we are still in charge. Second, I couldn't pass up the opportunity to cash in on ready bait."

"You're going to bargain with the human for him."

It wasn't a question.

"Don't let anyone ever tell you you're not a smart man, Tobias."

The side of Tobias's mouth tipped up, and he shook his head. "You think the girl will come for him?"

"I'm counting on it. Did you not see the way she responded to his removal after she freely gave her blood to him in front of all of us to tame the most primal part of himself? He went completely feral." He chuckled.

"She is quite remarkable."

Angelo scoffed. "For a human."

He wouldn't openly admit it, but during Vincent's trial, when the human broke away from her friends to throw herself into the heat of a Vasirian battle with no regard for her own safety, she impressed him.

Lost to his need for vengeance against the man who wronged his Korrena, Lukas snapped, unleashing the brutal fury of one half a pair bond. That, in itself, was a spectacle with which Angelo couldn't bring himself to intervene.

"You have to admit the fight leading up to that moment was rather entertaining for the other men. I'm still unsure if Vincent being completely lucid would have helped or hindered the entertainment value for them. I personally don't see the draw of watching two grown men act like animals."

Not only was it entertaining, but Angelo knew firsthand the overpowering need to avenge his Korrena.

When petty jealousy took his sweet Madeline from him weeks after birthing Clarissa, he'd taken his own brand of justice out on the woman who thought she held the right to destroy that which he loved the most outside of his daughter. The Vasirian woman—whom he would not honor by recalling her name—had been jealous of Madeline's pregnancy. Because of her inability to bear an heir, the woman's pair bond suffered for a long time. Seeing Madeline pregnant with Clarissa drove her to the edge. He could only thank the gods she waited until after the birth. Had he lost both of them, he probably wouldn't be sitting in this chair today.

Angelo took a generous drink of his scotch, emptying his glass. He stood and stalked across the room to refill his glass with something stronger.

"So, what's the plan?" Tobias asked, likely sensing the change in the atmosphere with Angelo's darkening mood. Tobias was always good at reading him, another reason to keep the man close.

Taking a pull from his Glenlivet Winchester, closing his eyes, he savored the spike of whiskey on his tongue. "You sure you don't want a taste? Only one hundred bottles ever made." He lifted the transparent bottle containing a deep amber-hued liquid. He expected Tobias would refuse, but not offering such a rare taste of luxury would be criminal.

Tobias rolled his eyes, not entertaining Angelo with a response.

"Suit yourself." He set the bottle on the bar before striding across the dark hardwood floor to relax back into his plush chair. "As I said, I intend to use Lukas as bait to tempt our little human into trading herself for his freedom. Aside from a simple suspension, which wouldn't remove him from the academy, considering he lives here, there isn't much we can do for punishment. His 'crimes' of fighting a student—albeit, he did nearly kill him—don't warrant something as extreme as banishment to Cresbel Asylum. Perhaps expulsion, but the trial to push for it would be more trouble than it's worth."

Dealing with a parent's cries, bargains, and threats over their adult children always grated on Angelo's nerves. With substantial sums of money and family legacies tied into the populace of Blackthorn Academy from such a young age, the parents of the university-level students had a hard time letting go.

Tobias shifted in his chair, switching to his alternate leg, crossing his ankle over his knee, waiting for Angelo to continue.

"When she's within our grasp, we'll be able to conduct as many experiments as we'd like without repercussion. Before, we needed to be careful in taking her blood, sending low-level goons to retrieve the skin sample, nearly killing the poor girl when our lab rats clearly could have done a better job. If she's with us willingly, then we can take samples and experiment in a controlled environment."

"What does it matter to you?"

"Well, if we have another mishap like what occurred over the summer, we may lose our opportunity to study the girl. Dead women tell no tales." When Tobias shook his head slowly, Angelo added, "I'd like to see what the extent of this magic is. If we can use it, manipulate it to our disposal, it could prove useful in enforcing order amongst the Vasirian in the Americas."

"I didn't believe we had a problem. There haven't been reports of rogue Vasirian in years."

"No, but wouldn't you like to be ready should the need arise?" Angelo's brow arched as he lifted his glass to his lips, extending his index finger to point at Tobias before taking a drink.

"Seems extreme. Reminds me of the doomsday prepping humans

do."

Angelo chuckled.

Tobias wasn't wrong. It seemed excessive to harness a magic they didn't understand simply to tighten their dominance over a group they already held a firm grip on, but seizing the magic merely scratched the tip of the iceberg. If they could unlock the mysteries of the magic running through the human's veins, then perhaps they could exploit it for their own use. The idea of wielding such power made his skin tingle with anticipation.

"And if she doesn't come to trade herself?"

"Oh, she will. She doesn't have a choice."

Shaking his head, Tobias didn't argue with Angelo's confident reply. It wouldn't have mattered. Once he decided on something, little swayed him to alternative paths.

"There's always the chance nothing comes of the experiments. What then?"

"I'm sure if such a disappointing outcome occurs, she would prove an excellent sacrifice."

Tobias's brows pinched together in confusion. "Pardon?"

Angelo spent time perusing the archives after they discovered Vincent performed such a dark ritual on the human and found quite a collection of long forgotten rituals. One particular ritual stood out to him, one not used in millennia. A primitive act: sacrificing a human to the gods to extend both life and prosperity. If they couldn't harness Blaire Wilcox's magic, then she could at least be useful for something.

"Sacrifice," he repeated. "For our longevity. The texts I've read held a piece of information you might find interesting."

Tobias inclined his head forward as if to say, "Go on."

"A deity of magic. Apparently, Vasirian long before our time believed not only in the gods, but in specific gods. None of interest today, save for one of magic. Magic, Tobias. It truly exists."

"I thought we established that. Besides, fairy tales of a god of magic do not make it true. Have you ever read Greek or Norse mythology? Do you think those gods and goddesses exist?"

Angelo rubbed his temples with his hand. Whenever they got into a discussion about the gods, a headache lingered around the corner. Tobias didn't believe in a multitude of gods or even a singular god. What Tobias did believe in Angelo didn't know, nor did he honestly care.

"This isn't about whether the god exists. It's about knowing magic was part of our world at one point. That it existed to such a point there was a belief in an entire deity around such a thing. It is something more substantial than the words of an old woman whose memories are fleeting, who rambles about an alleged Celestial Conclave and the simple experiments on a human girl. This dates back long before either ever existed."

Tobias sat back and rubbed a hand over his mouth. "Yet, you think performing a sacrificial ritual like a cult of mad men is appropriate to this… non-existent god?"

Angelo ground his teeth, tossing back another swallow of alcohol. "If there isn't any further use for the girl, there is no harm in at least humoring the old ways. Who can say if the god isn't real? Does it matter? Should they exist, we reap the benefits." He ran his tongue over the front of his teeth, setting his empty tumbler on his desk.

Tobias sighed. "May as well put the abandoned temple to use."

"That's the spirit."

2

SACRIFICE

Flickering candles in ornate sconces barely lit the cavernous, vaulted hallways of the administration building leading to the winding stairwell in the main tower as Blaire and Professor Velastra made their way to where they last saw Lukas a few days ago during Vincent's trial.

The main floors of the administration building matched the gothic vibe of the staff building and central interior of the main building. Dated—not in a retro, grandmotherly sort of way, but in a Dracula's castle sort of way. The space was beautiful, if not downright eerie.

Blackthorn Academy's exterior matched the outside world with its modern university layout, but still held true to the refined Renaissance and Gothic architecture this region of Georgia was known for, with arched windows and overlaid tracery. They had restored many of the centuries-old academy buildings, both inside and out, but Blaire could easily imagine what the place looked like a hundred years ago. Especially on the interior of the administration and staff buildings, which didn't have the same updated feel as the rest of the school. The upper floors of the main building and the dorms were the only spaces that felt completely brought into the current times, designed with the sleek and modern furnishings university students required and wanted.

Stained glass in shades of red and black covered the high-standing walls to allow as much natural lighting into the space as possible. If it were daytime, the windows would bathe the entire space in crimson, casting the area in the same blood-soaked appearance as the main building's bottom floor did from its beautiful windowpanes. She didn't know what unnerved her more: the bright sunlight amplifying the red to the point of making the space look like a horror show, or the moonlight filtering through the panes in dappled, muted red patches on the marble floor, leaving dark shadows where the light didn't touch. Nothing lurked in the shadows, but the hair on her arms still stood when her eyes shifted to the darkened alcoves the moonlight failed to reach.

Vaulted ceilings stretched high overhead, amplifying the echo of their footfalls on the polished marble floors they walked across.

"Like with Vincent's trial, try not to speak unless spoken to. The less ammunition you give them, the better the likely outcome will be," Professor Velastra said quietly, pulling Blaire's attention away from the detailed oil paintings that lined the hallway.

Blaire turned her head to the professor. "What do you think is going to happen in there? I'm not on trial, am I?"

"No."

Blaire frowned when the professor didn't elaborate or answer the first question. They walked in silence for what seemed like ages before stepping into the narrow winding stairs up to the lofty tower of the administration building.

The professor finally broke the tense silence. "I have considered many possibilities of what we might face once inside, but I could not settle on one simple theory. The one thing I am positive about is this has to do with Lukas."

Blaire stopped short in the stairwell and closed her eyes as memories assaulted her of Blackthorn Security dragging Lukas away from Vincent's trial after Lukas nearly killed him. Their last interaction was strained with Lukas's feral reaction, the horror of the murderous rage in his eyes reflecting Tennyson's "Nature, red in tooth and claw." Even if he resisted the urge to turn her, he had done the very thing she feared he would do to her. The thing that kept her from the claiming ritual for so long. He crossed a line that fractured the trust she felt with him, yet when he attacked the man responsible for turning her life upside-down for two straight months, the cracks had filled again. She needed time to explore that with him and find perspective. But he was immediately whisked away and locked in a holding cell. They had barely reconnected since Clarissa and Vincent tried to tear them apart, and now this.

How were they supposed to grow together and get past their issues if they continued to be separated?

Professor Velastra looked over her shoulder to where Blaire stopped, and her face softened at whatever look she found on Blaire's face. "I'll do everything in my power to not allow them to harm you," she said lightly, as if coaxing a small child to accept getting a shot at the doctor's office. It was going to be uncomfortable, but maybe not hurt as much as she feared.

Despite the assurance Blaire gave when Riley insisted on coming with them, Blaire now wished the professor allowed her best friend to come along. The moral support alone would make the process bearable.

Blaire resumed moving until she stood on the stairs next to the professor. Giving a sharp nod, the professor turned and continued up the stairs, her stilettos tapping the marble with each delicate step.

Pausing before the large doors that featured stunning relief artwork of a murder of crows and thorn branches that caught her attention the last time she stood in this spot, she looked at the professor, who rested her hand on the door handle. Blaire licked her lips nervously.

When had she started sweating?

"Ready?"

Blaire huffed a harsh breath that was part strangled laugh. "No." She didn't think she would ever be ready for this. She tugged down the sleeves of her sweater to ensure all the bruises from her time with Vincent weren't on display. The Order knew about the marks, but she still didn't like the reminder out in the open.

"I won't leave your side." The professor pushed the doors open, the sound from the action echoing into the large room beyond them.

The council room's atmosphere differed from the last time Blaire was there.

Moonlight spilled from the large window overlooking Blackthorn Academy's campus, highlighting the central chamber, and leaving the seven throne-like seats in shadow. The moon barely breached the stained glass behind them, and the contrast in lighting made the seven men sitting in those seats appear more intimidating. Only the soft glow of the tiered candles on the tall, ornate candelabras positioned along the floor reached their faces. Their silent appraisal as Blaire moved to the podium in the center of the room to stand next to the professor did nothing to take away from the aura of intimidation. The strange woman who kept drawing Blaire's eye during Vincent's trial was absent this evening.

Angelo's sharp eyes narrowed, and his lips tilted at the corners slightly, as if amused.

"So good of you to join us," a man with dark blond hair to the left of Angelo drawled, disdain dripping in his voice. "I was thinking we hadn't sent an invitation for how long it took you to arrive."

"Now, now, Maxwell," Angelo chastised. "I am sure Miss Wilcox didn't deliberately delay our meeting. After all, I'm sure she doesn't wish to keep her Korrena waiting." His gaze cut from Maxwell to Blaire. "No?" Subtle amusement laced his Italian accent, giving the question a sing-song quality.

When Blaire didn't respond immediately, a deep voice boomed, startling her. "Answer, human!"

She couldn't hide the way her body reacted. Her shoulders jerked in a flinch, head dropping quickly. "No," she answered Angelo in a shaky voice.

Without her friends with her, she felt out of sorts. The way the imposing figures on the dais watched her, as if she were something to eat, made her skin crawl with anxiety. Without Aiden and Riley by her side as a buffer, the confidence she felt when confronting the Order at Vincent's trial vanished into the air like steam. Then, she'd only feared the man who held her captive. Now, with seven powerful Vasirian staring her down, she feared everything.

Angelo sighed and tilted his head to the side. "Mm, I didn't think so. Though, Nathaniel… I think frightening our dear human when we are merely here to help her isn't necessary."

Professor Velastra cleared her throat. "If you wish to help Miss Wilcox, perhaps we can address the reason we're here?" She'd had enough of the intimidation game the men were playing with Blaire.

A low chuckle drew Blaire's eyes to the man with alabaster skin to Angelo's right. When he winked at Blaire, her eyes widened and she dropped her head, which made the man release a heartier laugh.

"Well, yes, I suppose we should proceed with the reason we are here." Angelo waved a hand adorned with golden rings decorated in gemstones that caught the candlelight. "Tobias, how is Mr. Virtanen faring in our accommodations?"

Blaire's head snapped up at the mention of Lukas's surname.

The man with alabaster skin who sat with his elbow propped on the armrest stroked his chin before speaking in a low, smooth voice. "He's angry. Refuses to eat. His 'accommodations'"—he chuckled—"are still a mess. The last time security tried to enter and straighten up from where he had a fit the first time, he lashed out at them and required sedation."

"Sedation?" Professor Velastra's voice held an edge of alarm that made Blaire uneasy.

Tobias sat up straight in his chair and nodded. "Lukas Virtanen isn't happy with being locked away from his Korrena. When security first placed him in confinement, he took out his rage on his surroundings, but not the staff. I assume he is smart enough to know it wouldn't help his case."

"Obviously the boy is not smart enough. The next time they came to his cell, he struck a guard," a man toward the end of the dais said in a thick Russian accent.

Tobias ignored him, continuing, staring directly at Blaire. "He didn't sleep for a long time. Angelo had to make him drink a blood packet to avoid *sanguis manie* setting in."

Blaire's brows scrunched, and she spoke before thinking better of it. "*Sanguis manie?*"

"Blood mania," Professor Velastra said quietly.

"Yes. If our kind go too long without… nourishment, we succumb to a type of mania. We get extremely ill—fever, aches, tremors—nothing pleasant to speak of. We eventually lose control of ourselves, reverting to nothing more than the monsters found in human media. I've always suspected that is the true root of where the fear of vampires came from. Perhaps a human witnessed something they shouldn't have centuries ago, and the rest is history? You know how urban legends go. How the humans came up with the term 'vampire' is beyond me. The origins of the myth have been speculated for many years."

"Tobias. The point," Maxwell snapped.

Tobias slid his aquamarine gaze to Maxwell and lowered his brows. Clearly, the interruption wasn't welcome.

"The point is that your Korrena," he said, looking back to Blaire with a relaxed expression again, "isn't happy. He eventually gave in to sleep, and that is when Blackthorn Security tried to tidy things. They underestimated how light of a sleeper he was, and in startling him awake, let's just say he… lost control."

Lukas isn't a light sleeper.

Blaire held her retort; it wouldn't be welcome or even necessary to the conversation. But the phrase hit her all wrong. It wasn't what she knew Lukas to be.

Lukas woke quickly when she had nightmares or was in danger, but before they bonded, when he slept most of the day, he barely stirred no matter what was going on in the room—when she was nearby. Except once, when Riley startled him awake. Maybe he could sense danger? Or didn't fall into a deep sleep while locked away? Maybe his change in sleep habits came down to the comfort of being near each other. That he couldn't even get true rest right now upset her.

"He's lucky he's not being expelled," another man said from the far left, pulling her attention away from her unsettled thoughts.

"You can't fault him for acting on reflexive instinct," Tobias reasoned, and Angelo shook his head slowly in agreement. "I'm sure whatever provoked him to punch the other guard was merely a lapse in judgment. No one was seriously injured. He received a tranq dart to the neck and slept like a baby."

Blaire's stomach clenched. They were treating Lukas like a wild animal. It was her fault Lukas sat locked away, trapped in this situation. If he hadn't protected her, if she had been stronger—one of them—Vincent wouldn't have been able to get her. Lukas would never have been so on edge to attack him. She wouldn't be standing in front of the Order now.

"As you can see, Miss Wilcox, your Korrena isn't faring well, being locked away and all," Angelo said with what struck her as mock sympathy. The way his eyes twinkled with the same spark of amusement from before gave away his true feelings.

Professor Velastra straightened her shoulders and placed her petite hands on the podium. "Taking into consideration maintaining the well-being of our students, how do you propose we proceed?" The question made it clear she was not amicable to Lukas being locked away if he suffered the way they implied. Another way to play their game of power and control: give them the keys to steer, but make it clear the current way didn't work.

Angelo sat back in his seat. "What the boy did violated our rules, Professor Velastra."

"I hardly feel the punishment fits the crime."

"Oh, but there hasn't been punishment yet," Angelo said matter-of-factly.

"Locking him away is punishment enough."

Tobias bit on the pad of his thumb. He returned to his relaxed position with his elbow on the armrest of his chair. "How are we to be certain he won't attack another student?"

"Lukas only attacked Vincent Brandt because of the threat to his Korrena." She cut a look at Angelo. "You, of all people, should understand what a threat like that can make you do."

Blaire didn't understand what the professor meant, but the way Angelo stiffened in his seat meant she crossed a line.

"Silence!" Angelo stood and pointed at the professor. "You speak too familiarly, Soomin. Do not speak of things you do not understand." He sat back down with a flourish of his robe.

Professor Velastra lowered her head in acquiescence. "My sincerest apologies, Angelo. I spoke out of turn."

Angelo snorted a harsh breath.

A cold baritone voice spoke from the other side of Maxwell. "The human's blood clearly drove Mr. Brandt to a madness none of us can comprehend." The bald man with skin the color of milk chocolate tapped his gloved fingers impatiently on the armrest of his chair. "I think she poses the greatest risk. Not some hormonal young man."

Blaire stepped back reflexively at the way his piercing eyes focused on her, his brown irises briefly flashing with a golden glow. Her heart hammered in her chest.

"Caspar is right," Nathaniel said, the deep bass of his voice snaring her attention. "The human presents a threat to the student body."

Angelo stroked his chin thoughtfully, eyes sparking with something Blaire couldn't place. He seemed to relish in his colleagues' distrust of her. When he finally licked his lips and a menacing grin crossed his face, the time for decision-making was at hand.

"Of course, we cannot risk our students with such a temptation." Angelo glanced at Maxwell, who rolled his eyes. "So, what are we to do in such a situation?"

The men kept their faces mostly unreadable. There was more to this meeting than Blaire's blood being a temptation to one lone student. She didn't believe others would react the same way; and even if they did, she wouldn't be offering her blood freely to them, so it was a moot point. No, something about the silent communication passing between the men on the platform screamed they knew more than they were conveying to her and Professor Velastra.

"You already know my opinion," Nathaniel snapped impatiently.

"We're not killing the poor girl," Tobias said with a sigh. He gave Blaire the same sympathetic look he'd given her back at Vincent's trial. She didn't know what to make of it.

Nathaniel tightened a fist on the armrest. "You are too soft. Too young. I still do not understand why the Blackthorn Clan allowed you to join council."

Tobias sucked his teeth, and Angelo raised a hand.

"Now isn't the time to discuss such matters." He turned his attention back to Blaire, who stood ramrod straight, her hands fisting the fabric of her clothing. "To ease your mind, no one is going to kill you. What good would it do us in understanding your… condition if we were to kill you? I, for one, am quite curious to understand what about your blood appealed in such a way it altered Vincent Brandt's mind. And how you are a Korrena to one of our kind—when it is unheard of? Oh, it would be a shame to destroy such an oddity."

Blaire didn't know how to react. On one hand, she was relieved her summons would not result in her death, and Angelo's words gave reassurance the Order wasn't out to kill her—at least, not all of them. Her gaze shifted to Nathaniel briefly. He still eyed her like dirt on his shoe. But in not killing her, how far would Angelo's curiosity take him? His words made her feel like she belonged in a freak show, or on display at Ripley's Believe It or Not! over at Myrtle Beach.

Maxwell shifted in his seat and rolled a hand at Angelo to get on with it. Angelo glared at him. Apparently, he didn't like being pushed. It made sense. The man seemed to enjoy listening to the sound of his own voice.

"Lukas Virtanen is facing expulsion, Miss Wilcox. With his expulsion comes no need for your presence on Blackthorn Academy grounds, and I'm sure you understand you cannot walk freely in this world with the knowledge of the Vasirian."

Blaire's body tensed, and Professor Velastra moved closer to her. She could not miss the unspoken threat behind his words. If Lukas wasn't at the academy, not only was her contract useless, they would end her along with it.

"Miss Wilcox would not reveal our secret," Professor Velastra said with certainty.

"We cannot know that," Nathaniel said. "You would risk our kind for the sake of a human girl?"

A tick at the corner of the professor's mouth betrayed the emotion she must have been struggling to suppress.

Angelo frowned and tapped his lips. "I'm sure Soomin is merely looking out for her students—*all* of her students—as is her job, yes? I'm sure it is not a matter of loyalty or betrayal of our kin."

Professor Velastra gave a tight nod but said nothing.

The way Angelo dragged things out, dancing around the point, made Blaire nervous. If they didn't intend to kill her, then what else could they do if they expelled Lukas?

"I'd like to propose an alternative to Mr. Virtanen's expulsion and possible banishment to Cresbel Asylum. A way to put your mind at ease." A smile graced Angelo's face that didn't meet his eyes as he looked at Blaire. "A trade, if you will."

"What trade are you proposing? I thought only expulsion was on the table."

Angelo's eyes slid to Professor Velastra. "Nothing that you or I wouldn't have done for our own Korrena," he said flatly, returning his attention to Blaire, effectively dismissing further discussion with the professor. "While it would be a stretch, an argument could exist for Mr. Virtanen's exile to the asylum based on his volatile behavior. He did attack Blackthorn Security, after all. You want to set Lukas free, don't you, Miss Wilcox?"

Blaire lifted her chin. "Yes. I'll do anything." She was grateful her voice didn't crack with the words.

"Excellent." Angelo sat back, clapping his hands together, a wide grin spreading over his face.

"You said he couldn't be faulted for his actions against the security team."

"Tobias said that. The Blackthorn Clan would likely have a different stance on the matter," Maxwell interjected with a sharp glare at Professor Velastra.

Angelo exhaled a quick breath from his nose as if exasperated. "I—*we*"—he motioned to the other six men on the platform—"are in the position to allow Mr. Virtanen to return to his studies without informing the Blackthorn Clan. In exchange, we ask that you humor us with a bit of testing."

"Testing?"

"Yes, Miss Wilcox. I would be most pleased if you would allow us to run a few tests on your blood to determine what possibly went wrong with one of our students. You see, while we do not condone the harm of a human, we still feel for the mental loss that befell one of our kin. Preventing a recurrence would go a long way in easing our minds. Wouldn't you like to help with that? Wouldn't you like to keep other students safe?"

His premise was already false. They'd harmed a human plenty since she arrived at Blackthorn Academy. She looked down at the scar on her arm from the stitches she received. While she didn't intend to let another student drink from her outside of Lukas, she didn't want an accident to happen that would harm others, either. There was no way this wasn't a trap, but to free Lukas, she'd have to walk right into it.

"I think you must also be curious about your own connection to our kind. After all, it isn't exactly an everyday occurrence a human and a Vasirian are pair-bonded. Won't you help us discover these secrets?"

Blaire glanced at the professor, who stood tense at her side, before meeting Angelo's eyes. "What would I need to do?"

Angelo waved a hand. "Oh, it isn't much of a hardship. We would ask that you stay in our facilities for the duration of testing, and once completed, you would return to your studies like before."

It sounded too good to be true. There had to be a catch. Something more they planned to do. The alarm bells ringing in her head told her to walk away, but she couldn't abandon Lukas. She wouldn't.

"How long would I have to stay?"

A growl sounded from the end of the platform, and the man with a Russian accent snapped at her. "You ask many questions, human. Be grateful you live."

Angelo huffed loudly. "Ignore him. I do."

Another growl came from the Russian man.

"You are well within your right to ask questions, Miss Wilcox," Angelo said. "While I would like to give you a straightforward answer to this question, I cannot. Research is not our specialty, so we cannot accurately predict how long our team would need to study the samples you provide."

Professor Velastra, regaining her resolve, stepped to the podium. "Is it necessary for her to be physically in your presence for the entire duration? Can she not return to her dorm and classes, only to show up to provide you with blood samples? I fail to see the benefit of twenty-four-seven observation."

Angelo's head tilted, and he pinched the bridge of his nose.

Tobias glanced at him then spoke up. "I believe having her available should the need arise would go further in helping us come to a speedy conclusion than setting appointments. If she was at hand, then if they run out of samples, there wouldn't be a lull in testing time. Professionals would handle her in this situation."

As opposed to the times you sent your goons to butcher me…

Blaire felt like a science experiment. But she couldn't deny her own curiosity about why the strange connection existed between Lukas and her. Why her blood drove Vincent to such devastating lengths. She didn't particularly like the idea of being cloistered someplace while they experimented on her blood, but at least everyone would know where she was. Right?

"Um. Will I still be able to see Lukas? Where will I be?"

"Sadly, no." Angelo tried to look contrite, but didn't hit the mark. "To keep a controlled environment, we need you to be away from the rest of the student body, so you would not be able to see your Korrena pair until we finish. That said, we are happy to let you see him before this begins. A pair should not stay apart for long, we understand. You endured a long time apart prior to this, and we wish not to bring undue stress to your bond."

He didn't answer where she would be, but arguing with the men in power seemed like a bad idea in this case.

"What is your answer, human?" Maxwell sat up straighter in his chair, turning toward Angelo. "I have things to do, and all this discussion is unnecessary when we can just make her." He waved a hand at Blaire. "She's a student. A threat to us. It's enough reason to bring her in."

"Now, Maxwell, while you are correct,"—he cut his eyes in Blaire's direction—"I believe we will get better results if we have her cooperation."

The men looked as impatient as Blaire felt with the song and dance Angelo led them in. It seemed he sensed he was losing the earlier flow of things as his gaze shifted over the dais.

"I think we've said all that needs to be said," Angelo finally conceded. "Your decision, Miss Wilcox?"

Taking a deep breath in through her nose and releasing it slowly from her mouth, Blaire met Angelo's scheming gaze and lifted her chin. He laid a trap before her, and maybe he knew she was aware of it, but the thing they both understood was Blaire would walk freely into that trap for her Korrena.

"I'll cooperate."

3

Insecurity

When the door opened, Blaire looked up from the bed where she waited in the safe room in the staff building Lukas and the others had taken her to after her rescue from Vincent.

The Order agreed to allow Lukas and Blaire one night together before they began whatever sampling and experimentation they deemed necessary.

She didn't like the idea of becoming a pincushion, but the alternatives painted a grimmer picture in her mind.

Lukas expelled, or worse, sent to Cresbel Asylum simply because security caught him unaware, and he reacted on instinct. If they allowed him to return to his studies, and she did not agree to play ball, the Order would send their underlings to take her blood without her consent. At least in this scenario, she held some level of control. She chose this to free Lukas. No one else decided for her.

Sea-glass eyes met hers from across the room as Lukas stood in the doorway, two members of Blackthorn Security at his back.

"*Blaire.*" Relief rang clear in his voice.

Before she could even stand from the bed, Lukas crossed the room and pulled her up into his arms in a tight embrace, burying his face in the crook of her neck and inhaling deeply.

The door to the room closed, and Blaire looked over his shoulder to see they were now alone. Lukas pulled back only a fraction, holding onto her upper arms as he peered into her eyes. Even without their empathic bond, his emotions were clear on his face. His guilt for what happened when they tried to restore their Korrena mark sat heavily between them, etched into his features stronger than before.

"I'm sorry," he said, his voice barely above a whisper.

"For what?"

"For everything." He let go of her arms and ran a hand across his jaw to the side of his neck, dropping his head forward. "I don't regret attacking Vincent, but the consequences…" His eyes met hers. "Seeing your face as they led me from that room was one of the hardest things I've ever had to see. Hearing you cry for me…" His hand went into his hair on reflex. "Shit, Blaire. I almost lost you again. They could have sent me to Cresbel for what I did to Vincent."

Blaire reached up and untangled his hand from his hair. His nerves were on edge.

He squeezed her hand and rested his forehead against hers. "I don't know what happened, but I'm so glad it's over. I'm ready to go back to our room and keep you there for the next week." He offered a half smile.

Did he not know? Had they not told him anything?

Blaire stepped back, looking up at the dark circles under his eyes. She sighed and prepared for the argument that would follow her next words. Already her stomach muscles cramped with nerves.

If he took this badly, it would only further push a rift between them; they might never get their bond back. She *needed* the bond back. She hadn't realized how much she needed that connection with him until they tried to bring it back once before and everything fell apart. She was certain they had more than a biological bond tying them to one another, but it still didn't stop the self-doubt from creeping in. Especially when silence echoed back at her through their broken empathic connection.

"It's not over," she finally managed to say through the nerves bubbling up inside.

"What do you mean?"

She sighed heavily. "Lukas, the only way they would allow you to return to classes was if I agreed to…" She turned her head and stared at the bedspread to her right.

"Agreed to what? What did you do?"

His rising anxiety finally touched her directly, though it was faint with their wavering connection, and her stomach clenched. When she didn't speak right away, his fingers curled around her arm gently, and he tilted his head to see her face, his eyes searching.

"I agreed to let them test my blood."

His lips parted, but no words came.

"It was the only way they would let you go. It was either that or expulsion—"

"I don't care about being expelled!" He turned and paced across the room, putting his hands on the dresser, dropping his head forward between his shoulders. He lowered his voice, speaking in a measured tone as he fought against the anger rising in him. "I don't care about that. I care about *you*."

"It wasn't just expulsion. Because of what happened between you and the security team, the Order said they could exile you to Cresbel

Asylum."

He turned to face her, and his eyebrows pulled together. "What?"

She lowered herself onto the edge of the bed and knotted her hands in her lap. "The Order said Blackthorn Security took you by surprise while you were sleeping. It's weak, but it's enough of an excuse to banish you."

"That's bullshit." His hand sliced through the air.

Blaire rolled her lips in between her teeth, unable to say anything. Nothing she could say would change the reality of the situation. While she didn't trust Angelo or the other members of the Order, being a willing participant in the trap set for her was the only way to ensure Lukas's freedom and safety.

"Blaire, please tell me you're not going to go through with letting them do that."

She lifted her head and looked at him. She hoped her conviction showed in her eyes as she spoke her truth. "It's my turn to protect you."

Lukas slumped against the dresser and curled his fingers against his stomach, his t-shirt bunching in his grip. After several beats of silence, he stood upright and rubbed a spot above his brow. "So, what? You just have to go to the health department and make donations?" His hand dropped as he breathed out heavily. "Something tells me that's not all there is to this agreement… There's more, isn't there?"

Blaire nodded once and looked down at her hands again as he turned to face her. He wouldn't like this arrangement. Would he still want to be with her after she made the choice she did? Had she gone too far?

"Tell me."

"They're giving us this night and tomorrow together, but then I have to go."

"Go?" Her heart ached at the confusion and pain in Lukas's eyes. "Go where? When? *Why?*"

"I don't know where I'll be staying, but it'll be late tomorrow sometime. They want me available at all times in case they run out of samples. Something about it delaying their research. I think they gave other reasons too, but honestly, I can't remember it all... I'd already made up my mind."

"How could you decide this for me?" His countenance darkened. "You talk about wanting to decide for yourself. You talk about how you don't want others—*Blaire*. What if I didn't want this? I *don't* want this."

She flinched. That wasn't the reaction she expected. She hadn't thought about the decision that way, but it wouldn't have changed things if she had. This wasn't controlling him. Lukas would have accepted expulsion—accepted going to Cresbel Asylum—but she couldn't let that happen. She couldn't consult with him before deciding. The Order knew what they were doing when they cornered her the way they did. Angelo knew she wouldn't walk away from Lukas.

"It's done. I don't regret, and won't feel sorry for, saving you. I won't."

His swallow was so hard it was audible.

"Please come here." Blaire outstretched her hand toward him, desperate for his touch. She needed reassurance he wasn't lost to her. "We only have tonight. I don't want to fight."

Lukas closed his eyes and took a slow, deep breath in through his nose and exhaled, as if steeling himself against the reality of their situation. He didn't protest any further, but his discomfort about her decision still thrummed in the air. Sighing, he moved to the bed, toed off his boots, and climbed over the covers, reaching out and pulling her down to lie with him. His strong arms banded around her, and he tucked her head against his chest, resting his chin on the top of her head, holding her to him tightly.

"It's not the end of the world," she said against his t-shirt. "And this way, they won't sneak around and hurt me to get what they want." A squeeze was the only response. "Lukas, please…"

"What do you want me to say?"

"I want you to not make this into a big deal."

"It *is* a big deal."

Blaire burrowed into the security of his arms and breathed in the apple spice scent of his body. If it were possible to stop time and stay in this moment, she'd ask for nothing else.

"I'm sorry. I know it's a big deal, but I just want to be with you right now and not think about it." Her fingers trailed over his stomach. "I love you, and I don't know how long they'll need to do this, so I just want to enjoy this time we have left." His abs tightened beneath his shirt as her fingers reached the hem.

Lukas's hand stilled hers, and he kissed the top of her head. She turned her gaze up to look at his face, and her eyebrows lowered in confusion at his pained expression. Did he not want her?

"We can't. I want to, but we can't," he finally said with a resigned sigh.

"Why not?"

He licked his lips and closed his eyes. "I don't trust myself."

She sat up, using one arm to hold herself propped up on the bed as she stared down at him. "What? Why? I trust you."

Lukas rolled onto his back and ran a hand over his face before resting his forearm over his eyes. "I… Shit. Blaire, I nearly killed you. I wanted to turn you."

"You stopped."

"It still doesn't change the fact that deep inside, I wanted to do what I did." He lowered his arm to look into her eyes, pleading without words.

"Lukas, I trust you. You wouldn't hurt me. You protected me."

Blaire didn't know how to convince him she wasn't afraid of him the way she used to be. In truth, she should be afraid. He'd nearly done the one thing she feared most before they bonded. The difference between then and now was how well she knew him. Knew him in a way that spoke to her soul. He wouldn't hurt her. It was why he stopped himself. It was how he overcame the darkest parts of himself during the trial. He just needed to understand that himself.

Her fingers tingled with the need to touch him again. With Vincent's violating touches still lingering in the back of her mind, she needed Lukas to burn it away. Brand himself on her skin. He could make it better.

She swung a leg over his body and sat astride his hips, resting her hands gently on his stomach. "I trust you," she repeated softly, giving a slight rock of her hips over the obvious arousal under his jeans. He wanted her. Even if his mind was in turmoil, his body was on board. She could work with that.

The next thing she knew, she was on her back beneath him, his lips trailing kisses up the side of her neck and across her cheek to murmur against her lips, "I've missed you."

Blaire closed her eyes as his breath floated over her lips where they hovered inches apart. The relief that washed over her was instant. He still loved her. Needed her. He wouldn't touch her if he didn't. Assurance he didn't resent her for being locked away settled something inside, but it wasn't enough. She needed more.

Lukas's hands slowly eased over her hips, sliding beneath the hem of her sweater. His warm fingers grazed over her sides as he worked the knitted fabric up her body and over her head. He tossed the sweater to the floor. Blaire stared up into heated eyes that glowed faintly around the edges of his iris. His gaze briefly flickered to the bruising on her shoulders and arms, but as quickly as she felt his irritation, it faded back into the desire she mirrored back at him.

Lukas pulled his black t-shirt over his head and tossed it aside before diving back in to take her lips in a slow and tender kiss.

Her hands slid over the soft skin of his back, contrasted by the hard muscle that flexed beneath her fingers where she touched. Their foreplay felt different this time. She relaxed and trusted Lukas to take care of her. Would their Korrena mark reappear this time?

Blaire tugged on the button of Lukas's jeans, but he pulled away, standing from the bed, and removed his jeans and boxers himself. She didn't wait for him, making quick work of her own jeans, bra, and panties. They only had so many hours together; she didn't want to waste them.

When his body molded to hers, his erection resting against her center, a soft moan passed between her lips.

The last time they made love was a frantic reconnecting to reunite their bond after being apart for months. While desperate and reckless, the sex was incredible, perfect—until she started losing consciousness. But Lukas freaked out. So caught up in her own desires, she hadn't sensed the internal war within him, or that their empathic connection was weakening with each passing moment. Only when she stirred had she realized something was wrong.

Lukas slid lower as he kissed over the skin of her breasts, his tongue flicking over her nipple when it hardened under his attention. Her soft moans of encouragement had him raking his teeth over the sensitive nub, his hand lavishing attention on the other with little twists and pulls.

When her legs opened farther, he rocked himself against her, sending zings of pleasure throughout her body.

"Lukas," she breathed. She didn't want him to just tease her.

His head lifted, and the flash of vivid green that glowed around the edges of his eyes made her pulse kick up a notch in anticipation of him giving in to his need for her.

"I want more," she said.

His answering smirk made her shiver with anticipation.

Without a word, he lowered his head and dragged his tongue between her breasts, then across the flat plane of her belly. When his tongue moved over her hip, his blunt teeth sank into her skin gently. The groan that left her throat was one of needy frustration.

She didn't want love nips; she wanted his fangs.

"More."

Lukas's breath ghosted over her hip as he chuckled at her impatience before kissing down to her thigh, using his hand to push it up and to the side. His eyes flashed brightly again as they met each other's gaze before he lowered his head and sucked hard on her inner thigh, causing her to throw her head back and let out a long, guttural moan. If she were in her right mind, she'd be embarrassed to have him hear the sound.

His mouth trailed kisses up her thigh to her center. When he latched onto her, suckling, and twirling his tongue, her entire body jolted. He had to wrap his arms around the tops of her thighs to keep her from pushing farther up the bed.

Groans vibrated through her core as he feasted on her like a man starved. She clutched his head with her hands, tangling her fingers in the long strands damp from sweat. When he released one of her thighs and slipped two fingers easily inside the heat of her body, her hips bucked up against his face.

Lukas lifted his head from between her thighs, sat back on his heels, and licked the wetness glistening around his mouth. A cocky grin curled his lips as he looked at her with heated, glowing eyes.

Yes. He was letting go.

Blaire sat up and reached for him, resting one hand against his thigh, and wrapped the fingers of her other hand around his erection. His head fell back with a groan.

The skin of his cock was warm and silky in her grip, and she delighted in the heaviness that came with how hard he got when aroused. Every time she touched him felt like the first time. The various things she tried to bring him pleasure always brought about different reactions, and it made her want to explore, to map his body with her hands, lips, and tongue.

When her thumb moved over his slit where moisture gathered, his thigh shuddered beneath her hand, and he hissed. Feeling emboldened by his reaction, she leaned in and flicked her tongue over the head of his cock.

"Shit, Blaire."

The strain in his voice made her smile, encouraging her to go farther.

Her grip firmed, and she wrapped her mouth around the leaking tip, giving an exploratory taste. Salty, sweet, and a bit of her own flavor from where he slid over her earlier, but she didn't mind it. This close to his body, the smell of his body wash was stronger. He must have showered before security brought him to see her. She took a deep breath of the spicy apple scent and slid lower, her tongue pressing to the underside of his shaft.

When she was halfway down his length, unable to take more of him into her mouth for fear of scraping him with her teeth or choking, she turned her eyes up to look at his face. Lukas's eyes were heavy-lidded, and he slid his tongue out over his lower lip before swallowing hard as he watched her bobbing her head, using her hand to stroke what she couldn't fit into her mouth. He looked at her not only with lust, but with awe and unmistakable love.

His hand came up to cup her cheek as he whispered reverently, "Mine." She hummed around him in reply, and his hips jerked in response to the vibration. He cursed before pulling away, leaving her mouth with a *pop*.

Lukas stroked himself as he looked at her sitting back on the bed, staring up at him.

"I've… never done that." She looked down, cheeks flushed with embarrassment. "Sorry if I did it wrong."

Fingers on her chin lifted her face upward. "Only me."

Before she could assure him there would never be another for her—he leaned in and captured her lips with his, pressing her back into the soft bedding as he lined his cock up with her entrance and pushed his way inside. Her arms wrapped around his neck, holding him close to her, feeling the slide of his skin against her heated body as he moved inside her with slow and languid thrusts.

The kisses between them grew tender as Lukas tilted Blaire's body, one hand squeezing her hip. He buried himself inside her, rotating his hips in a slow grind that had her toes curling. He was savoring her as much as she savored his every touch, kiss, and thrust into her body that stirred her down to her soul.

Soft moans, groans, and their mingled heavy breaths drowned out any other sound as they entwined, maintaining as much body contact as possible.

Lukas kissed across her throat to the side of her neck where her mark used to be. He sucked the flesh between his teeth, making her gasp at the sharp pain that melted into pleasure as he laved his tongue over the tender skin in a soothing gesture. He continued to pepper her skin with kisses and gentle bites, and when his pointed fangs finally grazed her skin, she whimpered.

"Please."

His thrusts grew frantic, and his hands bunched the covers on each side of her head as he panted against the skin of her neck, not moving his head as he slammed into her relentlessly. She wrapped her legs around his waist and held on for the ride. That familiar tingle in her lower belly stirred, and her muscles tightened around his shaft. His sudden change of rhythm and pace brought her so close to the edge she could taste it.

As she reached the precipice, his needle-sharp fangs, pressed so close by his position, inadvertently pierced the delicate skin of her neck. Blood trickled across her skin.

Lukas stiffened and lifted his head to look down at her. His chest was heaving, his glowing eyes wild and wide. He looked freaked out, and fear radiated from him so strongly it made her chest hurt, her orgasm long forgotten.

"Lukas? What's happening?"

He shook his head quickly, as if to clear it, returning his gaze to hers. His eyes blazed with that bioluminescent green she loved, but panic overrode other emotions. She reached up and touched his face, but he flinched, slipping out of her, and stood from the bed. He was no longer hard. Whatever freaked him out had flagged his erection. A small voice in her mind pointed out this might be a good thing, as they hadn't even considered a condom.

She pushed herself up to a sitting position and watched him intently. He wouldn't look at her. He stood with his back to her, hands balled into fists at his side. Alarm bells clanged inside of her in warning. This couldn't be happening. She couldn't lose him.

"Please tell me what's going on. You're scaring me."

Lukas sighed heavily and slumped his head forward, but his muscles remained tight like a spring coil. "I can't do it."

"What?"

"*This.* I can't even make love to you."

Her eyebrows met, and she bit her lip. What was he talking about? Wasn't that what they were doing?

Lukas stalked across the room into the ensuite and turned on the faucet of the sink. After a minute or two, he came back with a wet washcloth and stood beside her, holding it out in front of her. "Please get rid of it." His pained expression confused her.

"Get rid of what?"

"The blood," he said miserably, his voice breaking as his eyes gleamed with unshed tears.

Blaire took the offered cloth and wiped at her neck, pulling it away and looking at the traces of crimson staining the fabric. Her heart sank. Why hadn't he just licked it? Why didn't he bite her, like always? He did it at the trial and stopped. She couldn't stop the fear that trickled in and made a home in her heart. Everything was falling apart, and she didn't know how to get their relationship, or the situation, back on track.

"Tell me what's happening," she said softly, trying not to sound as broken as she felt.

When he didn't respond, his eyes locked on the cloth in her hand, she stood from the bed abruptly, stalked across the room to the bathroom, and dropped the stained rag on the counter. She didn't know if she was angry about having to wipe the blood away or just sad. Maybe both. Lukas felt a thousand miles away from her, and she didn't know how to navigate bringing him home again.

When she returned to the room, he hadn't moved from his tense position beside the bed. His despair thickened in her lungs like sludge, threatening to suffocate her.

Get it together. He needs you.

She moved to stand in front of him, resting her hands on his chest, gazing up into his eyes. "Talk to me," she whispered. His eyes closed. She unfurled his hands with hers and lifted them to her waist. In reflex, he wrapped his arms around her, pulling her body into his, and she rested her head against his chest as he buried his face against the top of her head.

"I don't want to hurt you."

Blaire shook her head against his chest. "You didn't."

His sigh stirred the hair on top of her head. "Not yet. I can't touch you like that without wanting to…" His words trailed off, but she understood the meaning. They couldn't make love without his wanting the connection that came with sharing blood. As a Vasirian, he needed that part to deepen their emotional connection.

Blaire understood that. She hadn't realized how much she relied on their physical intimacy to give her the same security. Things were too fragile between them. With a sigh, she finally asked, "Then why did you stop?"

Lukas pulled back, holding her waist, meeting her eyes. "I don't trust myself to stop anymore." Blaire's mouth parted, but he continued before she could say anything in response. "Whatever this is inside of me, it gets louder when we're like that. It won't stop. It wants to protect you, and the only way to do that in its mind is to, well, you know."

"It?"

"This *thing* inside of me. The Vasirian."

Blaire's eyebrows pulled together, her nose scrunching up. "What? Aren't you completely Vasirian?"

"I am; but when we're together like this, there's this disconnect in my brain." He stepped back and raked a hand through his hair, dropping to sit on the bed in front of her. "I get these intrusive thoughts. Thoughts that tell me to do things I wouldn't normally do."

"Like what?"

"Like turn you. Kill for you. All things to protect you."

She didn't know what to say to that. How could she understand or help him with this sort of thing? Humans didn't think of killing for each other—at least in proper society. They certainly didn't entertain thoughts of changing someone's species.

He groaned into his hand and rested an elbow on his knee. She picked up his t-shirt from the floor and pulled it over her head, not wanting to have this conversation while stark naked. She sat down beside him and curled into his side, wrapping her arms around one of his.

"I think you should talk to someone about this. Maybe this is normal for your kind? They said you'd be more volatile in the early stages of a bond."

"But to the point of wanting to kill? All I could think of was ripping Vincent's throat out until you stopped me. It was so much worse than when your stepbrother tried to take you away." He sighed. "And what about turning you? I promised I wouldn't force you into anything you didn't want. What you were most worried about was what I did. I nearly killed you, and I didn't want to."

"But you wanted to turn me, right?"

The muscle in his jaw ticked, telling her that her assumption was correct. The guilt passing through him to her spoke volumes.

"Hey." She sat up and put a hand on each of his cheeks, turning his face toward hers. "I'm not upset. I don't fault you for wanting me to be a Vasirian. When you put pressure on me, I have a problem, sure. But I've never faulted you for wanting it. Your feelings are valid. You're allowed to want that. Don't you know that?"

He pressed his forehead against hers. They sat in silence, breathing each other's air in the room's stillness.

Blaire had a feeling that until he came to terms with whatever he was fighting inside himself, they wouldn't be able to connect like they once had. That the empathic bond they shared wouldn't be constant until they got past the trust issues, the guilt, and found acceptance in what they both needed out of their relationship. As it stood, their connection remained fragmented. In some moments, like earlier, she could feel everything. His fear. Guilt. Desire. But in other moments, like now, nothing passed between them. It left her feeling empty and sad. Lonely. That he couldn't—or wouldn't—touch her deepened the loneliness that settled like lead weights in her belly.

"Please don't do this," Lukas whispered against her lips softly, breaking the silence. "Stay here with me until we can figure this out together."

"I'm not leaving you." Blaire sat back. "I'm only going to be gone for a little while to appease their curiosity."

"You know there's more to it."

Lukas wasn't stupid. Blaire knew that. They both knew Angelo's intentions weren't purely of scientific curiosity.

"I'll be okay," Blaire mumbled as she stood, pulling back the covers. She wasn't sure if she believed those words, but she had to accept them as the truth. Anything else took her away from Lukas, and the entire point of this agreement with the Order was to protect Lukas. She needed to focus on that. Not desires of the flesh. Not ridiculous intrusive thoughts taunting her, reminding her that if Lukas didn't make love to her, he didn't love her as a person.

When had she started talking to herself so badly?

Had she always done that?

No. She hadn't. It started with Vincent.

Even with Caleb's mockery, she wasn't insecure about being wanted by anyone else. Even if she couldn't be with another, she wasn't undesirable. People cared about her, and she didn't need more than their words to convince her.

Vincent's deception had slithered into her mind like a snake and poisoned her perception of herself, Lukas and his wants, and what she needed to feel whole. Vincent's "evidence" had manipulated her into believing she wasn't wanted. *He* started this. Did recognizing the truth of the situation change her perception? Not really. But it gave her something to focus those negative thoughts on. A place to shift the blame until she could teach herself to overcome the insecurity resulting from her time with Vincent. Specifically from the severance of her bond with Lukas that was in part voluntary because she'd believed Vincent's lies.

Lukas deserved a partner who wasn't a basket case of insecurity.

When Lukas settled under the covers, pulling her against him as they snuggled into the warmth together for their last night for who knew how long, he whispered against her neck, "I won't stop until I can set you free."

Would it come down to that being necessary? Would he need to free her like before? She hoped not. She wanted to give in to denial and believe the Order only wanted to satisfy the same curiosity she had about why her blood tempted Vincent and why she was a Vasirian's Korrena despite being a human, but she knew better. There was something more to this arrangement. She hoped it was something simple. Something she wouldn't need to be rescued from like some damsel in distress again. She hated feeling so weak.

Maybe being a Vasirian wouldn't be so bad in the end. She

wouldn't have to feel at such a disadvantage in this supernatural world she was now indelibly part of.

4

Separation

The ticking of the clock on the dresser across the room taunted Blaire as she stared at the ceiling of the safe room, nestled safely in Lukas's arms. She didn't know when, but before the day was over, she would leave him. For the first time since agreeing to the Order's proposal, she truly questioned her decision.

Sunlight filtered into the window through wooden blinds above the bed, leaving lines of the rising sun across the bedspread and Lukas's bare chest. Blaire traced her fingers along the lines on his skin as her thoughts drifted to the night before.

Before her insecurities had the opportunity to take hold, Lukas turned and wrapped his arms tightly around her, pulling her into his chest. His spiced apple scent settled her, and she snuggled closer into his embrace as his sleeping breaths puffed over her hair.

Blaire hadn't slept well, but she found it difficult to rest with only a handful of hours remaining before she had to leave. From the darkness that shadowed the skin beneath his eyes, Lukas hadn't slept well either. Even after talking longer before they fell asleep, the mood remained strained while they both tried to ignore the Sword of Damocles above their heads.

Lukas's eyebrows pinched together, deep lines etching his forehead and the edges of his eyes. His eyelids rapidly flickered. Whatever he was dreaming about didn't look comforting. When he mumbled, making a sound of discomfort, Blaire kissed his jawline near his ear and whispered his name.

His eyelids fluttered, then he opened heavy-lidded eyes. "Blaire." His voice came in a rasp, and he relaxed, the muscles of his face softening. "I dreamed you were already gone." He tightened his arms around her.

"Not yet." Blaire pressed her forehead to his chest and sighed. She didn't want to say that, but there wasn't any sense in pretending the elephant in the room didn't exist.

"I'm sorry."

She lifted her head from his chest and looked up into his eyes. "For what?"

"Last night I said some things without really thinking about it. After you fell asleep…" He took a deep inhale through his nose and rolled over onto his back, leaving one arm hooked around Blaire's shoulders, holding her body close to his. "While I still don't like the choice you made, I see why you made it. I can't fault you for doing that. I mean, how could I fault you for doing something because you love me and want to protect me?"

Blaire laid her head on his chest, listening to the steady beat of his heart.

"It just hit hard, you know? I haven't seen you in a week, and then I come to find you're leaving me when I think it's over… It was too much." He sighed. "It still is, but fighting about it isn't going to get us anywhere."

The change from how tense and shielded Lukas had been the night before to now took her by surprise. Last night, she wondered if she was losing him after everything that had happened between them, what Vincent had done to her, and the mark not returning—especially when it all led to his imprisonment, no matter how brief.

"Talk to me. What are you thinking?"

She stared at his hand resting on his stomach over the covers, not able to meet his eyes. "I'm afraid to lose you."

His body stiffened, and his hand pulled on her shoulder to encourage her to look at him. When she shifted to look up at him, he said, "You're never going to lose me. What gave you that impression?"

Blaire pulled from his hold and sat up, looking away from him when he frowned at the move. She needed space to think and find the words to articulate her feelings without it devolving into an argument. She didn't want to upset him by not being clear; they both deserved clarity.

She sat with her back to the wall, resting her hands in her lap, and chewed on the inside of her lip. "I guess part of me thinks you're going to get tired of me. Tired of dealing with a human who can't heal—who has a harder time healing than normal humans." She winced at the way the reality that she wasn't normal settled inside her. It wasn't a comfortable feeling.

When Blaire didn't offer more words, Lukas spoke. "It doesn't matter that you're a human. You're my pair. That's enough."

"Don't lie to me."

"What?" Lukas squinted in a genuine look of confusion. "Why would I lie to you? I'm not lying."

Perhaps he compartmentalized the beastly side of himself that he hated from the Lukas before her now to the point he didn't even realize what his actions meant.

"If that were true…" She paused, and her lips twisted as she tried to find the right words. "If you were honest with yourself, you'd know my being a human bothers you more than you're willing to acknowledge. You've said on many occasions you want me to be a Vasirian because you feel it would be safer for me. Subconsciously, the need for me not to be a weak little human pushed you into actions you didn't even want to do."

Lukas chuckled. "Look at you, embracing the therapist role already." His amusement died with a heavy sigh, and he scrubbed a hand over his face, leaving his forearm across his eyes. "You're right, though. I guess what I should be saying is, I don't want it to matter. I want this to be enough."

"But it's not."

"No, I guess not."

Blaire's head dropped forward, and she shrank in on herself, arms wrapping around her waist. Lukas would never be happy with her like she was. He told her he could do it, and maybe he hadn't lied when he told her. She didn't think him a liar, but the reality that came with their time together spoke of her need to be a Vasirian for this to work and his discomfort that she wasn't.

Lukas lowered his arms and sat up abruptly, hands going to Blaire's shoulders. She looked up at him. "What?"

"Don't do that."

"Do what?"

"Retreat into yourself. When I said I guess not, it doesn't mean you have to change a thing. It means I have to work on myself. It isn't fair to expect you to become a Vasirian like me. It's like if I said I didn't like blonde hair." He smirked when Blaire's nose scrunched at the comparison. "Okay, it isn't the same, but the point is even if your hair was purple, you'd still be the same person on the inside. This connection through the Korrena bond aside, I like the person you are. You infuriate me sometimes, but you're amazing."

"I am?" She refrained from sharing that he was equally infuriating; he likely already knew that. The thought made her smile briefly.

"Of course you are." Lukas laughed, and the tightness in her chest eased. "You're warm, friendly, loyal…" His hand moved to cup her cheek. "Protective of those you care about, and even those you don't know. Before we knew of that asshole Vincent's intentions, you still defended him and gave him the benefit of the doubt. You have a good heart."

Blaire frowned and gave him a flat stare. "Fat lot of good that did me."

"Don't let him destroy the good in you. It wasn't your fault."

"Isn't it? If I had listened to you, none of it would have happened."

"But then you wouldn't be you. I want you to listen to me, of course, but I also want you to tell me what you're thinking. Your opinion and feelings matter as much as mine."

The words were right, but how long would they hold? Lukas wasn't exactly one to stick to his rational words when his emotions ran volatile. Still, he didn't speak rational words often, so she would take it. She trusted him, but her trust wasn't blind. That wouldn't be good for either of them.

"You don't resent me for spending that time in the dungeon?"

"What? No! Why would you…" He shook his head. "That was my own fault. I made the choice to attack Vincent, and I'd do it again. Don't get me wrong. It sucked down there. I only had a bucket to piss in." He laughed at her sour face. "But I did it to protect you. Like you made this choice to protect me."

Lukas sat back and sighed, his expression shuttering. If she could sense more than bits and pieces through their empathic bond, whatever he felt in that moment would be screaming at her; as it stood, silence echoed between them.

Before she could ask him to share his thoughts, a knock on the door interrupted. She tensed. Weren't they going to pick her up later that evening? She looked out the window. It couldn't be any later than early morning. They hadn't even had breakfast.

Lukas put a hand over hers and kissed her forehead. "It's breakfast. After you fell asleep last night, Professor Velastra came by the room and said someone would bring breakfast."

Blaire's shoulders dropped as the tension ebbed from her muscles.

Lukas stood from the bed and went to collect a bag from someone at the door she couldn't see from where she sat. When he padded back from the door in nothing but a pair of boxers, she ogled him without restraint. She squirmed as warmth spread through her and centered low in her belly. She needed to get her libido under control.

She moved over as he climbed on the bed to sit next to her with his back to the wall, opening the bag and setting bottles of orange juice, wrapped biscuits, a small container of mixed berries, and a blood packet on the bed.

His shoulder bumped into hers as he leaned into her, sticking a small straw in the blood packet like it was a Capri Sun. "So, what do you want to do today?"

"I don't think they'll let us go anywhere." She picked up a biscuit and opened it. Sausage, egg, and cheese. Her appetite wasn't there, but she needed to eat something. "I mean, I'm a flight risk, right?"

"We could make a run for it."

Blaire's mouth dropped open. "What?"

He shrugged, taking a sip of his blood packet.

"Lukas, that's… No, we can't do that. We don't have money. No place to go."

"I have access to money through my parents. We can go to their beach house on Tybee Island."

"They'll look for us there."

While she didn't have family binding her to Rosebrook Valley, and it was true she didn't have a reason to necessarily hide out at Blackthorn Academy anymore, she had friends here. Riley and Aiden were almost like family now. Mera, Seth, Kai. Blaire was just getting to know Rue and Liam better. Charlotte and her mothers would lose their minds if Blaire took off without telling them.

"I'm sure Mom and Dad would hide us somewhere. They know it hasn't been easy since you came here…"

Blaire sighed when his voice trailed off and his head dropped. His parents were a touchy subject; she didn't like the way their relationship with him sounded. Ditching him at boarding school year-round when he was barely old enough to enter kindergarten. Her hand moved to rest on his thigh, and he lifted his head to look at her.

"I'm happy you're willing to not only run away with me, but also approach your parents for help," she said. "But I need to see this through. I don't want to spend the rest of my life on the run, and I have a feeling they won't stop. I know the secrets of your kind, and I doubt the powers that be will sit idly by while I run around the world with that knowledge unchecked."

"You know I'd do it, though. I'd go off-grid for you."

"I know you would." The thought he would drop everything to get her away from the Order warmed her heart, but it wasn't realistic for them to run. "But Riley would have our asses. I think she'd do a better job hunting us down than the Order would." Blaire relaxed further when Lukas chuckled at her words. She finally took a bite of the biscuit held in her grasp.

They finished their breakfast, dressed, and were sitting on the bed together, sharing the container of mixed berries, when Lukas finally broke the comfortable silence that settled between them.

"I want you to know when this is all over, I'm not going to pressure you into anything."

Blaire looked up at him. "I know you won't." After everything that happened when he attempted to turn her, and then how he changed and protected her, she trusted he wouldn't push things. Not after how badly it impacted their relationship. At least she rationally knew this when she wasn't viewing through the lens of insecurity.

Lukas rolled a raspberry between his fingers, staring down at his hands. "I don't know how to let it go." When Blaire didn't respond, waiting for him to continue his thought, he glanced over his shoulder at her. "I can't forgive myself."

She set aside the container of berries and moved to kneel on the bed next to him. Wrapping her arms around his shoulder, she pulled him to her and settled back on her feet. He collapsed against her chest with a heavy sigh, his cheek to her sternum.

"You already know I forgive you," she said, "but I know that might not be enough for you. I wish I could stay here and help you work it out."

He made a disgruntled noise low in his throat.

"I'm serious. I know you won't go to my therapist, so I figured maybe I could use what I've learned or something."

When he lifted his head to stare at her, she sat back, her face flushing. She hadn't learned a lot, considering everything with Vincent, but she had read books before coming to Blackthorn Academy, and her own experience in therapy long ago was more than Lukas had in his arsenal. If she could help him come to terms with his feelings—make it easier for him to accept what couldn't be changed and understand he could move on from that—she would do it.

"You'd do that for me?"

"Of course. Why wouldn't I?"

Lukas looked at the raspberry he still held. "No one has ever—never mind."

"Don't do that to me." She nudged his arm. "I thought we were past that stuff."

He tossed the raspberry in the small trash can beside the nightstand, huffing a breath through his nose. "I'm not used to people going out of their way to help me sort my shit." He scratched his jaw. "I mean, Aiden kinda does, but I guess it just hits different from you."

Blaire tilted her head. "In a bad way?"

"No. I like it."

"I'd hope so." She smiled, shaking her head.

If he viewed the way she treated him in the same light as the way Aiden acted with him, she'd have to ask questions. Like, did he want just a romantic relationship, or a friendship with her? Though she always thought good love relationships needed friendship. Charlotte's last boyfriend started as her friend two years before he ever asked her out. The relationship didn't last, but the relationship was good, so when it ended, they stayed friends until he moved to Arizona for college.

"What do you want for Christmas?"

The words broke through her thoughts, and she blinked at the change of subject. "Huh?"

"Christmas."

Would she be done with the Order's stupid games in a week? She decided against bringing it up and ruining the mood. "I don't need anything." At his flat look, she laughed. "Uh... the new Emley Rison novel coming out? It's actually a preorder, so it would be a late

Christmas present."

"Anything *now*? Something more than a book?"

Blaire shrugged. She didn't need material things. "Know what I'd really want?"

"That's what I'm asking." He waggled his eyebrows at her.

"Smart ass." He shrugged, and she shook her head with a small smile. "I wanna leave."

"Leave?"

"Uh huh. Once we're done with all this, I'd like to go somewhere and relax. I don't have to worry about my stepbrother or his grandparents anymore, but even so, I want to go somewhere beyond Rosebrook."

"Like a vacation?"

"Yeah!"

"Weren't we going to Tybee Island with everyone?"

Her lips pursed. "I mean..." She fiddled with the comforter on the bed absentmindedly. "Just us." When he didn't respond right away, she chanced a glance at his face and found his brows raised high and his jaw slack. "What?"

"You want to take a trip with me?"

Blaire flattened her lips, resisting the urge to giggle. "You need to stop sounding surprised by everything. I care about you. I *love* you. Of course I want to do things with you." She sighed. "There's just been so much happening. We haven't gotten a lot of alone time when shit isn't falling apart unless we're in the dorms, because we're always with everyone. I think it'd be nice to spend time as just the two of us." She laughed at the bright smile that seemed so out of place on his face. "What? I think we need it."

"Y-yeah. Yeah. You're right. We do." He nodded. "I think that's a great idea."

His overly eager response threw her off, and her cheeks warmed. The smile he gave her was gorgeous and blinding. She'd never seen him so happy and eager.

"Anywhere you want to go," he said.

"Not really. I don't have a lot of money—"

"Covered. Seriously. And please don't argue it. We didn't get to spend your birthday together, and this could also be your Christmas. Let that be an excuse for accepting it, since you need one." He gave her a knowing look.

She couldn't argue with that fact.

"When you're back, we'll plan something for just the two of us for a weekend or something."

She smiled.

"But I still did get you a birthday present. I've had it since long before your birthday, and I haven't had the chance to give it to you."

"What? Lukas," she spluttered and laughed.

"What nothing." He leaned in and kissed her lips softly, taking her hand in his. "Let me do something for you. You'll like it."

Lukas seemed so happy with himself that she couldn't bear to argue about his spending money on her. If she had access to the kind of money the kids of Blackthorn Academy had, she'd probably be more inclined to treat him and her friends to more, too. She couldn't fault him, or any of the others, for wanting to do nice things for the people they cared about.

When a soft knock came, Lukas sighed and let go of her hand. "What now?" He stood and went to the door, opening it to a frowning Professor Velastra. "What's going on?" He stepped back and allowed the professor to enter.

Professor Velastra crossed the room and stood in the center, her black stilettos sinking into the plush area rug in the center of the room. She folded one arm over her waist, resting her opposite elbow on her forearm as she cradled her chin and cheek with her forefinger and thumb. "Blackthorn Security came by my office this morning after they delivered your breakfast and informed me that Angelo is demanding your immediate transport to the testing location."

"What? I thought I had until later today, or even tonight."

Lukas crossed to the bed and sat next to Blaire, taking her hand in his and squeezing tightly. A faint spike of his anxiety and anger flickered between them. "Hey, it's going to be fine."

Her hand was shaking. She agreed to this, but it still didn't rid her of the nervousness that settled in over what the Order planned for her.

"Turns out, the original order was that you were to go last night after seeing Lukas. Angelo only conceded to you two seeing one another, not spending the night together." She glanced toward the door. "Security is waiting outside for you."

"He didn't want us to restore our mark," Lukas said, more to himself than anything, but they heard him.

"I thought the same. If you stayed overnight, then the likelihood of a successful claiming ritual happening seemed high." Professor Velastra's eyes settled on their necks. "I see that didn't happen, but if he didn't want the bond fully restored, it makes sense he would deny the extended time together."

Blaire huffed. "But why would he do that? What does it matter?"

Professor Velastra looked at her. "Perhaps a stronger bond might influence whatever tests they want to perform? I'm as in the dark as you are. We can only speculate. The only thing we know for sure is there isn't a choice in this, so you must go now."

"There's a choice." Lukas stood.

"Not if you're staying out of Cresbel Asylum, there's not." Blaire pulled him back down to the bed.

Lukas growled under his breath and put his elbows on his knees, burying his face in his hands.

No matter how much they talked about things, no matter how well he understood the need for this, and no matter how much he expressed how he understood she made the choice to protect him, Lukas was angry. Maybe he wasn't angry with her, but he couldn't hide his feelings about the situation—and he shouldn't. She preferred openness. But his upset made her uncertain of her quick acceptance of the Order's coercion. Maybe something else could have come of the meeting. Now she would never know.

Professor Velastra moved to the door as Lukas stood and pulled Blaire up into his arms.

"I meant what I said," he mumbled into her hair. "I won't stop until I can get you out of this situation."

Blaire looked up at him and sighed. "I want to believe it'll be fine." Her hug on him tightened when the door opened, and she buried her face against his chest. "Please don't stress about this. I'll be back before you know it, and then we can plan our trip." She lifted her head. "Okay?"

Lukas cupped her cheek and kissed her forehead. "Yeah. Sure." The muscle in his jaw jumped, showing he was only agreeing to not add more stress to the situation. It was foolish to ask that of him. "I love you, Blaire."

"I know. I love you too." She pulled away and took a step back. "Hug Riley for me?" When Lukas grimaced, she laughed. "Oh, come on."

"Fine."

She stepped around him and moved toward the door where a member of Blackthorn Security was waiting in the hall. Professor Velastra lightly touched her shoulder blade as she passed.

She knew in her heart this exchange was the right thing to do, but Lukas's reaction left a seed of doubt that tried to take root in her mind. Blaire glanced over her shoulder, and her heart ached in response to the devastated look on his face as he watched her from inside the room until the door closed and cut off her view of him.

5

CAGED

Footsteps echoed as Blaire, and three members of Blackthorn Security, made their way through the space. She couldn't see anything. When Blaire reported to the administration building after breakfast as required, Blackthorn Security waited for her on the steps. Professor Velastra tried to reassure her as they made the exchange, but Blaire still felt uneasy. The female security officer provided her with a thick black sack and told her to place it over her head. She didn't know if the location they were taking her to was a secret, or they simply didn't want her to find her way back.

They walked for at least five to ten minutes, and she became disoriented by the loss of her sight. She tried to listen to her surroundings as they moved, but nothing seemed familiar.

The sounds of the doors closing shortly after she put the bag over her head, followed by the sound of her footfalls on the marble flooring, made Blaire aware they had entered the administration building. Beyond that, she remained clueless to her surroundings. They traveled down a long staircase that felt like it went on forever. The farther down they traveled, the colder the air felt. She was thankful she put on a sweater that morning after being informed she was to meet security outside. With a week to go before Christmas, a chill lingered in the air, and she didn't want to risk getting sick.

Stagnant, cold air greeted her when they finally came to level ground and passed through a heavy door, judging by the loud sound that reverberated through the silent space when it closed. She guessed hardly anyone had been in the space in a long time, or there wasn't much ventilation. Based on how far down they descended, they were deep underground. The dungeons? Were they locking her away? Her steps slowed as tendrils of uncertainty crawled down her spine.

"Keep moving," a woman to her left said. She didn't speak in harsh tones, but the command in her voice rang clear.

Somehow, Blaire got her feet to cooperate, and she trudged forward, acutely aware of how the floor differed from the smooth marble in the administration building halls. The floor wasn't as rough as the cobblestone of the main courtyard of the academy, but her shoe caught on the occasional bump. The lack of clear echo also let her know the floor wasn't marble. Still, in the quiet of wherever they were, their footfalls filled the air, scuffing across the floor.

A hand grasped Blaire's arm, halting her movements. She flinched, instinctively withdrawing.

"Easy," the woman said gently.

The bag over Blaire's head was removed.

She squinted, expecting bright light but finding the opposite. She peered around the space and her stomach tightened.

The dungeons.

They stood in the center of a long hallway between cells with wrought iron bars on the sides and fronts on each side of her. She would have thought them cages if not for the stacked stone wall reminiscent of medieval castles from fantasy as the back wall of each cell. It wasn't far from the truth, though. Each cell held a basic single bed with a thin mattress and threadbare linens, but not much else. *Is that a metal bucket in the corner?* Her mind flashed to what Lukas told her. She would not be peeing in a bucket. Nope. Not happening.

Because of the dim lighting from candles on iron sconces and old, barely working bulbs, she could only see the two cells on each side of her, the shadows beyond swallowing what she assumed were more cells.

"Why are we here?"

"This is where you'll be staying for the foreseeable future," the woman to her left said. When Blaire looked into the woman's somber brown eyes, she could easily see the woman's discomfort. After a beat, the woman turned her face away from Blaire, her bob of brunette hair hiding her eyes. "Council's orders. You will remain here unless summoned for research. I'm sorry."

A snort drew Blaire's attention behind her. A large man peered down at her with a cock-sure grin on his face. Blaire had to tilt her head back to look at him; she only came up to his armpits in height. "Don't see a reason to apologize, Katie. She's just a human. She should feel lucky Angelo didn't have her put in a hole someplace." He crossed his enormous arms over his barrel chest.

"Don't be a dick, Marcus." Katie flicked Marcus's ear, and he reached up to swat her away. "Nothing wrong with humans."

"Whatever you say." He rolled his eyes.

Blaire looked around. She expected to find dampness and filth—at least, that's how most dungeons from fairytales were represented. Instead, the space looked clean, like an unused basement. Old and worn, much like the expected fairytale dungeons, but clean. No visible rats, straw on the floors, or puddles of unknown origin. She didn't know if there were bugs or spiderwebs; the corners of the cells were too shadowed to see clearly.

"Seriously, Kate, humans are nothin' but trouble. Crawlin' with disease. Dangerous. Somethin's wrong with this one's blood." The third man of the group shuddered, averting his gaze as he unlocked the cell to Blaire's right. "I steer clear of 'em. Order my groceries online to be delivered an' everythin'."

"You both are absurd. Does she look dangerous to you, Jackson?" Katie gently put a hand on Blaire's arm to lead her into the cell. "Don't mind dumb and dumber. Not all Vasirian have issues with humans."

"Yeah, an' the ones that don't are playin' with fire." Jackson ran a hand over the top of his head, giving it a little shake. "You think if they knew about us, humans wouldn' be at our gates with pitchforks an' torches?"

Katie turned to face Jackson with her mouth gaping. "This is not the Middle Ages."

"J has a point," Marcus said with a frown, crossing his burly arms over his chest.

"Children. The both of you." Katie turned to Blaire. "Ignore them."

Blaire shuffled to the back of the cell, her back toward the stone wall, keeping her gaze moving between the two men. She didn't trust them. Even if their conversation and mannerisms with Katie were relaxed, they still had no problem expressing their clear disdain for humans. From her experience, the Vasirian who held prejudices against humans didn't exactly handle them well.

Katie frowned. "Look at what you two idiots did. You have the poor girl scared."

"I'm not afraid."

Marcus laughed, and the deep, rumbling sound echoed through the dungeon. "Sure, you're not."

"I'm not." Blaire lifted her chin. Why was she arguing with him like a child?

"Quit playin' around. I wanna get this finished an' get outta here. I still hafta stop by the toy store an' get Lizzie's Christmas gift that came in."

Marcus looked at Jackson. "You didn't finish your shopping yet? I finished ages ago."

Jackson pointed back at him. "Only cause Tiffany woulda tanned your hide if you hadn't." He laughed and dodged when Marcus swiped a large hand in his direction.

"You think now is the time for this kind of talk? We're literally locking a damn student up in the dungeons. This is the third one in the last couple of weeks. While the first deserved it, and the other was questionable, I don't enjoy locking this one up."

Both men fell silent, heads lowered as if they felt genuine remorse. Blaire didn't know what to make of it. They both seemed to take such extreme issue with her existence, but expressed the good sense that locking her away when she voluntarily agreed to work with the Order didn't sit right.

Katie motioned to the small bed pushed against the bars dividing Blaire's cell from the next. With no walls to separate the cells, prisoners could reach through and touch each other if they felt so inclined. Blaire was thankful she didn't have a neighbor. "The blanket isn't much, and it gets cold down here, especially at night, so I'll bring you an extra blanket. Angelo can kiss my ass if he has a problem with it."

Blaire offered a faint smile, relieved someone seemed to be on her side. "Thank you," she murmured. Despite the obvious dislike rolling off the two men, the easy-going vibes between the three made an otherwise frightening situation not overwhelming. The banter between them gave her something to focus on.

Katie waved a hand in front of her face. "No sweat." Her gaze moved to the metal bucket in the cell's corner, and she grimaced. "Shit. That's unsanitary and not gonna fly." She looked around as if searching for a solution. When her gaze landed on a cell across the hall and to the left, she paused. "There."

Marcus looked over his shoulder, and Jackson frowned, moving out of the cell with his keys held up. "All this fussin' over a damn human."

"Yeah, but I'd rather her be in the cells with their own bathroom cubby and toilet than have her peeing and dumping in a bucket."

"It's not like anyone else is down here. Why the need for modesty?" Marcus looked genuinely confused.

Katie pinched the bridge of her nose. "Doesn't matter." She looked at Blaire. "The only reason the cells on the right have buckets instead of actual proper bathrooms is because we hardly have use for these cells. They've been slowly updating things down here, but haven't gotten around to that side, nor the temperature control."

Blaire followed Katie across the main hall to another cell on the opposite side. This cell appeared like the other, except in the back corner stood a rough wooden addition about the size of an old phone booth.

Marcus opened the narrow door and gestured to the interior. "This work for her highness?"

Katie smacked the back of his head.

The interior was the stuff of claustrophobic nightmares.

Inside the center of the "bathroom" sat a small, stained toilet with a roll of toilet paper perched on the back tank. The walls were so enclosed that even though there was space for a toilet paper hanger on the wall, it wasn't big enough to hold a full-size roll of paper. What was the point then? Prisoners weren't going to move it onto the roller when they used half a roll. Clearly someone didn't think ahead. The ceiling of the glorified phone booth was lower than it looked from the exterior, likely for ventilation additions. Still, it was better than the bucket. Anything was better than the bucket.

Blaire stepped away from the open door as Marcus shut it, turned, and left the cell, grumbling something about a lump on his head.

"Someone will bring you food an' drink at the proper times, an' whenever the Order is ready for whatever arrangement y'all have come up with, someone will swing by an' get ya," Jackson said as he stepped out of the cell, swinging his keys on his forefinger.

Katie turned before exiting the cell and smiled pityingly at Blaire. "The lights stay on most of the time." She looked around. "At least, what little light there is."

"Most of the time?"

"Eh… The wiring down here is older than my mother—maybe as old as electricity itself." Katie laughed with a shake of her head.

"It's not that bad," Marcus said.

"Close enough." Katie shrugged. "I'm just saying that should the lights go out, it shouldn't be for long."

"Not afraid of the dark, are ya?" Jackson asked, locking the cell door once Katie passed through, and his eyes glittered with amusement.

"Not really, no."

"Pity."

"Doesn't matter either way, so stop trying to scare the poor girl." Katie smiled at Blaire. "The power situation is another reason we have slow-burning beeswax candles around." She motioned to the iron sconces. "The bigger ones can last a week before needing replaced."

Blaire watched from behind the bars as Jackson turned and walked down the hallway into the shadows. His jingling keys gave away his position as he moved farther away. Her gaze slid back to the two remaining guards.

"You'll be alright." Katie nodded, but Blaire wasn't certain if she was trying to convince her or herself. "Might come check on you at some point if I can."

"Let's go before the council questions why it's taking so long."

Marcus frowned at Blaire and led Katie away from the front of Blaire's cell, their footsteps fading into the distance.

Exhaling long and heavily, Blaire looked around her home for the foreseeable future. She rested her forehead against the bars of her cell, closing her eyes.

Had she made the right decision? Lukas was angry she made the choice to exchange herself for him without asking his feelings about it. She knew in her heart it was the right thing to do, but his initial reaction left a seed of doubt that tried to take root in her mind. Had she done more damage to their relationship than good? Wouldn't he have done the same? Of course he would. He couldn't be upset over her choice to do something he would have done himself.

She didn't know if they intended to keep her down here for a day, a week, a month, or even longer. The Order hadn't found out what was special about her blood in the nine months she'd been a student at Blackthorn Academy. Who could say if the process of discovery would go faster because she now willfully took part in the experiments?

6

Regret

The letters on the page in front of Lukas bled together in a nonsensical blur as he tried to focus on what the professor said at the front of the classroom. Two days had passed since he saw Blaire last, and while he thought their time apart prior to this would have made this separation easier, it didn't. With their pair bond not fully restored, his entire being was in turmoil. Much worse than before they ever bonded for the first time. He hadn't been emotionally ready to return to classes after the weekend.

"You alright?" a girl to his left asked.

Lukas glanced her way, and the girl shifted in her seat to face him. He'd seen her before in class, but they'd never spoken to one another. For the life of him, he couldn't remember her name. Professor Burgess had rearranged seating assignments a couple of weeks ago, placing this girl next to Lukas. Only a week later the Order locked him up, so they hadn't spoken to one another. Blaire's disappearance had plagued his mind, so it wasn't like he was in his right mind during that week to have much of a conversation, anyway.

When he failed to answer her, she leaned toward him, peering intently at his face. His head recoiled, eyebrows raised.

"You don't look so good."

"I'm fine."

The girl sat back in her seat, frowning at his clipped response. Her frown made her look childish; she didn't look old enough to be in university. With a button nose, a smattering of freckles across her cheeks, and large, expressive, honey-colored eyes, her face looked youthful. She looked no older than a high school freshman. She looked smaller than Riley.

The Comparative Approach to Literary Criticisms class' seating wasn't like his classes last year. Instead of individual desks, long tables created several rows with two students per table. Professor Burgess said it promoted cooperation between students and healthy dialogue in the theoretical approach to exploring aesthetics and criticism. His penchant for randomly changing the seating assignments added to the "get to know your classmate" approach. But right now, Lukas's proximity to his desk partner made him feel suffocated.

"Look, I'm sorry," he offered. It wasn't her fault he felt like he did. "I'm just not having a good day."

She set her pen on her notebook and turned again to face him. She kept her distance, for which he was thankful. "I'm sorry if I bothered you. Um…" Her lips twisted, as if to contemplate what to say next. "You just have had this look all week that said something was bothering you."

Was he that transparent?

Lukas sighed heavily.

"Listen, if you don't wanna talk about it, that's okay."

Did he want to talk about the guilt eating away at his insides?

Would sharing it with a total stranger help him? He doubted it, but he couldn't bring himself to tell Aiden, Seth, or the others. They'd lecture him. Tell him it wasn't his fault. But he didn't see how Blaire's imprisonment wasn't his fault. Though that wasn't the biggest thing he felt. Shame for what he did to Blaire loomed larger than anything else. He wasn't sure he'd ever get over it.

He hadn't even talked to his friends about Blaire volunteering to be a guinea pig, but he assumed Professor Velastra told them. Riley hadn't come knocking on his door looking for Blaire, and they were giving him space—or maybe his active avoidance of everyone for the last couple of days forced them to. They had to know.

"Does it have something to do with why you were gone last week?"

Lukas looked back at the girl, dragging himself out of his gloomy thoughts. He didn't think anyone had noticed his absence. "Yeah." He tapped his fingers on the desk's surface lightly, looking up at the clock. Fifteen minutes to go.

The girl sighed when he didn't elaborate, the sound implying he came across as a jerk. Lukas hated when he gave that impression just because one-on-one talks with people he didn't know made him uncomfortable. He put his elbow on the table and held his forehead, keeping his eyes on the table's surface, exhaling heavily.

"I got into a fight."

He couldn't go into details. The Order hadn't forbidden them from talking about it, but he was sure if they found out he'd shared everything that happened, he'd be back in the dungeon before nightfall. Besides, he didn't know if he could trust this girl. She was a social butterfly. He remembered that much. He'd seen her laughing and talking with her other table partners. The other students' ease with her didn't erase his apprehension after everything that occurred with Clarissa. He didn't need another level-ten clinger.

The girl's eyes widened, and her small hand covered her parted lips. "Really? Were you hurt or something? Is that why you weren't here?"

He almost laughed at the way her voice pitched higher with each question. She latched onto the one thing he gave her and ran off a cliff with it. He couldn't imagine being hurt badly enough to miss school like that. He'd have to be near death for his healing abilities to not have him back to form within a day.

"Layla Crowley." Professor Burgess stood next to their table and frowned down at the girl. She spun around so quickly, her mocha brown ponytail almost slapped Lukas in the face. "Can you tell me what is so exciting that you felt the need to disrupt the class?"

"Um… I… You see—"

"Spider." All eyes moved to Lukas, and he wanted to slide down in his seat, but he didn't. He shifted, sitting up straighter and clearing his throat. "She was thanking me for killing a spider. Probably afraid of them." He had no idea if Layla feared spiders, but it was the first thing he could think of. Blaire would have responded loudly too. She had before. Her arachnophobia would be comical if it didn't bother him so much that she feared something.

"Right." Professor Burgess cleared his throat. "See that you try to keep your exuberance to a minimum. I know Christmas is fast approaching, and we're all excited for the break, but we still have this week's material to get through."

"Yes, sir." Layla looked down as the olive skin of her cheeks flushed. When the professor walked away, she turned wide eyes on Lukas. "Thank you," she mumbled.

Lukas shrugged, uncomfortable. He hoped his helpfulness didn't once again come back to bite him in the ass. Clarissa's obsession started when he helped her pick up fallen books.

He wasn't exactly excited for the two-week winter break they got for Christmas and the New Year, but at least it would give him a reprieve from acting like he wasn't aching inside. Though, based on the assessment of the girl next to him, he was doing a stellar acting job.

"So, what happened?"

"Huh?"

She glanced toward the front of the class. The professor was busy chatting with another student. "The fight."

"Oh, uh…" He tried to remember her questions. "I wasn't hurt or anything. Just got in trouble. Had to take time off."

"Oh, wow. And you're depressed because of that?" She bit down on the end of her pen cap and studied him.

"I'm not depressed."

"Your eyes say you are."

This girl acted way too forward for his liking. Maybe he made a mistake talking to her and helping her out. He looked at the clock. Two minutes.

"I'll be fine." He started packing away his books.

"Well, if you want to talk to someone…" Layla left the unspoken implication to linger in the air as she stood from the table, adjusted her plaid skirt, and picked up her book and notebook. "See you Wednesday?" They only had Comparative Approach to Literary Criticisms twice a week.

"Sure. See you."

Lukas watched the girl move to the door with the other students who filed out of the classroom. His stomach growled, and he closed his eyes. He'd forgotten to eat breakfast again. At least it was lunchtime.

"Lukas, wait up!"

Riley ran across the courtyard, waving her hand in the air. Lukas lay his head back, face to the sky, and closed his eyes. He carried his lunch in his hands, hoping to make it back to his room where he'd been eating his meals. Eventually, he'd have to face his friends, but he wasn't ready yet. But nothing stopped Riley when she was on a mission, and judging by the look on her face as she drew closer, it was time to pay his dues.

She came to a stop in front of him, holding her side, panting heavily. "Give me… a minute… please." Her breath made little clouds in the chilly December air.

Seth sauntered up behind her with his hands tucked into the pockets of his black uniform slacks, casting Riley a side glance with a smirk on his lips. Riley lifted a hand up in front of his face to stop whatever playful jab he likely had prepared. He chuckled softly.

Aiden came to stand beside them, unbuttoning his black blazer. The cold finally warranted wearing cardigans and blazers. Wearing the blazer made Lukas feel like a stuffy prep-school tool, but the school's new policy required them to wear the designated cold weather attire instead of their own jackets. Why, he had no clue, but he didn't like it. They could still accessorize—like Riley's buckled boots and fishnets—but the school required them to wear all the key pieces of their uniform.

"Okay… This ends now." Riley posted her small hands on her hips as she gave Lukas a challenging glare. "You've had the chance to mope. Now it's time to do something else."

Lukas rolled his eyes and held up the wrapped chicken burger and blood packet in his hands. "I have no idea what you're talking about. I'm going to have lunch."

"Do I look stupid to you?"

Lukas sucked his teeth.

"Exactly. When Professor Velastra told me and Aiden what happened, I wanted to come see you, but Aiden thought you needed space to process."

"I did. I *do*."

"Nope. You can have more space when you're dead. I'm not about to watch you spiral out like you did when Blaire was kidnapped. It's time to get out of your head."

Lukas turned and walked toward a bench at the edge of the hedge maze, sitting down and unwrapping his burger. Riley plopped down right beside him. Seth shook his head, glancing at Aiden, who shrugged.

"While she's not exactly using a delicate approach, she's right, man." Aiden came to sit on Lukas's other side. "I don't think I could handle seeing you slip back to that place you've lived in for the past couple of months."

Seth crossed his arms, standing in front of them. "It's not like Blaire is kidnapped this time. You know where she's at, right?"

Lukas lowered the burger, swallowing down the bite he'd just taken. It slid down his esophagus like a rock. "No." His voice cracked with the strain the emotions that knowledge brought him.

"What?" Riley's eyes widened. "How can you… What did…" Her mouth opened and closed, but she didn't finish her sentence, her eyes narrowing.

"Why didn't they tell you?"

Lukas looked at Aiden, wrapping the remaining half of his burger in its paper. "Hell if I know. All I know is when I got out of the damn dungeon, and after they let me clean off the stench from not showering for a week, I wanted to see Blaire. Only, they had her in the room down the hall from Professor Velastra's office." He set the half-eaten burger on the ground between his feet next to his blood packet, no longer hungry. "Then, she drops this bomb on me…"

Riley frowned. "What bomb?"

"That she made the stupid fucking decision to be a lab rat."

"She's not stupid."

He tilted his head to look at Riley. "I didn't say she was."

"No, but saying her decision was stupid implies it."

"What? No, it doesn't."

"Kinda does, man." Aiden nudged Lukas's shoulder with his. "We know you don't think Blaire's stupid, but sometimes you say things that sound like you think less of her." He held his hand up when Lukas opened his mouth to protest. "Again, we *know* you don't, but you really need to rethink your word choices."

Lukas dropped his head forward and rubbed his face, resting his elbows on his knees. While he understood what they were saying, he didn't think his words implied Blaire was stupid.

Seth shook his head and looked at Aiden. "The decision was kinda stupid, and calling it like it is doesn't mean he's calling *her* stupid. Truth's the truth." His steel eyes settled on Lukas. "Though, I agree you have a piss poor way of showing you *don't* think she's dumb."

He never meant to make Blaire feel less than, or even make it seem like he thought poorly of her. He didn't. Blaire didn't always decide things the way he wanted, but that was the thing about being together. They each were their own unique person. He needed to get used to being in a relationship. To not having control over everything around him. Especially if his reactions made others think he thought badly of his Korrena.

The argument he had with Blaire before Vincent kidnapped her filtered into his mind. He implied a monkey was smarter than she was. He cringed at the memory. As soon as the words left his mouth, he wished he could have snatched them back. It was the worst thing he could have said. In reality, he was the stupid one. Not her.

Another regret to add to the list of growing regrets he had about how he handled their partnership so far. He rubbed his aching chest.

"Anyway," Aiden said, "we heard what happened from Professor Velastra about Blaire agreeing to allow them to experiment with her blood, and that she'd have to stay somewhere while they did it. Beyond that, we don't know anything. And you've been MIA, so we've been in the dark."

"Yeah, sorry. I wanted time to process."

"I get it. Sort of. What's going on?"

Lukas sat up and took a breath. "I know what you know." He turned eyes to Aiden and saw the concern in his friend's dark green eyes. "I guess they didn't tell me where they planned to keep her because they assumed I'd come for her." He shrugged. "They wouldn't be wrong."

"What if they hurt her?" Riley squeezed her hands into fists on her lap, gripping onto her plaid skirt. "What if they kill her?"

"They won't kill her," Seth said.

"How do you know that?" Her voice wobbled.

"They need her alive to do their research, right? As long as she's useful to them, they'll keep her alive."

Riley stood quickly. "Then we need to find her before they don't need her anymore!"

"Hey, now." Seth stepped forward, hands gently grasping Riley's arms. "She'll be okay. We'll figure it out."

Riley swiped the tears from her cheeks, and Seth pulled her into his arms, where she buried her face against his chest.

Aiden clapped his hand on Lukas's shoulder. "We should at least try to find out where she is. That way, if things go sideways, we can get to her easily. But if she made an agreement, and everything is handled humanely, then there isn't much we can do—or need to do, whether we like the situation or not." His gaze moved to his sister.

"I haven't spoken to Professor Velastra since the day Blaire was taken," Lukas said.

"Then let's start there."

7

Unforgiven

Tugging his tie loose, Lukas turned sideways in the small leather seat in front of Professor Velastra's desk, throwing his leg over the arm to hang. He'd already ditched his blazer over the back of the chair. The school day was over, and he could finally relax. He bit back a laugh of derision. Relaxing wasn't even on his radar at the moment. It hadn't been for almost a year, except for fleeting moments wrapped up in Blaire's arms. He squeezed his eyes shut at the stinging feeling there.

Seth sat on the seat opposite him, rolling up his uniform sleeves to his elbows while Aiden leaned against the bookshelf to his left, arms crossed. Riley paced around the room, their earlier conversation likely the cause for her unsettled behavior.

"I spoke with the health department, and no one has received any information about possible sampling of Blaire's blood," Professor Velastra said, scooting forward in her desk chair to rest her hands on her desk.

Riley stopped pacing and blinked. "What does that mean?"

"The Order's council has likely hired their own team to handle this to keep the school out of the loop. If everything was legitimate, something like that wouldn't be necessary, but I no longer put anything past these people."

"Is there a chance they're doing the sampling and experiments themselves?"

Lukas looked at Aiden, stomping on his visceral reaction to his friend's words. If the Order took matters into their own hands, Blaire's life was in danger. They nearly killed her once before with their inferior methods of retrieving her blood and skin. Lukas cursed under his breath. Despite his relaxed posture in the chair, his entire body vibrated with restless energy.

"It is a possibility."

"They'll kill her," Lukas bit out through clenched teeth.

Professor Velastra closed her eyes, breathing slowly through her nose. "I won't lie and say that isn't a possibility, but they have promised her safety. They have no intentions of killing her based on the arrangements made prior to Blaire's concession to cooperate with them."

"Then we need to do something. Like, yesterday!" Riley strode between Lukas and Seth's chair and put her hands on Professor Velastra's desk, leaning forward to look the woman in the eye. "We can't just leave her in that situation!"

Seth put his hands on either side of Riley's small waist and pulled her back until her calves bumped his legs. Once assured she wasn't going anywhere, he released her. He sat back in his chair, spreading his legs so Riley could stand between his knees.

"She's right. If Blaire's life is in danger, leaving her like that isn't an option. I won't do it," Aiden said.

He looked as wound tight as Lukas felt. Though he looked relaxed with his arms crossed as he leaned on the bookshelf, the strain in his forearms, his raised shoulders, and the tightness of his uniform shirt on his biceps from where he held himself rigid and flexed—as if poised to fight—spoke volumes about his true feelings.

Fighting was what landed them in this situation in the first place. But it didn't stop the thing from crawling around under Lukas's skin, urging him to once again fight to protect his pair.

"No, we can't leave her in a situation like that." Professor Velastra sighed. "I should have known better than to allow her to accept their proposal." She looked at Lukas. "We could have found another way to get you out of the dungeons."

Lukas's jaw worked, but he said nothing. It wouldn't be productive to acknowledge how senseless the choice was, and like with Blaire, he needed to reign in his judgment, even if the decision to let Blaire exchange herself for his freedom was really stupid.

"So, what can we do?"

Professor Velastra looked at Riley. "Can you speak with Mera to see if she's heard anything in the health department? Perhaps those I've spoken to aren't aware, and a level of discretion is being used. If that is the case, not everyone would be aware." She sat back in her plush leather chair, crossing her legs. "I want to get in touch with the Blackthorn Clan directly, but typically, only the councils in each sector of the world have a direct access line to the monarchy."

"Is there not a way to bypass the chain of command?" Aiden asked.

"That's what I have to figure out. The Order has spent too long unchecked, and they are putting students at risk. Something has to give."

The question remained: what if the Blackthorn Clan had

something to do with this?

If the Order regularly reported to the Blackthorn Clan, then wouldn't they be aware of Blaire's strange blood? Lukas didn't know if trusting the king and the other members of the royal family would yield anything positive. Maybe they sanctioned these tests. Maybe they were behind the entire thing.

"Are you sure we can trust them?"

The professor stood from her chair and turned to the window, looking out at the small garden behind the staff building. Rays of the setting sun filtered through the cedar tree next to the window, making the silken material of her champagne blouse shine. She took a long inhale through her nose and huffed it out quickly. "I think so. King Adrian has made his stance on human interactions clear since he took the throne. While it was always our rule, he has set forth a no tolerance policy for Vasirian who harm humans."

"So, what the Order has done to Blaire so far would get them in trouble?"

"Yes, Lukas, it certainly would."

"Then why haven't you reported them sooner?"

She pinched the bridge of her nose. "As I said, I don't have the authority to contact them on a whim. It's not like I haven't considered it, but asking around when I didn't know who we could trust on staff wasn't an option. You know this."

"What about that one professor?"

Professor Velastra looked at Riley with a questioning brow raised.

"You know, the one who tried to compel Blaire—"

"What?" Lukas jerked upright in his seat. "What the fuck are you talking about?"

Riley winced.

"Shit," Aiden muttered under his breath. "Lukas, calm down,

man."

"No, tell me what you're talking about, Riley."

Professor Velastra sighed. "Blaire came to me while you were in the dungeons and expressed her concerns about something Vincent tried to do."

"He tried to compel her?"

Now Lukas really wished he had killed the asshole.

"Before he drugged her, yes. The reason he drugged her in the first place was because the compulsion failed. He later realized he could still bind her body with his abilities, but Blaire apparently has a resistance to control of her mind beyond immobilization."

"Okay… but what does that have to do with another professor compelling her?"

"My colleague is one of our most gifted Vasirian on campus. His compulsion abilities are top tier. I wanted to see if Blaire had a resistance to the act of compulsion, or if Vincent's abilities weren't as strong."

"Did she agree to that?"

Lukas didn't think Professor Velastra would force Blaire into something that would traumatize her, but in the search for answers, it seemed the older Vasirian around him weren't acting like they were supposed to. The Order were prime examples of this.

"Of course. Do you believe I would make her act against her will?"

"Not really, but…"

The professor held her hand up. "I get it. But no, I did not coerce Blaire into anything. I suggested the test, and with Aiden's physical support, and Riley's companionship, Blaire agreed to the experiment. I would never have allowed Professor Galloway to get near her had she expressed discomfort about allowing it to happen."

Lukas sat back in his chair and ran a hand through his long hair, exhaling a breath.

Aside from the relief of knowing Blaire hadn't been pressured into allowing someone to compel her, immense comfort came from knowing that while she remained out of his reach with the Order, they couldn't force her to do their bidding that way. But that knowledge didn't ease the frustration and guilt of knowing he was the reason she was in the situation in the first place. Even if he didn't regret attacking Vincent, what came of his actions wasn't satisfying.

"I believe Professor Galloway has connections that can allow me to reach the Blackthorn Clan."

"And you trust them?"

"Yes, Lukas, I trust him. As I told the others, he is my late husband's cousin. I've known him for fifty years, at least."

Aiden shifted against the bookshelf, tucking his hands in the pockets of his uniform slacks. "Aside from Mera, is there anything else we can do? I don't want to leave Blaire wherever she is longer than necessary."

"Even if we found her, we cannot act."

"Why the hell not?" Seth asked.

"Unless we have proof that something untoward is happening to Blaire, she freely accepted the experimentation. We have to trust their words until the Blackthorn Clan can get involved, or…" Professor Velastra glanced at Lukas and sighed. "Or until we get any sign that Blaire is in danger." She began shuffling papers in a folder.

Lukas hated the idea of waiting for something bad to happen. Leaving Blaire at the mercy of a council of old psychopaths didn't make him feel good. The longer he spent away from Blaire, the more their bond weakened. They'd already lost their mark. If they continued to be forced apart, would they lose the connection they were born with? He didn't know if he could handle it.

He rested his elbows on his knees, rubbing his eyes. With a resigned sigh, he looked up at the professor, finally speaking the words he needed to say now that they had a direction to go. "I need help."

At the broken sound of Lukas's voice, Professor Velastra's fingers stilled.

Aiden and Seth turned their eyes on him, and Riley faced him. He swallowed the bile rising in his throat. He needed help. Blaire needed him. He needed her. Even if she acted like she forgave him for what he did, he couldn't forgive himself. Instinct told him to withdraw and run away from it all, but he belonged to Blaire, and he had to do this for them.

They already knew what he'd done. He'd admitted to mortally endangering Blaire in a moment of weakness. But no one had told him what he could do about that instinct. How to keep from doing it again. He couldn't risk her life again; and when they slept together—or at least tried—when he got out of the dungeons, the thoughts that rode him when they tried to reseal their bond reared their ugly head again. He needed to stop before it went any farther; before he attempted to drain her again. He might not be as lucky as the last time.

A firm hand on his shoulder made him jolt.

"Hey," Aiden said softly. "What's going on, man?"

When did he move across the room?

Lukas sat back in his chair and closed his eyes with a sigh. "So, you all know what I did."

"What do you mean?" Aiden asked, propping his hip against the back of Lukas's chair. Lukas was glad his best friend could read him well enough to know that, despite his desire to run, he needed the closeness.

"When I almost killed her."

"You what?"

Lukas met shocked, steel-gray eyes. *Shit.* He hadn't told Seth what had happened yet. Riley and Kai knew because he told them later on. Lukas was sure Kai told Mera because of their bond. But Seth hadn't been in the room when he admitted what he did to Blaire.

"Things got out of hand when we tried to reseal our bond. I couldn't stop myself. The nagging thoughts of how much Blaire being a Vasirian would protect her, keep her from going through something like she went through with Vincent from happening again, raged in my head the entire time. The desire to not let her grow old and die. I lost it."

Seth cursed under his breath.

"As I told you before, your connection was already unstable. After losing her for an extended period, your psyche was damaged." The professor tucked the folder away and sat back in her chair. "What do you need help with?"

Here goes nothing…

"When I got out of the dungeons, and they allowed us to have one night together down the hall, things got…" He rolled his hand twice in a gesture to imply they could fill in the blanks. Judging by the way Riley's nose wrinkled, and Aiden chuckled behind him, they got the meaning. "So, while it was happening, those same thoughts started riding me again. I wanted to bite her—which wasn't abnormal—but I wanted more than that. The same protective need rose to the surface."

"Well, your connection wasn't any more stable than when you tried to reseal your bond. I'd venture a guess your fractured connection was in greater turmoil after the trial and being locked away from her for a week yourself. This doesn't sound surprising."

Lukas didn't consider any of that. It wasn't as if Blaire offering her blood to him during Vincent's trial to calm him fixed everything. He expected a shift in her behavior after that, but an underlying uncertainty remained between them about everything prior to that. Maybe not about what happened in their bed, but everything with Clarissa and Vincent.

Then came his separation from her. Every time something forced them apart physically, their bond weakened.

"What do I do about it? How do I stop these thoughts? I can't even make love to my pair without risking her life."

Riley dropped with a sigh to perch on the edge of the chair between Seth's legs, and he scooted back to accommodate her, hooking one leg over the arm of the chair.

"I truly feel that once you both are reunited, these thoughts will settle."

"No, they won't."

"What makes you believe that?"

Pressure built behind his eyes. His head hurt. How did he tell them he'd been fighting thoughts like this since after the first time they sealed their bond with the claiming ritual?

"When things were good… You know, back when we first bonded…" A supportive hand rested on his shoulder as he struggled with his words, strengthening him. He cleared his throat. "I had similar thoughts after our connection sealed. It was as if every possessive thought I had about Blaire intensified tenfold. Did you ever feel that?"

Professor Velastra folded her hands on her knee at the hem of her pencil skirt as she studied Lukas with a pitying frown. "No, I can't say I did. I also don't recall my late husband mentioning anything like that. In fact, this isn't something I've heard reported with Korrena pairs. Granted, we all experience a possessiveness and need to protect our Korrena that is stronger than with a compatible pair, or unbound lover, but not on the level you describe. Not in my experience, at least."

Lukas slumped in his seat, resting his elbow on the arm of the chair, holding the side of his head. Of course, things weren't going to be easy for him.

"But Lukas, you must understand one critical detail that is different for you than for other pairs." He met the professor's beseeching gaze. "Blaire is human. No other pair has experience with that. I suspect the most primal part of yourself is responding to that fact. As strong as we all know Blaire is, the fact remains that she's human. Humans are fragile. They don't live long. They get diseases we can only imagine. No matter how strong willed the human may be, the fact remains that humans are the weaker species. Couple that with the inherently possessive and protective nature of a pair-bonded Vasirian, it can be a recipe for disaster."

"So, what can he do?" Riley asked.

Seth leaned his elbow on the chair to peer around Riley. "I don't think there's much he can do. As long as Blaire is human, she'll be at risk. Not just from normal human ailments, age, or even our world, but from Lukas."

"Unless he can rein in these thoughts and control them, yes, he could pose a threat to Blaire." The professor frowned, as if she didn't like her own words.

"That makes no sense to me," Aiden said. "You're talking as if he's a lost cause."

"Oh, don't get me wrong. I fully believe Lukas can control himself, but only once the two of them reunite and there isn't a constant threat of separation looming over them. It's agitating the bond, which is agitating Lukas's baser instincts."

"You're saying he'll stop wanting to turn her once they're together again?"

"No. He said himself he had the thoughts before. The key thing about that statement is he never acted on those thoughts."

She was right. Despite the overwhelming desire to have Blaire become a Vasirian, he never once considered physically forcing the issue. Sure, he brought it up, and it led to heated discussions. It was one of the big catalysts in his belief Blaire had left the academy when, in reality, Vincent had kidnapped her.

"So, you're saying once this shit with the Order is over, things will go back to the way they were before my cousin kidnapped her?" Seth asked.

"Presumably."

Professor Velastra gave him a small pebble of hope. If they could get through this, and take things slow when the experimentation was done, things would work out. But only if things weren't so emotionally damaged between them that their bond would reseal, and the mark could return.

Even with the sliver of hope offered to him, he still couldn't forgive himself for what he did to Blaire.

8

Severed Realms

Blaire stood at the bottom of a worn and cracked stone staircase flanked by large rocks covered in moss, mushrooms, and overgrown grass. Peering over the edge of the natural stone wall, she looked at the drop below. It was impossible to make out anything below with fog swirling thickly beneath. It made the stairs feel like they were floating.

The Oracle was reaching out to her in her sleep. She half expected apprehension at finding herself in this strange dream world again after watching her mother melt in front of her last time, but as with all the other times she ventured into this space, a peace settled over her she couldn't describe.

She hoped she had more beneath her feet than just stone stairs, but she couldn't be sure with the way the bottom of the landing at the top of the stairs jutted out over the mysterious abyss. Lush ivy and vines dangled over the edge, disappearing into the fog below.

The air was quiet, but not in an unsettling sort of way.

Rays of the setting sun shone through a massive stone archway at the top of the stairs on the landing, calling to her. Strange markings were carved into the moss-covered stone.

A squawk caught her attention, and she looked up to see a large crow peering down at her from atop the arch, perched on what appeared to be an enormous emerald embedded in the center of the arch's curve. The golden sky with hints of pink cast its feathers in a soft light, making the corvid appear ethereal.

"Is she around?" Blaire felt silly talking to a crow, but they understood her before.

The crow cawed and swooped down from its perch to circle around Blaire's head and glide through the stone archway. She followed quickly up the remaining stairs. When she passed through the arch and around a bend on the edge of a mountain, she gasped.

She didn't know where the meadow and forest she'd seen before in this dreamscape went, but the new location was breathtakingly beautiful. She could have never conjured in her wildest imagination the scene before her.

A valley lay below another set of stone stairs surrounded by mountains on all sides. Lush forests skirted the edge of the mountains surrounding a small lake in the center of the valley with rivers trailing off in different directions. But that wasn't what held Blaire's attention.

Behind the lake stood an enormous gateway. Large chunks of stone floated on either side and above the structure as if suspended by a lack of gravity, but the faint purple and blue glow around them hinted at a more fantastical reason. At the base of the archway, an extensive set of stairs spanned the entire bottom, but she couldn't make out any details of what surrounded the stairs from this distance.

The center of the arch itself didn't look passable. She couldn't see the other side beyond a swirling black and gray fog filling the archway. Occasionally, a flash of lightning sparked in the mysterious clouds, as if the gateway contained its own private storm. The way the sky darkened, and the clouds converged over the structure made her wonder how far off her assessment was.

Another caw pulled her attention away from the massive structure, and she looked at the crow perched on the stones flanking the stairs leading into the valley.

"Where are we going?"

The crow made a guttural sound in answer before flying off down the stairs, and she laughed. She didn't understand a thing it said, but she knew to follow.

Once she left the steep incline of the stairs to walk among the lush flora, the air settled and warmed. Flowers she'd never seen before littered the edges of the path. Yellow blooms with orange streaks bursting from their center across petals the size of her hand grew in bunches against the base of several trees. Did flowers grow that large? None she'd ever seen.

Small glowing mushrooms dotted the pathway, illuminating her steps with their blue and green light. The dim luminescence was a welcome help as the trees surrounding her as she made her way from the edge of the mountains toward the empty valley blocked out the sunlight.

Moving deeper into the forest brought the sounds of birdsong and the rustle of leaves as wildlife moved through the foliage. She hoped it was only small wildlife and not the kind that could eat her.

Overhead, the canopy of tree branches twisted together, creating a blanket for the forest floor below. Vines and glowing blooms dangled like guiding lights through the shadowed forest. The place was stunning, and Blaire wondered why she never dreamed of something this beautiful before when she'd met with the Oracle.

The crow stopped occasionally, perching on rocks, logs, and larger mushrooms as if checking to see Blaire still followed.

"I'm coming. I'm coming. Just… this place is amazing. Where are we?"

Blaire's gaze followed a group of small glowing butterflies flitting in front of her from one side of the path to the other, a trail of sparkling blue and white floating behind them. Her gaze moved from the butterflies to the surrounding forest, where trails of the same sparkling lights floated in the shadows in various colors over the lush vegetation. Large leafy plants, ferns, clusters of clover, and foreign flowers hid the floor of the forest entirely. The only visible ground was the mushroom path she walked along. She could get lost in this place and not care. The entire area soothed and relaxed her.

"The forest that surrounds the Shimmer Gate's valley is a place of peace."

Blaire whirled around at the familiar feminine voice.

What greeted her standing in the center of the path made her pause. She knew the Oracle's voice, but the guise of her mother wasn't what awaited her this time.

This woman had long, wavy black hair that flowed to her hips. Streaks of silver cascading through the strands shimmered against the glow of the flora that swayed on the vine to her right.

She didn't look familiar, but her eyes sparked a memory. The trial.

"You were at Vincent's trial."

"I was."

"And you're… the Oracle?"

"I am."

"But—"

"I felt coming to you in my true form now was more appropriate after the traumatic vision you witnessed before the trial. I apologize for not having a better grasp of the situation to prevent you from seeing that."

The image of her mother's skin melting from her face as the storm raged around them in her last dream of this world flashed through her mind. She pushed it away, swallowing down the horror that followed.

"Why are we here?"

"The more you awaken, the stronger my connection to this world becomes. The stronger my connection becomes, the more the Celestial Conclave reveals to me."

"But why am I here?"

"You need to see what is at stake should you choose to turn away from Lukas."

"I don't understand."

The woman stepped forward. Her white gown, tied at the waist with braided gold rope, dragged the forest path with each step she took toward Blaire.

"Your indecision about your humanity, and his instinctive need to protect you, are at war with each other. As long as there is an upset in the balance between you both, the balance of our kind cannot be restored. This place will remain locked away to my kind."

"This place isn't real."

The Oracle held up her hand and a large bird landed on her fist. Blaire had never seen a bird like that in her life. A fat red bird with eyes like garnet and a long, pointed orange beak dappled with black spots. Its long tail feathers flowed a good two feet from its back, tipped with orange and yellow fluff.

"It is."

"But you said it was also a dream."

A gentle smile graced the woman's face as she cocked her head to the side. "It is that, too."

Blaire's lips twisted like she'd sucked a lemon. The ring-around-the-roses way the Oracle spoke irritated her. Why couldn't the Oracle just say it like it was?

Laughter tinkled, and the bird made a tittering sound that sounded too much like a snicker.

"I apologize if my delivery is not to your expectations."

Blaire had forgotten in this world her thoughts weren't completely closed.

"With more open to me, and the longer you remain in my kind's world, the more I can share with you. I still cannot tell you what this space is where we meet, but I can tell you it exists in reality."

Blaire was sure she'd have seen it on TV, or heard something about a massive structure sitting in the middle of a fishbowl valley surrounded by mountains and actual glowing flora and fauna. Her crow guide squawked as it came to land on the Oracle's shoulder, followed by its mate, who perched on her opposite shoulder near the strange red bird who studied Blaire with intelligent eyes. All the birds perching on the Oracle started to feel like a scene from a Disney movie. If the Oracle broke into song, Blaire was done.

"This place doesn't exist on the same plane of existence we do, and as of now, it is cut off from that plane."

"Why?"

The red bird's head lowered in sadness. It tucked its beak against the fluffy plumage of its chest. How did she know it was sad?

"Long ago, a balance broke between two species, and in turn, two worlds ripped apart from each other." The Oracle held her hand up, and the unique bird spread its wings wide before launching itself into the air and disappearing through the canopy overhead. "In consequence of choices made long ago, the connection between these worlds severed, and as long as the balance stays in disrepair, they will remain forever lost to one another."

Blaire listened to the Oracle's words, but she wondered what any of it had to do with her and why she was being exposed to this place. If it was a different plane of existence, wouldn't that mean it was a different time and space altogether? Her head hurt from trying to wrap her mind around it.

The smell of coconut and wet earth hit her nose, and she looked around for the source of the new scent that permeated the air.

The Oracle's gaze moved over Blaire's shoulder as she continued to explain. "This place doesn't exist at a different time. As our world moves, so does this one."

Blaire shook her head, and her mouth parted before she sighed. "I still don't understand any of it. What does any of that have to do with me and Lukas?"

"Your blood, child. The secrets dwelling in your blood are tied to a past that shaped the current tragedy which has befallen this world and ours."

"What tragedy?"

"Severance of the Shimmer Gates."

Blaire blinked. The Oracle mentioned that name earlier. "What are the Shimmer Gates?"

The Oracle closed her eyes, and she remained quiet for several beats, her eyelids fluttering rapidly, and her mouth moving as if she were speaking, but no sound escaped her lips. Finally, she opened her eyes to look at Blaire.

"The bridge between our world and this one."

"Wait..." Blaire squinted at the Oracle. "You weren't lying about this being an actual place?" She looked around at the fantastical environment again in disbelief.

Soft laughter was her answer.

"I'm serious."

"I never lie, child."

"You mean to tell me I can come here when not dreaming?"

The Oracle gave a slow shake of her head. "No, you cannot come here while awake. Not anymore. And possibly never again."

Movement behind Blaire caught her attention, and she spun to meet a pair of the brightest blue eyes she'd ever seen. She didn't know wolves could have blue eyes.

Stalking toward her slowly, the gigantic wolf with white and gray fur kept its eyes focused on her. Again, like the deer from previous dreams, the creature showed an intelligence she hadn't seen in any of the animals in her world. Why did the creatures of this place seem more than animal?

Once the wolf reached her, she was taken aback by how massive it was. Not like the dire wolves she'd seen in television documentaries, but much larger than modern wolves and dogs. The wolf's back came to her hips, which was quite impressive against her five-foot-eight height. Its head alone was the width of her hips.

She took a hesitant step back and the wolf stopped, slowly lowering itself into a seated position, remaining eerily still. Blaire let out a relieved breath. At least the animal had the good sense to know when it scared the daylights out of someone.

Blaire swallowed, keeping her eye on the predator sitting there watching her intently as she spoke. "Why can't I come here?"

"The connection between the worlds was severed long ago, and that is the only way to cross between the two realms."

"Again, though, what does that have to do with me and Lukas?"

The wolf stood and padded toward her again, and Blaire tried not to act on instinct and run like hell when it didn't seem the wolf meant her any harm. She was still dreaming, right? Even if it was a real place, she couldn't die in the dream—right?

Coming to a stop at Blaire's side, the wolf sat again, leaning into her, knocking her off balance from the weight.

"I cannot tell you much."

What else is new?

The Oracle chuckled. "But I can tell you if you turn away from Lukas, the bridge remains closed forever."

Blaire looked down at her feet.

She would never turn away from Lukas. She loved him. Despite the trials of their relationship, and the brief hesitation she felt when she considered being in a committed relationship at nineteen—not sure if the love she felt was real at first—the truth existed deep in her soul. With the losses she suffered from an early age, and the continued curve balls life kept throwing at her, she had to grow up fast. Did she know it all? No. Were all of her decisions rooted in the seasoned maturity of an adult who'd had plenty of relationships? No.

But when you know, you know.

Blaire almost laughed as she recalled Vincent using the same words.

She doubted another living soul could make her feel the way Lukas did. No one could arouse her, make her feel safe, and frustrate the hell out of her at the same time, still leaving her wanting more. If that wasn't love, she wasn't sure she wanted anything else.

At this point in their relationship, she understood what parts of Lukas's personality were his own prickliness, and what was the overbearing instability of a Vasirian in the early stages of their Korrena bond. Her eyes lifted to meet the Oracle's. Staying with Lukas wasn't the only issue at hand. No, it had everything to do with her humanity and her blood.

The more she remained in Lukas's world, the more she saw the benefits of becoming a Vasirian. Maybe once they got past this with the Order, and dealt with calming down their bond, she'd discuss it with him again. But even if this strange world connected with her decision to become a Vasirian, she couldn't change who she was for that reason alone. Besides, it didn't sound like the world would cease to be if she stayed a human.

"That's correct. This world remains no matter what happens to you, Lukas, or the balance. But there is so much more to it than merely existing."

Blaire's hand stilled in the wolf's fur. When did she start petting it?

"What do you mean?"

"I have told you all the Celestial Conclave will grant me the ability to say. Anything more I share will influence your decision. The information thus far is not enough to sway you into making choices about who you are or what you want."

"So, if my decision to become a Vasirian or not is what's important, then why do you keep mentioning a balance?"

"More than you becoming a Vasirian is key to the future of our kind and the connection between these worlds. But again, this is beyond what I can share with you at this time."

The wolf nudged Blaire's hand, and she absentmindedly stroked the soft fur on its head.

"As for the balance, it is connected to many distinct elements. Your blood, your humanity, what you carry within you. There is a balance between these worlds, the past, our bloodlines, and more that I am not at liberty to discuss. These things are reliant on the choices you make."

Peachy. More confusion.

Blaire muttered, "It would be nice if I knew which choices I was supposed to be making. You're not making this any easier. Don't you need my help or something? I can't do anything if I don't know what to do."

The wolf snuffed her hand with its wet nose.

"Oh, child. I cannot influence your decisions or make you make choices in the name of the balance. I can only guide you toward making choices you truly desire."

"But what if I mess up? What if I make a decision that hurts someone or this beautiful world?"

The Oracle smiled warmly at Blaire. "That is how life works. Not all choices we make will benefit everyone around us. Sometimes we make mistakes. I am merely here to give you the tools and information the Celestial Conclave grants me permission to share as my memories return. They deem what is essential in guiding you toward making the choices that are true to you but also helpful for the future."

"What if it doesn't restore whatever balance you're talking about? What if the worlds stay apart?"

"Then that is what happens. Should such sad outcomes arise, I am certain there is a reason for such a thing. Perhaps the methods we believe are key to the restoration of the balance are not accurate. Perhaps there is more to it than what we believe. This is why I can only share bits of information with you to not alter the path you are on."

She stepped forward and gently touched the side of Blaire's face with a soft hand. Her eyes were warm and filled with affection as she spoke.

"I am but a guide. I will do everything I can to guide you and be a support as you traverse this unfamiliar world with Lukas. But I cannot force your hand. I cannot reveal everything. That isn't how it works."

The wolf at Blaire's side circled around the two of them before sitting back and howling at the canopy above. The Oracle sighed.

"It is time."

"Time for what?"

"For you to wake up."

9

Change

Wednesday morning, Lukas walked into his Comparative Approach to Literary Criticisms class more relaxed than he had been the past several days. Knowing that Professor Velastra was reaching out to the Blackthorn Clan for help eased his concerns. If they found something wrong with where the Order had Blaire and what they were doing to her, he had to believe the clan would intervene. Anything else would send him back into a tailspin.

"You look better."

He sat on the chair behind the long table, dropping his backpack between his feet. Layla already sat in her seat, watching him intently, a big smile on her baby face.

"I guess?" He didn't mean for it to sound like a question, but he didn't know how to respond to this girl. He still wasn't sure of her motives.

"Did something good happen?"

He shrugged.

"Well, I think this look suits you bet—"

"Settle down everyone." A woman Lukas had never seen before walked from the door of the classroom to stand in front of the whiteboard at the front of the class. Her lips pressed into a thin line, and her features remained tight as she frowned.

Layla leaned over and whispered, "Wonder what's going on?"

He didn't know, but the grave look on the woman's face set him on edge.

"I have unfortunate news to share," the woman said, adjusting the jacket of her pantsuit. "Professor Burgess will no longer be teaching this class."

"Why not?" a guy in the front row asked.

With a resigned sigh, the woman said, "His Korrena was involved in a tragic accident and could not heal quickly enough to survive." Murmurs filled the air. She raised a hand. "And, as you all are aware, the loss of your Korrena is sometimes too much for the other half of a pair bond to handle…"

"Oh no, really?" A gasp of disbelief came from the girl behind him. She said to her table partner sadly, "They were together for sixty years."

Then the woman dropped a bomb. "He had no other family, so no one was around to know what happened until it was too late."

A couple of girls in the class broke down crying, and the murmured whispers elevated until the entire class buzzed. The woman waited until the noise died down before she spoke again.

"Until we find a replacement for this course, you all will have your Monday and Wednesday mornings free. Should you choose to switch your course to something else you're required to take, you can opt into this class at a later time." She sighed again. "For those of you who feel you need someone to speak to about this news—especially those with Korrenas yourselves—then I encourage you to seek the psychology department's guidance."

A couple of marked Korrenas were in the class. The girls who broke down crying were two he knew of. Lukas didn't wish the loss of a Korrena on anyone. Blaire had not died, yet having her kidnapped, thinking she left him, nearly destroyed him. The separation now, despite being voluntary on her end, was awful. To lose her forever? He wondered if he wouldn't do the same thing Professor Burgess did.

"What are you gonna do?" Layla looked at Lukas. "I think I'll just take it as a free period for now. There's a possibility we could get a replacement next week. I'd hate to rearrange everything if it ends up being a few days missed, or none at all, if they find someone by Monday. Especially with the holiday break coming."

Despite the circumstances of how it came to pass, Lukas was grateful for the reprieve from the class. With everything happening, he was having a difficult time concentrating, and the social aspect of this class didn't do him any favors.

"Probably will do the same."

"Yeah? Wanna go to the cafeteria and hang out, then? At least we can get a decent table before lunch starts this way."

Students were already leaving the class, still talking loudly about Professor Burgess's death. Their disrespectful gossip about the dead, especially of someone who took their life under such painful circumstances, bothered him.

Lukas shrugged. He didn't know why the girl wanted to hang around him, but she provided a decent distraction. At least in a crowded cafeteria she couldn't do anything to him.

As they made their way from the classroom, a group of girls followed close behind.

"Look at that. She's already moved on to her next mark."

"After everything that happened with Brandon, I can't believe it."

"I can. She cheated on him, and now she's going after someone already bonded. If she'll cheat, I doubt she'd care about a Korrena bond."

Lukas couldn't tell who was saying what. He wasn't going to bait them into conversation by looking back, but Layla curled in on herself, holding her books tightly to her chest and hunching her shoulders. He didn't want to ask about it, but he didn't like how bothered she looked.

He tuned the girls out as they made their way to the end of the hallway, but before they could take the stairs, the three girls shoved past Layla, knocking her forward. Her books tumbled down the stairs, but before she could go down with them, Lukas snatched her around the waist and pulled her up against him. He growled as the girls continued down the wide staircase giggling and talking amongst themselves.

Lukas was still glaring after the girls when Layla wiggled out of his hold, straightening her plaid skirt and button-down blouse. She rushed down the steps and gathered her books as he stood staring at her. She ducked her head, her ponytail falling forward and shielding her face, but not before he saw the shiny marks from tears on her reddened cheeks.

Lukas raked a hand through his long hair and huffed. He didn't know what to say, but it seemed like the right time to reassure the girl. In truth, he wanted to go after the girls who tried to knock Layla down the stairs and demand to know what their problem was. He hated bullies.

Layla cleared her throat, and their eyes connected. He frowned when he saw how wet her lashes were.

"Are you okay?"

She shrugged. "Used to it."

"What? This happens a lot?" Lukas stepped down the stairs to where Layla waited, and when she turned and continued down the steps, he followed.

"With those three, yeah."

"But why?"

"Crystal thinks I stole her boyfriend back in high school and has had it out for me ever since." She sighed. "I've only had one boyfriend. Brandon." She glanced up at Lukas. "I wasn't the one who cheated." Her gaze moved forward again, and she tightened her hold on the books in her arms. "The reason it became such a big deal to Crystal and her friends is because Crystal liked Brandon. I didn't know that. Freshman year of high school, there was a boy who liked me—her boyfriend—but I rejected him because he was with Crystal. She and I were friends at the time. I told him I wouldn't date a boy who had a girlfriend, so he dumped her."

"Did you date him next?"

"Oh, no way. There's too much ick there. He would dump a girl just to be with someone else? That's gross." She looked up at Lukas. "What if he did that to me next?"

"Fair." He tucked his hands in the pockets of his uniform slacks and let Layla talk. She seemed to be calming down the longer she talked.

"She was my friend, you know? I wouldn't do that to her. The thing is, Crystal found out that Shane—her ex—liked me, and she was convinced he dumped her to be with me." She laughed. "Well, he *did*, but I didn't agree to be with him." She sighed. "She didn't believe it, and it became this big thing, and our friendship was ruined."

They reached the end of the hallway of the second floor where the cafeteria was located and stopped outside the doors.

"When I finally got my first boyfriend my senior year of high school, I didn't even consider Crystal would do anything. We hadn't had anything to do with each other for three years." Layla glanced through the glass on the cafeteria doors. "I didn't know she had a thing for him, but she took the opportunity to do to me what she thinks I did to her. Unlucky for me, Brandon was just like Shane. He went for it because I wouldn't sleep with him. I hadn't slept with anyone at that point." Shrugging, she spoke casually, but tension stiffened her stance. "They had sex, and,"—she took a shuddering breath—"Crystal sent me the video."

"That's disgusting."

She nodded, squeezing her books.

"Hey," Lukas said softly.

Layla looked up at him.

"It wasn't unlucky. It's better to know his true colors than stay with him and end up sleeping with him."

"I guess you're right."

"So why the hell are they saying you cheated on him?"

"I don't know. Probably just to be mean and scare you off." She turned quickly to him, genuine worry in her eyes. "I'm not trying to 'go after you' or anything. I've heard about your Korrena." She shook her head. "I don't understand why guys and girls can't be friends."

"We can. You just have to overlook the assholes." He pushed open the door to the cafeteria and motioned for Layla to enter first.

While he wasn't quick to trust the girl, he felt bad for what she'd been through, and he wasn't going to reject her the way those girls had.

"So, what's it like having a human for a pair?" Layla asked, sitting across from Lukas at the round table in the cafeteria's corner against the floor to ceiling windows overlooking the forest backing the academy.

Lukas grimaced. It wasn't a secret that Blaire was his Korrena. Everyone and their mother knew about it. Not that the academy was small, but the fact that a human freely walked their halls paired to one of their own wasn't easily missed.

He sighed. "What's it like having a Vasirian for a pair?" He shrugged. "I can't really answer that because I don't know the difference between the two." Well, that wasn't entirely true. Key elements about Blaire and his pair bond set them apart from the other pairs he'd encountered. How he sometimes felt like a monster around her being one of those key differences.

The volatile beast living inside of him remained subdued lately. Buried beneath the guilt, bitterness, and shame churning inside of him.

Lukas had never thought of the Vasirian part of himself as a separate being, but with the way everything occurred when they tried to reseal their bond, how he kept losing control, it felt like he was two people. The docile Vasirian and the bloodthirsty beast prowling the depths of his very being, hungering for so many things he never thought he'd crave.

"I don't know. I don't have a Korrena. As I said, only one boyfriend." She sighed. "I get your point, though. I just wondered if it was different from what we've learned about the pair bond."

Lukas sat back in his seat, sliding a small straw into his blood packet. "A little bit," he admitted, taking a sip. At least she didn't seem jealous of his Korrena, or hateful of humans.

"How so?"

"You're in here early," Kai's voice pulled his attention from Layla.

Kai's timing couldn't be better. Not that Lukas didn't want to talk to Layla. She seemed nice—a little lonely. But he wasn't about to spill the crazy feelings he'd been experiencing to a total stranger.

Mera stopped and eyed Layla with raised brows. "What are you doing here? I thought you ate with your friends in the courtyard."

"Mera!" Layla jumped up. When Mera set her tray on the table, Layla immediately wrapped her in a hug. At least she wasn't upset about the bullying incident anymore.

Lukas's brow arched as he watched Mera's arms go around the small girl, before turning his gaze back on Kai. "Our professor passed away. No one to teach the class."

"Really? What happened?" Mera pulled from Layla's hug and took her seat at Kai's side.

Kai's eyebrows pinched. "It had to be something bad if they didn't heal from it." He cut into the beef tenderloin on his tray.

"He killed himself," Layla said quietly, lowering herself back into her chair.

"Who killed himself?" Riley said, dropping into the chair next to Layla. "Hi, I'm Riley Easton." She smiled brightly. Riley always introduced herself using her full name, and Lukas never understood the habit.

"Hi. I'm Layla." A blush spread across Layla's cheeks, making her freckles pop. "Layla Crowley. Lukas's classmate, and Mera's cousin."

"Any relation to Professor Crowley?" Aiden asked as he set down his tray, taking a seat next to Lukas. Seth moved to sit on Aiden's other side, beside Riley. At Layla's nod, he said, "She's alright. A bit strict."

"My aunt is like that outside the classroom, too."

"My condolences."

Layla giggled.

Mera shook her head. "Aunt Vivian isn't that bad."

"Sooo?" Riley prompted, looking at Layla.

"Oh! Yeah, um, Professor Burgess in our Comparative Approach to Literary Criticisms class killed himself after his Korrena pair lost their life in an accident."

Aiden cursed under his breath, and Kai set his fork down, taking Mera's hand as she reached for him.

Riley frowned. "That's terrible."

No one said anything for a long time as the cafeteria filled with the noise of students breaking for lunch.

Kai rubbed soothing circles against the back of Mera's hand, before expelling a breath. "It happens so rarely I don't give it much thought."

"What do you mean?" Riley asked, finally scooping a forkful of baked macaroni and cheese into her mouth.

"The death of a Korrena pair. I think we take for granted our ability to bounce back from injury and avoidance of most diseases. The rare times it happens, we aren't prepared. Mind you, no one could ever be prepared for losing a loved one, but to lose a Korrena…" His Adam's apple bobbed in his throat. "I think there should be a course that prepares students for the possibility. The emotions linked with a bond like this are too strong to navigate without a support system."

Kai's words resonated deep inside of Lukas. If he knew more about the bond and how to deal with the emotions that came with it, it would have been easier to navigate the strange curveball of his pair being a human.

Currently, Blackthorn Academy's elementary, middle, and high school divisions prepared them for what a Korrena bond was, the biological aspects, and the expectations, but nothing on the strange cocktail of emotions and struggles that accompanied it. It wasn't all sunshine and rainbows like they presented it. Maybe once the bond was secure, but there remained a huge time frame where it was like wading through sludge to get to that elusive peace. Should one pair pass, they lacked guidance on what to do, but it was well known the pain and devastation resulting from that loss was more than what came with the death of a friend, family, or other loved one.

"Heard anything from Professor Velastra?" Seth asked Lukas, changing the subject.

"Not yet, but it's only been a couple of days."

Seth took a drink from his blood packet and nodded.

"Did you find out anything from the health department?" Aiden looked at Mera across the table as he poured Italian dressing on his salad. Lukas wrinkled his nose. That stuff was nasty.

"Actually, yeah." Mera set her water bottle on the table. "I spoke with a woman in her last year who works directly beneath the head of the department, and she told me Blackthorn Security paid the department head's office a visit. She was in the back sorting files and overheard the conversation."

"What'd they say?" Riley said through a mouthful of macaroni.

"They were asking for supplies. Said the Order's research team had an accident in their lab and several supplies they needed to extract 'the human's blood' were destroyed."

Lukas sat up in his chair. "Research team? Lab?"

"I don't know any more than that, but in a way, it relieves me."

"How so?"

"Well, if they have a proper lab, and a team of actual researchers, and not some goons running around in robes in the night, then maybe they are treating Blaire right."

Lukas had to concede to that thought pattern. He still didn't like the idea of Blaire being a pincushion, even if he was curious about the secret to their connection himself. His curiosity wasn't so strong that he wanted her to be hurt, though.

But the mention of a lab set him on edge. Other than the science and health departments, he wasn't aware of any labs on the academy grounds. Where had they taken Blaire?

"What are you talking about?" Layla looked at Mera and Lukas, her eyebrows scrunched together.

Shit. He'd forgotten about Layla. She'd been so quiet, eating her lunch as they talked. He'd let his guard down concerning her after hearing she was Mera's cousin and not just a random girl trying to weasel her way into their group, like a certain obsessive whack-job he didn't care to think about. What had he said? He looked around the table, his eyes searching for the answer to his unspoken question in his friends' eyes.

"The administration wants to learn more about why Blaire can be a Korrena, find out what makes her special," Kai answered smoothly. "I mean, I'm sure we all would love to know the secret behind the mysterious human who found herself as a Korrena. No?"

Layla shook her head. "It is interesting. So, they're testing to find out?"

"Yes, but hopefully it won't take too long. They should know pairs shouldn't be apart very long."

"Is that why you've been so sulky?" Layla asked Lukas before taking a drink from her blood packet.

Riley snorted. "He's always sulky." She glared at Seth when he nudged her with his elbow. "What? It's true. He's a salty—" The rest of her words became muffled when Seth stuck a cookie in her mouth off his tray. She bit the cookie and pulled it from her mouth. "Careful. Next time, I'll bite your fingers off."

He leaned in and whispered something in her ear, and Riley's eyes widened.

Layla giggled, watching them. She had no idea this was normal banter between the two. Lukas was thankful their back-and-forth distracted Layla from the topic of Blaire and the Order's experiments.

They continued to eat their lunch, joking, and discussing plans for the upcoming weekend. Lukas didn't have any interest in going out, but he didn't expect everyone else to stay holed up at the academy. He hadn't expected it during the fall when Blaire went missing, but losing Blaire then had been too much for all of them. Now, with Blaire not in any immediate danger that they knew of, things were different. He still couldn't find it in himself to socialize and do things he would normally find enjoyable. Not until she was home and in his arms again.

"Layla?"

Lukas looked up to see a girl with a short black bob and olive skin looking expectantly at Layla.

"Ah, crap! I'm so sorry, Miko!" She quickly pushed back her chair, scooped up her backpack, and picked up her tray. "I'm sorry to eat and run, but I forgot I promised Miko I'd help her with this thing." When she didn't elaborate, Miko's face flushed.

"I didn't do so well on my final… Layla has already taken the class her freshman year." Miko shrugged. "It's okay to tell them. I'm not embarrassed by it."

"Right. Sure. Sorry. I didn't know if it'd bother you."

The two girls said their goodbyes and made their way across the cafeteria. When they were finally gone, Riley slid her chair closer to Mera. Seth slid his chair over to almost the same distance from hers again, but it gave Aiden more elbow room between Lukas and Seth.

"So, who was that?" Seth asked, settling back in his chair after finishing his food and pulling out his cell phone.

"She's Mera's cousin and Lukas's classmate. Weren't you listening?"

Seth looked at Riley and shook his head. "Not really, no." He tapped at his screen.

Riley grumbled. "Maybe if you paid more attention to what's going on around you instead of texting girls, you'd have a clue." Lowering his phone, Seth stared at Riley until she snapped, "What?"

"Nothing. But if you must know, I'm responding to an email."

Riley shrugged. "Not my business."

"Yet you're so invested," Aiden said with a chuckle, and Riley glared at him.

"You've changed." Mera's words pulled Lukas away from the lighthearted bickering. She was looking at him curiously.

"Huh? Me?"

She nodded. "I don't think I've ever seen you voluntarily sit and openly chat with another student without a valid reason."

It was true. Lukas avoided interaction with strangers. Not that he hated people, or desired being antisocial. He actually wanted to feel more comfortable around others, but trust didn't come naturally to him. He didn't want to be alone, but he didn't want to be disappointed, either.

He shifted in his seat and shrugged lightly. "She asked to sit together when we were dismissed from class early. I wasn't going to be rude to the girl."

"Blaire has really changed you."

Mera shook her head at Kai. "No, I don't think it was Blaire directly. I think it's the way their unique situation has forced Lukas into facing parts of himself he's avoided for years."

Lukas's eyebrows pinched together. "What the hell are you talking about?"

"You haven't been able to shrug off Blaire and retreat into yourself like you've done since I've known you."

Aiden spoke up. "She's right. You're also forced into limitations and boundaries you've never dealt with before. Not just hers, but yours."

"Not to mention the Order and Blaire's stepbrother," Kai said. "You've had to act against everything you'd normally do. Whether you've liked it or not, having a Korrena has pushed you into a different way of thinking."

"I don't think I'd ever seen you cry until Blaire came along," Aiden said. "Except maybe once or twice at best when we were little. And that's from physical injury, not feelings."

"He's definitely let his emotional side surface," Riley added.

Lukas loosened his tie and sighed. His friends' assessment of him wasn't far off. Even if he hated being under the microscope.

While he'd always been protective and cared for his friends and those around him, he wasn't one to go on the attack if they were threatened. Being with Blaire, he'd had to face the fact that he sometimes could be a real asshole. Not that he wanted to come across that way, or even felt that way inside, but his actions and words painted a different outward picture.

A rush of guilt and shame tightened his chest as he recalled things he had said and done to Blaire when they were first getting to know each other.

Being aware of these things and being able to change them were two different things. Had he changed? Sure. But it wasn't enough. Not yet. Lukas still had a long way to go before he would feel worthy of being Blaire's Korrena."

10

Motive

Christmas music and excited chatter echoed throughout the cafeteria as Lukas and his friends sat around their usual table. Vanilla, cinnamon, and other delicious scents filled the air from the dozens of baked treats lining several of the buffet tables.

A couple of girls ran by their table laughing, carrying gifts in their arms, heading toward the large Christmas tree decorated with an assortment of beautiful ornaments and colorful twinkling lights. Those same twinkling lights wrapped around the edges of the buffet tables, doorways, and even the trim of each and every window that made up the cafeteria wall. With the night sky as a backdrop, the lights cast the room in a kaleidoscope of color.

"They outdid themselves this year with the tree," Mera said as she took her seat with Kai. She held a small plate of frosted sugar cookies in one hand, passing Kai a packet of fresh blood with the other.

Every December, Blackthorn Academy hosted a small Christmas

party for students to kick off their two-week winter break. Even though he never took part in any of the festive party games, or socialized with anyone outside his friend group, Lukas always attended. This was probably the first year he didn't want to go. He didn't feel festive without Blaire.

"I can't wait for the dinner buffet to open," Aiden said.

Riley clapped her hands. "I can't wait for the presents."

Seth snorted at her.

She elbowed him. "What?"

"You know those presents are for the staff, right?"

Lukas glanced at the large Christmas tree at the far end of the cafeteria. Gifts with colorful wrapping paper, bows, ribbons, and baubles to accent them cluttered the floor beneath the tree.

"I know." Riley rolled her eyes, popping a bite-size treat with powdered sugar on it into her mouth. "I just like seeing people opening gifts. How happy they get. It's contagious."

"You're always happy," Seth said. "If you perked up anymore, I might catch diabetes."

Riley glared at him. "You can't catch diabetes, dingus."

Seth gave her a "duh" expression and stole a cookie from her plate. He was sarcastic, not stupid.

"Besides, the way the last few months have gone, we could all use a little holiday cheer."

Lukas could appreciate his friends going about their lives and making the most of a shitty situation, but he couldn't do it. Something in him told him the situation with Blaire and the Order's little research project wasn't as simple as they made it sound.

"Oh, wow," Riley said, standing. "Look at the size of those hams."

The kitchen staff carried trays upon trays of steaming hot dishes from the back rooms to the empty buffet tables accented with garland,

Christmas lights, and holly.

"Aiden, they have your favorite." When Aiden looked up at his sister with an arched brow, she added, "Deviled eggs."

His face split with a huge grin and he jumped to his feet. "Let's go before they're gone."

The siblings headed for the buffet as students crowded around before the staff had even finished placing the dishes.

Seth stood and chuckled. "Want me to get you anything?" he asked Lukas. "I wouldn't blame you for wanting to avoid that mess."

Seth was more perceptive than he sometimes appeared. He hadn't understood the Korrena bond when Lukas and Blaire first got together, but he learned really fast the impact everything had on Lukas.

Lukas shook his head. "I'll get something soon."

"You sure you're alright to wait?" Kai asked, standing, and pulling Mera up gently to her feet.

"Yeah, I'm fine. Go."

Lukas needed a minute to process and take in the surrounding festivities without feeling like people were watching him, waiting on him to snap—or worst yet, become a blubbering mess of tears and heartbreak again. He wasn't that far gone. At least, not anymore.

Once everyone gathered around the table again, and most of the crowd had cleared, Lukas finally went to the buffet. Students chatted, and the sounds of them eating carried through the space under the continuous melodies of Christmas carols playing over the PA system.

He filled a plate with spiral ham, turkey breast, stuffing, green bean casserole, cranberry sauce, and a roll, then sat back down at the table where his friends were already digging in.

"Hungry?" he asked Aiden, noting a plate heaped with enough food for three. Well, maybe two, considering it was a holiday feast. Everyone overindulged for the holidays.

Aiden shrugged and swallowed the bite of sweet potato casserole with marshmallows on top. "I love Christmas dinner."

"Blaire would love this," Mera mumbled, but Lukas heard her. He looked down at his plate, suddenly unsure if he should enjoy such an extravagant meal.

Seth nodded. "She'd probably give Aiden's holiday appetite a run for its money."

"Don't make fun of her eating habits," Riley snapped.

"I'm not."

"Better not. She told me about how that creep handled food in her old home." She threw her hand out over the table toward the buffet on the other side of the room. "If she wants to eat every single thing on that buffet, she should be allowed without comment."

"Hey," Seth said, gently placing a hand on Riley's arm. "I was pointing out that Blaire likes to enjoy good food, not fat-shaming her. You know she'd be trying a dab of everything and giving her opinion on the flavors and textures—some of the stuff she says is hilarious."

Aiden shook his head. "It hits different without Blaire here to laugh with us, don't you think?" He picked up his third deviled egg when Kai nodded in agreement.

"Yeah. Shit." Seth scratched his jaw and started poking at his potato salad with his fork. "Too bad she has to miss it, though."

They ate to the sound of music and laughter around them for about fifteen minutes before their meal was disturbed.

"Excuse me." All eyes shifted to a woman dressed in a black and white wraparound dress with long sleeves and a tight bun high on her head. "Lukas Virtanen?"

Lukas swallowed the food in his mouth and cleared his throat. "That's me."

"For you."

Before he could ask what she was talking about, the woman placed a cream envelope with a familiar wax seal of a raised feather design in front of Lukas and walked away.

He didn't hesitate.

He tore into the envelope and pulled out the crisp parchment within.

What did this mean?

"What is it?" Kai asked after Lukas sat there staring at the parchment in his hands for too long.

"The Oracle."

"Huh?" Riley perked up in her seat. "What does she want?"

"To meet us. All of us. Tonight."

The walk to the library was quiet. The school kept the main building unlocked at all times for students who wished to access the library or canteen, but at two in the morning, most students were in bed after the Christmas dinner party dragged on until midnight. The staff who lived on campus had retired to their housing units in the building beside the main staff building where Professor Velastra's office was located. With no one around, the deserted library seemed like a fitting place for a meeting with the Oracle, if she were avoiding the Order. Lukas assumed this was the case, considering the letters he and Blaire received. He didn't think the Order would condone her encouragement, or the strange messages for Blaire they still hadn't fully deciphered.

Aiden pushed the double doors open and stepped inside the massive library, and they followed him inside. The interior was mostly dark, except for moonlight filtering in the windows on the far wall away from the floor-to-ceiling bookshelves that surrounded them.

Riley glanced around, squinting at the darker parts of the library. "Should we turn on the lights?"

"Not sure that's a good idea," Aiden said.

"Why not?"

He motioned to the windows with a view of the staff and administration buildings. "Don't want to draw attention to ourselves."

"I guess..." Riley said, looking up at the chandeliers that held tiers of crystals in all different shapes, from tear drops to tiny balls. During the day, they sparkled and cast an amber light around the space with their faux candles.

Lukas looked around. He wasn't sure exactly where they were supposed to meet the Oracle; several paths could take them through the archways away from the spacious main chamber, or the stairs to the upper floor of the library gave a lot of options to choose from.

"There's a light on back there." Mera pointed to the back corner of the library, where a small hallway was lit by the soft glow of light.

"Let's go," Lukas said.

Passing under the pointed archway, exiting the main chamber of the library, they moved into a narrow hallway where the hardwood flooring had a burgundy carpet runner down its center. The soft light from the open door at the end of the hallway illuminated the painted portraits of past and current members of the Order. The dates on the golden placards beneath a few portraits dated back hundreds of years.

Apprehension coiled inside Lukas when he reached the end of the hall and stepped inside the small room. All communication so far from the Oracle came in the form of letters. What was so important it needed to be said in person?

Standing in a long burgundy robe accented by black feathers embroidered at the bottom around the feet and dainty silver chains tipped with small rubies, the Oracle gave him a warm smile. The smile disarmed him; he didn't expect the reception. Especially now that he recognized her from Vincent's trial by her unique robe and silver-streaked black hair in a tight bun.

"Thank you for joining me. Please, sit. Relax. No one knows we are here."

The others filed into the room about the size of his dorm room. The layout of the furniture made the space feel cramped. A long table surrounded by chairs filled much of the room, and along the walls were carts with various books stacked high.

Once everyone sat, the Oracle tucked her hands into the bell sleeves of her robe and looked around the table at each of them. "I'm sure you wonder why I've called you together at this hour."

Riley was the first to speak, as always. "Is this about Blaire?"

At the Oracle's nod, Lukas sat up in his seat. "Is she in trouble?"

She gave another smile that made him uncomfortable. There wasn't anything wrong with the expression. It wasn't a sinister smile. But he didn't know why someone of her standing would be so… he didn't even know how to describe it. Casual? Cryptic?

"Your Korrena is unhappy, but she is not in danger as of this moment."

"As of this moment?" Aiden frowned. "Where is she?"

"She is being kept in the same dungeons they held Lukas in until the laboratory team needs her for their research."

Lukas narrowed his eyes and tightened his fists on the table. Blaire shouldn't be kept in such a cold and lonely place. With the poor excuse for a bed, lack of a real bathroom, and the isolation, he didn't wish a stay in the dungeons on hardly anyone. He stood up.

"Where're you going?" Riley asked.

"To get her out of there."

"You can't. We agreed that unless something bad was happening, we wouldn't interfere."

The Oracle moved around the table and placed a delicate hand on Lukas's shoulder, looking up at him. "Patience, child. She is safe right now. We must not act, or the consequences could be dire."

"I can't leave her alone like that," he whispered, his voice strained with emotion.

"She won't be alone for long."

"What do you mean?"

"I cannot say much else, but she will be protected during her time in the dungeon. As long as she is there, I have seen no harm befalling her during her time within that space."

Lukas's shoulders slumped, and he lowered himself back into his seat. While he didn't like Blaire being locked away, if she was safer in a cell than outside of one, then he wouldn't fight against it. At least, not right now. The thing that prickled at the back of his mind was the second half of the Oracle's statement. Was Blaire in danger once she left the cell?

"So, why are we here?" Kai asked from the other end of the table.

"I've come to warn you all to prepare." The Oracle crossed to stand at the head of the table. "Blaire is a key element to restoring a lost balance between our kind and hers, and the secret to that restoration lies dormant within her blood."

Lukas's mouth went dry, and he had difficulty swallowing around the lump in his throat.

"When she first arrived at Blackthorn Academy, I sought the old texts to try to find out why she came. My memories have been gone for a long time, only returning in bits and pieces in the past year. With the death of King Adrian's father three months before Blaire came to Blackthorn Academy, much has been revealed to me. Things that, at this time, I cannot share with you."

"Why can't you tell us anything?"

The Oracle tilted her head at Riley and offered her a sympathetic expression. "Should I reveal too much, it could upset the path of events that are to take place." Her gaze shifted to Aiden briefly before settling back on Riley. "Revealing events can make others alter their course. While you may think it a good thing, it can backfire in catastrophic ways."

Riley crossed her arms and sulked.

"Then what can you tell us?" Mera asked.

"My search of the archives uncovered texts that triggered more of my memories to return, but those same texts would create chaos—not only within the academy, but also the Vasirian world. It was not the time for such revelations, so I took the pages and hid them away."

Mera nodded. "That explains why when I did my own research when I first heard of a human Korrena, I found tomes with torn pages."

"Yes, that would be my doing."

Seth's eyebrows knotted and his forehead creased. "But why didn't you destroy them to keep someone from finding them?"

"There has already been enough destroyed history about our kind. I simply couldn't remove the only pieces that remain from the time of King Adrian's great-grandfather Rosendo Blackthorn's reign. Only the latter thirty years of his reign remain documented. We've lost most documentation of his three-hundred-year reign and have absolutely no records of the time before that. I couldn't play a role in taking more of our history away."

Riley slid to the edge of her chair and stretched her arms out on the table in front of her. "So, what did the pages say?"

"When it is time, the truth will be revealed."

"That's so not an answer."

Aiden barely suppressed a snorted laugh with his hand.

"It is all I can offer, child. Until more comes to light and the appropriate time reveals itself, this information is best kept a guarded secret."

Kai crossed his ankle over his knee. "Well, if you can't tell us much, then what are we doing here?"

"I need you all to understand that conflict is coming. When the truth comes to light, it will throw the Vasirian world into disarray, and Blaire will be at the center of it all. Each of you has been placed in her path for different reasons. Some intended for a deeper connection than others."

Lukas raised a brow. "What do you mean by placed?"

"Your parents could have enrolled you in one of the other academies around the world, yet you ended up here." She looked at Riley and Aiden. "You two, born locally, were already in a prime position, yet your siblings ended up all over the world. As for Blaire herself… her mother and father are not from Rosebrook. While we control our fate mostly, sometimes there is a higher guidance to set certain events in motion."

Riley shook her head. "What are you talking about?"

"The timing of King Adrian's ascension to the throne. The uncanny way his father, Luciano, died of the same mysterious illness his great-grandfather Rosendo succumbed to put that into motion before expected. Lukas being part of Blackthorn Academy's Georgia location. Blaire's family and life events… it is all connected. None of what has happened, or what is to come, could come to pass without each of those occurring. Had even one moving piece on the board changed their course, the outcome for our kind would have been very different."

"What is to come?" When the Oracle gave Riley a sympathetic look, Riley rolled her eyes. "Let me guess. You can't tell us."

"Blaire will need each of you to guide her through what is coming to our world. Her indecision and fear of the unknown must not stop her, and with your companionship, she will endure until the end."

"The end? What end?"

The Oracle looked at Lukas. "The time that either she chooses to join us and restore the balance or not."

Lukas knew better than to ask how Blaire becoming a Vasirian would restore whatever the balance was. The woman's words sometimes were crystal clear and other times so muddy with riddles he couldn't get out of the muck—if she even granted them a response at all.

"She doesn't want to be a Vasirian, and pushing her isn't right," Mera said.

"Of course. If you push her, you will only drive her away." The Oracle turned her attention to Lukas. "Pressing the issue will cause not only her rejection of the gift, but also a loss of a bond."

"Our bond is already—"

"No. You misunderstand. Your bond exists. You feel her still. She is still part of you, as you are part of her. The balance of the Vasirian world is not the only thing in chaos. There are things you must overcome within yourself to restore the balance within your connection with her. You must learn to let go."

"Let go?"

"Yes. Let go of many things. Your expectations. Your need to control what is around you." She took a breath. "You must come to terms with other things like this within yourself. In time, with the help of those around you, you will learn. As long as you do not give into the darkness that seeks to steal your bond."

"How do you know anything about Lukas or Blaire, and what they're feeling?" Aiden asked and Seth nodded, clearly wanting the answer himself.

"Much is revealed to me through dreams and visions, and I am allowed to share a portion of this information. Not everything, as there is also a balance to maintain in the timeline of our lives, but enough to be a guide."

Seth's brows furrowed. "How do we know you're not on the Order's side? Aren't you one of them?"

"It is disconcerting." Kai folded his arms over his chest. "You advise us not to seek Blaire out, even though she sits imprisoned in a dungeon. You dangle bits of information before us but hold onto key pieces of information that would make our steps forward not so blind… What do you have to gain from this?"

The Oracle shook her head. "I have nothing to lose or gain. My only allegiance is to our creators and our monarchy. I can be privy to the Order; and by rights, have a position connected to them, but I have my own standing." She looked at Kai. "My advice is only to guide you. You can take my advice at face value and do what you will with it. If you wish to forgo the knowledge that Blaire is safe while she remains locked in the dungeon and risk the consequences of what it means to take her out of there before the time is right, then you are free to do so."

"So, you're a good guy, then?" Riley scrunched her nose. "No, wait… Good girl—woman?" She frowned deeply. "That sounds odd."

The Oracle chuckled; the sound was almost musical in quality. Seth shook his head, and Aiden sighed at his sister.

"Things are never black and white, good, or evil. I merely wish to see our kind flourish. And if our kind needs the secret within Blaire's blood to once again flourish, I will do what I must to bring that to fruition."

With that last piece of cryptic information, the Oracle exited the small room without another word, leaving them staring at one another.

Lukas was still hung up on the information regarding his bond and how it wasn't completely lost to him. While it would be a herculean task to avoid going to the administration building and demanding entrance to the dungeons to take Blaire home, he would do it if it meant she stayed safe.

11

EXPERIMENTS

Fifteen, fourteen, thirteen…

The rubber snapped tight, and Blaire breathed through her nose slowly, trying to avoid looking at the tourniquet at the top of her arm. She focused her eyes on the buzzing fluorescent light over her head and startled when chilly dampness touched the crook of her arm.

A soft voice spoke. "It's only an alcohol wipe for sterilization."

Blaire flexed her fists, her muscles aching from the tension she carried throughout her body.

Twelve, eleven, ten, nine…

Where was that coconut smell coming from? It was nice.

"I told them sedating her for this was a good idea," a short man who approached her seat said. He crouched down in front of Blaire, pushing a pair of wireframe glasses up his nose. "Are you sure you don't want to go that route?"

Eight, seven, six…

"I'm fine," she lied through clenched teeth.

Five, four, three...

There had been a point in her life where getting a shot or blood drawn didn't send her body into flight mode, but since her ordeal with Vincent, she couldn't control the visceral response. It took everything in her not to punch the woman prepping her for her latest donation. This was her second offering in as many days.

Learning from her experience in captivity with Vincent, Blaire proactively tracked her time. She didn't know how long the Order planned to keep her, and instead of assuming she'd get to go home soon, she took it upon herself to scratch the walls of the back of her cell with a spoon she kept from one of her delivered meals.

"Right." The man stood to his full height, which wasn't that tall compared to most of the men she'd encountered at the academy. He was about the same height as her. "Well, at this point we don't have the time, if we want to get any work done today."

She cringed. His tone and the shift in his willingness to do the additional steps to make her comfortable said he didn't like her short answer. She couldn't help it, though. It took everything she had to maintain her composure. She wasn't trying to be rude. The researchers had been nothing but nice to her, even if some of them gave her strange looks and a wide berth. What that was about, she didn't know.

It was uncanny. Despite being kept in a cage, the people she'd been forced to interact with—except for a couple of security guards who ended up not being so bad in the end—weren't cruel to her. She expected poor treatment given how the Order's goons had treated her months ago. Maybe submitting to the experiments voluntarily would not be as bad as she feared.

As he moved to the other side of the room where the woman stood labeling vials, Blaire looked around the room.

The lab they brought her to looked like something out of a forensic crime show. Beakers, racks of vials, paperwork, books, and various pieces of lab equipment littered the white, sterile surfaces. Men and women in white coats stood, or sat on stools, hunched over microscopes and notebooks, jotting down their findings for whatever they were experimenting with.

Her nose wrinkled at the smell of the room the first time she entered. The air held a medicinal odor, edged with other scent notes she was unfamiliar with, but a soothing coconut fragrance lay under the others.

"We won't have to take as much as last time. We still have some vials left."

Blaire squinted at the woman. "Then why am I here?" Her arm was going numb from the tourniquet.

"Because those vials will probably be gone by morning, and unless you'd like us to wake you up in the middle of the night, doing it now keeps us with a stock to avoid slowing our research."

Blaire didn't know if the woman's words meant they were being considerate of her need for things like adequate sleep, or if they simply didn't want to slow down their experimentation, but she welcomed the courtesy. If the woman felt like being generous, then Blaire decided to try her luck and get more information than what they'd given her so far, which had been nothing at all.

"Why do you need so much of my blood? What research are you doing?"

The man made a tsking sound from somewhere behind her chair. "You're a human." When Blaire looked over her shoulder and inclined her head forward, opening her eyes wider to prompt him to continue, he said, "But not just any human. A human bearing—" He cleared his throat and waved a hand at his faux pas. "Well, who once carried a Korrena mark."

Blaire turned back in her seat to face the woman. She had already spent the past week of her captivity going over the probable reasons their mark didn't return. She didn't think it had anything to do with Lukas's desire to turn her into a Vasirian. He had felt that way before they first sealed their bond, but maybe the problem lay with how strong the desire had become. Thinking about it made her head hurt. Going in circles in her mind about all the what ifs and possibilities behind why the Korrena mark hadn't returned wasn't going to help her right now.

The woman crossed to the sink and washed her hands, then tugged on a pair of latex gloves with a snap at the wrist. The sound made Blaire tense.

"You need to understand, you're a fascinating anomaly in our world," the man continued, oblivious to Blaire's stressed state. "You can't expect a room full of scientists to pass up the opportunity to study such a rare find, can you?"

She assumed the question was rhetorical, so she didn't respond.

"Ready?"

Blaire gave the woman a flat stare, hoping to convey how not excited she was by the prospect of being poked and drained for their curiosity. The woman frowned and rubbed an alcohol wipe over the crook of Blaire's elbow again, tapping at the skin to produce a vein. Blaire felt this was unnecessary, seeing how long they kept the rubber tie on her bicep. Surely her veins were visible with how numb and tense her arm felt. She wasn't about to look to confirm, though. Nope.

The woman frowned when Blaire flinched, wincing at the sharp pain. She hadn't felt that the first time they took her blood.

"It hurt?"

"A little bit."

The woman frowned. "The area must still be tender from a couple of days ago. Strange."

It wasn't strange to Blaire. With her slow healing, the lack of bruising on the surface didn't mean there wasn't internal damage or lingering sensitivities. She shrugged it off as the woman pressed a cotton ball to her arm after taking several vials of blood. She asked Blaire to hold the cotton until she sealed the vials and retrieved a strip of medical tape to hold the cotton ball in place.

"This one might bruise if it hurt. I'm sorry."

Blaire studied the woman's face. It was hard to come to terms with the caring nature of several of the Vasirian she'd encountered after agreeing to be part of the Order's game, but they weren't the ones responsible for her captivity, so she worked to mentally separate them from those who deserved the blame. She offered a small smile.

"You look pale." The woman spun her chair toward a mini-fridge and opened it, pulling out a small box of orange juice with a foil covering and a tiny straw in plastic glued to the side. It reminded her of the juice boxes her mother used to pack in her school lunches when she was little. "Drink this. I'll get you some cookies." She left Blaire sitting with the man, who was tapping on a tablet computer in his hand.

"Don't get used to this," the man finally said after about five minutes of awkward silence.

"Used to what?"

"Cookies. Juice. Providing simple blood samples."

Blaire perked up. Were they finished with her? Did she get to go back to her dorm to Lukas?

The man set the tablet on the counter and moved to take a seat on the stool in front of her. "From the look on your face, I can see you misunderstand." He looked up as the woman reentered the room with a packet of Oreo cookies.

"These might not taste too good with the orange juice, but I couldn't find anything else in our break room." She opened the packet and handed it to Blaire, who still sat staring at the man in confusion. "What's going on?"

Blaire pulled out an Oreo and took a bite. A glass of milk sounded great right about now.

"I was just about to explain to Miss Wilcox that we're stepping up our research efforts."

The woman paused, gaze darting quickly between Blaire and the man.

Blaire didn't like the look on her face. "What do you mean?"

"The samples we obtained from Vincent, and what we've gathered so far, have taken us as far as we can go. From now on, we want to test our findings."

"Findings?" Blaire asked.

"Yes, findings. We've discovered disconcerting things in your blood."

"Disconcerting?"

He hummed his confirmation. "I'm excited to test directly at the source."

"The source…"

Like a parrot, she echoed everything the man said as she tried to process and find meaning in his words. She was truly at a loss.

"Yes. We want to test our theories in relation to how the reactions we've been able to achieve may alter if the blood is freshly spilled—or hasn't left your body at all—versus blood that has been outside of your body for extended periods. I'm most interested in witnessing the physiological reactions that might occur if the blood remains in the source."

Blaire set the cookies down. The casual way he spoke about experimenting on her made her queasy. Her thick swallow was audible. She suddenly didn't want to know what they'd found.

"C-can I go back to my bed?"

"Oh, yes, of course."

He waved a hand in the air, and two members of Blackthorn Security approached. Blaire knew the drill. She stood and held her hands out in front of her expectantly. The man closest to her placed a black bag into her hands and waited silently for her to pull it over her head. They never let her see what was beyond the lab room or the cell blocks of the dungeon. She had no way of knowing where either was located or how to get to or away from them.

As the guards led her back to her cell to sleep off the lingering discomfort that always came with donating blood, her thoughts raced through her head on a loop. Obviously, the scientists knew the answer to what made her blood so special, but they were less than eager to share. She didn't know if that should make her more concerned or not. It did.

"We're here," a man murmured behind her.

Blaire pulled the bag from her head. She was facing the open entrance to her cell.

"Katie will be down in about an hour with dinner. Get some sleep until then," Marcus said. She hadn't seen him in the lab, but apparently somewhere in the journey back to the dungeons he'd replaced one of the original two guards.

He'd softened toward her in the last week, saying how she didn't seem like such a bad human. Jackson still held an aversion to her, but he at least engaged in civil conversation when they needed to be in each other's presence.

The guard behind Marcus tipped his head to him and left them alone.

The members of Blackthorn Security were numerous. She'd seen them at the lab, during Vincent's trial, and the night Lukas pounded her stepbrother to a pulp in the alley behind the nightclub Haven. She wondered if the reason only Katie, Jackson, and Marcus kept rotating duty with her had to do with making this situation easier on her.

She shook her head.

It was doubtful the Order would make a call like that. But Katie? Something told Blaire the woman may have had a hand in it. She already took it upon herself to bring Blaire nicer bedding, brought snacks outside of mealtimes, and soft, triple-ply toilet paper. Not the thin, one-ply disaster typically found in institutional bathrooms—and apparently also in dungeons. The stuff shouldn't be legally able to call itself tissue. When would companies learn it didn't save money if people had to use more to get clean and avoid accidents on their hands?

Rubbing her eyes as a wave of lethargy washed over her, she nodded at Marcus and crossed to the bed with the thin mattress, made somewhat comfortable by the plush duvet and soft sheets her guardian security angel left for her.

Marcus eyed the bed for a beat then chuckled. "She's treating you like you're gonna break if you're the least bit uncomfortable." He scratched at the light stubble on his jaw. "I guess I don't blame her. Not sure I'm really caring for all this either at this point." He shrugged when Blaire blinked at him. "What? You're an alright kid."

"Kid?" she deadpanned.

"Mmmhmm."

"How old are you?" He didn't look older than twenty-two at most. She tried to remember the aging process Riley explained before, recalling vaguely how physiological decay slowed in their twenties, and how most Vasirian appeared in their early thirties well into their seventies, but in her tired state, she couldn't come up with much of anything else.

"Thirty-nine."

"Not that old." She yawned.

"Old enough to be your dad. So yeah, kid." His warm chuckle echoed in the empty dungeon as she slid beneath the cozy blanket muttering about being a young father.

"Sleep well. Katie will be down soon with food. She wanted to bring clothes, but she didn't want to press her luck. Maybe later."

Blaire pressed her back against the bars to the neighboring cell, the duvet providing minimal cushion against the metal bars. She didn't like the idea of keeping her back to the main area of her cell in case someone came in. Sure, they could enter the other cell, but they couldn't grab her and take her away from there. She wanted to see what was coming—if she woke up soon enough to know it was happening.

12

Camaraderie

The gang gathered around their usual round lunch table. Lukas sat between Riley and Aiden, Seth on the other side of Aiden, and Kai next to him, and then Mera. Two seats remained empty in spite of the crowded cafeteria, an unspoken placeholder for Blaire and an invitation for new friends like Layla, though she was elsewhere today. Lukas had little appetite today but welcomed the company of his friends—his chosen family.

Riley sighed in contentment, stuck a straw into her blood packet, and proceeded to suck noisily through the tiny tube, eyes rolling back in her head.

Seth snorted. "Wow. Do you and the bag need a room?"

The blood bag in question crinkled as Riley finished drinking. She released a satisfied sound on an exhale, smacking her lips before turning her glare on Seth. "Nope. All done."

He rolled his eyes. "What was that all about?"

"Starving." At his brow raise, she added, "I missed breakfast and lunch. Haven't drunk blood since last night."

"That's dangerous and unhealthy," Mera said.

"Sorry, *Mom*."

Kai laughed, and Mera shook her head. "I'm serious. You know what can happen if you go for extended periods without feeding. I'm surprised you've lasted this long."

Riley sighed and looked down. Her hands rested on each side of her tray on the table, a slight tremor belying her nonchalance. Things had become bad before she had that packet.

Clearing his throat, Lukas slid his packet across the table toward her. She looked up, surprised.

"I don't need—"

"Just drink it."

Grumbling about everyone motherhenning her, Riley stuck the straw in and took a sip, drinking at a normal pace after demolishing the other packet.

Aiden frowned at his sister with obvious concern. "So, why hadn't you had any blood since last night?"

"I've been busy."

"Doing?"

"Busy things."

"To the point you skipped breakfast *and* lunch with no snacks or blood in between?"

She shrugged, finishing Lukas's blood packet, and moving on to the beef stew and buttermilk biscuits on her tray.

"Uh-uh. You're not gonna shrug me off. I'm not above calling Mom."

"Stop acting like a caring big brother. It's giving me the creeps."

Lukas rolled his eyes. What would be out of character—not necessarily creepy—was if Aiden didn't try to pry information out of

Riley. His care for his little sister ran deep, and it extended to those around him. Aiden was a brother to all of them.

"She was with me."

All eyes moved to a blond guy standing a few feet away with a concerned look on his face. If Lukas remembered correctly, his name was Liam. Rue's Korrena pair. He'd gone out with them a couple of times, but didn't talk a lot.

"With you?" Seth said in a low, measured tone.

"Yes, she was… helping me. With, ah… investigating. Yes, that's it." His accent was thick, though still understandable, but it made Lukas understand why he hardly spoke when around them. It'd been a while since they'd seen him or his Korrena.

Riley nodded to the two chairs between her and Mera. "Have a seat, Liam."

"Ah, no. I still need to search more."

"We were searching all day. Have you eaten?"

He shook his head.

"Sit." Riley stood and marched away from the table as Liam lowered himself awkwardly into the chair she directed him to, looking at her retreating form like a lost puppy briefly before turning his attention back to the table.

"I am sorry for disturbing your mealtime."

Aiden shook his head. "Not a big deal, man. What's going on? What have you two been searching for?"

"Rue, my Korrena pair."

Kai raised a brow. "You don't know where she is?"

Liam shook his head emphatically. "She… she is gone."

"Gone?" Mera and Kai said at the same time.

"A week, yes. She did not return to our dormitory room this morning exactly one week ago."

They exchanged wary glances around the table. The panic Lukas had felt when he'd searched for Blaire when she first disappeared during fall term still stung like a fresh wound. The same thing couldn't have happened to Rue; Vincent was on the other side of the world in Cresbel Asylum.

Riley set down a tray with beef stew, buttermilk biscuits, a small bowl of peach cobbler with a scoop of vanilla ice cream, and two blood packets in front of Liam. "Eat. Drink. You're shaking as much as I was."

Liam didn't argue, nodding and picking up the blood packet before anything else.

Riley plopped a fresh blood packet in front of Lukas as she resumed her seat, then set a plate of mini cakes and cookies in front of herself, before proceeding to stuff her face.

"I'm confused. What did you need Riley for?"

Liam looked up from his meal. "My English is not very good when I get nervous. Some words are already difficult for me when calm. Humans… sometimes they cannot understand me. They get angry I do not sound like them."

Lukas shook his head. Liam wasn't stupid. Rue had mentioned his final exam scores put him in the top percentile of his program, but people underestimated him because of the language barrier. The thing was, Liam had a decent grasp of the English language and used vocabulary unexpected of a foreigner. Lukas could only recall one or two instances in their interactions where Liam had to stop and consider his word choice or fumbled a pronunciation.

Lukas's mother faced the same problem a couple of times when she'd visited him in his early years at the academy. Her Finnish accent was thicker than it was now, and her English was broken, so she spoke mostly in Finnish to his father. It didn't go over well with locals who felt she should use the language of their country or leave. While she'd gotten better over the years, and could communicate better with him, he still didn't like the idea of her being discriminated against based on her accent.

"So, Riley assisted in translation?" Kai asked.

Liam nodded. "Yes, she has been very helpful today."

Mera cocked her head. "Why didn't you search sooner?"

Liam broke apart a biscuit into his stew and sighed heavily. "I have much regret for not doing so. I started searching the second day, but only asked Riley for help after I checked all places I could on my own."

"Yep. He thought since Blaire and I are friends with Rue, we'd either know where she was or would help search."

"Yes. I do not know where she is, and I no longer feel her as strongly as before."

"How long have you been bonded?" Kai asked.

"Three years."

"And how old are you?"

"Twenty."

Kai sat back and nodded. "Quite a long time to be with each other and then be separated."

Lukas couldn't imagine what it would be like to lose Blaire after experiencing their connection for three years. The two-month span of her kidnapping, after only six months in each other's company, was enough to let him know he couldn't handle it.

"Did she say anything before she disappeared?" Mera asked, putting her spoon into the empty bowl on her tray. "Or perhaps give any indication of anyone who might want to hurt her?"

"Hurt her?" The flash of panic in Liam's eyes made it clear he hadn't considered that possibility. It made Lukas wonder what he had thought happened to his Korrena.

"I didn't mean someone hurt her," Mere clarified. "Merely, a possibility someone who didn't have good intentions toward her might have something to do with her disappearance. Did she have enemies?"

"None that I knew. Her uncle would not allow them to hurt her."

"Her uncle?"

"Yes. He is on administration council. Though, I cannot remember his name."

Mera and Kai exchanged a look, and Lukas glanced at Aiden's uneasy expression.

If the Order was connected to Rue, then was she really on Blaire's side, or had they done something to Rue too? Lukas didn't know what to think. Surely they wouldn't hurt their own relatives. Angelo didn't do anything bad to his own daughter. He'd let her run around like she owned the place and certain people in it. Rue hadn't acted like that, so maybe she wasn't close to her uncle.

"Have you met him? Or asked him if he's seen Rue? That would be a good place to start," Lukas said.

Liam shook his head. "I have never met him, and in the three years we have been paired, Rue has not mentioned him more than letting me know about him in the beginning. I do not think they talk."

"Then why are you certain of his protection of her?"

Liam looked at Kai. "Are family not supposed to take care of each other? Even when they are… how do you say this… estrangled?"

"Estranged," Kai corrected. "And I suppose you're right."

Seth's phone pinged on the table. He picked it up and groaned in frustration.

Aiden leaned over. "What?"

"I don't know how she got my number. I never give out my

number. Now she wants to go out to Haven together tomorrow night."

"Girlfriend?" Liam inquired, and Lukas could tell he was trying to divert his thoughts from the meltdown he was likely having inside.

"Fuck, no."

At Liam's shocked expression, Riley cleared her throat and said, "No, just one of his many bed buddies." She didn't sound bitter at all. "Can't put up with him long enough to be a girlfriend."

"Piss off. I don't want a girlfriend, is all."

"You're not being fair to them."

"They know what this is."

"Obviously not." Riley motioned to the phone on the table.

"Sometimes they think they can change my mind."

Liam's gaze ping-ponged between them. It was obvious he wasn't used to the back and forth between Seth and Riley by the way his brows stuck to his hairline. "So, what is this?"

Seth looked at Liam. "Huh?"

"You said 'they know what this is.'"

"Oh. Uh. They know I don't want a relationship."

"What do you want?"

Riley's face turned ten shades of red, and Aiden bit back his laughter. Kai's shoulders shook with the force of his repressed laughter, and Mera turned completely to face Liam. Even Lukas had a hard time keeping a neutral expression.

"Sex," Seth stated.

"Huh." Liam's expression shifted to stoic as he dug out a bite of ice cream with his spoon.

Seth sat up straighter. "What is it?"

"I never understood meaningless sex." He ate the bite of ice cream. "I have read about it. Heard about it. Never experienced it. It sounds like someone chasing something they cannot have or wish to find."

Seth narrowed his eyes. "You know nothing about me."

"Oh, pardon me. I am not referring to you. It was a… Hmm. I apologize, I do not know the word. But I do not know your feelings."

Seth crossed his arms, leaning back in his chair. "It's not about feeling anything. It's about not feeling."

"What does this mean?"

"Nothing." Seth stood and grabbed his hoodie off the back of his chair before heading toward the exit.

"I hope I did not offend him. He was nice to me at Haven when we all went together."

"You didn't. He's just dealing with stuff." Aiden frowned. "So, Rue…"

Riley lifted her head from where she'd been staring at her empty stew bowl as if it were the most fascinating piece of kitchenware on the planet. She looked relieved at the change of subject. "We're gonna check around town again tomorrow."

Aiden nodded. "I'll come with."

"We can ask around our departments." Mera looked at Kai, and he nodded.

"Will you and Blaire also join us?" Liam asked Lukas.

Aiden cursed under his breath, and Riley slumped her shoulders again.

"Did I speak wrong again?"

Lukas shook his head. "No. Blaire isn't around right now."

He explained in brief everything that had taken place from before Blaire's kidnapping through the exchange Blaire agreed to. It didn't feel wrong to share the information with Liam. Sure, they didn't know him well, but Rue had become a friend to Blaire, so Liam belonged in their circle. With Liam missing his pair, Lukas felt a strange camaraderie with him.

13

Waiting Game

Shrugging off his leather jacket and laying it over the back of the chair in front of Professor Velastra's desk, Lukas took a seat and hooked his leg over the arm of the chair. Aiden took the chair next to him. The fireplace burning in the corner to ward off the chill from outside made the room hot and stuffy. Thankfully, the school didn't force students to wear their uniforms during winter break, or he would have been uncomfortable. The dress slacks, belt, and button-down already made him feel overheated most days. The clothing by itself wasn't too warm, but wearing it to the school's standard—all tucked in and neat—made him feel claustrophobic.

She asked, "You said there was information you wished to share?"

Lukas nodded. "Yeah, I got another message from the Oracle."

"Another letter?"

"Not really. A request to meet her in the library."

"When is this meeting?"

Lukas folded his hands over his stomach. "Already happened."

The professor sat forward and looked between him and Aiden. "And? When did this happen?"

"After the Christmas party at the start of winter break," Aiden answered. "A few days ago."

Frowning, the professor settled her gaze on Lukas. "Why didn't you inform me?"

"Well, we didn't get the message until we were at the party, and she wanted to meet right after." Lukas shrugged. "Didn't have time to really think about it. We're telling you now."

The professor gave a subtle shake of her head and sat back in her chair, crossing her legs. "What happened?"

Lukas tried to think of everything said in the small room at the back of the library. The Oracle had said nothing and a lot all at once.

Aiden spoke up, no doubt picking up on Lukas's confusion about where to begin. "She mentioned Blaire's blood."

"Her blood?"

"Yeah. She said something dormant in Blaire's blood is some sort of key to a balance. Yeah, something like that. A balance between Vasirian and humans." Aiden crossed his arms and looked up at the ceiling in thought. "Oh, and she admitted she personally destroyed some of the archive papers."

"What?" The professor's normally stoic expression shifted into one of surprise.

"Remember when Mera said she tried to research about humans and our kind when Blaire first arrived?"

At the professor's shake of her head no, he continued.

"Well, apparently, the pages Mera said were missing from several tomes were ripped out by the Oracle. She didn't destroy them, but she removed them from the archives."

"Why would she do that?"

"Something about what she found creating chaos in the Vasirian world. She was vague about it. Said it would disrupt stuff to talk about it." He shrugged. "I didn't understand, but I don't mess with things like that. If she said it wasn't time to know, then I didn't intend to argue."

"Blaire's also in the dungeons," Lukas added, trying to keep the agitation over the situation out of his voice.

"I thought they were taking her to a facility for research."

"The Oracle said Blaire was being kept in the dungeons until the researchers needed her. So I don't know if she's still there or not."

"I don't know of a lab on campus, but there are many areas I'm unfamiliar with in the administration building, and the lower levels are completely foreign to me beyond the rooms where we found Blaire held captive. I've never even seen the dungeons."

"They're not great. But I don't know either; security kept a bag over my head until they had me in the hallway full of cells, so I don't know how to get there or how to get out."

"Right now, we don't need to know how to get out," Aiden said. "The Oracle said as long as Blaire was in her cell, she remained safe."

Professor Velastra stood and walked to the window, fogged with condensation from the drastic difference in temperature from the warm office to the chilly air outside. She looked out past the old cedar tree to the garden. "Was there anything else?"

"She warned us that when the truth does come out, the Vasirian world will be in a mess. Said Blaire will need us. That was after she dropped on us that we're all here at Blackthorn Academy for a reason—Blaire included." Aiden gave a sidelong glance at Lukas. "And she mentioned their bond."

"What about it?"

Lukas shrugged. "Just some stuff I need to work on."

The professor hummed, and he could tell by her face she wasn't satisfied with his lackadaisical answer. Before she could say more, the door swung open, and Riley rushed inside.

"What'd I miss?"

"Where were you?" Aiden asked.

Riley looked at her brother. "With Charlotte."

Lukas hadn't told Blaire's human friend Charlotte about the new situation. Aiden said he'd given her a basic rundown of events, enough to make her aware but without exposing the Vasirians' secrets. He'd met with her before Vincent's trial but after Lukas failed to reseal their bond. Aiden told Charlotte a student had become infatuated with Blaire and locked her up in an abandoned room on campus for two months. He told her they caught the guy, but Blaire wasn't up for talking to anyone yet. Charlotte was shocked, to say the least, but thankful Blaire was okay.

Aiden didn't tell her about the physical damage Vincent had done. They weren't sure when Blaire and Charlotte would have time to meet up, and they hoped by that point, the visible bruising would have faded. At least in December, sweaters and hoodies made hiding the marks a lot easier.

"What'd you say to her?" Lukas asked as Riley perched on the arm of Aiden's chair.

"Told her Blaire hasn't felt that great since what happened with Vincent, which is true. I didn't have to say anything else. She pretty much drew her own conclusions that Blaire probably didn't feel like coming out after something like that, so I didn't have to lie to her."

Riley didn't like the idea of lying; it wasn't her style. But Lukas worried she could be honest to a fault.

"Sooo? What'd I miss?"

"We were just telling the professor about what the Oracle said,"

Aiden said, standing so Riley could take his chair. He leaned against the bookshelf to her left.

"You mentioned something about being at Blackthorn Academy for a reason," the Professor prompted, sitting back down at her desk.

"Yeah, she said Lukas could have ended up at one of the other academies but didn't. That Riley and I were meant to be here. That Blaire's parents weren't from here."

"They're not. They moved down from the Carolinas before having Blaire, from my understanding."

Riley nodded. "Yep. Blaire's mom and dad were from North Carolina."

"So, the Oracle said all those things were connected. Even the new king's ascension to the throne. That the death of the two kings before him was part of the chain of events leading to whatever is to come."

The professor turned in her leather chair to look back out the window. "I can't help but wonder what all this means. Both Luciano and Rosendo died under mysterious circumstances. Our records show members of the Blackthorn Clan discovered Rosendo sitting at his dinner table face down in a bowl of soup."

"He drowned in the soup?" Riley asked.

Professor Velastra shook her head. "No. Strange markings—like a rash, not drawn on—covered his neck and arms. They could never determine the true cause of death. At the time, the lack of understanding was merely chalked up to an absence of medical advancement. They assumed a disease affected him, and he fell victim. But after King Adrian's father died at the beginning of the year before Blaire joined us with the same markings, at his own dinner table as well, I am not the only one suspecting something more sinister is at play."

"Assassination?"

She tilted her head at Lukas as she contemplated his question. "Perhaps. It has to be more than mere coincidence. Assassination is one theory that has circulated within the Vasirian world. A more fantastical theory suggests the Blackthorn monarchy is cursed."

Riley sat up in her seat. "Cursed? But why? How? Curses aren't real, are they? That's, like, magic stuff." She looked at Aiden. "This sounds like your video games."

Aiden chuckled, despite the seriousness of the conversation. Riley had a way of lightening any mood. "I doubt it's like a video game," he said.

"No, this is reality." The professor frowned at Riley. "And while I don't believe in magic, curses, or anything else related to the occult, many Vasirian long ago did. The old tomes I lifted from the archives document sacrifices and worship of a magical deity."

"Yeah, but people don't actually believe that stuff now, do they?"

"Oh yeah, they do," Aiden corrected. "Tons of humans are into the occult. A lot of their beliefs fuel the myths and legends around supernatural creatures. Supposed sightings and interactions with magical beings. You know, the stuff you read in your books. Some people actually believe in that stuff."

Riley's face scrunched as she considered Aiden's words.

"Belief in things of that nature isn't the problem. It goes hand in hand with the belief in various gods. Everyone wants something to believe in. The problem occurs when these beliefs become so all-consuming people will destroy others over them. Either to defend them or force their beliefs on others."

Lukas wasn't sure he believed in anything. He hadn't given consideration to the gods. Not that he didn't believe, but he didn't give faith any thought except in the times where he thought he was losing

Blaire. Then, he'd prayed to any being that could hear him to save her. Maybe he was cynical, but even as a child, he didn't believe in things like Santa Claus or the Easter Bunny, despite Riley's insistence they both existed. He hadn't had it in his heart to tell her the professors were the ones leaving presents and baskets filled with candy. He'd seen it.

"So, what do you think happened to the former kings?" Lukas asked.

"I lean more toward the theory of assassination, but it isn't something to discuss in casual company for obvious reasons. With the way Luciano died, I can't help but wonder if his death resulted from a copycat killer."

Considering it had been one hundred and fifty years since Rosendo's death, the idea it was the same person—if there was a killer—made little sense. Wouldn't they kill him earlier in his reign while there wasn't an heir to step up?

"What I find a fascinating coincidence," the professor interrupted Lukas's thoughts, "is both Adrian and Luciano were fifty years old when they ascended the throne."

Riley's head tilted. "Doesn't that support the whole 'everything happens like it's supposed to' thingy?"

"I don't know about that, but it is interesting. Speaking of the Blackthorn Clan…" Professor Velastra sat back in her chair with a heavy sigh. Lukas didn't like the look on her face. "I encountered resistance when I tried to reach out to them."

Lukas's brows pulled together. "What do you mean?"

"The Order pulled both Professor Galloway and I into a disciplinary meeting once they discovered we hadn't gone through the chain of command."

Aiden cursed under his breath. "What happened?"

"Well, I don't know how they discovered we were trying to contact the Blackthorn Clan, but Professor Galloway used an excuse that exonerated us."

"Huh?"

The professor looked at Riley. "He told them we were seeking information on an extended family member of his who moved to Europe whom he hasn't heard from. Of course, this is all a fabrication, but it was enough to sway them into understanding why we dared to go straight to connecting with European administration over our local one." She sighed and looked out the window. Something about her posture and mood made Lukas suspect there was more to the story. "While they claimed to buy the excuse, we're now under their scrutiny, and I don't believe I'll be able to reach out to the Blackthorn Clan without dire consequences."

"What? Why?" Riley asked.

Professor Velastra's voice turned sharp. "This does not leave this room." At Riley's rapid nod, the professor turned in her chair and tapped her fingers lightly on the desk. "They dismissed Professor Galloway, and Angelo told me that while he didn't truly believe his excuse, they had no evidence to the contrary. I was told in not so simple terms that should they hear of my attempts to contact the Blackthorn Clan again, they will take me to Cresbel Asylum for acts of treason."

"Holy crap." Riley shook her head. "They'd do that? What's treasonous about that?"

Aiden's eyebrows slammed together. "What evidence of treason do they have if you contacted the Blackthorn Clan? That doesn't make sense."

"It does not. Several of the members on the council didn't seem to share the same vehement reactions to what we did and seemed even less inclined to punish me for it… Angelo runs the show. What he would do, or say, to the Blackthorn Clan to get a proper conviction is beyond me. I had no idea our Order was so corrupt."

Lukas had been taught the Order looked out for the Vasirian of the Americas and ran the affairs of the school. He'd met none of the members before, but there had been no sign of anything untoward happening at the academy. No other Vasirian reported problems to the Blackthorn Clan that he knew of. No one from the clan came to the academy campus. If there was corruption, wouldn't the monarchy intervene?

Aiden scoffed. "It's leadership. Of course, they're corrupt." At Riley's surprised expression, he clarified, "I'm not saying they're all bad. Realistically, there's always corruption when power is involved, even if it's just one person. When someone like Angelo is running the show, it spreads through the ranks like a plague."

"An unfortunate reality," the professor said. "That said, I cannot make a move toward the Blackthorn Clan. I won't be able to help any of you if I'm locked away, and I don't want to be locked away either, so we'll have to find another way."

If the Order's corruption ran into the staff of Blackthorn Academy, who could they trust? Someone apparently was watching Professor Velastra's actions if the Order got involved, thwarting her attempts at getting help so quickly. Were they stuck waiting for the experimentation on Blaire to reach a conclusion, or would they be able to find another way to get help?

"I hope they finish with Blaire soon," Riley said quietly. "I don't like this. I don't trust them."

"I don't think any of us do," Aiden said.

"What can we do?"

The professor's jaw hardened, and she folded her arms over her chest. She didn't seem happy to not have answers for them. "I won't give up. I promise you three I will not give up on Blaire. But for now, the best course of action is to wait. To watch and listen. Anything more might bring about consequences none of us are prepared to deal with. You said Blaire is safe as long as she's in the dungeons, correct?"

Aiden nodded.

"Then all we can do is trust those words. For now."

14

STRANGER

A tickling sensation moving across Blaire's arm stirred her to consciousness. She didn't want to get up yet. She was having the nicest dream about taking a road trip up to Myrtle Beach for the weekend with her mother. The same weekend her mother dropped the shocking news that she was marrying another man. A man who wasn't Blaire's father. Blaire had expected to be upset by the news, but she wasn't. She wanted her mother to be happy. When she heard he had a son who was a little older than she was, that made her happy. She had always wanted an older brother. Too bad it didn't turn out the way she wanted.

The grazing tickle moved from her forearm to her cheek.

"Stop it," she mumbled, swatting her face.

The cell she called home for the last week and a half came into focus. The low light made it easy for her eyes to adjust quickly upon waking, and she slowly sat up on the thin mattress. Rubbing her eyes, she sighed as her stomach growled. Despite what the scientist had told her, they called her in once more to the lab for another blood sample yesterday, and she felt too sick to eat dinner afterward, so now she was hungry.

As she lowered her hands to her lap, something brushed across her fingers. Looking down, she froze. Crawling across the bedding pooled in her lap was a large wolf spider. Throwing the covers off the bed, she shrieked and stumbled out of the bed, crawling farther away from the bed to get away from the vicious thing.

Her eyes darted around the cell, looking for anything she could use to destroy the hell spawn sent to disturb her rest. When the spider crawled across the stone floor toward her, she screamed again and scrambled to her feet, running to the other side of the cell.

"What's going on? Are you okay?"

Blaire whipped her head around toward the cell next to hers so fast she flinched at the ache it caused in her neck.

A young guy who looked an awful lot like Seth, but with hair dyed silvery-white with dark roots, eased himself into a sitting position on his bed, which was jammed against the bars of the cell adjacent to hers. The resemblance to Seth was uncanny. Aside from his hair color, everything else was so similar. She'd have thought he was Seth's brother instead of Kai, who didn't favor Seth outside of a few facial features.

The guy scratched his head and shoved the longer hair on top of his head out of his eyes. "Well?" His voice was deep and scratchy from sleep. "What has you screaming loud enough to wake the dead?"

She'd forgotten about the spider in her surprise of finding someone else in the dungeon with her. Her gaze darted around the cell, trying to find the sneaky thing, but she didn't see it. She quickly rushed to the bed and jumped up on it, tucking her feet beneath her to get them off the floor, shaking the covers out on the floor before piling them onto the bed with her.

"Okay, then. Don't tell me."

"Huh?"

Blaire turned on her bed to look at the guy who sat only a couple feet away on the other side of the bars. If she wanted, she could reach out and touch him.

His deep chuckle echoed in the space, and he shook his head. "What. Has you. So frazzled?"

"Spider," she mumbled under her breath, looking at the floor again in search of the spawn of evil. She wasn't sure what to be more focused on: the spider, or the stranger within touching distance.

"Come again?"

"A spider," she said, louder this time, looking back at the man. Her cheeks heated in embarrassment that her arachnophobia was so extreme.

His brows rose as he peered into her cell. "I don't see anything."

She followed his gaze to the empty floor. "I think it's gone." She felt even more embarrassed by the lack of proof to support her freak-out. The spider was huge. Anyone would be afraid of it—or at least they should be.

The man yawned. "Who are you?"

Blaire turned in her bed to study him. His chocolate brown eyes assessed her, but she couldn't tell what he was thinking. She didn't like that. This close, it was easier to see the differences between him and Seth. Seth's eyes weren't as wide, and the piercing steel color made her feel like he could see her very soul. This guy's eyes were soulful, wide, and chocolate brown. His head tilted slowly as he raked his gaze over her face and her body, pausing on her arms that were still littered with bruises. She grabbed the sweater she'd worn the day the Order locked her up and pulled it over her tank top to hide everything. She'd thrown it off when she got too hot under the covers, but the air was too cold outside of the covers.

"Blaire. Who're you?" Her words were clipped. Unfriendly. Wary.

"Dom." His brows pulled lower. "You're not…" He paused, his lips twisting as he looked to be considering his next words. "Why are you here?"

She didn't know how to answer that question. She didn't know if the guy was dangerous, and if even sitting this close to him was a bad idea. Her gaze moved into the cell again as she considered her chances with the spider. She slid to the foot of the bed, putting distance between them. Not that he couldn't move to her end of the bed and reach through the bars, but it was the statement behind the move that mattered. She didn't trust him.

"I'm not going to hurt you."

"Didn't say you were." Her words came too quickly, too defensive sounding to be believable. She didn't want to believe someone would hurt her, but considering the last couple of months in Vincent's grasp, she didn't put anything past anyone. She pulled the covers over her lap, her hands clasped tightly beneath them.

"No, you're not saying much of anything."

"And you are?"

"Touché." He moved on his bed to sit with his back to the bars, obviously putting himself in a disadvantageous position for her. If she wanted to hurt him, she could easily do it. Either he underestimated her, or he was trying to show her she didn't need to be afraid of him. She wasn't sure which, but it allowed her to lower her guard a bit. At least enough where she wasn't feeling like she would jump out of her skin. "I got myself into a bit of a situation and pissed off the wrong people. Not sure when they'll let me out of here."

Blaire's brows knotted. Did he think she would just start talking if he did?

"I didn't notice you sleeping there when they brought me in earlier tonight." He stretched his arms. "I was kinda out of it. Compulsion is a hell of a thing." His eyes cut to her so subtly she would have missed it had she not been scrutinizing his every move.

She gave no reaction.

His head dropped back against the bars as he exhaled heavily. "Oh, come on." His laugh caught her off guard, and a slight accent entered his voice, but she couldn't place it. He wasn't Southern, but most people she'd met at the academy were from outside the area, so that didn't mean much. "Give me something." He turned on his bed, propping his shoulder against the bars. "You know what I am, don't you?"

"Dom?"

He groaned and dropped his head forward, the longer strands of his hair flopping over his forehead. "*What* I am, not who. You know damn well that's what I meant." He chuckled and lifted his head. "You're a human, aren't you?"

Blaire flinched.

"Easy. I'm not going to hurt you. I already told you that."

So did other Vasirian. She bit her tongue to avoid saying the retort aloud.

"That's why you have"—he motioned up and down at her midsection where her arms were beneath the covers—"all that. You can't heal." He took her silence as confirmation because he continued. "The question is… Do you find it strange I ask if you're a human? Or do you know the truth already?"

Blaire sighed. She had spent a week of solitude in this place. All things considered, aside from the brief time between when they found her in the diplomat wing, and a week ago, she had lacked social interaction with anyone sane for months. She was honestly dying for a social connection with someone who wasn't a nut job. "That you're Vasirian? I know."

His brows lifted at her confession. "And you're still alive?"

"Last I checked."

His loud laugh echoed around them, and she couldn't help but smile at his genuine amusement. What did he expect her to say? From the way she understood it, humans weren't supposed to know about Vasirian, but she didn't think humans were outright killed for knowing their secret. Didn't they just compel them to forget? Of course, that wouldn't work on her for reasons that made little sense to her, but not much made sense when it came to her existence in this world.

"So, why are you down here?" His quiet question brought her out of her thoughts.

Blaire toyed with the hem of her sweater beneath the covers as she contemplated how to answer him. She could tell him the truth. That she agreed to be a guinea pig for scientific research. Maybe be vague about the reasons. She didn't want to lie. Not only because it wasn't something she took pleasure in doing, but also because Dom seemed genuinely curious and non-threatening.

"You're doing it again."

"What?"

"Falling silent when I ask you a serious question."

Her lips pursed, and then she pulled them between her teeth before taking a deep breath through her nose and exhaling sharply. "Because they want to know more about me?" She frowned at the way her words came out like a question. *Way to be confident in your answer, Blaire.*

"They?" He shifted on the bed as he removed the covers he'd had over his lap.

Blaire shrugged lightly.

Dom was dressed nicely in black slacks, a peacock blue button-down shirt rumpled from sleep, and polished leather Chelsea boots. While he looked to be not much older than Blaire, she knew better than to judge his age based on that. But the way he accessorized his look with a couple of earrings on his left ear and an eyebrow piercing spoke of his youth.

He wasn't a student, that much was clear from the lack of a school uniform. But maybe school wasn't in session… They were supposed to be going on winter break. She looked over at the wall where she'd been scratching hatch marks into the surface to track her days. Yeah, they should be in the last week of winter break. She'd missed Christmas.

But he also had been guessing she was a human and didn't seem to know her name. It was common knowledge at Blackthorn Academy who she was. She stood out like a sore thumb.

"You're killing me here." He groaned in apparent exasperation.

"Why are *you* down here?"

He'd been awfully nosey without revealing much about himself. Other than he made someone mad and got compelled.

"Because I stuck my nose where it didn't belong." At her snort of laughter, he arched a dark brow. "What?"

"I was *just* thinking you were sticking your nose all up in my business."

His lazy smile relaxed her. "Yeah, well, I guess I'm curious to a fault."

"How so?"

"Well, I'm down here, aren't I?" He waved a hand at his cell. "Take pity on me and share."

Blaire shook her head slowly, a small huff of laughter slipping free. "You're like a dog with a bone." When he leaned his head toward her and flourished his hand for her to say something more, she rolled her eyes. "The Order. They want to see why I have a Korrena."

All the humor on Dom's face faded as he stared at her with hard eyes and a serious expression. She swallowed. Maybe she shouldn't have revealed that part.

"You're pair bonded?"

"I was," she whispered.

"I don't follow."

"I…" She drew her knees up and wrapped her arms around her shins beneath the covers, resting her chin on her knees. "I think it's still there, but the Korrena mark is gone."

The man's frown deepened.

"A professor told us the bond isn't fully gone even though it was broken—"

She startled as Dom suddenly grabbed the bar closest to her, turning on his bed to get on his knees, facing her.

"Broken? What the hell are you talking about?"

She eased completely to the foot of the bed, leaving him at the halfway point. His brows slammed together at the move, and then he looked down at himself and cursed.

"I didn't mean to scare you. You just surprised me." He lowered himself to sit again, leaning a shoulder against the bars, facing her. "What happened? How are you a human Korrena?"

Wasn't that the big mystery of the year?

"Well, we don't know how I'm a Korrena, but it's one of the things the Order is trying to figure out." She reached up and lightly touched the side of her neck where her mark used to be. "As far as what happened to my mark… Someone performed some taboo ritual on me. It disappeared."

A low growl made her gaze snap to his.

"That ritual should be forbidden."

"You know of it?"

"I've witnessed it." He shook his head. "From what my mother told me, what she felt was much worse than what I saw." His jaw hardened, and the muscle twitched. "The ritual is barbaric."

His mother? His own mother went through the ritual? She wanted to ask for the details, but the haunted look on Dom's face made her hesitate and decide against it. They didn't know one another well enough to go into details about such a traumatic event. She sure didn't want to share the details of her own blood ritual. She hadn't even told Lukas the details of what she went through during it.

"Did you choose it?" he asked.

"Huh?"

"Did you ask for the ritual to be performed?" His voice was low, measured, as if he were restraining his anger until he had her answer.

"No, I… At first, I agreed to it because I was told that if one pair doesn't want the bond, the bond could be broken. I was manipulated into thinking my pair didn't want me." She looked down as emotion bubbled up inside and burned her eyes. "But then I second-guessed it. By then, it was too late. I was forced into it."

Dom relaxed, turning on the bed and sitting with his back to the bars again. The anger in his features fading by a fraction. She wondered if he had expected her to say she wanted the bond gone and was angry about it. He didn't ask her who performed the ritual. Didn't ask why. Didn't ask for any additional details. He only stared into the darkness on the other side of the cell for several minutes in silence, his arms crossed over his stomach.

Blaire's stomach growled, breaking the awkward silence. Her face warmed as his gaze slowly slid back to her. Now wasn't the time for this. The topic at hand too serious for food cravings.

"Sorry," she mumbled.

He snorted his laughter. "Are you seriously apologizing for your body's involuntary response?" When Blaire glared at him, he brought a knuckle up to his mouth to mask his amused smile, clearing his throat. "You can't exactly control when that happens. When's the last time you ate?"

Blaire looked up in thought. "Um… lunchtime?" She nodded. "Yeah, lunchtime," she repeated, more sure of herself.

Dom shook his head. "I don't think it's wise to skip meals while locked in a dungeon." His features pinched. "Or wait…" He turned his face back to her. "Are they not feeding you regularly?"

Blaire laughed as Katie the guard passed through her mind. "Yeah, I just… was too tired to eat." And too dizzy from giving blood. But she didn't say that aloud.

Katie made sure she regularly brought Blaire meals, snuck her snacks when possible, and even brought the occasional bottle of peach tea. It surprised Blaire how kind the woman was to her. She toyed with the thick duvet that wasn't normal furnishing for the cell, glancing over at the threadbare blanket on Dom's bed.

Katie felt guilty for locking her down in the cells, but it wasn't her fault. She was merely following orders, and if she defied those orders, the consequences probably wouldn't be pretty. The Order didn't seem to take kindly to defiance of any kind.

"Too tired to eat? There isn't much to do down here but sleep. Why so tired?"

Blaire twisted the ends of her hair and looked at her lap.

"You know, you're really transparent."

"What?"

Dom pointed at the hair in her fingers. "You have various ticks when you want to avoid answering one of my questions. It lets me know the answer isn't simple. Maybe even uncomfortable." When she released her hair and tucked her hands beneath her thighs to keep from fidgeting, he chuckled.

"You don't have to answer. You can say you don't want to."

Blaire frowned at him. Logically she knew that, but it was something she still struggled to put into practice, even after everything she'd done to get her freedom. Consequences for going against what someone wanted never went well for her. Still, since coming to Blackthorn Academy she found saying what she did or didn't want came easier. She wasn't quite there with strangers, though.

Dom yawned. "Still, I can't believe it's true."

"Hmm?"

Dom turned his gaze to her. "What?"

"You said you can't believe it's true."

"Oh. I did, didn't I?" He rubbed a hand over his mouth. "I'd heard something about a human at the academy, but wasn't sure if I believed it or not."

"Well." Blaire gathered her hair and pulled it up into a messy bun, using the elastic on her wrist to tame the long strands. "It's true. I don't know what you've heard about me, but I've somehow found myself caught up in all this, and I don't know why."

"No clue, at all?"

"I mean, I know what the Order wants… but I don't know the answer to their questions."

He tilted his head back against the bars to stare at the dark ceiling. "At the risk of sounding like an ass, I'm going to ask. What questions do they have?"

Blaire's lips pulled down in a frown, and she shook her head. "Why would you sound like an ass?"

"Because I keep asking you invasive questions that you've avoided.

An asshole would keep asking questions." He waved a hand in an exaggerated flourish. "Human, meet asshole."

Blaire huffed a small laugh and shook her head. She had avoided most of everything he'd asked. What was the worst that could happen if she answered? They were locked in the dungeons, and it wasn't as if his knowing the information would do any harm beyond what had already taken place.

"They're curious about my blood." She rolled up her sweater's sleeve to show the crook of her elbow where a cotton ball and medical tape covered the area. A purple bruise had formed around the bandage from the frequency of donations. The other arm looked worse. The bruises from her time in captivity with Vincent were still there in shades of yellow and green, but at least they were healing finally.

"They've been taking my blood to run tests or something. Apparently, it isn't normal for a human and a Vasirian to be fated Korrena pairs." She shrugged, pulling down her sleeve. "Your guess as to the reason is as good as mine."

Dom's eyes lifted from her sleeve to her face. She couldn't read his expression. "Did they do all that?" He nodded toward the now covered bruises.

Blaire shook her head. "No. Well, the purple around the bandage, but not the others." She put a hand on her neck, regretting putting her hair up, knowing more bruises lay under the collar of her sweater.

"Why are there bruises from that? Why do you have so many other bruises? Are they abusing you?" He'd seen the ones on her arms and shoulders before she threw on the sweater. Thankfully, her clothes concealed her stomach and thighs. The concern on his face was a little disarming.

She looked down. "I don't heal properly. Ever since I was born, I've had a problem with healing like other humans. I bruise easily.

Cuts and other injuries heal slowly. And before you ask… No, I don't know why. Doctors have tried to find out, but all the normal causes for something like this don't apply to me."

"Maybe it has to do with why you're able to be a Korrena."

The thought had crossed Blaire's mind. If her blood truly was special, did it conflict with her humanity? The idea had always seemed preposterous, but with how her blood affected Vincent, and the Order so intent on experimenting with her, the idea couldn't be entirely dismissed.

Even if the idea of her body rejecting its humanity sounded absurd, if there was any truth behind the theory, it only added to the becoming a Vasirian argument.

Blaire yawned and rubbed her bleary eyes.

"You look exhausted. Get some rest. There's always another time to chat. It's not like we're going anywhere anytime soon, yeah?"

Blaire hummed noncommittally and tugged her sweater off over her head. He'd seen the bruising anyway. She moved up the bed and lay down with her back to the bars—to him—and pulled the covers over herself.

"Goodnight, Blaire."

She heard rustling behind her as he lay down on his own bed. Her eyelids grew heavy. It was strange to sleep so close to another man who wasn't Lukas, but she wasn't about to risk the floor. The cell was cold, and the floor was made of stone. She opened her eyes to look across the stones.

"Think the spider will come back?" she whispered. She was surprised he even heard her, but his chuckle let her know he had.

"I think your screeching scared it away."

Blaire mumbled, "Asshole."

"Apparently."

15

RUE

The smell of herbs and spices stirred Blaire back to consciousness, and she cracked her eyes open. In the night, she'd turned to face Dom's cell. He sat cross-legged with his back to her against the bars, eating a bowl of something steaming and delicious smelling.

She watched him quietly, wondering who the man locked away with her was. He didn't seem dangerous. Was he waiting to go to Cresbel Asylum? Had he harmed a human? Blaire wasn't familiar with enough other laws of the Vasirian to speculate further.

Her stomach growled, and he glanced over at her. When their eyes met, he chuckled and held up the bowl. "Chicken noodle soup." He looked toward the hallway running along their cells as the sound of a door opened in the distant shadows.

Blaire slowly rose to sit on the bed and pulled her sweater on over her head as the chill of the dungeon air met her skin. She took the elastic out of her hair and let her hair down. It'd become less of a messy bun and more of a rat's nest in her sleep. She finger-combed the blonde waves, trying to tame them, until movement in front of her cell pulled her attention and made her fingers still.

"Rue?"

Her friend Rue lifted her head from where she was arranging items on a tray, sliding it through the slat at the base of Blaire's cell. She offered a stiff smile and looked away quickly.

Blaire scrambled out of the bed and rushed to the front of her cell. "Rue! What are you doing down here?" She grasped the bars of the cell.

Rue shook her head, her dark ponytail swishing from side to side as the forced smile turned into a frown.

"Rue?" Blaire reached out and touched Rue's arm. She flinched, and Blaire pulled her hand back hesitantly. "What's going on? Where's Katie?"

Katie was the one who usually woke her with breakfast. If the scent didn't wake her, Katie's humming or cheerful singing did. It kept Blaire's spirits up to be faced with such brightness when all around her was gloom and shadow—both literally and figuratively.

"She got in trouble," Rue said softly. Her usual perky voice rang hollow.

"Trouble? How? Why?"

Rue slowly turned teary eyes to Blaire. "They found out she brought you things." Her gaze moved to the bedding in Blaire's cell. "She's been reassigned. Uncle said she's lucky they didn't end her employment with Blackthorn Academy."

Blaire dropped her hands from the bars of the cell. What Katie did was outside the usual treatment, but when Blaire questioned it, Katie blew her off. Now she was in trouble because of her kindness. Her brows pulled low. "Did you say uncle?"

Rue swiped her cheeks and nodded. "I don't really know him, but my uncle is part of the Order." She looked at Blaire with pity. "I didn't know," she whispered.

"Know what?"

"That they wanted to… That they did all this to you." Another tear raced down her cheek. "I don't really have a relationship with my uncle, so I had no clue. He's my dad's older brother." She looked at the tray. "You should eat while it's still warm."

Blaire picked up the tray from the floor and moved to sit on the bed as Rue watched her. She looked over at Dom, who continued eating his soup, not looking at them, but surely, he was listening. How could he not hear the conversation happening a few feet away?

"How did they find out what Katie was doing?" She took a bite of the warm soup and closed her eyes as the flavors of chicken and herb broth washed over her tongue.

"She went to get you clothes from your dorm."

Blaire hadn't changed clothes since she got here. They'd allowed her a shower at the lab, but hadn't provided her with clean clothes. It seemed counterproductive to put on clothes she'd worn for over a week after a shower, but she wasn't about to argue the sliver of hospitality in allowing her to clean her body every other day.

She took a bite from the buttermilk biscuit that'd come with the soup. Her eyes widened, and she set the bread down as a thought occurred to her. "Did she see Lukas? How is he? Have you seen him?"

Rue shook her head as Blaire resumed eating her breakfast. "No. It was during a meal service. She hoped to sneak in and out, but they'd been watching her. I haven't seen Lukas for a couple weeks. I've been in the diplomat wing for the last week."

Blaire paused with the spoon in front of her mouth. The diplomat wing was where Vincent had kept her during the last two months.

What was Rue doing there and not in her dorm with Liam? She frowned. "Why?" She took the bite before it fell from the spoon. She was too hungry not to have a conversation and eat at the same time.

Rue looked down at her polished shoes. She wore her uniform, which seemed out of place during the last days of the winter break. Students weren't required to wear them outside of class.

"Rue?"

Sighing, Rue looked up, tears building again. "They'll hurt my parents." She swallowed. "With what happened with Katie, they decided to keep the knowledge of you being here restricted to just the lab researchers, the Order, and the few security guards who already know. Now me. Because I'm a relative, and I know you, they think I can keep you cooperating."

"That's insane."

Rue shook her head. "They won't even let me see Liam." Her tears trailed down her cheeks again. "They won't let me see my pair, Blaire. I don't know what to do without him."

Blaire put her tray down on the bed and moved to her friend, reaching through the bars and pulling Rue against them, trying to hug her the best she could. "I'm so sorry."

Blaire couldn't even say she couldn't imagine, because she could. It was the hell she currently lived, and had lived, for two months before this. Being without Lukas made her feel like a parasite was gnawing at her insides, threatening to pull her into the pit of despair that had made a home in her stomach.

Rue pulled from Blaire's embrace and took a deep breath. "My parents are all I have besides Liam. I don't know what they'll do to them, but Uncle says if I don't tend to you while you're here…" She sighed. "Nothing good'll happen."

Blaire didn't know what to say. Her being here tore apart people she cared about. But it wasn't her fault. It wasn't her fault a group of psychopaths felt the need to poke and prod at her to find answers to something that might lead nowhere. It wasn't her fault she showed the Korrena mark. It wasn't her fault Vincent wasn't all there in his head. Yet, the knowledge didn't stop the guilt from occasionally creeping in when things connected to her harmed her friends.

"I don't know what they plan, but I heard Uncle talking with Angelo and Tobias. They think there's ma—"

"That'll be all, Rueanna."

Blaire's gaze snapped to the left. A man with alabaster skin and platinum blond hair stood watching them, expressionless.

"T-Tobias." Rue backed away from Blaire's cell quickly and stood ramrod straight. "I-I was just…"

Was Tobias dangerous? Even without the Order's cult-like robe, Blaire recognized him as the man who seemed the most sympathetic to her during the trial. She'd seen it on his face. He didn't wholly agree with what the Order did, but not enough to stop it. Not enough to avoid barking his own orders.

"It doesn't matter. Go back to your room. Nathaniel is looking for you."

Rue nodded quickly and bowed slightly before giving Blaire one last look, pain floating in her hazel eyes. She hurriedly rushed into the shadows down the hall, and Blaire heard the door slam closed.

Blaire looked over her shoulder into Dom's cell when a low growl echoed into the space.

"Dominic," the man—Tobias—chastised. "Growling like an animal is beneath your pedigree."

"Shove the pedigree bullshit up your ass, Tobias. You and I both know you don't subscribe to that fake shit any more than I do."

Blaire blinked. She'd not heard Dom speak so crudely, and it sounded so wrong coming from him with what he'd presented so far.

"Is that any way to talk to someone who holds your fate in his hands?"

"You know my cousin will be looking for me."

"Mm, perhaps."

"How do you plan to explain to him your insubordination?"

Tobias shook his head and *tsked*. "I'm playing my role as intended."

Dom set down the empty bowl on the tray on his bed. "What do you call locking me up?"

"An inconvenience."

Dom shook his head, and Tobias sneered at him.

"I am not about to throw the past twenty years down the drain to keep your reckless ass out of the flames."

Blaire looked between the two men. She didn't understand what they were talking about, but it was obvious they knew one another.

"Why are you down here if not to help me?"

"Not everything is about you." Tobias turned his gaze on Blaire. "I was merely fetching Rueanna for Nathaniel."

Blaire studied Tobias as intently as he did her. Tobias had the body of a runway model; lean, but not too skinny, with long legs in neatly pressed black slacks. His shoulders were broader, and filled out the button-down plum shirt he wore, but his body wasn't bulky, judging by the way his clothing fit tailored to his body. His sharp, chiseled facial features added to the model aesthetic. He looked only a few years older than her.

"Are you comfortable?"

Blaire's breath hitched at the question. It surprised her. She didn't think anyone on the Order's council cared about her comfort level, only getting answers. Maybe there was more to the look of discomfort she'd seen in Tobias's expressive aquamarine eyes during the trial as

Blackthorn Security led Lukas away.

"As much as I can be, all things considered." She tried to go for a lighthearted tone to mask the surprise at his question and the urge to yell at him for keeping her locked up this long. She thought she'd be allowed to go home already. Back to Lukas.

"What do you need?" His tone was flat, but his eyes showed genuine interest.

She wanted to say, "to leave," but that would be a waste of breath and would likely lead to a less than accommodating reaction. Instead, she made a reasonable request.

"A change of clothes would be nice. I appreciate being able to wash myself at the lab, but..." She looked down at her rumpled sweater and jeans that didn't look dirty but felt dirty. She definitely didn't like how her panties felt. Her eyes found Tobias's again. "I've been wearing this since I agreed to come here."

Tobias tilted his head slightly then nodded. "Fresh clothing isn't an unreasonable request."

She wanted to ask if that was the case, why was that the final straw for Katie, but refrained.

"Anything else?"

Blaire's brows lowered. She couldn't think of anything else off the top of her head that she needed. Katie had already done her best to make her comfortable in the dungeon. She also didn't want to push her luck. "No, thank you."

He nodded tightly. "I'll see that Rueanna brings you clothing to sleep in and proper lounge wear."

Blaire's gaze darted over to Dom's cell. Was Tobias going to ask him if he needed anything?

"Finish your breakfast. You will participate in a different kind of experiment today. You'll need your strength."

Again. The look in Tobias's eyes again indicated discomfort.

Before she could give him a response, Tobias turned away and moved into the shadowed hallway. Moments later, the door to the dungeon fell shut.

"So, Dominic, is it?"

Dominic chuckled. "Caught that, did you?"

Among other things.

"That's your real name?"

"Yeah, but so is Dom. My friends call me Dom."

Blaire stirred the soup on her tray but couldn't bring herself to finish her breakfast. What had Rue started to tell her before Tobias showed up?

Blaire's laughter echoed in the dungeon.

"It really isn't that funny."

"You jumped into a lake while fully clothed to escape a goose… An innocent little bird… That's hilarious, actually."

He frowned. "Canada geese are vicious domestic terrorists that should be taken seriously. I could have *died!*"

When Blaire burst into another fit of laughter, clutching her stomach as she doubled over in her lap on the bed, Dominic's frown cracked into a wide grin. He wasn't serious.

Dominic had spent the morning sharing stories of his childhood in Canada, and Blaire had become fascinated with the little differences. Like bagged milk. She'd never heard of such a thing, but apparently Canadians bought their milk in bags instead of gallon jugs.

The conversation remained lighthearted, and he hadn't prodded too much into Blaire's past, keeping the questions to superficial things like her favorite foods and her thoughts on the mountains versus the

Eventually, he had opened up about his situation.

Dominic was visiting the academy when he'd overheard something he shouldn't have, and the Order locked him up until they could decide what to do with him. How he got into a position to hear something serious enough to land him in a cell below the school, she didn't know. He hadn't shared what he heard or what he was doing at Blackthorn Academy, and Blaire didn't want to push for the information and ruin the unexpected friendship she had started forging in the most unlikely places.

Who came to a dungeon to make friends?

She also learned he was the same age as Lukas—twenty.

Lunchtime rolled around, and Rue brought a tray with a plate of country ham, scalloped potatoes, and fresh green beans. A bottle of water accompanied it. The time of tea and juice from Katie was over. She gave Dominic the same thing, with the addition of a blood packet.

As Blaire stabbed a few green beans with her fork, she watched Marcus direct Rue toward the dungeon's exit. Apparently, the Order no longer trusted her not to overshare with Blaire. At least that was her theory.

As they left, Marcus made eye contact with her and gave her a pitying look. This situation sucked for everyone. "She'll be back with clothes when she collects your dishes," he said before leading Rue away.

Would Rue be alone then? Blaire wanted to ask if Rue knew anything more. What the Order's intentions were beyond this point and if they'd found anything. She wanted to know if they'd shared any of their plans for their experiments, and if she'd be able to go home soon. She missed Lukas.

With a full belly, Blaire lay back on the bed and closed her eyes, sighing.

Moments like these, when physically sated by food, made her feel uncomfortable. She didn't want to slip into accepting the daily routine as normal. It surprised her she could even find any form of relaxation given her situation, but in the last who knows how many hours, Dominic had given her something to focus on.

Her eyes opened as air stirred around her face when Dominic collapsed on his bed next to her cell. She glanced over at him.

He lay on his side facing her cell, his elbow on the bed, and his head cradled in his palm. "Napping?"

"No."

"Sure looks like it."

"I'm thinking."

"About?"

Blaire dragged her eyes away from his and looked at the dark ceiling. "How long I'll be stuck in here. I'm ready for it to be over with so I can go back."

"You miss your pair?"

She swallowed. "Yeah."

"Tell me about your Korrena."

A small snort of laughter escaped her as she thought of how to describe Lukas. Their time together had been so chaotic. There were so many red flags as they got together that it made no sense for them to be in a relationship, but the circumstances of how it all started and came to be had a lot to do with those red flags. She'd given a lot of concessions to Lukas's behavior she would likely not have given a human. It didn't mean she was a pushover. No. She put him in his place when necessary.

"Blaire?"

She turned her head. "Huh?"

"You kinda spaced out there." The corner of his mouth lifted in a half smile. "You don't have to tell me about your pair. I only thought it might make you feel better."

The man was kind. Genuinely kind. She couldn't detect an ulterior reason behind his questions or attentiveness. Dominic genuinely wanted to know, and honestly cared, about her thoughts and feelings.

"I was just thinking about how to explain to you that Lukas is an asshole, but a good asshole."

Dominic's bark of laughter made her smile. "An asshole? Do tell."

"He's jealous. Possessive. He likes to talk about me like I'm property instead of…" Her lips pursed as she tried to search for the right words.

"A human?"

She huffed air in through her nose. "Yeah, that."

"Sounds like a paired Vasirian to me."

"So I keep being told."

"I'm sure that isn't all there is to this Lukas."

"It's not." When he said nothing in response, she turned on her side to face him, tracing her index finger over the sheets beneath her. "He's fiercely loyal. Something I questioned once and regret." She sighed. "He's caring. Not just for me, but for those he lets in his circle. Which isn't many people. But those he lets in, he cares for in a way many people don't care about others, you know?" She looked up at Dominic.

"He's antisocial?"

"To a fault sometimes. Knowing what I do about him now, I'm not as surprised he stopped to speak to me the day we met and ran into each other. But for a while there, it didn't fit the impression he gave. Turns out, he'll talk to a stranger if necessary, and he won't be a jerk to them if they aren't rude to him, but he won't seek people out."

Dominic frowned. “What do you mean?”

“Like you, for example. You’re warm and extroverted—at least that’s the impression you give me.”

He smiled and she dropped her gaze.

“Lukas is the type to make you think he’s angry with you when he doesn’t even know you if you somehow catch his eye. He’s just got this presence…”

“Back off and don’t fuck with me?”

“Exactly.” She looked up at him again.

Dominic hummed, shifting on the bed.

“But it’s all a mask. I can tell. He’s so unbelievably loving and pure-hearted, even if he has issues with his anger and all that… Vasirian, growly, touch-her-and-die nonsense.”

Dominic snorted and held a hand up. “Sorry, sorry. I’ve never had a pair, but I’ve seen the ‘nonsense’ in action. It is pretty intense with new pairs.”

Blaire clenched the sheets in her hand and sighed. “I think something is missing.”

“Pardon?”

She wondered if it was wrong to open up this way about Lukas to a stranger, but it wasn’t like she could talk to Riley about it. Riley and Lukas were close, so Blaire wasn’t sure how she’d take any of this. Besides, sometimes Riley had a problem with keeping things under wraps. Not the big stuff. Riley learned from past incidents, at least. Blaire couldn’t go to Charlotte either; the risk of accidentally revealing something incriminating about this world was too great.

Blaire sighed. “I think there’s something he’s missing in his life, and it keeps him the way he is. The reason he holds everyone at arm’s length. Even his friends. Despite the feelings I know are there through the empathic bond we share, he doesn’t always share them. There’s always this underlying loneliness I don't understand. It's not as strong since we did the claiming ritual." Her face warmed. "But, it's there. Strangely, I feel it a lot when we're with his best friend and mine."

Dominic shifted to sit up on the bed. "What about just one of them?"

"Huh?"

"You said when you're with both of them. Did you mean either of them, or both of them together?"

Blaire thought for a moment and her brows lowered. "Together. Not so much when it's just one of them."

"How do they know each other?"

"They all grew up together."

Dominic scratched the light dusting of dark stubble on his jaw that grew overnight. "So, they're like family, eh?"

"Well, Riley and Aiden are actual siblings."

"Oh, yeah?" Dominic was silent for a few moments before he met Blaire's eyes. "Does Lukas have siblings?"

"No. He's an only child. Been at the academy since he was five."

"So, he doesn't have a family?"

"He has a mom and dad, but they only see him once a year at the holidays, if that."

Dominic pointed at her. "There's the problem."

"What?"

"Your pair wants a family. Seeing his best friend with his sister makes him long for that familial bond. I mean, I don't know for sure, obviously… I'm merely speculating. If you feel loneliness when he's faced with a real family dynamic, and his parents never come around, it only makes sense."

"He says they are his family."

"Yeah, but a makeshift family doesn't always squash the desire for the real thing."

Blaire looked down at the bed. It made sense. That same lonely feeling from their empathic connection would crawl over her whenever she mentioned her mother, or when she asked Lukas questions about his parents. Until he made a family of his own, or connected more with his parents, she wondered if Lukas would ever stop feeling so lonely—even with her by his side.

16

Corruption

Blaire's head slumped forward as prickles of awareness teased her at the edge of consciousness. Voices were arguing, but she couldn't make them out. She wanted to speak, but her awareness wasn't part of her body. She wasn't in control of her vital functions to make her mouth move. She stood at the edge of her mind as an observer who couldn't do anything.

The blackness was disconcerting. The burning in her veins alarming. She welcomed sleep's embrace when it wrapped around her again.

Another week had passed since Tobias told her they were going to start new experiments, and no amount of food they could give her would have prepared her for what she endured. She didn't even know what they did to her. Shortly after they began each experiment, she'd pass out from the pain that wracked her body. Then she'd wake up in her cell weak and disoriented.

Rue had come several times to help clean her up when she had been too weak to take a proper shower at the lab. She'd brought Blaire a pair of soft pajama pants as well as a couple pairs of jeans, t-shirts, a warm hoodie, and a pile of fresh, clean panties. A security guard always stood watch when Rue came, so Blaire couldn't ask for any information, but her friend was suffering. Rue hadn't been back to see Liam. Blaire's heart hurt for her, but she couldn't focus on someone else's plight when struggling to grasp her own situation.

It always started with blood being drawn and ended with presentation of various stones smeared with runes in blood. Whose blood, she didn't know. But when they spilled her blood on her skin and lay the stones on her body, she no longer cared. The pain was so intense her body revolted against itself. She screamed and everything went black. It happened every single time; today was no different. At least they didn't cut her open to get the blood.

This time, a bolt of searing pain shot down the side of her neck, making her eyes fly open. Her lips parted on a soundless cry; the shock stole her breath. She dug her nails into the armrest of the chair she was bound to with leather straps.

"Get the stones off her!"

Hands swept across her arms and thighs. The noise of several objects clattering across the floor reached her through the echo of blood rushing in her ears. Tears tracked down her face as she gasped, drinking in the air that had been stolen from her as the burning sensation dissipated and the smell of burnt meat faded from the air. She slumped in the chair, her vision hazy and black around the edges. She struggled to stay conscious, focusing on the nice coconut scent she kept smelling when she came to the lab.

"Did you see that?" a man said, panicked.

Blaire squinted, still panting, at a woman—or maybe it was a man with long hair—standing over her.

"Ben." A long pause stretched as the two hazy figures stared at one another. "According to the photos we have on file, that symbol was her Korrena mark," the woman said.

"But it was practically on fire!"

The hysterical nature of the man's yelling put Blaire on edge, but she didn't have the physical strength to move or respond. She closed her eyes, focusing on breathing slowly through her nose, trying not to pass out.

"Yes, I saw that. But look." The woman lifted Blaire's hair from her neck. "No burnt flesh. No remnants of the mark. You would expect a brand from the way it smoldered against her flesh, but nothing remains." She dropped Blaire's hair. "The burning mark left her hair untouched. It's as if the fire burned from within."

"This differs from the vials of blood," the man said, calmer, but his voice remained pitched high and uncertain.

"What did you do differently from the last test?"

Blaire's hair lifted again, and she cracked her eyes open to see the man pointing at her neck. "Made a small incision here. I wanted to test a hypothesis running around in my brain for days."

"That is?"

"That blood flowing from the source would elicit a visceral response to the stimulus of runes and Vasirian blood."

"Well, you certainly got your answer."

"What are we going to tell Master Moretti? He'll want to cut her open, if he knows that is the only way we can get new returns from her."

Blaire's vision dimmed further. She wasn't sure if it was from blood loss, the physical strain she endured, or fear over the information she overheard.

"You say that like it's a bad thing," the woman challenged.

"I don't... I didn't become a scientist to hurt people. I... I barely cut her neck. I can't do this if it goes that far. I won't."

Blaire's head fell forward.

"Good answer," the woman said softly. "We won't allow them to hurt her while under our care."

"What if they find out?"

"They won't. We won't lie, but we won't reveal everything. We note what responses we've had to the other tests, and that's it. This test never happened."

"But—"

"Never. Happened."

The man cleared his throat. "I'll document the three tests we did prior to that one. It should account for the time lost with us if we consider the time she spent unconscious. A pity, really. If we could get a sample of her Korrena's blood we could see if there would be any impact on her reaction, but that would require disclosing this experiment to Master Moretti."

By the sounds around her, objects were moved during another beat of silence, but she didn't have the strength to lift her head. Her eyelids felt glued shut.

"It's a shame she's suffered this much from simple blood donations. She certainly piqued my curiosity," the woman finally said.

"I've never seen a condition like hers outside of cases of menorrhagia, but the health department noted that wasn't the situation after a brief consultation last school year. Further, the symptoms extend beyond her menstrual cycle. Have you ever seen a human bruise this severely? For this long?"

Blaire wanted to flinch away from the rough hand that lifted her arm after removing the restraint. She was so tired. All she wanted to do was sleep. The severe burning pain had receded, but her body still protested like she had run a marathon while being pelted with tennis balls. Muscles she didn't even know she had ached.

The woman sighed. "No. There are rare conditions that manifest bruising in this way, but her medical records from her youth all turn up negative results. Previous doctors reported issues with low or abnormal blood platelets, but it isn't a consistent issue to warrant a proper diagnosis."

Cool fingers pressed against her neck as someone moved her head back to rest against a cushion on the back of the chair. "Ben, stop touching her. Look at her face. She's in pain."

The man gently returned her arm to the armrest.

Darkness took her.

A girl's cries interrupted Blaire's sleep.

Why wouldn't she stop crying? What was wrong with her?

Blaire wanted the girl to stop crying. She pulled the covers over her head and whimpered as pain seized her muscles. The crying stopped at that moment.

"Shh." A hand touched the top of her head, stroking her hair. "You're safe."

Blaire's eyebrows pinched tightly. *Who is that?* The voice sounded familiar, comforting. Sniffling, Blaire slowly cracked open eyes full of grit.

Dominic removed his hand from the top of Blaire's head, pulling his arm back through the bars. He smiled down at her, but it looked strained. He had dark circles under his eyes.

"What's going on?" Blaire tried to sit up and gasped when her nerves pinched at her shoulder. She wasn't getting up anytime soon. "How long have I been out?"

This wasn't the first time this week she'd woken up disoriented on the bed in her cell. Dominic had witnessed more than she cared to count her response to the loss of blood. But this was a first. She'd never woken up in tears. Never felt like all of her muscles were completely spent.

"I don't really know," he said. "No way to tell the time… but it's been hours."

"How do you know?"

"Haven't slept."

"Why?"

Dominic grimaced. "Well…" He scratched his jaw. "You've been crying a lot."

"I'm sorry."

"No, no, don't be sorry. I want to know what happened this time. This isn't normal. What did they do to you?"

"I can't remember much. I couldn't stay awake. There was so much burning." She winced as she rolled on her side.

"Why can't you move well?"

Blaire sighed and licked her chapped lips. "I dunno. The last thing they did to me made my entire body hurt."

"What did they do?"

Blaire explained the vague memories of stones on her body, and the burning beneath the surface of her skin. How the scientists stopped whatever they were doing. How they said they would hide this experiment from the Order because of how badly she responded to it. She even explained her medical issues in more detail to help Dominic understand some of the things the scientists said. Needing someone on her side, she took the chance of trusting Dominic. Trusting he couldn't hurt her with the knowledge.

"I don't understand." Dominic lowered himself to lie on his back, yawning. "Did they even find anything? It doesn't sound like they did." He turned his head toward her. "Is it just the reaction?"

"I'm not sure. I wasn't completely with it, so I only really remember the conversation about the Order."

"I wonder why they're keeping it a secret."

"It doesn't make sense they're protecting me. Wouldn't scientific curiosity win out?"

"Morals."

Blaire studied Dominic's face in the dim lighting of the dungeon. Was the only thing keeping her from being sliced into ribbons a strong moral compass? It stood to reason that if Angelo ordered other researchers to do experiments on her, they might not have the same moral resolve. What would happen to her then? She could only hope they didn't get an idea to cut her open if that's what elicited the reaction the two scientists she was last with were so concerned about.

"We're not all bloodthirsty monsters, you know."

"Huh?"

Dominic reached through the bars and gently pushed between Blaire's eyebrows with his index finger, smoothing out the skin there. "You have this look, like you find it hard to believe. Not all Vasirian take pleasure in locking people away and hurting them." He chuckled. "Most don't."

"I know that."

The time spent with the friends she's made since coming to Blackthorn Academy was enough to tell her that. While a few of them had it in them to inflict harm, the Vasirian she knew would never hurt indiscriminately. They would never bring harm to another, human or not, without good reason. That didn't make her blind to the Vasirian who would—and had—harmed her. But from her experience, there were more Vasirian with good intentions than bad.

"I was actually thinking about what will happen if different researchers get involved. Not everyone has good intentions."

A line formed between Dominic's brows, and he shifted his gaze over Blaire's shoulder, staring into the dimness of her cell.

"I'd like to promise I'd protect you, but I'm just as trapped in here as you are." His gaze settled on her face. "But should I be in the position to stop them from harming you, I'll do just that. You have my word."

"Why?"

The question was simple, yet so complicated. This man didn't know her. He had no reason to risk himself on her behalf, and she didn't even know why he was locked away. She didn't think the Order locked people away on a whim—or did they? Maybe it was like he explained regarding the scientists. Maybe Dominic's own moral compass wouldn't allow him to let her come to harm if confronted with it.

Blaire nestled into the bedding, trying to settle and get comfortable despite her protesting muscles.

"It's not right, for one." He yawned. "For two… Well, let's just say I have a vested interest in your wellbeing now."

"That sure doesn't sound ominous."

"It's not. You're a human in this world, and a Korrena. Like others, I'm curious."

Something about his word choices didn't strike her as plain curiosity, but she didn't push.

"This isn't working."

Blaire's brows knotted, and she groaned, coming back to consciousness again. She wanted this to end. Ever since they stepped up their experimentation, her body had a difficult time keeping up. While she hadn't felt the same pain she did a few days ago when she overheard the conversation between the researchers, they continued to draw her blood daily.

Humans replenished their blood quickly, but not this much. Charlotte donated blood before, and Blaire remembered them telling Charlotte she had to wait two months if she wanted to do so again. Somehow, Blaire doubted the medicine they kept providing her with was enough to see her through. She felt weak, and by the look on Dominic's face when he'd give her lingering glances, she didn't look the best.

"I'm aware. You've been doing the same thing all week and nothing changes. Just cut her open and see if anything occurs directly from the source."

She recognized the Italian accent.

"Master Moretti, the human is weak. She has a medical condition we do not understand; if we cut into her body rather than extract her blood into vials, the likelihood she scars is high."

"Do I look like I care about that? I want answers, Ken."

"Ben."

"What?"

"Uh… Well, you see… My name is Ben, not Ken."

"That's what I said."

Blaire didn't move, didn't breathe, didn't draw attention to herself. This was the first time she'd woken during their experiments, and she wanted to see if she could learn anything about what was happening to her, or what they'd discovered.

"Her hemoglobin levels are low, much lower than should be for her to continue. She needs weeks to recover—if not more, considering her unique design. We can't even take platelets at this point now, since there was a mix-up with her medication, and she received aspirin. If we continue this way, there is a possibility she will—"

"Enough. I want answers. I need something I can actually work with, Gen."

She heard an exasperated sigh. Rustling. Papers shuffling.

"Master Moretti, if we continue this way, we will merely waste time." He cleared his throat. "And money."

That seemed to get Angelo's attention, because his tone shifted. "Yes, well, we have a limited budget. What do you propose we do, then?"

She wanted to yell at them to say something of substance, but she refrained. A scientist would desire answers more than they would care about their financiers' budget, especially if said financier had the kind of money the Order likely had at their disposal. Her gut said this was a move to protect her. Another surprise from the Vasirian world. Another person who possibly cared about her well-being.

"This is unfamiliar territory. We don't have a direction to go in to try to replicate what we've achieved with her blood in vials. Despite a clear physical response from the human, it yields no results worthy of documentation. Her blood and the runes elicit the same response as our lab tests. Being near the source only creates a physical response of pain to the point she loses consciousness. Beyond that, there is nothing worthy of note."

What response were they talking about?

As much as she suspected agreeing to work with the Order to save Lukas was a trap, she didn't grasp the depths of how far Angelo's need for more could go. He seemed to lack any empathy for anyone. She understood it didn't matter if she was human or Vasirian. When he wanted something, no one stood in his way. She'd witnessed enough of his posturing, and heard plenty of his twisted desires, to know his appetite for more knew no bounds.

"We are getting nowhere, Angelo," said a man with an extremely deep voice Blaire didn't recognize.

"I'm aware of that, Nathaniel."

"We should proceed with the next step. Chalk this up to a mistake of nature. It is unlikely we will encounter another human like this. I've said from the beginning that removing the issue was the best solution. Why waste our time, and that of our researchers, on something that matters not? This witch nonsense is just the ramblings of old. Let us put it to bed and move on."

Witch? She must be a mess in the head. She wasn't hearing conversations correctly. What did witchcraft have to do with anything?

"I was hoping we would have more answers before we proceeded with the sacrifice."

Blaire tensed, but she tried her best to remain as still as possible. What sacrifice were they talking about? Surely, they couldn't mean her. She was supposed to take part in experiments and go home. That was the agreement. They promised they wouldn't kill her.

"You get ahead of yourself, Angelo. Do not allow your lust for the power she holds inside cloud your judgment."

Angelo scoffed. "Oh, you misunderstand me, my friend. I am very much in control of myself. I merely see the benefit of tapping into the little surprise our project has within before disposing of her. Can you imagine what we could do with an active source? How are we to know we can harness the magic and make use of it once she passes? It might not even be possible to extract it."

Blaire's breathing quickened. She must be delirious. Nothing they said made any sense.

"I never believed it possible. This whole magical deity nonsense you expect us to entertain is absurd. What do you expect to happen?"

"From what I've read, at the time of her death, the magic should pass from her body to a willing vessel."

"A willing vessel? Who do you expect to fill that role?"

"Me, of course. It is the least I can do for dragging each of you into this."

A deep chuckle that didn't suit the seriousness of the bass voice rang in Blaire's ears. "I'm sure your motives are purely diplomatic."

"Come now. I'm thirsty."

Movement and footsteps retreated from her, and she relaxed slightly, but she couldn't control the pounding of her heart in her chest.

"They're gone," Ben whispered, gently placing his hand on her arm strapped to the armrest of the chair. He fidgeted with the restraints. "I've done everything I can to avoid another incident like what happened on Monday, but I won't be able to stop what they plan next. I'm sorry."

She swallowed. "Why?" Her voice cracked, the words a hoarse whisper. Her throat felt so dry.

"Because whatever they have planned has nothing to do with scientific research."

She wanted to tell him her question wasn't related to why he couldn't stop the madmen who were convinced of fantastical things, but her face hurt. Lacking the strength to talk, she only wanted to sleep.

Yes, the Order was corrupt, but to the point of a sacrifice? Sacrifice to who? To what? Magical deity? With the blood loss, and whatever strange experiments they did while she was unconscious, she was missing key pieces of information. Sweat rolled down the side of her face as her heart hammered in her chest and her head spun.

17

Dominic

Blaire sighed, looking down at the mottled bruising across her arm. The purple and blue marbling pattern over the faded yellow and green from weeks ago looked ghastly. She hated being on display for Rue to see, but required her help to stay clean when she wasn't able to shower in the lab if she passed out. Her eyes cut to the security guard, Marcus, standing just outside of her cell. At least he had the decency to keep his back to them to give Blaire the privacy to be undressed and wasn't witness to the terrible state her body was in.

"So, what's his story?" Rue asked as she gently eased a washcloth over Blaire's arm.

"Who?"

Rue looked into the next cell where Dominic lay with his back to them, presumably asleep.

"Oh. I don't know. He's Canadian?" Blaire didn't know enough about his situation to give Rue much information. He'd made someone upset, but that didn't say much, given the Vasirian punishments for other infractions. She was thankful she'd made a friend to make the time spent here bearable.

Rue frowned. "That's all?"

"Well, we've talked, but mostly just distracting ourselves from this situation."

Three and a half weeks had passed since she first set foot in the cell. Despite having moments where she could barely stay conscious, she never wavered from marking the walls. She would not lose time. Not again.

There wasn't even a point in asking to go back to her dorm after what she'd heard a few days ago. The Order didn't intend to set her free. No, they planned to kill her in some messed up sacrifice. Maybe the rumors spreading around Rosebrook Valley about a cult running this school didn't stray far from the truth. It wasn't true of the students and staff, but Blaire was beginning to get that impression from the administration.

"He's handsome. Not as much as Liam, but I can appreciate his looks without wanting to sample."

Blaire snorted a laugh. "You're ridiculous."

Dominic was a handsome guy, but he wasn't her type. Riley, on the other hand, would likely think he was hot. He favored Seth in some ways, after all. Even if Riley wouldn't admit to it, it was obvious to everyone but Seth and Riley they were attracted to one another. Seth wasn't an ugly guy either. Both men were objectively handsome. They just lacked the key physical attributes that worked for her. Lukas had those traits.

"I don't know what he did to end up in here. He said something about crossing the wrong person or making them upset. Something like that. I can only imagine who it was to end up here. It had to be one of the seven members of the Order. Does anyone else send people down into the dungeons?"

"No. Well, actually, yeah. Typically, whenever a Vasirian is to be put on trial, is awaiting transport to Cresbel Asylum, or is being held until the royal guard can claim them, they are sent here. So really, this guy could be anyone."

"His name is Dominic."

"Okay, Dominic." Rue shrugged. "I'm just saying he could be a hardened criminal. He could have hurt a human."

Blaire didn't believe that. Dominic had been nothing but kind to her so far. He looked out for her as best he could from his cell. Talked to her about her worries. Soothed her fears and spoke encouraging words when the experiments dragged her morale down into the gutter.

When Blaire didn't respond, Rue continued. "I don't know, though. He seems nice. Funny, too." She wet the washcloth in the metal basin on the floor beside Blaire's bed before squirting a dollop of body wash onto the cloth, reaching for Blaire's foot where she lay on the bed.

"You know I can clean myself, right?"

Rue paused with Blaire's foot in her hand. She turned her gaze to Blaire. "Really? Because it looks like you can barely keep your eyes open."

Blaire looked away and squeezed her hands into fists to stop their shaking. She hated being so weak. Didn't like everyone catering to her like an invalid. She couldn't even stop the involuntary twitches and spasms from her protesting muscles that kept her hands shaking. If she tried to wash herself right now, she'd probably fall out of bed.

Rue's voice lowered as her eyes shifted to Marcus. "I'm working on a way to help you. I can't handle seeing you like this."

"Don't get yourself in trouble for me," Blaire whispered, her eyes tracking to Marcus. He seemed to be in his own little world, tapping at the screen of his cell phone, occasionally chuckling at whatever he was looking at. "I'll be fine."

But that wasn't true. If Blaire didn't find a way out of the dungeon, she was as good as dead. If whatever the Order planned didn't kill her, then the experiments would. She wasn't as battered as her time with Vincent, but the multiple places they'd drawn blood left unsightly bruising along her forearms and the tops of her hands. At least she wasn't riddled with bite marks and bruising in finger patterns anymore.

"You and I both know that isn't true."

"I'm not ready to die," Blaire said, mostly to herself, but Rue made a small sound and sniffed. Rue may have heard that, but she didn't know about the sacrifice.

Blaire cleared her throat. "Does blood not bother you?" She looked at the pink-tinted soapy water from where one experiment reopened a wound on her upper arm. If they were only drawing her blood and laying stones on her skin, she wasn't sure how they'd torn her flesh.

"Hmm?" Rue lifted her head from her focus on lathering the washcloth and passed it to Blaire. "Here, for… you know. The girly bits." She looked away as Blaire took the cloth from her. Blaire always took care of her own private areas whenever Rue came to help her bathe. It was difficult, but she couldn't handle having someone clean her so intimately.

"The blood," Blaire repeated. "How are you not bothered by it?" She finished washing up and dropped the washcloth into the basin, reaching for a pair of panties and sliding them on, followed by plaid pajama pants. She slowly sat up, and Rue stood, helping Blaire ease a baggy t-shirt over her head and arms.

"Doesn't bother me too much." She tucked a strand of dark hair that had fallen from her braid behind her ear. "I mean, it isn't the most comfortable thing in the world, but I'm not wanting to turn you into a meal, if that's what you're worried about."

Blaire laughed. "I'm not." She put a hand to the side of her head as a wave of dizziness swept over her.

"Here. Let me help." Rue cradled Blaire's elbow and guided her down onto the bed again. "This is ridiculous."

Dominic stirred on the bed, turning over. "What's ridiculous?"

Rue sighed in frustration and waved a hand at Blaire. "That they keep going, even though she can barely stand."

"How long have you been back?" Dominic sat up and rubbed his eyes.

"Not long. Was able to get my bath done before you woke up." Blaire sat back against the bars and closed her eyes.

"How do you feel?"

"Tired. Dizzy." She didn't like how her words slurred.

Marcus opened the cell, eyeing Blaire warily. "She alright?" He lifted the basin of water and shifted with uncertainty, glancing back at the open cell door.

"No, she's not. They are torturing her. Would you be alright?" Rue snapped and lines formed between Marcus's brows.

"Don't blame him. It's not his fault. He's just doing his job."

"If he really gave a damn, he'd get you out of here."

Marcus's hands tightened on the metal basin. "I don't like this any more than you do, actually. But I can't do anything about it. I have a family to support. If I lose my job..." He snorted derisively. "You're just a kid. You don't get it."

Rue glared at him.

Blaire groaned. Her head hurt.

"Maybe it'd be best if you both let it go?" Dominic looked between

Rue and Marcus. "Our security friend here is just doing what he's told. He's not directly responsible for what those researchers are doing to her. Besides, arguing isn't helping her." He looked at Blaire as she slumped to the side against the bars with heavy eyelids.

"I'm going to get rid of this water. You." He pointed at Rue. "Stay put."

"Where else am I gonna go?"

Marcus muttered several disgruntled things Blaire couldn't make out as he stepped out of the cell, set the basin down, and locked the door. He lifted the basin and disappeared down the corridor that ran the length of the cells until shadows swallowed him.

"So, you." Rue pointed at Dominic as she settled on the foot of Blaire's bed. "Spill."

"Pardon?"

"Ugh. Your accent is nice." Rue laughed as a faint blush stained Dominic's cheeks. "Why are you here?"

"I don't think that's important."

Blaire wasn't used to seeing Rue with snappy comebacks and silly retorts as frequently as she delivered them this evening—or day—Blaire didn't know what time of day it was. Dark circles sat beneath Rue's eyes and her caramel skin appeared paler than usual. She looked tired and worn. The loss of Liam affected her, and Blaire suspected she used over-the-top responses to distract herself. What else could she do? Allow despair to sink its claws into her so deeply that when she did reunite with Liam, she'd be a hollow shell of herself? Blaire didn't think Rue operated like that.

"I think I'd like to know who the person who sleeps so close to my friend is."

"Fair." Dominic sighed. "I was sent here to check into things."

"Things? By who?"

"Yes, things. I can't go into detail, and it doesn't matter to her safety."

Rue sighed and waved a hand for him to continue.

"The person who sent me here wanted me to find out information on the Order. How they operated. What they were up to. If everything was on the up and up. You know, sniff out any corruption."

Rue huffed. "There's plenty of that. More than I ever imagined." She peered at Blaire. "I had no idea they were doing what they were since you've arrived."

"It's not your fault. I didn't tell anyone."

"I discovered exactly that information in passing. Nothing is recorded in writing—at least from what I could find."

"You acted like you didn't know if the human rumor was true," Blaire said, frowning.

"Well, I didn't. I didn't know the person they were talking about was human. I heard they were performing experiments on blood."

"Oh, so you don't know what she went through?"

"What do you mean? I thought you were talking about the experiments."

"Nope." Rue folded her arms over her stomach. "Apparently, my uncle and his merry band of evildoers decided to sic their henchmen on Blaire to steal blood from her in the night like blood burglars. Nearly killed her."

Dominic turned narrowed eyes to Blaire. "She serious?"

"I wish she wasn't."

Dominic cursed. "I had no idea it was that bad, and now this? No wonder they put me in here to silence me."

Who did Dominic work for? Why did they choose now to investigate the Order when the likelihood of their wrongdoings extended farther back than when Blaire came to Blackthorn Academy?

"Well, after they locked her Korrena away because he tried to kill the asshole who kidnapped his pair, they had Blaire right where they wanted her. I heard my uncle talking about it. It was an elaborate bait and switch situation."

"I don't think that means what you think it does."

"No?"

"Blaire wasn't given something of lower quality by being baited for something of higher quality."

"But isn't that what it is?"

"Huh?"

"Well, she ended up with this terrible outcome in exchange for freeing Lukas. She thought she'd get to go home with him after a volunteer blood donation. Like the humans do for the Red Cross all the time. But what they actually gave her is all this. Baited her with something good and gave her something bad."

"I suppose I can see that."

"Whatever it's called doesn't matter. What matters is figuring out how to get out of this situation. And now that I know you're not a bad guy—"

Dominic raised a brow.

"I have one more person to consider." She glanced over at Blaire.

"Blaire?" Dominic asked, concern in his voice.

"Mm?"

"You still here with us? You've been awfully quiet."

"Mm."

"I don't like this. She's lost too much blood," Rue said softly. "This can't continue."

"But what can we do?"

Blaire collapsed to her side on the bed.

18

Father's Will

Blaire snuggled into the warmth that surrounded her, sighing happily. A coconut perfumed breeze moved over her face, and she deeply inhaled the comforting scent. She'd always liked the smell. She had candles like that in her room growing up, and even the school had given her a candle for the dorm bathroom with the same scent. It had helped her get through the experiments as well. She didn't know what caused it, but the lab also had a coconut smell.

Sunlight teased her through her eyelids, and birds sang in the distance, but she didn't want to get out of bed. The blankets she lay on were too cozy—even fuzzy.

Fuzzy?

With hesitation, she slowly opened her eyes to look at where she slept.

The enormous wolf she'd seen before lay curled around her on the forest floor, and Blaire had nestled herself against its stomach.

Gasping, she sat up quickly and scooted away. Yawning, the wolf opened its mouth wide, revealing large sharp teeth. Blaire slid another few inches away. He licked his muzzle lazily and yawned once more, oblivious to her freak-out.

"You should know by now he won't harm you."

Blaire's head snapped around to see the Oracle sitting daintily on a fallen log surrounded by small purple, red, and blue flowers with glowing stamen. The crow pair perched quietly next to her on the end of the log.

"Why was I sleeping with him?"

"He likes you."

Blaire looked back at the wolf, who lay watching her with intelligent eyes. "But that doesn't explain how I got in that position with him."

"Giving too much thought to trivial things when there is so much more to consider places an unnecessary burden on the soul."

Blaire didn't see how being concerned about using a massive wolf as a bed was a trivial thing. It wasn't a trivial thing when the bed had the potential to eat you.

"He's not going to eat you. He's not like wolves from the waking realm."

The wolf huffed as if offended.

"I doubt he would do so," the Oracle said, "even if he had that type of hunger."

"Why?"

"A Guardian serves a purpose. To watch over their chosen soul. Killing them would be the antithesis to that."

"Guardian?" Blaire looked at the wolf.

"I suppose we should go back many years first for you to understand." The Oracle clasped her hands in her lap and took a breath. "I think now is the right time for you to know the truth."

"The truth? The truth about what?"

"Your father."

Blaire's brow furrowed. "What do you mean?"

"With the return of my memories, the Celestial Conclave has revealed new truths to me. About my kind. Yours. Your past, and your potential future."

Blaire clenched the strands of grass beneath her hand.

"Long ago, long before I was even a sparkle in my parents' eyes, magic existed."

"Magic?"

"Yes, magic. It flowed freely in the veins of many mortals and Vasirian alike. These special beings had gifts beyond that of Vasirian compulsion and strength. Depending on how they harnessed and shaped their abilities, they could do great things."

Blaire stared in awe. Was the Oracle seriously trying to tell her that magic—the kind of things she'd only seen in movies and read in stories—existed on Earth hundreds of years ago?

"But alas, all good things must reach their end—be it temporary or not."

"What do you mean?"

"When King Rosendo made his move, unable to harness this power for himself, he severed the flow, bound my memories, and set forth the events that have led us here."

"But why? Why would he do that? I don't understand."

The wolf whined low and eased forward on his belly until he lay beside Blaire. He nudged her hand in the grass. Her hand automatically moved to pet the fur on his back gently.

"The plague of avarice affects us all," the Oracle said with a sigh. "Transcending reason, discriminating against neither age nor species, it casts the hearts it infects into ruin. Such is the truth of Rosendo Blackthorn's true downfall. He lusted for material wealth and sought to become more powerful than those around him. His dark ambitions led him down a path of pain and destruction. His hatred for a species not his own contributed to more bloodshed than I wish to remember."

"What does this have to do with my father?"

"Some humans carry remnants of this ancient bloodline. Potential doors to restore the balance lost between the two species. Your father brought such a door into existence."

The wolf whined again and nudged Blaire's arm. He eased his massive head into her lap. She scratched at his scalp with her fingertips as she tried to take in the Oracle's words without reacting too much. She didn't understand. Everything sounded so out of left field it was hard to comprehend.

"Your father's death has a darker truth than what you believe occurred."

"Huh? But—"

"You were only a toddler, I'm aware. But there was still the possibility of reaching you that young and putting a stop to everything the Celestial Conclave desires to come to fruition. Your father discovered a plot to take your life and did what he could to stop this—to his detriment."

Blaire's heart banged against her chest so hard she wondered if it would escape. "What are you saying?" Her voice sounded strained. Impatient.

"He did not have magic, child. At least, not that he knew. But someone, somehow, made him aware of things even I didn't know. Warned him of deadly intentions that would rid this world of your existence before you'd come into your own." The Oracle took a breath. "Your father gave his life so you could live yours."

The world shifted beneath Blaire. She tried to get up, but the wolf's heavy head kept her in place. A low growl from him was the only warning not to run like she wanted to.

"You're wrong. He died of a heart attack."

"Of course. But behind such a tragic event was a nefarious plot. If your father hadn't discovered what he did, you would not be here, but he would."

The beautiful forest around Blaire blurred as her eyes filled with liquid emotion. She grasped the wolf's fur with shaking hands. Her father died to keep her alive. Her father, whom she'd never had the chance to know. A man who loved her enough to give his life to protect her from something she still didn't understand.

"Why did whoever it was want to kill me? Who was it?"

"Those of my kind who seek to disrupt the balance. Seek to prevent events that are unfolding now from occurring. If you didn't exist, those events wouldn't happen, and many future events that could be possible would cease to be a possibility."

One tear after another tracked down Blaire's cheeks as the information settled in her stomach like a stone at the bottom of a river. Magic was a real thing, and for reasons she couldn't understand, her father had a connection to the Vasirian world. She remembered the mention of witches. Maybe she hadn't been as delirious as she'd suspected.

"Before your father died, the Celestial Conclave heard his plea."

"What plea?"

"That you live. That your mother and you wouldn't be left alone."

Blaire swallowed thickly and looked at the canopy overhead. Sunlight streamed through the branches, lighting patches of the forest floor. Even at his death, her father thought more of protecting them than himself. Her mother told her of his selflessness. Told Blaire how he'd give anything for them. She told the truth.

"They answered his last request through a Guardian."

Blaire's gaze dropped back down to the Oracle as the wolf lifted his head and sat up on his haunches. "I don't follow."

"His protection lives on in Ciro."

"Ciro?"

The wolf's tail swished excitedly.

Blaire's features pinched. "Ciro?" she repeated, and the wolf turned his head toward her as if he understood.

"Ciro has been cast to be your Guardian until you come into your own."

"I don't understand."

"In time. More will be revealed in time. Right now, you need to understand Ciro is your father's wish made manifest."

Blaire's eyes widened. "Wait…" She peered into Ciro's startling blue eyes. "*Dad?*"

The wolf huffed loudly out of his nose, and the Oracle laughed softly.

"No, child. Ciro is not your father reincarnate. Ciro carries your father's will deep within. What carried through your bloodline made such a transition possible."

"Is that why he seems intelligent?"

"No." The Oracle looked at Ciro. "Ciro is more than what you see. He's chosen to stay in this form for now to avoid frightening you."

"*Avoid?*" Blaire blinked. Did they not get how massive the wolf next to her was? "Wait. Are you telling me he's not a wolf?" She looked at Ciro. "You're not a wolf?"

"I think the term you'd be familiar with is wolf shifter—or werewolf."

Blaire's mouth fell open. She'd seen werewolves in movies, read of wolf shifters in the novels she liked. *Why am I even surprised?* Vasirian, magic, sacrifices, magical deities, strange realms… Everything in the last ten months Blaire encountered should have softened the blow, but it didn't. It was just as shocking as finding out beings existed that aligned with vampire myth.

At least she didn't pass out this time.

"So, that means you're also a man?"

Ciro lowered his head as if to nod.

"I don't even know what to say to that."

"There are others like him in this realm."

"Guardians?"

"Shifters. In this case, wolf shifters. But none with the power or purpose he has. When he fulfills his role, he will have a choice. To move on, or return to his life, and possibly have a family, should he choose to. He is still young, after all."

Several small orbs of light drifted between them, and Blaire squinted. Not orbs. Bugs? Tiny creatures with wings engulfed in a purple glow moved as a group around them and into the forest that had darkened around them as the sun set.

Blaire's attention moved back to the Oracle, and she frowned. "You said move on…" She looked at Ciro. "Do you mean die?"

"Being a Guardian can tax the mind. I have only heard of it happening a handful of times in my lifetime. Many seek to move beyond this reality when the vessel they are meant to protect fulfills their purpose."

Blaire didn't like that. Not at all. To know that when she did whatever was expected of her, this beautiful wolf—who apparently was also a man—would die.

Ciro lowered himself to the ground again slowly, moving his paws forward inch by inch until his nose bumped Blaire's leg. As if he sensed her uncertainty.

"So, he's been around since I was a kid? Why haven't I seen him?"

"He can't leave this realm."

"What? Then how's he protected me?"

"Your mind. You've endured so much since your father passed. Ciro has been able to fortify your mind. Not reshape your personality or control your actions. Merely lend his mental fortitude to help you face the battles you've experienced and those yet to come. The ties you have to the magic of old, and your father's will, make it possible for this connection to exist."

"So he's like a guardian angel?"

"Without the wings."

"So that's why you say it taxes the mind…"

The Oracle nodded; her face soft with empathy. "It takes a lot to help shield a mind. Especially in cases where the vessel is under constant threat from the world around them."

After losing her father, life wasn't too bad, but when her mother married into the Wilcox family, and after her death, Blaire faced so much adversity that often she feared she would snap. In those moments, she thought of her father, and it gave her the will to go on. She looked down at Ciro, who stared up at her with large, inquisitive eyes. Had that been his protection? Saving her from giving up?

"Can I… see you?" She wanted to see the face of the man who'd watched over her since she was a toddler.

Ciro rose to sit on his haunches and tilted his head at the Oracle.

"If you are comfortable with that, Ciro. It is your choice. She is your vessel to protect."

A firm pressure compressed Blaire's chest and pain shot up her arm. She doubled forward.

"They have come to her cell."

Ciro whined anxiously and got up, pacing the forest floor. Low growls reverberated, speaking of his discontent. The smell of coconut grew stronger.

The Oracle closed her eyes as Blaire held her arm, trying not to panic.

After only a minute that felt like much longer, the Oracle opened her eyes. "They are taking a small vial. Nothing like before. There was damage in the lab, and they lost part of their supply."

Ciro growled.

"They are leaving. The pain Blaire feels is residual, and likely from previous incidents based on the bruising she carries in the waking world."

Another growl.

"She is safer in the cell for now."

How was she safer? Blaire was being treated like a lab rat. She didn't feel safe. She felt pain. A lot of it. Constantly. She bit the inside of her cheek to keep from shouting, her anger simmering beneath the surface. She spoke through gritted teeth, "I'm not safe. They plan to sacrifice me."

Ciro padded over to Blaire, his eyes boring into hers fiercely.

"What?" the Oracle asked.

Blaire looked away from Ciro's intense stare and met the Oracle's confused expression. Did she not see this coming? "I heard Angelo say he was going to sacrifice me… Something about a magical deity, Nathaniel said."

"By the stars."

Blaire's breathing quickened, and her pulse increased at the genuine distress on the Oracle's face. Ciro collapsed onto the ground, dropping his head into Blaire's lap, and nuzzling to distract her. Apparently, in this realm, he could physically interact with her and was going to take advantage of helping her out beyond the mind. At least that's how she looked at it. She dug her fingers into his fluffy nape. It helped. Her breathing slowed.

The Oracle's eyes closed, and her mouth moved as if she were talking to someone without sound. She'd done that once before.

When the Oracle finally returned to them, she sighed.

"Let me guess… you can't tell me?"

"I'm sorry, child. The—"

"The balance. Yeah, I know the routine at this point."

"I truly am sorry."

Apologies didn't save her from certain death.

Blaire sighed and looked at her hands. "So, if I have magic, what does that mean? I don't know how to control it. Where did it come from?" She didn't feel different. Through her life, she never felt anything special, so it was still strange to think of herself that way. But she couldn't stick her head in the sand and ignore the events surrounding her. The Order wanted to experiment and sacrifice her. She was somehow a Korrena mate to a Vasirian. None of that tapped into what kept happening when she woke up in this dream world that physically existed somewhere out there.

"Magic has been around since the beginning of time and is the base of creation for every being of this realm as well as the Vasirian of your world. As far as controlling it… I wish I had the answer for you, child. But I am not all-knowing."

Blaire's brows lowered. "Then why me? If the magic has always been there, what's so special about me?"

"The original child of power born thousands of years ago was a human witch—you are one of her great grandchildren. The only surviving one. When Vasirian came into being, the Celestial Conclave spread their magic into the human world, planting the seeds for the future and allowing for Vasirian to find their Korrenas in those humans with magical blood. With these pairings, stronger children were born."

Would Korrenas not exist without the magic?

Vasirian could procreate without the bond, but the guidebook the school provided to her clearly stated that children born from a pairing were stronger and had abilities children of compatible pairs couldn't manifest.

What did that mean for Vasirian and their bonds if she didn't become a Vasirian and bring back this mysterious balance between Vasirian and humankind?

19

GUILT

A chilly breeze swept through the tree grove. Lukas pulled his leather jacket tightly around himself as he breathed in the scent of camellias blooming early at the base of several trees.

He'd been coming to the grove at the front of the academy grounds across from the hedge maze for the last week after he'd noticed several times in passing powerful emotions that didn't align with his current state of mind.

Sadness. Fear. Confusion.

Aside from sadness, those emotions weren't common for him—especially as of late.

Knowing Blaire was in the dungeons somewhere beneath the academy, and the strange feelings that would come and go, he suspected the tree grove was located near the dungeons.

Once classes ended, he changed and came outside—that was thirty minutes ago. The sun was well on its way to setting, and the temperature was dropping. He didn't want to go back to his dorm until he felt something—anything. But with their connection fractured, Blaire's emotions came to him in bits and pieces. Some days he felt nothing.

Sometimes he wanted to curse the Korrena bond. The fact that it worked to allow him to sometimes feel his pair—and for her to feel him—but didn't allow them to push their emotions to each other when they wanted to sucked. Over their first six months together, he had learned that if he felt a strong enough emotion she would feel it too, but not because he wanted her to feel it. Projection to each other was all up to chance, and he couldn't pick which emotions passed through the empathic connection. It was maddening.

His phone chimed with a text message.

Lukas sighed, his breath fogging in front of him.

Charlotte.

She wanted an update on Blaire.

The night before Blaire went to become a guinea pig for the Order, Blaire spoke with Charlotte from Professor Velastra's office phone before Lukas arrived. She explained to Charlotte that administration wanted to have Blaire do special testing. After the kidnapping—knowing there had been a crazy student infatuated with Blaire—Charlotte accepted that.

It wasn't exactly a lie, but it was far from the whole truth. So much so, Lukas felt guilty having to keep the secret about what he was. He hated knowing Blaire had to keep the secret from her friend.

Charlotte was important to Blaire. She was a nice girl. Riley had even grown to like her. Despite centuries of obfuscation from humankind keeping his kind safe, it wasn't fair to Charlotte, Blaire, or anyone else that they kept her in the dark.

He tapped on the screen, replying honestly that he hadn't heard anything. Charlotte had been told they wouldn't allow Blaire back into the dorms after she went to do her testing. Who knew what Charlotte thought the reason was, or even where Blaire was staying. Thankfully, she hadn't asked, and they hadn't had long that morning to get into the nitty-gritty of things.

"You're so full of it," Aiden said to Seth, laughing as he approached.

Seth rolled his eyes, tucking his hands deep in the pockets of his jacket and pushing down, pulling his shoulders inward, huddling to shield himself from the chill. He looked at Lukas. "How are you sitting out here? It's so cold."

Lukas shrugged one shoulder. January was the coldest month of the year even in Georgia.

Aiden propped a shoulder on the tree Lukas leaned against, looking down at him. "Anything from Blaire?" Lukas had told Aiden about the tree grove and his theory about being near Blaire.

"How would he have heard from her? She's still in the dungeons."

"Something about this area triggers their empathic connection. Lukas thinks the dungeons might be close."

"No shit?" Seth raised a brow. "I thought your connection was busted."

"Not entirely," Lukas said.

"What do you mean?"

"Ever since the trial, it would come and go. So, like Professor Velastra said, it's there, but not stable and whole." He missed the connection to Blaire. She made him feel whole.

Another strong breeze passed through the grove where they stood. The air was already chillier under the shade of the trees, but with the sun slipping behind the horizon, Lukas probably should move inside. His nose was already numb.

Aiden zipped up his coat. "Any luck on figuring out why it's like that?"

Lukas closed his eyes and tipped his head back against the bark of the tree. He had his theories. There were so many reasons their Korrena bond could be damaged. Pinpointing one wasn't an effortless task, but one thing stood out to him after the things he'd heard from the Oracle and Professor Velastra.

"I think it's my fault."

"How's it your fault?" Seth squatted, huddling into himself. He had decent muscle mass to keep himself warm, but he was leaner than Lukas. Neither of them was as broad and muscular as Aiden, and even he looked like he was freezing. Yet, Lukas still couldn't bring himself to leave the tree grove if it meant missing a single thump of life through his and Blaire's empathic connection.

"I can't stop blaming myself for what happened." He lifted a hand to pinch the bridge of his nose, head still resting against the tree. "I nearly killed her. I tried to take her choice away."

"She knows you didn't mean it. You told her what you thought. You know, she likely felt what you felt. Like, I'm sure the emotions were strong enough."

Lukas dropped his hand and opened his eyes to look up at Aiden. "It still doesn't change the fact that I did that to her. It was the one thing she was most afraid of about the claiming ritual. I couldn't do that one simple thing." His chest tightened. "I couldn't stop."

"Listen, man, what you did was fucked up." Seth held up a hand and waved Aiden off when he opened his mouth in protest. "But, you stopped. You were still with it enough to recognize the mistake you were making. Sure, Blaire was upset and likely scared out of her mind. But she forgave you."

"How do you really know that?"

"Dude. Seriously?"

At Lukas's blank stare, Seth sighed. "This bonding shit is so obnoxious," he muttered, exasperation clear in his tone. He wet his lips. "Look, Blaire ignored everyone at that trial. She risked herself and thought nothing of the consequences when she ran to you and offered her blood. That's not the actions of someone—human or not—scared of you. Not something someone who didn't love you would do."

Lukas blinked twice. Seth wasn't one to get heartfelt, but here he was, using reason to reassure him. Lukas looked down at his hands resting on his thighs, curling them into fists against the black denim as he remembered the moment at the trial where he'd lost himself to his rage.

Blaire had thrown herself into him with all her strength. Thrown herself in the path of two angry Vasirian trying to tear each other apart. She'd clung to him like both their lives depended on it. Maybe they had. She'd reached out to him and connected with the beast within, calming the storm that raged inside, and trusted him to take her lifeblood without an ounce of fear in her eyes. He'd felt everything. Her love. Her resolve.

He scrubbed a hand over his face.

Aiden's phone pinged, and Lukas looked up at him.

"Riley's hungry."

Seth's brows drew together. "Tell her to go to the canteen and eat something if she can't wait until dinner. It's only, what?" He pulled his cell out of his jacket pocket, looking at the screen. "Like, thirty minutes from now? Why's she telling you?"

"She wants to go to Hushpuppies. All of us."

Seth's face screwed up. "I hate seafood."

"They have other stuff," Aiden said, pushing off the tree and tapping at the screen of his phone. "They make a killer chicken fried steak with white gravy."

"Yeah, I know, but the smell of fried fish is so strong there."

Hushpuppies was a family-owned restaurant on one of the eastern wings of the Valley Center Plaza. The outlet shopping center had everything. Even locally-owned businesses thrived. Lukas visited the restaurant a couple of times, but he hadn't made a habit of eating there. The diner was his go-to until Blaire dropped into his life. Hushpuppies was a small restaurant, but the food tasted decent. The menu was mostly seafood, but they also carried a selection of Southern homestyle dishes.

Aiden smiled. "Looks like not just Riley wants to go." He looked up from his phone. "Riley apparently asked Charlotte and Layla to go."

Lukas squinted. "Layla?"

"Yeah, the girl from one of your classes. You brought her to the cafeteria."

"I know who she is. I'm wondering how, and why, Riley—You know what? Never mind. Riley could make friends with a houseplant if left alone with it."

Seth burst out laughing and stood.

"Anyway, I'm hungry and cold. I don't care." Lukas stretched his arms over his head before getting off the ground that had grown cold beneath him. His legs had gone numb from sitting for so long. Disappointment at not connecting with Blaire settled heavily in his bones.

"You coming?" Aiden turned to Seth.

Seth glanced over his shoulder at the dorms, and then down at his phone screen.

"If you're trying to decide whether to use our room to get laid or come with us to eat…"

Seth glared at Aiden. "Nah. I'll go." He sighed. "Besides, it's not working anymore, anyway."

"Did it ever?" Aiden asked quietly.

Seth shot Aiden a look of irritation laced with sadness in reply, not something normally seen on his face. Lukas wasn't sure what it meant.

The restaurant was humid from the plethora of dishes coming from the kitchen at the back. For such a small place, Hushpuppies stayed packed. Even with the loud country music spilling out the door into the street, patrons weren't deterred by the volume.

They'd had to wait outside for twenty minutes before a table was available for them, and Lukas thought his toes were going to fall off despite the thickness of his leather boots.

When one of his classmates said something similar earlier in the day, their professor had laughed. Apparently, Southerners were too delicate, and forty-five Fahrenheit was mild compared to where they were from up north. He would never move to New York if that was the case. They could keep their below-freezing temperatures. He couldn't wait for the predicted warm front to come, as heard over the radio playing outside while they waited for a table.

Once they'd settled at a table in the back and placed their drink orders, he'd finally warmed up enough to remove his leather jacket and hang it on the back of his chair. Others followed suit.

"I'm starving," Riley groaned, flipping through the menu.

Layla scanned the menu then looked across the table at Riley. "What's good here?"

"What?" Riley looked up. "You've never been?"

"Nope. Mom is allergic to shellfish, and I don't enjoy going out to places like this by myself. Miko and my roommate like to stay on campus."

"Allergic to shellfish?" Seth raised a brow.

Layla nodded. "Yeah, I was surprised too. I didn't think Vasir—"

Aiden started coughing and took a drink of his soda. Layla's eyes went wide at her near slip-up as she cautioned a hesitant look at Charlotte, who was studying her menu in blissful ignorance. It wasn't common, but Vasirian could have allergies. Professor Velastra shared that information when Lukas lost his Korrena mark and thought it might be an allergic reaction until the grim truth revealed itself.

"The frog legs are pretty good," Charlotte spoke up, still focused on the menu. "But I think I'm gonna get the stuffed crab with a side of clam strips and a side salad." She looked up after deciding.

"Frog legs?" Layla's forehead crinkled as her eyes widened.

"Uh, yeah?"

"I've never had them." Layla's features scrunched up, making her look even more childish. "I can't get used to the idea of eating something that looks so… real. Dad loves them, though."

"They taste like chicken," Charlotte said.

Riley snorted. "Everything tastes like chicken."

"Well, they actually do, I think. But the added breading and salt and pepper seasonings gives it an added edge."

"Yeah, I'll pass. I don't think I can do it." Layla's nose was still wrinkled as she flipped through the menu. "Oh! They have shrimp and grits!"

Lukas tuned out the girls as he turned his attention to the menu. It was hard for him to focus on what he wanted when his mind kept drifting back to the tree grove and the conversation with Aiden and Seth.

This entire time, Lukas had focused on what took place between him and Blaire. He'd blocked out what happened at Vincent's trial.

But that was a key bit of information to assess Blaire's motivations and feelings in that moment. How she felt and acted afterward. Maybe he couldn't completely forgive himself now, but if they got through this, he could prove to her his only motivation was to protect her. If only he could lay the guilt down entirely.

Seth hadn't magically fixed him, but at least he had something to help keep focus. To keep hope alive.

The server came and took their order, then they shared funny stories about their classes for Charlotte's amusement.

Once their meals arrived and they began eating, Riley spoke up, glancing at Aiden. "Do you think I should go back to my natural hair color?"

"What? Why?"

Riley pushed pinto beans around her plate with a fork. "Eh. It's nothing."

Aiden's brow rose. "Oh, come on. What happened?"

"Just this guy…"

"What guy?" Seth asked, his tone sharp.

"A guy in one of my classes." Riley shook her head, her eyes fixed intently on the fried catfish on her plate. "I can't even remember what he said."

Whatever he'd said to Riley was enough to bother her. That much was obvious. Not much bothered Riley. Especially regarding her appearance. She wore her eclectic style with pride. Her personality suited her in-your-face fashion sense.

Seth's eyes narrowed. "Then what's the hangup with your hair?"

"He said something about my hair color."

Lukas suspected she remembered exactly what the guy said.

"I don't think I could ever pull off your style. I love the pink. I don't think you should change it," Charlotte said, setting her fork down and popping a battered clam strip into her mouth.

Layla nodded, drinking her sweet tea through a straw. When she finished, she said, "I agree. You're super pretty."

Riley perked up. "Think so?"

"Doesn't take much to bring her back," Aiden said, chuckling.

Riley grinned. "Flattery will get you everywhere with me."

"Careful. Flatter her too much and her head won't fit through the cafeteria doors," Seth sniped, but the upturn of one side of his mouth showed he didn't have malicious intent with his words.

"Who needs enemies when I have a friend like you?" Riley teased, leaning toward Seth, and giving him a saccharine smile, but Seth's fist clenched on the table.

Charlotte pulled air through her teeth. "Friends. Riiight."

"Huh?" Riley turned to Charlotte.

A blush spread across Charlotte's face, and she covered her mouth. "Oh my goodness, I did not mean to say that out loud."

Aiden snorted. "It's bad when people not around us all the time see it."

"See what?"

Aiden looked at Riley. "Seriously?"

"I'm so confused."

"Don't worry about it," Seth said, voice sharp, jaw tightening. "Of course we're friends. I've had to put up with her since she was a snot-nosed brat chasing after her big brother all the time."

Riley elbowed him.

Charlotte looked down. "I didn't mean to offend anyone, I…" She looked up at Seth. "I sometimes say things when I shouldn't."

Seth gave a subtle shake of his head. "Already forgotten. Just drop it."

Aiden shook his head. "Don't stress it," he said to Charlotte. He cut into his country fried steak smothered in white country gravy.

Riley frowned. "I don't know what the big deal is, but don't be mad at her. She didn't do anything."

"I'm not."

"You are. You're sitting there all tight like you have a pole up your ass. You're brooding."

"I'm not," Riley mocked in a sing-song voice over Seth saying the same words.

Layla and Riley burst into a fit of giggles as Seth glared at Riley. Charlotte's mouth hung open.

Aiden shook his head, and said with exaggerated patience, "If you two don't figure your mess out…"

Charlotte had to cover her mouth to silence her own snickering.

"Nothing to figure out," Seth said with a shrug.

"Oh, there definitely is," Riley protested.

Seth's face paled. "What?" His voice cracked.

"That face." She pointed her finger and swirled it around in front of Seth's face. "You need to stop making it all the time."

"What face? I'm not making a face." Seth's voice had softened with his impatience. He rarely directed true hostility her way. They had been this way as long as Lukas had known them.

"Oh yes, you were! Like this…" Riley scrunched her nose and closed one eye, curling her lip and sticking her tongue out to the side.

Seth laughed. "What the hell are you doing?"

Riley's face lit up with a bright smile. "Mission accomplished."

"Huh?"

"You're not brooding."

Seth huffed a quick breath through his nose as he smirked. "You're impossible."

"You're right." She popped a piece of cornbread into her mouth.

"It's silly of me to think you could pull off a face like that. You don't have the features to pull it off like I do."

Seth shook his head.

Whatever that guy had said that had Riley feeling self-conscious had become a distant memory.

"So, I know you said you hadn't heard from Blaire," Charlotte said.

Lukas tensed. The entire table fell silent.

"But do you know when these tests will be done?"

"No idea." Lukas didn't mean for his words to sound short.

Charlotte sighed and brushed a few stray red curls from her face that had fallen forward when she lowered her head to pour ranch dressing over her salad. "I don't understand why she has to leave the school for this. Isn't she missing classes? I mean, I don't mean to come across like a helicopter parent, but I know how much she wants to get a degree. Won't she risk her semester by missing so much class?"

"I don't know about that," Aiden said. "We did just have two weeks off for winter break. It's only been a few weeks, and everything happened right after exams. It was a wind down period." He was trying to justify the time away from classes, but it still didn't look good to be gone for three weeks.

"I know, but..." Charlotte put her fork down and huffed in frustration. "Aren't any of you bothered by the fact that she just spent two months with some psycho fanboy, missing classes, and now this? What kind of ship is the admissions department running at that university? They could have given her a break before forcing her into tests."

Aiden stared at Charlotte, clearly at a loss for words. Riley tore pieces off the corner of her napkin. She shared the same habit with Blaire. Lukas wondered which of them influenced the other.

Layla kept her eyes on the table. Riley had given her a brief rundown of the events that happened before they all met up. Lukas wasn't sure it was such a great idea to share too much of Blaire's private business, but at the same time, if Layla was going to be around them more, she probably needed to know what she was getting into. Then she could decide if it was worth it to try to be his friend.

Seth cleared his throat. "I think so too, but they're strict. Too strict, if you ask me."

Charlotte deflated. "I'm just frustrated. I'm sorry. I didn't mean to bring the mood down. I just miss my best friend, you know?" Her eyes met Lukas's. "I'm leaving for college and won't get to see her hardly at all. I want to spend more time with her before I go."

Aiden reached over and put a hand on Charlotte's forearm. She looked up at him from her seat next to his. "We all miss her. I'm sure things will be wrapped up soon."

Lukas wished he could tell Charlotte everything. Things would be simpler if he could. She'd be just as frustrated, but at least she would understand why they had no information to offer her. He suspected to her it looked like they didn't care. Which was the farthest thing from the truth. He rubbed his sternum. Hopefully, one day they'd be able to tell her the whole truth.

20

Considerations

Dust and bits of dirt from the stone wall fell to the ground as Blaire etched another mark into the wall in the corner of her cell. It had been two days since she made the third week's mark and Blackthorn Security had stopped coming to get her for the researcher's experiments. Normally, something like that would make her hopeful that her time in the cell was coming to an end and she could go home, but nothing about this situation was normal.

At least having the last few days free of their poking and prodding had allowed her muscles to recover. She still looked like she'd been in a fight, but she didn't feel like it.

When the lab finished whatever last experiments they wanted to perform, they'd move on to the sacrifice. She didn't know what all was involved with that, but a sacrifice could only mean death. She wasn't dumb enough not to understand she was the lamb being led to slaughter.

Her thoughts drifted to Ciro, the wolf. Or man-wolf. Whatever he was. It was surreal to imagine such a creature existed. It seemed even more out there than Vasirian. At least Vasirian were one hundred percent humanoid and didn't shapeshift into something different. She wondered when she'd see Ciro again. She was eager to learn more.

"Ahh, that was nice," Dominic said from the next cell over, interrupting her thoughts. His hair was wet, and he was clean-shaven from the shower they'd let him have.

Blaire stood from her crouched position on the floor and walked back to her bed. "How long had it been?" she asked as she tucked the spoon away beneath the mattress.

Dominic finger-combed the wet strands of longer hair on top of his head, pushing them back to tame them. "Mm, I think I've been here for almost two weeks? Something like that." He rubbed his smooth jaw. "Feels good to get rid of the scruff. I looked like a caveman."

Blaire shook her head and smiled faintly. "I doubt cavemen wore slacks and tailored dress shirts."

He motioned at himself in a downward sweeping motion. He wore a pair of relaxed-fit dark-wash jeans and a charcoal gray t-shirt. "Not so refined looking now though, eh?" He winked.

Earlier, Jackson and Marcus retrieved Dominic saying he could shower and change out of the same clothes he'd been wearing since he arrived. While he was gone, Rue changed his bedding. Blaire wouldn't say it aloud, but she was glad they'd allowed him to shower. Sleeping so close to him, it was hard to not notice the smell. He wasn't gag-worthy smelly, but the pleasant aftershave—or cologne—he wore had gotten a muskier edge to it. One that wasn't pleasant.

Blaire collapsed onto her bed and stared at the ceiling.

While grateful the experiments had stopped, even if it meant something worse was coming, she couldn't help but view the peace as a double-edged sword. Not being so delirious from blood loss left her to her thoughts. Thoughts filled with Lukas. Thoughts of missing him and wanting to be with him. The doubts she carried from what he'd done to her after her kidnapping, when he allowed his primal side to take over, were a thing of the past. She trusted him. He'd broken that trust with his actions, but the realizations she'd come to during Vincent's trial changed everything for her.

"What's wrong?"

Blaire looked over as Dominic settled down on his bed, propping his head up on his hand, resting his elbow on his bed. "Hm?"

Dominic reached through the bars and swiped a tear from Blaire's cheek that she hadn't noticed. He held up his wet finger. "This."

She looked back at the ceiling. "It's nothing."

"Nuh uh. Don't shut me out like that. We've been through some shit together. Let me help."

Blaire sighed.

"Besides, what else do we have to do around here? Come on, it'll be therapeutic. Is it the experiments?"

"No." Blaire swallowed down the lump of emotion in her throat. "I miss him."

Dominic nodded. "I can understand that. What, with the kidnapping fiasco, and now this? And you were newly pair-bonded too… I can't imagine what he's going through."

Blaire wiped fresh tears from her cheeks. Lukas was likely suffering like she was. This wasn't like last time. With their separation then, she thought the worst. That he didn't want her. That he moved on to someone else. Vincent had painted a grim picture with the "proof" he provided her and the ritual he forced on her. Now she knew better. Lukas loved her. Trusted her. She didn't understand why their mark wouldn't return—aside from the fact that Lukas wouldn't fully make love to her out of fear. Maybe that was the problem.

"I know he's beating himself up about what happened, but I understand now. I forgive him."

"Forgive him for what?"

Blaire's eyes slid toward Dominic. He already knew most of everything, anyway. If not for her sharing it with him, then whatever sleuthing he did prior to being caught. Though, he also missed quite a lot if he hadn't known a human was a Korrena.

"He lost control, and it nearly killed me," she said quietly, trying to keep a steady voice.

Dominic sat up quickly. Blaire turned her head and grimaced at the worried look on his face.

"It's fine. Obviously, he didn't." Her laugh was dry and void of humor. "We tried the claiming ritual again. As you can see, it didn't work." She brushed her fingers over the side of her neck where her mark should be.

"What happened?"

"Well, after the first part..." Her face heated, and she felt it to the tips of her ears. "He bit me, and I drank from him. The problem came when he didn't stop. At least for a while. He snapped out of it, but I became disoriented."

Dominic cursed.

"He really beat himself up over it. When I left to come here, he was still beating himself up over it. And knowing him like I do, I'm sure he's still doing the same. I'm worried about him. I hope our friends are getting him out of his head."

"You're not afraid of him?"

"No. I mean, when we first met, and I found out what all was involved with the claiming ritual, I freaked out. You would too if you were a human, and a virgin." She muttered the last part under her breath. Dominic had the good sense to not comment on it, but the quick narrowing of his brow let her know he heard. "But after it happened, I realized I had been afraid for nothing. It wasn't a big deal at all—at least not a big reason to fear him."

She sighed.

"The problem arose when, in trying to reseal our bond a second time, he did the thing I most feared. He didn't stop. I had been so scared that he wouldn't stop, and I'd die, that when that actually happened this time—not dying, but his not stopping—I was upset."

"Rightfully so."

"Yeah, well, I told him I didn't trust him. It wasn't a lie. He broke my trust. I didn't know if I could trust he wouldn't try to do it again. Especially when he freely admitted his thoughts were leaning toward this incessant need to make me like him to protect me."

Dominic's lips turned down. "Is that so bad?"

"Being Vasirian?"

He nodded.

"Well, no. Not really. I thought so at first, but not so much anymore."

"Have you told him?"

"What?"

"That you're more open to it now."

Blaire sighed. "I had planned to, but then he did that… it sent me back into that guarded place of fear and distrust. I said something after, but I was heated, and I doubt he really grasped I meant it." This situation did nothing to give her the opportunity to have a genuine discussion about it, either. She wasn't fully ready to commit, but she could tell Lukas she was open to it, and at some point in her life was likely to accept that path.

"It's not so bad. I mean, I guess for a human it'd be scary. Drinking blood and all that."

Blaire snorted. "That's not the issue. I thought it'd be strange, but I actually like the way Lukas's blood tastes." Her nose wrinkled. "That's so weird to say."

Dominic chuckled. "He's your Korrena. As I hear it, your pair's blood is supposed to be not only like eating a delicacy, but an aphrodisiac. Mind you, it's stimulating to all of my kind, but something about the pair bond heightens it to a whole new level."

"You can say that again."

"So, what *is* the issue?"

Blaire sat up on her bed and leaned against the bars with her shoulder. With a sigh, she said, "I'm afraid of dying."

"Why would you die? You live longer as a Vasirian."

"Uh... because I have to lose almost all my blood and be near death before the change can happen."

Research had revealed there was more to turning a human than draining them of blood. It took a Vasirian's bite and an exchange of blood. Apparently, only Korrena-bound pairs could transition. Other humans would die—had died. Apparently, Vasirian tried to turn humans they wanted to be compatible pairs long ago and failed. Professor Velastra had discovered this information in a tome left in her office, and she'd relayed that information to Blaire and Lukas. Where she got the tome, Blaire didn't know, but she suspected the Oracle's meddling.

Dominic looked down, and his brows knotted. "I guess I can understand that, but can't something be done to make it safer?"

"What do you mean?"

"I don't know... Like, have blood on hand in case something goes wrong?"

Blaire's lips twisted. "A blood transfusion?"

"Yeah. Think about it. If by some chance the transition doesn't happen smoothly, and it looks like they'll lose you, why not have everything prepared to give you blood again to save you?"

"I don't know if it works that way."

"Can't hurt to look into it."

She'd never considered something like that. The entire center of her fear revolved around losing so much blood that she'd actually die. Slipping into whatever state was required to become a Vasirian as a result wasn't as frightening. She looked across the cell and sighed. She hadn't given this proper consideration. Which wasn't fair to Lukas. Allowing her hackles to rise and immediately go into a defensive state of thinking, expecting the worse, wasn't fair to anyone.

Maybe if she made it out of this, it'd be time to sit down with Professor Velastra, and maybe someone in the health department, to see what they could do to make this safer when she made the transition—*if* she made the transition. At this point, holding onto the fantasy that she wouldn't transition was pointless. Why couldn't she just be honest with herself? She wanted to be with Lukas for as long as possible. Did it really matter if it was as a human or not?

Vasirian weren't vampires. They weren't dead—or undead. They didn't have to sleep in crypts, avoid sunlight, garlic, or crosses. She could still have children one day.

"What has you smiling?"

"Thinking."

"Penny for your thoughts?" He patted his pockets. "Not literally, of course."

"About kids."

"Well, that's way off in left field."

Blaire shook her head and smiled. "Vasirian can have children."

Dominic tilted his head. "I wouldn't be here if they couldn't."

"I guess I still have hangups about vampires… that whole undead thing in media? Not able to have kids? I always thought it'd be nice to have children someday."

Blaire wondered if their children's eyes would be as pale as Lukas's. She hoped so. His beautiful eyes reminded her of sea glass.

Dominic propped both feet on the bed and stretched his legs out, leaning his shoulder against the bars, mirroring Blaire's position. "I kinda like being alive." He grinned. "Not sure about the kid thing. Not yet, at least."

"Oh no, I'm not ready to be a mom. I'm still trying to figure out my life."

She wasn't ready for children at nineteen, but thinking about sharing a life with Lukas, making a family together after considering Dominic's words about Lukas desiring one, made her feel warm inside. She wanted that if he wanted that with her. After losing her own family and learning what her father had done for her, she wanted to have someone to care for and protect the same way someday.

They both turned their heads as a door opened at the end of the line of cells.

Moments later, Jackson stepped out of the dark with a tray in each hand. "Grub time!"

Blaire left her bed for the cell front, where Jackson pushed a tray with spaghetti and meatballs through the slat. He passed a bottle of water through the bars when she stood.

"I'm so hungry I could eat a horse."

Jackson grunted. "Don't think that'd taste too good."

She sat on her bed and dug in. "Where's Rue?"

"Nathaniel's niece? Girl with the tan?"

"That's her, yeah." Rue didn't have a tan. She had beautiful caramel skin that was all natural.

"Don't know. Think her uncle called her in. I ain't gettin' involved in any of the Order's business." He slid Dominic's tray through the other cell's bottom slat, then passed a bottle of water and a blood packet through the bars.

Jackson didn't stick around, disappearing down the hall as Dominic returned to his bed. Blaire was already a quarter of the way through her spaghetti.

"You weren't kidding about being hungry." Dominic sat, and then speared a meatball with his plastic fork.

Blaire looked up from her tray and swallowed the large mouthful of spaghetti noodles. "I never kid about food."

Dominic chuckled, shaking his head. "If we get out of this in one piece, I'll take you to a nice dinner sometime."

Blaire blinked.

"Oh, shit." He waved his hand. "I didn't mean like a date or anything. I know you have a Korrena. You're sweet, but I don't mess with that. I heard what happened to the last guy who had a thing for you."

Blaire rolled her eyes at the ridiculousness of his remark. She'd told him what Lukas did to Vincent.

After polishing off the spaghetti, she took the tray to the cell slat and slid it outside to be retrieved after they'd gone to sleep, then went back to her bed. Dominic averted his eyes as she put on the pajama pants and long-sleeved pullover Rue brought her to sleep in. With nothing happening each day, she slept if Dominic didn't keep her entertained, so comfortable lounge wear was much nicer than sleeping in jeans.

She yawned and lay back on the bed, snuggling under the warm blanket. She wondered what Lukas was doing. If he was okay. She had been gone longer than she anticipated, and she wondered how Lukas was handling it. He would worry, but with their weak and broken bond, would he be as affected as Rue was about Liam? She hoped not. She hoped their fractured connection dampened the turmoil and pain.

It was probably one of the only upsides.

Blaire rolled over on the small bed and huddled deeper beneath the covers for warmth. It'd gotten colder in the dungeon in the last few days. Maybe it was a result of not leaving for experiments and staying in one place, but it seemed colder. She heard footsteps.

"Tobias. So good to see you, cousin. Come in. Have a seat. Sorry I have nothing to offer you, so you'll have to settle for my charming face as recompense."

Cousin?

"Getting yourself caught was the stupidest thing you could have done, Dom."

Blaire tensed and tucked her head down to keep her face hidden in case they could tell she was a wake. What were they talking about?

"Oh, yes, I came all the way to the states just to enjoy these lovely accommodations. How else was I going to get access?"

One of them sucked his teeth.

"Can't you be serious for once?"

Dominic sighed. "What do you want me to say? I didn't intend to be caught. I didn't think security patrolled the archives. I didn't even tell them you let me in."

Silence stretched.

Lowering his voice, Tobias said, "I'm not sure what I'm supposed to say to Adrian about this. He's going to be infuriated. I can't get you out of here."

"So what's going to happen? Am I going to trial?"

"No."

"Then what?"

Tobias sighed, frustration obvious in the huffed breath. "I'm trying to hold them off. But I'm running out of viable excuses. Angelo is on a warpath to find out how you got to the lower levels."

"Does he know who I am?"

"No. He's not even close to the truth. He thinks you're a rogue with an agenda against the leadership."

Dominic laughed.

"It isn't funny. I don't see a way to get you out of this. At this point, we may have to wait for Adrian to intervene."

Adrian… where had she heard that name before?

She thought furiously as they continued to talk in hushed tones until it clicked. She gasped. Wasn't the king of the Blackthorn Clan named Adrian? How would he intervene in any way positively on Dominic's behalf? Or did Tobias mean he would wait until the king approved Dominic's banishment to do anything more for him?

She froze. The talking had stopped.

Turning over on the bed, she groaned and rubbed her eyes, hoping it looked like she was just waking up. When she opened her eyes, Tobias stood inside Dominic's cell, and Dominic sat with his back to the bars. They both had their attention turned to her.

"W-what's going on?" She sat up slowly like she would if she were still half asleep.

Dominic smiled at her. "Bad dream?"

"Huh?"

"You gasped when you woke. Scared?"

Blaire shook her head slowly. She wasn't scared. She wouldn't lie, but she wasn't going to offer the full story.

"Is it morning already?"

"No. You can still sleep."

"I'm fine. What's happening?" Her gaze shifted to Tobias.

He crossed his arms over his chest, saying nothing. His eyes narrowed slightly.

"Our new friend Tobias offered to bring me a warmer blanket and thicker sheets, since it's so cold I'm freezing the family jewels off here."

Tobias whipped his gaze from Blaire to Dominic. "Excuse me?"

"Yeah. Don't you remember saying how it wasn't quite fair that Blaire had nice bedding while I had this?" Dominic held up the threadbare blanket.

Blaire mashed her lips together. He was lying, but Tobias didn't call him on it. Instead, he clenched his jaw and inclined his head.

"Marcus or Rueanna will see that you have adequate bedding delivered soon."

Dominic grinned ear to ear like the cat that got the cream.

He'd just manipulated a member of the Order, and he was smiling about it. Who was this guy?

21

Connection

Lukas pounded his fist against the door of the administration building Saturday morning after breakfast. He'd had enough. Three and a half weeks they'd kept his Korrena from him. He'd hardly had any time with her after two long months apart, and now he'd endured three and a half more agonizing weeks. Something had to give. He'd reached his limit.

Aiden grabbed hold of Lukas's leather jacket, pulling him back from the doors. "Stop. You're going to get yourself locked up again."

"I don't give a fuck!" Lukas jerked out of Aiden's grasp. "I'm sick of this! At least if I'm locked up, I'm with her."

Seth came up beside them. "How does that help her?"

"I don't know!"

"Calm down, man." Aiden put a steady hand on Lukas's shoulder.

"I can't. I can't do this anymore."

The large doors to the administration building pushed open and three members of Blackthorn Security stepped out, two men and a woman.

“What’s all this about?” A man built like a truck stepped down the short stairs lining the front of the building, thumbs tucked into his belt. When he reached the base of the stairs, he crossed his arms over his chest like a bouncer from the nightclub Haven and stared them down.

“I want to see Blaire!” Lukas broke away from Aiden and stepped forward.

Aiden stepped between the burly guard and Lukas, putting a hand on Lukas’s chest. “Chill.”

“Take your buddy’s advice, son. Nothin’ worth gettin’ locked up over.”

“Nothing worth… What the hell?” Lukas shouted. “That’s my Korrena!” He threw his arm up, gesturing toward the shorter man standing at the top of the steps.

The short man shook his head and said, in an incredibly thick Southern accent, “It’s too cold for all this nonsense. Y’all need to take it someplace else.”

“Look, kid,” the burly guard started, and while Lukas knew better than to provoke the man, he bristled at his tone, tensing for a fight.

Before it could go that far, the woman guard stepped forward and placed a hand on his large arm.

“Let me, Marcus.” She turned her attention to Lukas, Aiden, and Seth. “I’ve met your Korrena. She’s a strong girl. I did what I could to make her comfortable until they stopped me.” She met Lukas’s gaze. “I’m sorry this is happening to either of you, but this doesn’t help your case.”

“What am I supposed to do?” Lukas asked in a broken tone.

“Respect the agreement and wait,” said a new voice.

The guards turned, and all eyes looked to the top of the stairs.

Angelo Moretti stood glowering down at them with disdain. He wasn't in his robe. Instead, he wore a pair of gray pressed slacks and a pristine white button-down. He still had the gaudy rings on most of his fingers.

"I didn't agree to this!"

"No," Angelo conceded. "But she did." His sinister smile turned Lukas's stomach.

"It's almost been a month! What more can you possibly find? Haven't you had her long enough to get what you need?"

"Oh, you foolish little boy. What you fail to comprehend is this is much more than a bit of research."

Aiden turned his head, still keeping his hand steady on Lukas's chest. "What is it then?"

They were all under the impression Blaire agreed to let them test her blood. That she would be available on tap for samples as they needed them. Nothing more should be happening.

"Revelations have altered the direction we will take regarding the human girl."

"The human girl has a name," Seth bit out, crossing his arms.

Angelo shrugged casually. Two more security guards stepped out to flank him.

Lukas growled under his breath, and Marcus stepped forward in response. Lukas wasn't stupid enough to challenge a man of his size. "What are you planning to do with her?"

"Never you mind. But I suggest you return to your dorms before all three of you face trial for interfering with a Vasirian Order's investigation. I'm sure King Blackthorn would not take lightly to treasonous actions such as those."

"Treason?" Seth questioned in disbelief.

Angelo sneered and turned from them, disappearing back inside the administration building without dignifying the question with a response.

"Y'all ought to head on back to your dorms now." The short man gestured across the courtyard to the line of dormitory buildings. "Lunch'll be comin' soon."

Lukas knocked on Aiden and Seth's dorm room door after lunch. He couldn't be alone this evening. Being alone with his thoughts and guilt was his worst enemy. The door opened and Aiden stepped back to let Lukas in.

"What's up, man?"

Seth typed steadily on his laptop on his bed, not looking up as Lukas stepped into the room.

Riley lay sprawled across Aiden's bed. She frowned at him. "You don't look so hot."

"I'm not feeling so hot."

She sat up, and Lukas sat where her feet had been.

"What's going on?" she asked.

Lukas shook his head. "Need to get out of the dorm. What are you three doing today?"

It was the weekend, so he didn't have class to distract him, and going into town by himself wasn't something he liked doing.

"I thought about going shopping if I can convince Layla and Charlotte to go with me. I asked Mera, but she was packing her things."

"For what?"

"Something about the academy sending her to California for some medical conference. Kai has permission to go with her, so he's leaving too. I don't know the details. With everything going on, I didn't even know about a medical conference."

At least he wasn't the only one neglecting to pay attention to things because of everything happening in recent months.

"I thought about staying out and grabbing dinner while we were out," she said. "I came over to ask Aiden and Seth if they want to go. Aiden agreed, but Seth didn't want to peel himself away from his laptop. He's been typing away for the last hour like we're not here."

Seth closed his laptop slowly, cutting his eyes to Riley. "You have no idea. I'm working."

"On?"

"Noneya."

"Real mature."

Lukas's gaze ping-ponged between the two of them.

"Why do you need me to come?" Seth asked. "You're taking Charlotte and that new girl."

"What's with that look? I like Layla."

"No look. Nothing's wrong with her, but you'd like a copperhead if it smiled nicely at you."

Aiden chuckled. "That's… pretty accurate." He looked at Seth. "Come on, man. We need more supplies for the dorm, anyway. Weren't you wanting to pick up the new Resident Evil 4 remake? We can get that while we're out."

"Can I at least choose the restaurant?" Seth sighed. "I do not want to smell all that fried fish again."

Riley rolled her eyes and pushed off Aiden's bed. She crossed over to Seth's bed and flopped down next to him on her back, crossing her hands over her stomach, turning her head to look at him sitting against the wall. He stared down at her with wide eyes.

"If it gets you off the computer, fine. Whatever you want." She yawned.

"Why're you on my bed?"

"Because this is where I always slept when I stayed over with Aiden."

His brows drew together. "And?"

"Aaaaand this bed is sooo comfortable." Stretching her arms and putting her hands behind her head, she crossed her booted ankles over each other. "Might take a nap before we go, since Layla won't be ready for another hour."

Seth tore his gaze from Riley's exposed midriff, then groaned and thunked his head back against the wall. "Why must you test me like this?"

"I'm not doing anything." She reached up and pulled Seth's pillow down, fluffing it and resting her head on it, closing her eyes.

"That's my pillow," Seth mumbled, his eyes intently focused on Riley's face.

The corner of Lukas's mouth pulled into a half smile. He already felt lighter by witnessing the banter between his friends. He'd made the right decision by visiting them. Even if they never left the room, being surrounded by their energy made all the difference from sitting in an empty room that smelled like Blaire's jasmine perfume and had her things all over the place. Wallowing in his memories of her didn't bode well for his mental health.

"I've got an essay to work on, so I'm gonna get on that while we wait on Layla," Aiden said to Lukas. "Watch TV or break out a video game. Whatever you wanna do." He looked over at Riley. "She meeting us at the store, or what?"

Riley yawned. "Told her how to get to your dorm. She'll swing by when she's ready." She turned on her side, facing away from Seth, who sat against the wall at the head of the bed. He opened his laptop again and started typing quickly.

Lukas sat back against the wall on Aiden's bed. "Have you and Liam had any luck finding Rue?"

Riley opened her eyes and looked at Lukas. "None." She frowned. "We've asked everyone. Mera didn't have any luck checking with her department. I visited the Psychology department and met Professor Sinclair. She hadn't seen Rue either and didn't know what happened to her. There wasn't any information given."

"Has anyone asked her parents?"

"Liam did. They're worried sick. They haven't heard from her."

"What the hell?" Seth looked up from his laptop. "Is administration doing anything about it?"

"Liam says Professor Velastra notified the security team, and they opened an investigation, but they aren't sharing any details."

Lukas shook his head. He hoped nothing bad happened to Liam's pair. Rue was Blaire's friend, and he knew what it felt like to think his Korrena pair died. He couldn't imagine the reality of it being true. He hoped that wasn't the case for Liam.

Going out with everyone for the afternoon and dinner made his anxiety easier to manage, but once he returned to the dorm alone, the darkness swept in and gripped his heart with its claws.

Lukas placed his hands on the bathroom counter, staring at his reflection in the mirror. The patter of the running shower water did nothing to calm the storm raging in his mind.

Angelo's words from early in the day floated around in his head, refusing to leave.

The Oracle said Blaire was safe as long as she remained in the cell. How safe was that? Alive? Unharmed? What happened if they took her from the cell and moved her elsewhere? What if his actions earlier today influenced a decision that got Blaire removed from the cell and put into harm's way?

He rubbed the heel of his palm against his solar plexus to push down the sharp pain that tightened his chest and made his heart race.

Unable to look at himself in the mirror any longer, he turned away and stripped out of his clothes. He sighed as he opened the shower stall and stepped under the hot spray of water.

How would he explain the latest development with Blaire to his parents?

Reasonably, Blaire's decision to trade herself for him spoke of the love she felt for him, but the implication of what it meant still settled like a lead weight in his gut.

Everyone fucking leaves.

First, his parents when he was only five. Now her.

Time with those he loved and trusted was short-lived. He'd tried his hardest to convince Blaire to become a Vasirian—like him—to protect her, and keep her alive longer, but in the end, she walked away, leaving him much earlier than he could have ever guessed.

And it was all his fault.

This entire situation resulted from the actions he took at a council trial…

He breathed in deeply through his nose before dropping his head under the hot water spray.

His parents were going to be so disappointed. They'd blame him, and rightfully so. He didn't want to give them an excuse to have a lower opinion of him. They barely held a connection in the first place. He didn't want them to see him as a screw up who couldn't hold onto his Korrena.

His stomach roiled, and he placed a hand against his skin over it.

It was all too much.

Months of this had taken its toll.

Lukas was too young to feel as old as this situation made him feel. His body ached. His sleep schedule was all over the place. On the surface, he'd accepted that Blaire was okay and everything would end smoothly, but a deep, dark sense of foreboding weighed heavily on him now.

He hadn't felt Blaire recently when he went to the tree grove. He was lucky to feel something on the edge of his senses, but their already weak connection had diminished further. Something in his gut told him Blaire was in danger. This morning he finally snapped and approached the administration building.

Even without a sense of impending doom creeping into his thoughts, the time had become too long. He couldn't handle Blaire being gone for this long. He needed her back.

The walls of the shower stall closed in on him. A stall he often shared with Blaire.

He slapped the tile wall with a smack.

Lukas panted as the hot water hit his back muscles like tiny bullets until he finally doubled over, taking a gasping breath. The water poured from overhead, over his face, and blended with the tears streaming freely down his face.

He couldn't breathe.

Wrapping his arms around his waist, he hugged himself tightly, keeping his head down near his knees, trying his hardest to swallow air and not water.

If Blaire made it back to him this time, would she stay? He didn't blame her if she turned away from him after having to go through whatever she dealt with because of his stupid decision to attack someone. Worse, he'd do it again if the opportunity presented itself.

His knees hit the tile flooring, and his hands curled into fists in the water pooling around him as he retched into the drain. He stayed like that for several minutes until everything vacated his stomach. His wet hair matted to his skin.

In the other room, his cell phone rang. He didn't have the strength in his limbs to lift himself from the shower floor.

Lukas stayed on the floor for another several minutes before he found the fortitude to push himself up with shaking arms. He hadn't even properly washed himself. His hands trembled as he pumped out his body wash onto a loofah and made quick work of cleansing his body. If only his worries would swirl down the drain with the soap and debris of the day.

He padded from the bathroom on bare feet, a towel wrapped around his waist. Water trailed down his spine from his long hair that he hadn't dried properly.

Sitting on his bed, he checked his missed call logs. He tapped the screen and leaned forward, resting his elbows on his knees as he waited on the call to connect.

Riley and Layla's brightly smiling faces filled the screen.

"Oh, wow." Layla's face flushed red, and she looked away from the screen, one hand covering her mouth. Lukas didn't see the big deal. The only thing visible on screen were his bare shoulders and collarbone area.

Riley snorted, looking at Layla. "What took you so long?" Riley asked, turning her attention to Lukas. Her face fell. "What's wrong?"

"What are you talking about?" Lukas swiped away the wet hair dripping in his face.

"Have you been crying?"

Layla turned back to the screen and squinted. "Are you okay?"

"What's going on?" Aiden said in the background.

He should have pretended he'd already gone to sleep and called

Riley back tomorrow. He didn't expect everyone to still be together.

Riley panned the phone to Aiden, who sat next to her.

"It's nothing. I'm fine."

"Oh, I love it when you lie to me." Riley rolled her eyes, her words dripping in sarcasm.

Lukas rubbed his tired eyes. "Listen. It's just all this shit with Blaire. Nothing new. Some days are just harder than others, alright?"

Layla scrunched closer, sandwiching Riley between her and Aiden to peer into the phone screen. "I don't know you that well, and I don't know your Korrena at all, but I kinda get the idea of what's going on with everything you've shared and what they've told me. So, like, if you need to talk…" She picked at her plum nail polish. "I'm willing to listen. Like, I know they are too… obviously. They're your friends." She looked back up at the phone. "But you seem like a good person, so I wanna help if I can."

"You're so damn sweet." Riley leaned on Layla's shoulder. "Seriously. This girl is adorable."

Layla's cheeks turned pink again. She did look like a kid, especially when she blushed and pouted. "I'm trying to be serious."

"My bad. My bad."

Lukas chuckled and wiped a hand over his mouth. "I appreciate it. I think I just need to get some sleep."

"Okay, but if you need us, we're here. You don't gotta call. Just come downstairs. I'll leave the door unlocked in case we've gone to bed," Aiden said.

"Thanks, man."

They ended their FaceTime call and Lukas set the phone on the nightstand. He rolled his shoulders, trying to loosen his stiff muscles. They'd done enough today that he actually felt tired for once. After crying in the shower, and throwing up everything he'd eaten, exhaustion might allow him sleep.

It helped to know he had friends nearby if he needed them, both old and new. He'd always had a difficult time connecting with others, but being around Blaire made him want to try. He didn't want to live in limbo, just going through the motions waiting for the next day and the next like he had no purpose. That wasn't living.

22

Escape

The clanging of metal on metal stirred Blaire out of her dreams. She opened her eyes and listened intently, focused through the bars on Dominic sleeping next to her. He looked peaceful; his chest rose and fell with deep, steady breaths. She wasn't sure if she should wake him or not.

The cell door creaked as it swung open.

"Blaire?"

Throwing the covers back off her, Blaire sat up and looked at Rue. She stood in the middle of Blaire's cell, gripping a set of keys in her hand so tight her knuckles were pale despite her darker skin tone. It wasn't breakfast time yet. They couldn't have been asleep long. It hadn't felt long.

"What's going on?"

Rue's gaze darted toward the darkened hallway, then to Dominic, who continued to sleep, unaware. She looked at Blaire and bit into her lip.

"Hey..." Blaire climbed off the bed and moved to Rue, putting a hand on Rue's hands that held the keys clenched tightly in front of her stomach. "Talk to me. What happened?"

"I..." Tears brimmed over and ran down Rue's cheeks. "I can't let them kill you. I heard. You have to get out of here." Her voice rose with each statement. She seemed on the verge of a panic attack with her quick breaths. The keys jangled in her shaking hands.

"What's wrong with her?" Dominic shifted on his bed and squinted to focus as he woke.

"Come over here." Blaire led Rue by the arm to her bed and sat her down slowly. "Breathe."

Rue took a shuddered breath and dropped the keys in her lap, digging the heels of her palms into her eyes as she tried to get herself under control.

"That's it. Now, talk to me. Why are you here now? Where is Marcus or Jackson?"

"They don't know I'm here."

Dominic leaned on the bars. Blaire looked over Rue's head at him and they shared a concerned look.

"Blaire. They're... I heard my uncle say they're going to sacrifice you in some old ritual in this underground chamber located in a temple I'd never known existed beneath the academy."

"Sacrifice her?" Dominic grabbed one of the bars, squeezing it. "What are you talking about?"

Blaire sighed. "I know." She looked up at Dominic. "They haven't been experimenting lately because I suspect they were about to move on to that. I overheard them talking about it one day while I was out of it. Something about a magical deity. I didn't hear much, but I understood they planned to sacrifice me. I didn't know anything about a temple, though."

Telling them earlier wouldn't have done anything but create tension and fear. If these were her last days, she wanted to spend that time in peace, even if it was fake. Dominic kept her happy and entertained. Rue and Blaire distracted each other with lighthearted jokes to keep from thinking about their lost pairs. If she shared that the Order intended to kill her, that illusion of security she'd built would shatter.

"Why didn't you tell us?"

"I didn't want to freak either of you out. You see how Rue is taking the knowledge. We can't do anything about it."

Rue raised her voice. "Yes, we can! I can!" Her hands shook as she picked up the keys from her lap and thrust them at Blaire. "Take these."

Blaire held up the keys, and her brows pinched. "The cell keys?"

"Not just the cell keys." Rue looked back toward the darkened hallway. "They unlock the door out of the dungeon, and another at the far end of the hall on the right, which opens to a passageway down into another sublevel. Once you get down there, take a left, and at the very end, behind several crates, is a hatch that opens into the underground tunnels."

"Tunnels?" Dominic asked.

"Yeah. I checked. These tunnels stretch for miles, but they lead away from Blackthorn Academy. They were an emergency exit to escape attack hundreds of years ago. I think they come out near Swainsboro or something. It isn't far by car, but on foot… it might take a couple days. I checked that too. It's almost a hundred miles, with no way out until the end. If you walked without stopping, it'd take around thirty hours. But seeing as you're not exactly in top shape… I don't know how long it'll take."

Blaire had visited Swainsboro before. It was a small town about an hour and a half away by car, but it was nice. It acted as a crossroads to Macon, Augusta, and Savannah. If they could get there, they had the opportunity to head in a few directions with relative ease. Going back down toward Savannah wouldn't be wise, since Rosebrook Valley was only twenty minutes outside city limits.

Dominic whistled low. "That's a long time for a human. Hell, that's a long time for me. Thirty hours nonstop? That's not even physically possible."

"I know… Um," Rue started, glancing nervously at the hallway again. "I left a bag behind the crates at the tunnel entrance with foods that don't require refrigeration and bottles of water to get you through. I snuck it out of the lab's cafeteria. There's also a blanket. A warm front came in, and it's warmer than last week, but it'll be cold underground, and you'll have to camp since thirty straight hours of walking isn't likely. It'll probably take a couple days or more depending on how you handle it."

Blaire rubbed her thumb over the keys in her hands. "I don't want you to get in trouble," she said softly.

"I don't care anymore. They threatened me, using my parents, but I don't believe them. I'm not trusting their threat. Especially when I *know* what the alternative is. There's no guarantee they'll harm my parents." She sniffed and wiped her cheek. "They intend to do more than just harm you."

Blaire turned on the bed and met Dominic's worried eyes. "Come with me."

"What?"

"I don't want to leave you here rotting in a cell."

Blaire didn't have any clue who Dominic was. What his purpose was at the academy, but he seemed like a good guy. He didn't deserve to be stuck locked away until it was convenient for the Order to deal with him. Who knew what they would do to him once they made a move? He held a connection with Tobias, but it sounded like Tobias couldn't help him.

Dominic looked down at the bed and took a deep breath.

"Please come with me. You don't deserve to be here."

"Alright. I can't do much for anyone locked in here."

"You need to go before morning services start." Rue stood. "It was four when I came down here, so we don't have a lot of time. Do you remember the directions?"

"Honestly, no. I'm just so… I'm shocked. This is a lot." Blaire passed Rue the keys so she could unlock Dominic's cell. Blaire didn't know what key did what, and they didn't have time for her to fumble around trying to find out.

"I'll guide you both to the tunnel entrance, but then I have to get back to my room."

Dominic got up and pulled a fresh shirt over his head after removing the one he slept in. "Will you be okay?"

"Yeah, as long as we hurry." Rue let Dominic out of his cell while Blaire changed quickly into a pair of jeans and a hoodie. "We have to be quiet. As soon as we leave the dungeons, to the left there is a small stairwell up to a central hallway that connects to the diplomat wing and several offices. I don't know if anyone will be there."

Blaire stepped out of the cell into the hallway as Dominic also stepped out. Their eyes met, and he gave her a comforting smile.

"I told you I'd protect you. Time for me to shine." His jovial words settled the nerves that fought against the desire to stay calm.

"Let's go." Rue motioned for them both to follow.

Dominic extended his hand, and Blaire laced her fingers with his. He tightened his grip in reassurance before leading her down the darkened hallway, following Rue from the dungeon where she'd spent the last three and a half weeks.

It took time to navigate down to the sublevel with the crates Rue mentioned, but once they arrived, Rue motioned them to the corner of the room. "Over here." She pulled up a metal handle attached to a worn wooden hatch covered in dust.

"I climbed down in there to see what it was like. I wasn't sure you could even go in there at first because of the darkness, but there's an electrical box at the bottom of the ladder. If you flip the switch, it turns on a system of low-watt bulbs along the length of the tunnel. I don't know when that was installed, but it should see you through."

Peering down into the darkened space, Blaire shivered. She felt the spiders crawling on her skin already.

"I'll stay here until you flip the lights on." Rue motioned to a backpack and tote bag in the corner. A blanket sat on top of the tote bag rolled tightly. "I didn't know both of you were going, so you'll have to share the food sparingly and share the blanket." She twisted her lips, her gaze darting between them. "I'm sorry."

"Don't apologize. You don't know me. They hadn't planned anything for me. You were just trying to protect her." Dominic let go of Blaire's hand and patted Rue's head like she was a puppy. "You did good. I'm not hurt."

Rue swatted his hand and laughed. "You're weird."

"But I'm hot, eh?"

"Oh gods, get out of here before I change my mind." She laughed, but emotion clogged her throat. This situation affected her, but Dominic's joking softened the blow, alleviating the stress.

Blaire turned to Rue as Dominic climbed down the ladder into the darkened space. "You have to come with us."

"What? No. If they find I'm missing too, they'll immediately go on the hunt."

"What can you do to delay things? As soon as they see I'm gone, they'll start hunting."

Rue glanced in the direction they came from. "I don't know. But when it's time for the meal service, I'll do something. I don't know what yet, but I'll delay the dungeon visit. Besides, if my uncle comes to visit me before then, everything will seem fine. Trust me."

"Rue..."

"Come on, Blaire. There isn't much time." Rue put her hands on Blaire's arms and guided her toward the opening, her eyes sparkling in the faint light. "I'll be fine."

"You have no idea what this means to me." She leaned over and hugged Rue. "I promise once I'm free, I'll find a way to get you free from the Order. I'll tell Liam somehow. I won't be able to come back to Blackthorn Academy, but I'll figure something out."

Rue hugged Blaire tightly, fingers clutching the hoodie she wore, the fabric muffling her sobs. When Rue got hold of herself and pulled away, Blaire nodded at her.

She wasn't sure how she would connect with anyone from Blackthorn Academy once she escaped, but she would try. Public libraries had computers. She could use the same emails she did when she reached out from Vincent's phone. Her friends would check them. She wouldn't let Rue stay trapped. She would find a way back to Lukas and save her friend in the process.

"I've got it!" Dominic called from below. He climbed up the ladder and stuck his head out of the hatch. "Pass me the tote bag."

Rue handed him the bag, and he hooked it over his shoulder like a purse. Blaire pulled on the backpack and peered down the hatch. She hugged Rue one final time before descending the ladder. She looked up when she reached the bottom to see Rue staring down at them, tears swimming in her eyes.

"I promise I won't forget you, Rue. Hold tight. I'll make sure someone gets you."

Rue nodded rapidly, taking a breath to swallow down her tears. She lowered the hatch, leaving them to their escape with a solid, final clank.

Blaire hoped she could fulfill that promise.

She looked down the tunnel ahead of them.

Tightly packed dirt floors worn down and flattened from years of foot traffic stretched into the dimly-lit distance. The walls and ceiling looked the same: more dirt. A metal bar and cords ran along the upper area of the wall. Bulbs in metal caging flickered along the bar every ten or so feet, casting odd shadows. Not enough to illuminate everything brightly, but enough to see to navigate the space. The cool underground air tasted stale and sat unmoving.

"Looks like we have a lot of walking to do," Dominic said, shifting the bag on his shoulder.

A hundred miles? Blaire didn't know if she could do it, but she would try.

23

Spy

Gravel and dirt scraped under Blaire's dragging feet. Exhausted, hungry, and missing those extra hours of sleep she lost when they made their escape, she was running on fumes. She pulled out the watch she'd found in the backpack's front pocket; Rue had figured they'd want to track time, and cell phones couldn't get a signal down here. Not that she had one of those, anyway.

Ten in the morning.

By now, the Order knew they had escaped. She hoped Rue made it back to her room without being caught. Hoped the Order and Blackthorn Security hadn't suspected her.

Blaire glanced back down the way they came. She hoped security wasn't following them already.

It'd been six hours since Rue gave them this ticket to freedom. They hadn't walked the entire time. Dominic insisted they stop intermittently to drink water and rest. Blaire suspected he could go for much longer than she could even were she at full strength. Vasirian were stronger physically than humans, so maybe they also had more stamina. She'd never asked.

Dominic slowed his steps and turned around to look at Blaire. "Need to stop again?" He pushed a hand over his forehead and hair, wiping away sweat that beaded on his forehead. Despite the chilliness of the tunnel, they'd worked up a sweat from the constant physical exertion.

Blaire dropped the backpack and slumped down to sit on the ground, kicking her feet out in front of her and leaning back on her hands, panting. "I just… need a minute."

It had been so long since she ran or exercised, and she certainly felt it. If she made it through this, she needed to add running back into her daily routine—or at least a couple of times a week. She was so out of shape. The weeks spent losing blood didn't help her physical condition. Had they not stopped experimenting on her days ago, she'd be in a mess right about now. Even so, the walking exhausted her.

Blaire had taken the freedom at the academy to slack off and relax about obsessive exercise. Who wouldn't do the same if they got out from underneath Caleb's twenty-four-seven scrutiny and criticism? Lukas didn't care how much she loved carbs and that she didn't work out until her stomach was tight and leg muscles defined. Her physique had become softer, still slender with defined muscle, but not hard. She'd already put back a pound or two of what she lost from her time in captivity with Vincent, but not all of it, and not new muscle. She liked it; she felt more feminine without the athletic build she had in high school.

Dominic squatted and dug through the tote bag. He passed Blaire a bottle of water before taking a small sip of another. She was careful not to chug it down either, and fought her desire to pour it over her face. They could carry only so much water, and Rue had only prepared for one person. They still had days to go. Running out of water early wouldn't help them. Dehydration could kill either of them, defeating the purpose of this journey.

Dominic finally sat and stretched out his legs, mirroring Blaire's posture. "How long has it been? We're halfway, yeah?" He tilted his head back and closed his eyes.

Blaire huffed. "I wish. It's only ten o'clock."

Dominic groaned and dropped flat on his back, wiping his hands over his face. "Wanna eat?"

"I'm hungry, but the protein bar we had at eight can last me a little longer. I don't want to waste the food. If Rue estimates this will take us a couple days, there's no way this food is going to last the entire time if we eat too often. Not between two people."

Dominic sat back up. "We should keep moving, then. If we stop now, muscles are gonna seize up or something. I think. I don't know." He heaved a tired sigh. "I know if we stay still for too long, I won't be able to get back up." He laughed mirthlessly and pushed himself to his feet, extending a hand to help Blaire up.

When Dominic turned to lead the way again, Blaire dusted his back, covered in dust and dirt from lying on the ground. He paused.

"Get it all?" He dusted off the back of his jeans.

Blaire tore her eyes from the motion. "Yeah, you're good."

Dominic picked up the tote and slung it over his shoulder as Blaire put on her backpack. "Let's go for another couple of hours and break around noon for lunch. How does that sound? Think you can manage?"

"I think so."

She couldn't physically walk nonstop for that long, but they stopped periodically to rest their feet for a few minutes. He meant to stop at noon for an extended break. As long as they could keep the pace of small stops, with only a few longer stops for meals or proper rest, they might get through this.

Blaire looked at the watch for the hundredth time that day. "I can't anymore." She stopped walking and let the backpack slide from her shoulders. She rolled one shoulder at a time to loosen her muscles and took a deep breath.

The tunnel air was stale from lack of fresh air and signs of life for however long it'd been since someone graced the depths.

Dominic stopped and turned to face her, the first time he'd looked at her in hours. "What time is it?"

"Six."

"Fourteen hours since we left the cells. Even I can't keep going like this. Let's stop, eat dinner, and set up camp."

His facial features looked pinched, and he sweated more than she did. She guessed he was in pain, and his frown looked angry.

"You okay?" She sat on the ground and looked up at him.

"Yeah," he said with a sigh. "Why?"

"You look a little rough."

Dominic set the tote bag on the ground and let out a self-deprecating laugh. "Gee, thanks. Strike a blow to my ego." The words sounded like his usual joking, but the tone was grittier than usual, and he avoided her eyes. He knelt and pulled out an apple, a wrapped sandwich, and a bottle of water, passing them to Blaire.

Blaire narrowed her eyes on the slight tremor in his hands. He needed to eat more than she did.

She dropped heavily onto the ground, uncaring that she got filthy. She already had dirty jeans from previous stops, and after fourteen hours, she felt way overdue for a shower. She crossed her legs beneath her and set the water in front of her, putting the apple in her lap. She unwrapped the sandwich and lifted the bread. Peanut butter. She definitely appreciated the protein. She took a bite.

Dominic sat in silence across from her, chewing on a protein bar.

"Not gonna eat a sandwich?"

"No."

Blaire's brows creased at his sharp tone.

He finished his protein bar and stuffed the wrapper in the bag, scrubbing his face with his hands and making a frustrated groan. She'd never seen him act like this. Thinking about it, she didn't know him. Not really. She didn't know what he was like outside of the dungeon. The sharp-spoken, tense man in front of her might be the real Dominic. The sudden shift in behavior set her on edge; her hackles rose.

She flinched when he reached for his bottle of water next to her backpack.

He looked up at her, and his eyes narrowed. "What's wrong?"

"Why are you looking at me like that? Did I do something to piss you off?" She took a breath, proud of herself for sounding confident when she felt suddenly nervous around him.

Dominic's brows furrowed further in confusion. "I don't know what you mean." He sat back on the ground and opened his water, taking a small sip.

"You look angry."

His eyes widened. Genuine shock crossing his features. Maybe she read him wrong. They'd barely spoken, and he'd kept his focus on the tunnel ahead as they traveled, so she didn't know what had set him on edge, but she didn't like it. For the first time since she met him, she felt like prey. Her instincts told her to run, but her body had other ideas, staying firmly in place, though aware of every shift the guy in front of her made.

"I'm not. Not at all." He scratched the side of his neck. "I'm tired. Hungry, but don't want to waste food. I..." His eyes shifted away from Blaire, but not fast enough for her to see a look of anguish on his face. "I guess I'm struggling more than I thought I would."

Blaire tucked the wrapping of her sandwich into her backpack and stood. She crossed to the tote bag and pulled out the blanket. "I'm sorry." She crouched next to him and unpacked the backpack onto the ground. When she finished, she handed him her apple as an olive branch. She didn't need to get in her head about it. Suspecting him of nefarious intentions when all they had was each other wasn't the best thing to do in their situation. "The sandwich was enough for me. Please eat more." His hand shook as he took the apple.

Sitting next to him, she spread the blanket across both of their laps. At his raised eyebrow, she said, "It's cold now that we've stopped. We've basically been sleeping together for weeks." She fluffed the empty backpack behind her on the ground.

"We had bars between us."

"Are you going to hurt me?" She tried to make her words lighthearted, but couldn't mask a seriousness to the tone. She didn't think he would hurt her, but the reality of the situation still cautioned her from the edges of her mind: Dominic was a predator, and he wasn't bound by bars.

"What?" He reeled back. "I would never..." Shaking his head, he said firmly, "I'm not going to hurt you."

"If I actually thought you would, I wouldn't be doing this. Now, don't overthink it. Finish your dinner, and let's sleep. I'm exhausted."

Dominic quietly ate his apple as Blaire lay down on her side, her back to him, resting her head on the empty backpack as a makeshift pillow.

After several minutes, the blanket shifted as Dominic got comfortable. The warmth of his back against hers comforted her.

"Do you think we'll get out of this?" she asked hesitantly.

Dominic sighed. "I don't doubt we'll make it through the tunnels. What happens on the other side, I don't know. But I'll do what I can to keep you safe."

"How?"

Blaire didn't know how Dominic would keep her safe. Just because he was a Vasirian didn't automatically mean he could prevent anything bad from happening. It wasn't like he held a position of authority in Blackthorn Academy or law enforcement. He was the same age as Lukas. He couldn't do much other than physically try to protect her. Considering their situation with traveling through the tunnels and how tired he seemed, he was likely at a disadvantage.

The blanket pulled as Dominic moved, and Blaire looked over her shoulder to find him facing her. She turned toward him.

He tracked his hand through his hair to push it out of his face. "There's more to my story than you know."

She said nothing, afraid if she spoke, he would stop. Was he going to tell her about his connection to Tobias?

His eyes caught hers. "As I said before, I was sent here to investigate the Order."

"By who?"

"I can't reveal that information." His gaze dropped to the space between them. "I'm sorry. It's safer for you not to know."

"Hey, I'm not mad. I'm just trying to understand. So you're a spy?"

"Something like that. I guess?"

Blaire smiled at the uncertainty in his tone. Saying he was a spy made it sound like they were in a Bond movie or something. "I mean, spies investigate things and try not to get caught. But usually they're part of the group they're investigating—like a mole. I don't know the right word to use, but you get my meaning, right?"

He nodded and looked up at her again. "I was only supposed to get into the archives and access their reports of activities from the last two years. From my understanding, they kept that information filed down there. I certainly wasn't prepared to find out about you and everything they've actually been up to. I was only supposed to be looking for corruption like embezzled funds and a bit of power play."

"Surprise?"

Dominic laughed and shook his head. "You certainly were a surprise."

"So, what will you do now?"

"Once we're safely away from Rosebrook Valley, I'll have to find a way to contact the people who sent me. Beyond that, I don't know. I didn't expect this to happen. We'll also have to find out how to get in contact with your Korrena. Lukas, right?"

"Yes."

"Yeah, we need to get in touch with him. You two have been apart for too long."

Even with a damaged bond, the effects of separation wore on her psyche. She tried to push it aside in favor of surviving. But if she gave herself the time to focus on her feelings for Lukas, sadness crept in and strangled her to the verge of panic. She shook her head. She couldn't let herself go there. If she panicked now, she'd be no good to Dominic.

He yawned and when he covered his mouth, a faint tremor shook his fingers. "Let's get some sleep, yeah?"

"Sure."

Blaire pulled the blanket over her shoulder, and he tucked his arm beneath his head.

She didn't know who sent Dominic to Blackthorn Academy, or whether the errand he'd named was the only purpose he had there, but she didn't want to ask too many questions if it risked her safety once they got free. The only issue she had with their conversation was how Tobias fit into all of this. Was he really related to Dominic? He used the word "cousin" when they spoke. She couldn't have been that groggy. It wasn't a word easily mistaken for another. Did Tobias have something to do with his investigation? What did that mean for the Order?

She had more questions than she could get answers to, but now wasn't the time.

Dominic looked haggard, with shadows under his eyes. Even after eating, his hands still shook and sweat beaded his brow. She worried he was sick, but from her understanding of Vasirian, that wasn't a common thing.

Hopefully, a proper sleep would refresh him. She sure needed it.

"Stop thinking. Sleep," Dominic mumbled without opening his eyes.

"How do you know I'm thinking and not sleeping?"

"I can hear your brain working from here." He cracked his eyes open. "No, seriously, I can hear your little sighs and huffs. It's obvious you're contemplating the meaning of life or something. Sleep."

"You know everything, don't you?"

"Perhaps."

24

Trauma

Sighing, Blaire rubbed her face, staring down the endless tunnel. It would have been nice to get a few more hours of sleep, but with the way Dominic tossed and turned beside her, that wouldn't happen. She glanced at his face when he groaned. Sweat beaded his forehead, and his brows were crumpled. His lips pressed tightly into a grimace when she dabbed the sweat from his forehead with the sleeve of her hoodie. The heat from his skin came through the fabric.

Fever.

Reaching for the tote bag, she retrieved a water bottle. She dampened a paper towel that had once held a sandwich and lay it over Dominic's forehead. After a few moments, the tension in his face faded, and she breathed a sigh of relief. Hopefully the water, which stayed relatively cool packed in the tote bag in the chilly tunnel, would help lower his temperature. Vasirian didn't get sick like this—at least as far as she could remember.

She paced the side of the tunnel away from Dominic to allow him to rest without her body heat next to him. She shivered and rubbed her arms. If not for the fever, he might appreciate her body heat like she had his. It was probably around forty-five degrees down here.

So much had happened to her since joining Blackthorn Academy that it was hard to keep her thoughts organized. She tried to keep her focus on getting through the experiments with the Order, finding out they wanted to sacrifice her, and discovering the lengths they were willing to go to find out her secrets. Secrets she didn't understand herself. She tried not to focus on what Vincent had done to her, but it was hard to keep pushing those horrible thoughts away.

She slumped against the wall, resting her shoulder against it, and hugging her waist.

Professor Sinclair met with her several times in the week following the Order locking Lukas in the dungeons. The professor tried to help her get through what happened when Lukas could have killed her by sucking her dry when they made love, desperate to reclaim their bond. Tried to help her understand what compelled him to do it. Even if she trusted him, and knew intellectually he didn't mean to endanger her, it still happened, and she needed to sort through those feelings. She and her therapist had barely scratched the surface of what happened with Vincent before she met with the Order. Every time she thought she had moved past her trauma, being alone brought back the terrible memories.

Her eyes closed, and she returned to the windowless studio apartment, standing in the kitchenette looking at a table set for two covered in all her favorite foods. The smell of stale roses surrounded her, and her breathing quickened.

It isn't real.

Footsteps approached.

He's not here.

A firm hand grasped her shoulder, and she shrieked, reaching for the knife on the table to use in defense. Before her fingers touched the handle, everything vanished into thin air, and strong hands spun her around. The shift in scene, and the momentum of her movements, disoriented her. But she still struck at him with her fists. She wouldn't let him take her this time.

"Hey! Calm down! It's me!" Dominic reached up with both hands and held the sides of Blaire's face. "Hey, stop hitting me!" He took hold of Blaire's wrists as she punched at his chest.

She froze at the voice, lifting her gaze up to meet Dominic's. "Dom? What are you… Where…" Her gaze swept the tunnel around them then settled back on his face. "I…" She took a deep breath. "I'm sorry."

Dominic released her wrists, and she stepped back. "Don't apologize. Just tell me what the hell just happened. You freaked out on me."

Blaire put her back against the wall, sliding down the dirt surface to sit on the ground, drawing her knees to her chest, and burying her face in both hands against her knees.

"Blaire?"

She heard him move, felt the shift in the air next to her, and stiffened as he settled beside her on the ground.

"You're kinda freaking me out here."

He's sick, and you're having a panic attack. Get out of your head.

"I'm okay. Really." She lowered her hands and looked at him. His face looked paler than before, but he appeared more concerned than anything. Maybe his own worries were overriding his illness, or maybe he got better after resting. She sighed. "Just remembering what happened."

"When? What do you mean?"

"From the time I lost my mark, when I was kidnapped."

Dominic lay his arms over his knees, dangling his arms out in front of him as he leaned fully against the wall. "Does that happen a lot?"

"Remembering? Not really. But when it does…"

"You panic?"

How did she tell him he was the reason she panicked?

But he wasn't the reason…

When she didn't answer after a couple of minutes, getting to her feet, and moving away from the wall, he asked, "Blaire? You good?"

"Yeah, and no, I don't always panic. I heard you approaching, and I thought…" She licked her lips, tipping her head back to look at the dirt ceiling when he stood and joined her.

"You thought I was him."

"Yeah," she said with a heavy exhale.

"Do you want to talk about it?"

She took two steps back before walking around Dominic, giving him a wide berth. He would not hurt her, but she was shaken and wanted space. "What's there to talk about?" Hurrying to the bags and blanket, she rubbed her hands together. She stared in the direction they'd come from and closed her eyes, taking deep, steadying breaths.

Dominic wasn't dangerous. Dominic didn't kidnap her. Being trapped in the tunnel with him wasn't by force.

It unnerved her she needed to remind herself of these things. But with his behavior lately, and the flashes of memories of Vincent, she was having a hard time separating Dominic from a Vasirian who wanted to harm her. She hated it. A small whimper slipped past her lips as she tried to restrain her distress. Her eyes burned.

She'd been so good. Why was she falling apart now?

Was it because she was so close to freedom?

"Hey," Dominic's low, soft voice came from behind her—a little too close. She flinched when his hands gently rested on her shoulders. He released her. "What can I do?"

"Please don't touch me." She slowly turned to face Dominic, and his face fell into a severe frown. She must have looked terrible. She wrapped her arms around her middle and looked down at her feet.

"I don't understand. Things have..." His brows pinched tighter. "You haven't been like this." He clasped the back of his neck. "I mean... with me." His last words were barely above a whisper.

Blaire lifted her head. "What?"

"I just want to help you with whatever this is." He held his hand to the side. "I get you panicked, and maybe you don't want to be touched right now, but I would never hurt you—or anyone, really." He rubbed his eyes with his index finger and thumb. Sweat beaded on his forehead.

"Dom, I..." She dropped her arms from her waist. "I just need space. It's not that I think you'd hurt me." She chewed the edge of her lip. "Ever feel uncomfortable in your own skin?"

"Sort of."

"It's kinda like that. I don't want anything near me right now. It feels suffocating." She held her throat. "Like, I can't breathe." She dropped her hand and sighed. "Even my clothes feel suffocating. Or, well, they did. Before..."

"What can I do to help?"

"Nothing. I need..." She scratched her arm and paced away from him.

"What? Tell me." He stepped forward. "Let me help you."

She spun to face him. "You can't! You're not him!"

"Who?"

She flinched at the sharpness of his voice. She looked down and whispered, "Lukas..."

Dominic released a shaky breath. "I'm not, no." He swallowed and wiped sweat from his brow. "I'm not. I'm sorry I can't be him. I'm sorry I can't—*Fuck!*" He scrubbed his hands down his face. "Fuck, I can't focus." He crouched and dug his fingers into his eyes.

Blaire took a step toward him. "Dom..."

"I don't know what to do. This is too much."

"No, Dom, please..." Blaire's steps faltered when he lifted his head, and his eyes were glowing topaz. Her heart skipped a beat. "No. Don't do this."

His voice dropped, becoming a low rumble in his throat. "Do what?"

"Don't leave me. Don't hate me. I'm sorry." She knelt in front of him and held out her hands as her breathing quickened. The fear of him leaving her overrode any sense of self preservation. "I didn't mean to panic. Please don't leave me down here."

The glow faded from his eyes as his mouth dropped open. "What? Blaire—what? Why? I wouldn't—" Dominic moved forward on his knees and grabbed her around the waist, pulling her against his chest.

Blaire's nails dug into his back as she clung to him, her face buried against his neck as she began to cry.

"Why on Earth would you think I would abandon you down here?"

"You're angry." She sat back on her heels and swiped her cheeks. "I'm not your Korrena. I'm not anything to you. You"—she sniffled and hiccuped—"don't have any reason to put up with this. I'm broken, Dom. I need Lukas, and he isn't here, and it's getting to me."

"I'm not angry with you. I'm angry because I feel like death, and I can't give you what you need. But I'll try to get you back to him.

Can you trust me on that?"

Dragging her nails over her jean-clad thighs, she nodded. "Okay. Okay, I can do that." She swallowed and looked up at him. "Why are you so sick?"

"I need more sleep."

He was lying, but she didn't want to risk upsetting him by saying so. Not when she needed him. Not when he could change his mind and leave her to fend for herself when they reached the end of the tunnels. Especially not when he was there for her—supported her.

"Then let's sleep," she finally said, standing and reaching her hand for him. The panic from earlier, and her desire to keep a distance between them, finally faded away to a manageable level. He'd even held her as she cried. Focusing on the task at hand—on escaping together—would have to keep her demons at bay for now.

When everything was safe and normal, then she'd consider seeing a professional again. She laughed at the idea anything would ever be normal in her world again.

25

Sanguis Manie

Frustration and concern warred inside Blaire as she followed Dominic. Traversing the tunnel system with him had become a nightmare all of its own. After sleeping for three hours, they traveled for another twelve, stopping to rest periodically when her feet wouldn't allow her to move any farther. If she'd done the math correctly, and they were walking a casual two miles per hour, they were approaching the halfway point. If that were the case, and they could keep the same pace, they might get through to the end in another twenty-four or so hours—including sleep and rest stops. She silently thanked her old track coach for drilling distance and time information into her head long ago. Finally, a use for it outside of track and field.

Blaire stared at the back of Dominic's head.

Everything changed after last night. She didn't know what she could do to make him feel better. The situation wasn't ideal for either of them, but she could at least do something to show her appreciation for him looking out for her. He didn't need her, and with his Vasirian fortitude, he could have covered much more distance than they had together. She held him back, and that didn't settle well with her.

Being around him had become a practice of patience and delicate walking on eggshells. Somewhere around hour three after they'd awakened this morning, she decided casual conversation was out of the question. Every time she tried to engage him in normal banter like they'd become accustomed to in the dungeon, his tone was sharp, and his replies short and impatient.

She didn't know if he was still feeling ill, frustrated that he agreed to come along, hungrier because he kept insisting she take the lion's share of the food when they stopped to eat, or if his real personality had graced her with its presence, but she would not push him. Tempting fate while trapped underground with an angry Vasirian in a tunnel system that had hours upon hours of travel on either side of their location with nowhere to hide wasn't a good idea.

The lighting at the midway point flickered more often, and every fourth bulb didn't work. Blaire worried the lights would go out, and she'd be left alone in the dark with him.

Her steps slowed to allow extra distance between them, but when Dominic's steps faltered, and he stumbled, she paused.

"Dom?"

He dropped to his knees.

Rushing to his side, she knelt and slipped the backpack off her shoulders, pulling a water bottle out and thrusting it into his trembling hands. "Drink."

He growled low in his throat and looked up at her.

"What is happening? Talk to me."

Every instinct in her screamed to flee, but this guy had been so kind to her before. Had seen her through the pain and heartache she faced in the cell.

"I didn't realize," he rasped. His breathing came in labored pants. His pupils were pinpoint tight, and the chocolate irises glowed topaz at the edges. "I didn't know..."

"Know what? What didn't you realize? You're scaring me."

Dominic looked up at her with wide, pleading eyes.

She quickly opened the water bottle and held it up to his lips, and he took a long pull of water, coughing as he finished. She closed the cap and set down the bottle, reaching up to put a hand on his forehead to check his temperature. He was coated in sweat. His skin was pale and hot to the touch. She didn't know how to deal with a sick Vasirian.

He grabbed her wrist, and his eyes flashed brightly.

"Dom? W-what are you..." Blaire leaned back as he leaned forward toward her, taking a deep breath of the air in her personal space.

Before Blaire could say anything more, Dominic snarled and shoved her back. She fell onto her back in the dirt, and he stood quickly, moving to the side of the tunnel, far away from her.

"Stay away from me."

"Dom?"

"I said stay away!" He shouted the last two words and hit the wall of the tunnel. "I don't want to hurt you!" He clutched his throat and squatted, sitting on his heels as he doubled in on himself. But before long, that position wasn't enough, and he stood, pacing in circles until he stopped, faced the wall, and pulled on the hair on top of his head tightly.

What did he mean by he didn't want to hurt her? He just shoved her to the ground. He'd never done anything aggressive like that before. Never snarled or acted out this way. His behavior over the last day had to relate to his distress and sickness. The man from the cell still existed, but something was off. He acted borderline feral.

Blaire's brows crumpled. Something seemed familiar about the behavior he exhibited since a few hours after entering the tunnels. Fatigue and hunger made it hard for her to think, but she'd heard of this before. She lifted herself off the hard ground and tempted fate. She couldn't stand to see him suffering.

When her hand touched his back, he spun and grabbed her by her upper arms, slamming her against the rough tunnel wall hard enough to briefly knock the breath from her lungs. She stared up at him with wide eyes as he looked down at her, panting. His eyes glowed a bright citrine; his sharp fangs descended.

She breathed slowly through her nose to mask her fear, but she couldn't hide the tremor that passed through her. Hopefully, his own frantic shaking hid hers.

"I'm… thirsty." His voice sounded like he'd swallowed glass. "I…" His eyes lowered to the pulse point of her neck that beat a staccato rhythm. He likely couldn't see it with the bulky hoodie around her neck, but could he hear it? "I'm going mad."

"M-mad?"

"*Sanguis manie,*" he mumbled, leaning in, and dropping his forehead to her shoulder. "Blood mania."

She stiffened, and her eyes widened with realization. The Order mentioned that at the meeting while Lukas was locked away. That's where she remembered the symptoms from. Remembered the condition being the likely culprit behind the vampire myth. It had been maybe thirty-two hours since they left the dungeon. Dominic's last blood packet from dinner time had been hours before that. As the pieces fell into place, she was surprised he'd lasted this long. His entire shift in demeanor made sense now.

He needed blood, and she was the only source in the tunnel.

With Rue not accounting for Dominic coming with her, there wasn't a single blood packet in their bags. Blaire didn't know how long a Vasirian could go without blood before they died. They needed it to live. Was this what happened when a Vasirian was dying? Did *sanguis manie* come first?

Blaire took a deep breath and closed her eyes. Dominic had been there for her. He promised not to hurt her, but to protect her. If she didn't help him, he'd probably kill her anyway as he slipped further into delirium. She only hoped her blood didn't harm him. It had an adverse effect on Vincent. But the alternative meant they both might die.

"Dominic," she whispered, using his full name, keeping her voice steady.

He slowly lifted his head. Tight lines formed around his eyes, and his skin appeared gaunt despite his young age. His fangs cut into his lower lip, and blood trickled down his chin. He was restraining himself. Even with the glow in his eyes, he looked on the verge of crying. Whether from how awful he felt, or his fear of harming her, she didn't know.

"Hey," she said softly, keeping her voice low and soothing. She brought her hand up to push the hair from his sweat-slicked forehead and cupped his cheek, hoping to calm him.

Dominic's forehead creased in confusion. "What are you doing?" His voice dropped lower and sounded strained.

"Helping you." She gently pushed him back a couple of steps and tugged her hoodie over her head, clenching it tightly in her fists. She watched him, waiting expectantly.

"Blaire, no… I can't." Dominic stepped back even farther, shaking his head. "I don't… I… Your pair… We can't harm humans." He put a trembling hand over his face, his other hand fisted at his side.

"You can. I'm allowing you to do this. This isn't hurting me." She took a deep breath. "You need blood to live, and I know you won't hurt me. You said you wouldn't." She wet her lips anxiously. "If you don't, while you still have this much control, you might end up killing me down here. We're only halfway to freedom."

This wasn't a betrayal to Lukas. This wasn't a violation of the Korrena bond. She didn't feel the revulsion that came with Vincent's violation. This was about survival. For both of them.

Dominic lifted his head, lowering his hand from his face. The resignation on his face made her heart clench in sadness for him. He hated the idea, but he couldn't help what he was.

"How can you suggest this when…" He swallowed. "Your Korrena didn't stop. I don't want to scare you. Maybe I would act the same. Maybe I won't stop. How are you not afraid?"

"I am afraid."

"Then, no." His tone came sharp, with a finality to it.

"What?"

"I won't do it." He crossed to the bags, losing his footing briefly, before coming to a stop and squatting, picking up the water again and taking a small sip.

Blaire stood still, twisting the hoodie in her hands.

"Lukas wanted to turn me—not kill me for a meal. I'm more afraid of what is going to happen to me if you don't accept a small donation." She threw her hoodie to the ground as frustration rose in her voice. "Stop being so stubborn and bite me already! Don't be a coward!"

"Coward?" Dominic rose to his feet and turned, glaring at her. His mood was already volatile. She was playing with fire by provoking him. "How am I a coward?" Every word he spoke wavered and sounded like it took all his strength to speak.

"Don't treat me like glass. I've been through more than what a simple bite from you could do to me." She breathed in long and heavy through her nose and exhaled out her mouth. "You're a coward if you can't even do what you need to for survival."

Dominic dropped the water bottle on top of the tote bag and stalked toward her, closing the distance in long strides. He hemmed her against the wall, putting his forearm against the wall above her head, and took her chin between his fingers. "I don't want to hurt you." His words shook. "Why… won't you understand that?" Despite the way he had to force his words, sadness and uncertainty echoed in his tone. Pain laced his expression.

Blaire looked up into eyes that still glowed fiercely. "I do understand. You're not going to hurt me." She had to find enough conviction for both of them.

Dominic gently turned her face to the side, still holding onto her chin, keeping her face turned away from him as he leaned down to her neck.

"N-not there," she whispered. "The other side."

Her skin was littered with bruises. As much as she didn't want him to bite near, or where, her Korrena mark had been, anywhere else would likely hurt a lot.

Dominic didn't question why she made the request. He simply moved her head to the other side, respecting her wishes. His nose brushed the column of her throat, and she swallowed thickly.

"I…" His breath ghosted across her skin as he spoke. "I don't…" He took another unsteady, shuddered breath. "I won't… hurt you."

Blaire shivered as his lips brushed her skin before his fangs grazed the surface. An eternity passed before the sharp pinch of pain came with fangs piercing her flesh. She whimpered.

Dominic moaned against her neck at the first taste of blood, running his tongue over where he'd bitten her, before returning to suck the skin clean. His strong arm banded around her lower back and pulled her against his body as he drank from her without further hesitation. His trembling abated, and the tension in his body eased. He relaxed against her. His fingers dug into the bare skin of her lower back where her tank top had ridden up as he tightened his hold.

Fingers that held her chin now ran down her neck, over her shoulder, and down the length of her arm. Goose bumps rose on her skin and a familiar sensation stirred low in her belly. She opened her mouth to speak, but gasped when he shifted and his grip tightened.

"Dom," she breathed, her eyes rolling back in her head as her eyelids fluttered close.

It felt good.

It shouldn't feel good.

Why does it feel so good?

His hands dropped to her hips, no longer holding her head in place, and her hands clutched the front of his shirt, pulling him tighter against her.

When Lukas bit her, she felt good. More than good. She felt desire like she'd never known before. But that was normal for Korrena pairs. It heightened the connection between pairs and made blood exchange easier. Even as a human, that connection made her desire Lukas's blood. Not just a biological desire, but knowing what it meant to Lukas to connect that way made her want it.

When Vincent bit her, she wanted to crawl out of her own skin. No arousal. No emotional connection. She certainly didn't want to drink his blood in return. She assumed if any Vasirian other than Lukas took her blood, she would hate it the same way. Feel the same revulsion. Especially considering what sharing blood meant to Vasirian in a pair bond—not just what she felt with Lukas. It was that way for all Korrena pairs. Something she herself had started seeing as sacred. It was one of the biggest reasons she felt so violated by Vincent biting her.

But Dominic. *Oh God.*

As much as she wanted to lie to herself and say it wasn't happening, she was turned on.

The proximity of his body, hot against hers, and smelling so good, even after days of sweaty hiking.

His strong and comforting hold on her body, relaxed against her like a lover.

The tingling sensation coming from where he was taking her blood.

Dominic needed to feed, and she didn't want to push him away, but no way would she go that far with him despite what her body thought was going on. That would be a betrayal to Lukas, and not one she was willing to concede to.

Dominic drank his fill, oblivious to the internal struggle she endured. She felt slightly dizzy, but not enough to stop him. Not enough she couldn't recover. Not enough to feel fear. As long as he didn't take her physical reaction farther, she wouldn't push him away. Did he even know how she was responding to him?

When he leaned against her at the right angle where their hips pressed tightly together, and an uninvited moan broke her lips, she tried to squirm away from him. He froze at the sound and pulled away with wide eyes. His heavy breaths puffed over her skin.

Blaire swallowed and stared into his eyes while the glowing receded. Her eyes darted down to his blood-stained lips and heat spread through her core.

Why did she feel like this? Why couldn't she stop it?

"Hey, are you okay?"

She blinked a few times and shook her head to clear it. Dominic took a few steps back and wiped a hand over his mouth.

Blaire slumped against the wall, closing her eyes, breathing deeply. She needed a minute to get her equilibrium back after being fed on; thankful she hadn't donated blood recently. She tried to ignore the niggling problem of her arousal and focused on recovering from being fed on.

"Blaire?"

She opened her eyes to find Dominic staring at her in concern. His lips were parted, and his brows were drawn down. He looked lost and helpless. She needed to say something.

"I'm fine. I just need a minute. Little dizzy." She offered a half smile as he came toward her, picking up the hoodie from the ground and offering it to her. "Thank you," she murmured, shaking the dirt off before pulling the warm hoodie over her already heated skin, using the sleeve to wipe away any residual blood from her neck.

"What was that?" he asked.

"Huh?"

"You…" He frowned. "I don't know how to say this tactfully."

"Just say it."

"Did it…" He squeezed his eyes shut and lay his head back, groaning. His eyes met hers. "That felt good?" He sounded surprised. "Shit, I had no idea it was real."

Blaire's face warmed. She looked away. "That what's real?" She couldn't look at him.

"I… I'm sorry… I'm so sorry." Dominic took a heavy breath. "I didn't mean… I didn't want you to think I wanted…" He looked down, and a blush rose on his cheekbones and the tops of his ears when she looked back at him. He licked his lips. "If there is acceptance between the one receiving the bite and the one drinking, certain chemicals are released, making the 'victim' of the bite feel pleasure instead of pain. I've never had blood from a live body before, so I thought it was a myth."

"What? That can't be right. Vincent—"

"You didn't accept his bite."

"Well, no."

"Then it wouldn't stimulate the release of those chemicals."

She bit her lip. "I thought only Korrena pairs experienced pleasure."

He shook his head. "I don't know all the details, but it's not on the same level as pairs. It's temporary and only goes one way. Not for both parties."

"I didn't think you wanted anything more than food."

"Oh. Well, okay." He ran a hand over the back of his head and huffed a laugh. "That's good."

"It's not."

"What?"

Blaire crossed her arms over her chest. "You might not have wanted… but I did." She looked down, ashamed. "I don't understand. I wanted you to…" She took a shuddering breath, trying to keep her emotions under control.

"Oh. You can't possibly—"

"I know! I shouldn't want it. I shouldn't want you to touch me like that. Or kiss me." She looked up at Dominic as tears rolled down her cheeks. "I feel so guilty. Lukas and I…"

"Hey, no. Listen. I meant you can't possibly be thinking of blaming yourself for having a biological response to physical stimulus, or the dopamine rush released with my bite."

"I am!" She choked on her cry. "I didn't feel this way when Vincent did that to me, but you…"

"Come here," he said softly.

"What? No."

"Come here, Blaire."

Dominic's words were commanding, but they weren't harsh. The tone was one he'd used before. A tone that grounded her. She slowly walked toward him, her silent tears still trailing down her face.

"It makes sense," he said gently. He huffed a laugh. "I didn't think it was real. I'm so sorry. I would have warned you."

When she reached him, he took her hand and pulled her into his arms, wrapping her in a comforting hug. She sank into his embrace. There wasn't anything sexual about the feeling she got from being held by him this time. It was like night and day.

"You were afraid of the man who kidnapped you. He wasn't kind to you. You weren't friends." He stroked her hair. "You've depended on me recently and have gotten to know me. We get along. There's a bond there."

She looked up at him and squinted.

"Not like the bond you have with Lukas. We're friends. There's trust between us. You offered me your blood. I'm sorry if that feeling you experienced was uncomfortable."

"It wasn't. I mean, it was… a little. But mostly because I didn't want to feel it."

"That sounds confusing."

"You have no idea."

Dominic laughed and let her go. "It's definitely different, I won't lie—but blood is food for me. Please don't feel ashamed for saving not only your life, but mine too." He offered her a tired smile and moved over to sit down on the ground. "Come on. Let's eat actual food and get some sleep."

Just like that, he let the situation go. But she couldn't shake the guilty feeling her reaction brought. She needed to ignore the arousal and let it go, too.

If he could move past it, couldn't she?

He pulled out a can of Vienna sausages from the tote bag and held it out to her. "Hopefully, the next time we have to stop to sleep, we can be in a bed somewhere."

The mention of bed didn't help her mental imagery right now. "Doubt it. We're only halfway there. We already had to camp once, probably will have to one more time." Blaire rubbed her eyes and ambled over to him, taking the small can from him at arm's length. He returned to digging through the bag. Lethargy set in after he fed from her. Coupled with the hours of walking, once her head hit the backpack, she'd be dead to the world for hours. It also made it hard to overthink the awkward pattern of her thoughts. "Will you need more?"

"Pardon?" Dominic looked up from scrounging around in the tote bag. He pulled out two sandwiches, passing her one. "Last one. After this, there are a few more cans of Vienna sausages, more protein bars, and a couple of apples." They'd eaten the peanut butter sandwiches during "official" mealtimes.

She took the sandwich. "Will you need to drink more blood before we get out of here?"

He paused and turned his head to look at her, his mouth slack.

She wondered if he had considered how much time they had left. If this was how he responded to the time they'd spent on the run, and they were only at the halfway point, surely he would need to feed again to avoid the same manic state creeping in.

"I think to avoid an episode like today..." He cleared his throat. "Yeah, that might be best."

The top of his ears stained with his blush, but she chose not to acknowledge it. The situation was already awkward. If she got stimulated that far every time he drank from her, she would be in trouble.

She hoped Lukas would forgive her for such wantonness.

26

Misadventures

The next thirty hours went smoother than Blaire expected them to. They discovered that by allowing Dominic to take small amounts of blood each time they stopped for a rest, it didn't weaken her, and minimized the heightened state of arousal, though it didn't squash it completely.

He took her bruising problem into consideration and used her wrist and neck in rotation. The resulting bruises were light and wouldn't be there after a week. Unfortunately, every time he used her neck, her body reacted. The position was so intimate, it was hard for her to ignore.

The other problem came through dehydration.

Earlier, the tote bag Dominic carried had quite a few water bottles, along with the canned meat and other heavier items. Rue separated the items between the bags, but Dominic shifted the heavier things into the tote to make the journey easier for Blaire. Vasirian had added strength, after all.

Now, the tote bag he carried was much lighter.

They ran out of water a few hours ago, and Blaire felt it. Her mouth felt like someone stuffed it with cotton and soaked up all the saliva. She desperately needed water, a toothbrush, and pain medication for the headache that set in about three hours ago. She wet her dry lips.

Dominic had stopped drinking water when he started feeding from her. The water content of her blood was enough to sustain him. Had she not given him her blood, the water would have run out long ago.

In this section of the tunnels, the lights barely worked, so they walked blind. However, with no obstacles, larger pieces of debris, or tunnel branchings or turns, it was easy to navigate without the lights. One foot in front of the other. That didn't last long. Eventually, they were back to moving down a lit path.

"Is it me or is it getting colder?"

Dominic paused ahead of her and looked over his shoulder. "A little." He had draped the blanket they used for sleeping over his shoulders, since he only wore a t-shirt. She wore a hoodie, so stayed warm enough while they were moving.

Coming up beside him, she hugged herself. "I think there's a breeze or something. Do you feel that?"

Dominic glanced down the tunnel in both directions. "Maybe we're almost out."

"The timing lines up."

"Think you're good to go, or do you need a break?"

"I'm still fine from the last break. Do you need blood?" He hadn't taken from her the last time they stopped.

"Not yet. I think I'm fine to skip another stop."

The longer they remained in the tunnel, the more the physical toll wore on them. Frequent stops meant less time passed between each break. Blood at mealtimes was pertinent for Vasirian, from what Blaire understood, but she didn't know how badly physical exertion or other factors weighed on that. He also took far less than would be contained in a blood bag from a donor center. She couldn't hold up to that kind of constant demand.

"I do need to take a quick pee break."

Blaire nodded and dropped her backpack next to the tunnel wall then sat. She rested her back against the wall and tilted her head to rest against the hard surface as the sound of liquid hitting dirt reached her ears from farther away.

Bathroom breaks were a test of comfort down in the tunnel. She hadn't had to squat to use the bathroom since going camping and fishing with her friend's family at Lake Greenwood in South Carolina, when she was little. Rue had at least had the forethought to pack diaper wipes. Blaire already wanted a shower, but to also not have a clean backside? She had to draw the line somewhere, and that's where it was going to be.

"You ready?"

Blaire cracked open her tired eyes as Dominic sauntered toward her, hands tucked in his jeans.

"Five more minutes," she mumbled, already drifting into the space between sleep and awareness as her eyelids fluttered closed again.

Dominic sighed without exasperation and chuckled. "Five minutes. Sure." He dropped the tote bag and sat down next to her against the wall. He flourished the blanket out to drape over the both of them and pulled it up higher, moving close to share the warmth.

Five minutes turned into one hour. Dominic had fallen asleep, too.

Blaire's neck ached from the awkward angle against the wall, and her limbs were heavy. Sleeping against the wall or the floor of the tunnel didn't make a difference; there was nothing comfortable about tightly-packed dirt.

She drew deeply on her endurance to make it the rest of the way, but as they approached a set of worn wooden stairs leading up to wooden double doors like those attached to a storm cellar, she breathed a sigh of relief, a sob catching in her throat.

A strong draft carried from the gaps around the cellar-style doors, and Japanese kudzu snaked through the side gaps, consuming the dirt wall that flanked the small set of steps leading out.

"This is it," Dominic said, climbing the stairs. Blaire followed closely behind.

He gave the doors a push. They resisted the action at first. He had to give them a harder shove before the wood cracked and the hinges groaned from years of disuse. The doors finally swung out and opened fully, falling to the sides of the open mouth to the tunnel. Outside was darkness.

Dominic grabbed Blaire's hand. "I'm with you, no matter what happens." At her nod, he led her up the steps. The chill of the night slapped her in the face. She released Dominic's hand and tucked her hands into the front pouch of her hoodie.

Outside wasn't what she expected.

What had she expected?

Blackthorn Security en masse, ready to drag them back kicking and screaming? The Order themselves with their smug expressions filled with disdain?

Instead of the fight she'd prepared for, they stood alone in the middle of a dark forest. The light from the tunnels below spilled out into the forest, helping them see. Japanese kudzu had consumed the forest floor around them like it did much in rural Georgia. The stuff spread like a plague. Leave anything abandoned long enough, and the vines with large leaves would take over. Pine trees stood tall all around them with kudzu climbing the bases of many. Areas void of the invasive vine were barren and covered in dried pine needles, dimly lit by moonlight filtering through the treetops.

Dominic pointed toward a small single-family home with lit windows alongside a large barn. A smaller one stood farther away next to a silo. "Look. A farm."

"We can't just approach someone's home."

"We're not." At her drawn brows, he elaborated. "Where there are people and their homes, a road isn't far." He smirked and added slowly, "Roads lead to towns."

She glared at him, but the look didn't hold any bite. "Har har, smartass."

He laughed and tilted his head to motion for her to follow. "Come on, let's get out of here in case they know about the tunnels and come to this end."

Before they left, Blaire helped him close the doors to the tunnel again. Once the doors were closed, she discovered the other reason, aside from lack of use, that the doors resisted opening. The invasive plant had grown over the exit entirely. Broken vines lay strewn around the doors, but many still clung to the surface. If someone didn't know what to look for, they would completely miss it walking through the forest. Day or night.

The trek through the trees didn't take long, and after avoiding the curious stares of several unsuspecting cows who mooed at them as they passed through a pasture at the edge of the farm, they made their way to the long dirt driveway that ran alongside the pasture. The driveway led to the main paved road.

Blaire wasn't sure how much longer they walked before passing signs for Main Street, but her feet ached, and her calves burned as they walked into town.

"Look over there."

Dominic pointed at a brightly lit sign for an open motel.

The vacancy sign lit in neon green was a beacon of hope to her overworked muscles and mind. The temptation of a warm bed, hot shower, toothpaste—maybe not in that order—appealed to her more than she realized as a drawn-out groan of relief left her mouth.

Dominic chuckled. "Almost there."

Blaire froze when he resumed his pace. "Wait." She put both hands over her face and hung her head forward, her dirty, long hair falling forward. How could she be so stupid?

"Aren't you coming?"

She dropped her hands and met his confused gaze, sighing. "How do you expect to pay for this?"

"Hotels have telephones."

"Uh huh…" She dragged out the last part of the word.

"I can call who sent me and get them to pay for a room—maybe wire money in. I'm sure there's one of those stores that handle wire transfers and things like that around here."

"At this time of night?"

"Probably not. But they can pay for the room over the phone, and I'll just deal with the money situation in the morning. Besides, we have to see if we can even check in this late. Some places have check-in time policies."

Luckily for them, that wasn't the case here.

Dominic made a private call, and within minutes, he sauntered toward where she slumped exhausted in a chair in the lobby.

He held up a key card. "Got it."

"Thank God." Blaire laid her head back and sighed in relief.

"You can just call me Dom."

She squinted at him, and then her slow-firing brain caught up with his meaning. "Oh, shut up."

Dominic whistled. "Someone's cranky."

Blaire groaned and stood on shaking legs. When she reached for the backpack, he put a hand over her arm.

"I got it. Let's get to the room. The receptionist said we could have leftover items from their continental breakfast they have in the staff fridge. Once we get settled, I'm going to run back down here and get them."

Blaire gaped at him. "She's just giving it to you?" Not that she was complaining. They probably had a single can of Vienna sausages left to split between them. She hated those tiny, salty, rubbery things, but Dominic seemed to like the poor excuse for meat.

"Well, the breakfast is complimentary."

"Yeah, but it's late at night."

"I mentioned our car broke down miles outside of town and we've been walking for a while and haven't had the opportunity to eat or anything. She offered."

Blaire glanced at the front desk where a young receptionist no older than sixteen—possibly younger if her family ran the motel—with blonde hair pulled into a high ponytail sat staring at Dominic like he was the second coming. She snorted.

"What?"

"I can see the hearts in her eyes from here."

He glanced back toward the desk, and when the receptionist caught his eye, he winked. She whipped her gaze back to the computer screen, her cheeks flaming.

"Leave her alone. She's probably still in high school." Blaire limped toward the elevator. "I need a shower."

"Fine, grumpy pants."

Blaire didn't acknowledge him as she stepped into the metal box that would take her to sweet relaxation.

"Ideally, we'd each have our own rooms, but it's not safe. I'm not the only one who thought of that."

"Who else—"

"Confidential." At her incredulous look, he laughed. "Just my contact who sent me here. If we're being watched, it's safer to stick together."

She couldn't argue with that logic.

Once inside the room, she headed straight for the bathroom sink, completely ignoring the room itself. She turned on the faucet and ducked down to drink greedily.

"There's… glasses over there."

Blaire lifted her head and wiped her mouth, glancing at the corner of the counter next to her. She missed the small collection of glasses entirely. Shrugging, she pulled open the door next to the sink and peered in at the shower and toilet. "Dibs!"

"While you handle that, I'll go see what our friendly receptionist has to offer."

"No flirting!" Blaire called from the open bathroom, bursting into laughter as she failed to sound serious.

"What do you take me for? I don't mind a few years younger, but she's a kid." Dominic's laughter faded as the room door clicked shut and latched.

The first spray of hot water on her skin wrenched forth a moan of satisfaction that faded on a sigh. Never had she appreciated the invention of a shower like she did in that moment.

The hotel shampoo wasn't anything to write home about, but with how grimy her hair had gotten from lying in the dirt, she sang its praises, regardless.

She climbed out of the shower, eager to shake off the last seventy hours of another misadventure to add to the running list of "Weird Things Blaire Keeps Getting Caught Up In"—the title needed work. She shook her head and wrapped a towel around her body, twisting her long, wet hair into another. It still left Dominic a towel for his use.

Outside of the tiny bathroom that barely had room for a toilet and tub, she stood at the sink again. She looked at herself in the mirror, noting the faded bruises and markings from Vincent's deeper bites. Her gaze caught on Dominic's newer bite marks on her neck and wrists.

She turned away from the view, avoiding the visual reminder of what happened in the tunnel, and looked over the room.

Neutral Earth tones instead of garish, brightly colored décor made the room look modern. Soft green walls and white floral paintings in golden frames lent a touch of color. Two double beds with checked beige and white pattern comforters took up most of the room. A lamp sat on the nightstand between the beds with a landline phone, a small digital clock radio, and a remote for the TV, which was mounted on the opposite wall above a long dresser that spanned the foot of both beds. A small table sat next to the air-conditioning unit by the window with two small chairs upholstered in beige leather.

Cataloging the room helped Blaire push away her destructive thoughts. The dirty clothes on the bathroom counter made her nose wrinkle.

She hated putting on dirty clothes, but she had little else—and she would not sleep nude with Dominic in the same room. She put on the tank top she'd worn beneath the hoodie, and panties. Neither had touched the dirt of the tunnel, so they wouldn't soil the bed. She'd stay beneath the covers until morning and put on her jeans then.

Sliding between the sheets, she sighed happily at the feeling of soft fabric brushing over her freshly washed skin. It felt good to be clean. And hydrated. Add real food to the mix and she'd be a most happy camper.

But she wondered what tomorrow held for them and when she could reunite with her Korrena.

27

Understanding

The locking mechanism on the door beeped, and the lock clicked. Dominic opened the door and came inside carrying a bag in his hand. He held it up and grinned.

"Honey, I'm home."

His words were lighthearted, but tiredness filled his tone, matched by the fatigue on his face. He'd likely need to feed before bed. Unless he'd dallied illegally with the receptionist, or robbed a blood bank, he hadn't consumed blood in hours. She didn't want a repeat episode of the onset of mania.

Dominic ambled over to the bed, his steps slow and tired. He set the plastic bag on the foot of the bed and pulled out various items. Chocolate chip muffins, banana bread, pecan pinwheels, a plastic container with sliced fruit, small bottles of juice—both orange and apple, covered the bed in front of Blaire. Her brows rose as Dominic lifted the lid off a plastic container and delicious-smelling steam rose from the contents. He grinned.

"I was able to use the microwave." He lowered the container to show Blaire the scrambled eggs, biscuits, and sausage gravy within. "You Southerners make amazing country gravy." He grabbed two plastic forks from the bag and handed her one. "Eat up."

"She must've really liked you." Blaire stabbed a piece of cantaloupe with her fork.

He lifted one shoulder. "If I didn't know any better, I'd say you sound jealous."

Blaire's eyes widened, the fork pausing in front of her open mouth. She sputtered, "W-what? No, I—"

"I'm kidding. Jeez, you're so wound tight." He leaned forward and took a bite of the fruit from her fork, chewing while suppressing laughter at her surprised expression.

She wasn't overthinking it. It just caught her off guard after the weird tension that grew from his drinking her blood. He sat down heavily on the floor next to her bed, and she blinked. "Why are you on the floor?"

"I'm filthy."

"I don't care." Even if she stripped down to avoid getting her bed dirty, she didn't want him to have to sit on the floor. "Get up here." She looked down at the fork in her hand that he ate from.

He chuckled, and groaned as he pulled himself back up, collapsing on the bed beside her. "Happy?"

They both dug into the warm breakfast food, making small appreciative noises as they devoured the first proper meal they'd had in a while.

"I need a shower," Dominic said as Blaire chewed on a pinwheel. He set the empty container they shared breakfast from on the dresser under the TV. "Call if you need me."

"Yes, Dad." She shoved a sizeable chunk of honeydew melon into her mouth, rolling her eyes.

She left half the bowl of fruit and several pieces of baked goods for Dominic, putting them back in the bag and setting them on his bed before crawling back beneath the warm covers.

Blaire fell asleep until the bathroom door opened, waking her again, and Dominic stepped out wrapped in a white towel around his waist. He stood at the mirror, finger-combing his wet hair. She turned on her side, averting her gaze from his tight abs and cut v-line, her face warming.

"Asleep?"

She opened her eyes again to find Dominic standing between the two beds, wearing a fluffy white bathrobe. Her brows lowered. "Where did you find that?"

"Hanging against the wall near the sink. I'm only wearing boxers underneath so I don't get my sheets dirty." He shrugged. "I figured this would make you more comfortable."

Blaire appreciated the respect he showed her. Especially after what had transpired in the tunnel, and the strange feelings she fought ever since. She slowly sat up and moved her damp hair away from her shoulders. "Do you need to feed?"

Dominic sighed and sat down on the edge of her bed. "I should. I'm sorry. I don't like this, but I don't want to end up hurting you."

Blaire nodded. "I know. This time might be the last time. When you go out for the transfer in the morning, can't you stop by somewhere like the Red Cross?"

He chuckled. "I'm sure there's somewhere I can get a blood packet now that we're in town. Most places have medical centers."

"Then, don't stress it. Just take what you need. I'll be okay."

Dominic sighed again and shifted on the bed, leaning toward her with his hands braced on each side of her hips. She tilted her head, moving her hair to the side to give him access.

Like every single time his mouth met her neck, she melted into the sensation. But more and more, Lukas filled her mind each time as she tried to ignore the reaction she accepted wasn't her fault. It had the opposite effect. To counteract the way her body responded to Dominic drinking her blood—to lessen the guilt—she pictured Lukas. It was a double-edged sword. By picturing Lukas, she could blame the sensations on what her mind conjured and not what the person next to her brought out. But on the opposite end of things, her desire increased.

Unable to stop herself, she reached up and wrapped her arms around his shoulders as he drank. Her fingers slid into his hair on the back of his head, and he groaned, pulling away from her neck. They stared at each other, breathing heavily. His gaze dropped to her mouth.

This couldn't all be because of the dopamine reaction, could it? He said the chemicals didn't affect him, only the one receiving the bite.

Before she could think more of it, or question him, he leaned in and captured her lips with his. She tasted her own blood on his tongue as he teased her lips with it until they parted to let him in. She lay back, pulling him down until her head met the pillow. They continued to kiss until he was over the top of her.

He didn't press his body to hers, but his body caging her in was enough to snap her out of the haze of lust. Her eyes fluttered open to see the Vasirian looming over her, eyes glowing gold. Her vision blurred, and a flash of long black hair hung over her.

No, it isn't him. It isn't...

Her hands flew to Dominic's chest. She needed to escape.

"Stop," she said sharply, panic in her voice. Her nails dug into his bare chest where his robe gaped open.

Blaire shoved him, and he sat back on the bed, confusion crossing his features until he looked at her face. He paled.

"I'm sorry. I got carried away again," Blaire said quickly, looking to the side, flushing. She would not go in-depth addressing the fear that erupted when he had her beneath him on the bed. She couldn't tell him she envisioned Vincent. She didn't want to upset or insult him by implying she saw in him the monster who wanted to hurt her. He wasn't. "I was thinking about—"

"No, I'm sorry. I know it was just a physical response to the bite, not genuine feelings for me. I know you love your pair. But I… I did something stupid. I shouldn't have kissed you."

Her exhaled breath of relief rattled loose the remaining tension in her chest.

Blaire loved Lukas, and feeling even the littlest arousal by another man made her feel guilty. But Dominic was right. Anyone would likely respond to that much physical stimulus from someone they felt comfortable with. She'd never responded to Vincent that way, but he'd made her feel constant fear, anger, and violation. There was a vast difference between the two men.

Maybe it was the same for Dominic. She couldn't fault him for responding when she had her own reactions to him. He wasn't dead.

"But in all seriousness, how many Vasirian have drank your blood?"

"Three, including you."

"Sooo, your Korrena, a sick and twisted psycho, and me."

Blaire nodded. She wasn't seeing his point.

"Well, it's not hard to guess how you feel when the others drank your blood. The next question is, have you ever been close to another guy before?"

Her lips pursed.

Blaire grew up without her father, and her mother didn't date another man until her stepdad. She wasn't really close with him, and Caleb and his grandfather were a nightmare. She wasn't allowed to date once she joined their family, and before that, she never focused on boys. When she joined Blackthorn Academy, she was thrown in with Lukas, but then there was…

Her eyes opened wide.

Aiden.

"What is it?"

"There is this one guy…"

Dominic's brow arched.

"Lukas's best friend, actually. When I first came to the academy, we got close to one another. Talked a lot. He protected me. Was there for me when bad things happened. Kinda like you." She huffed an amused breath. "And I started feeling… things. When he made a move and kissed me, I let him. I kissed him back. I wanted to."

Dominic watched her intently, letting her talk without interruption.

"It was good. Maybe not as intense as this, but blood wasn't involved, so maybe there would have been more if that had been the case with the chemicals and all." She shrugged helplessly. "The thing is, I knew something was missing. I didn't feel right. Lukas wouldn't get out of my head." She looked up. "Just like this time."

"Because you love him."

"I didn't then."

"But you were beginning to connect with him?"

"More than I realized, I guess." Her head tilted to the side in concession. "But I don't know what makes it different."

"Don't you?"

"No."

His eyes smiled, but he kept his tone quietly serious. "You're telling me you don't know what makes Lukas different from this Aiden guy or me?"

Blaire toyed with the edge of the comforter. "There's a lot different."

He waved his hand for her to continue.

"It felt physically nice with you both, yeah, but I don't feel that need like I do for Lukas."

"For sex?"

"No! To just be together. Lukas and I don't have to say anything, and it feels right. With Aiden, I feel the awkward need to fill the silence. With you, I dunno. I'm comfortable, and I trust you, but not like I do Lukas. Or even Aiden, really."

Dominic sighed. "I won't kiss you again. We know why you acted on the chemicals now, and I'm not going to start betraying your trust by not controlling my own libido. In fact, I don't think I'll take blood from you the same way again. I've noticed it's worse when I use your neck."

"Yeah, me too."

"It's an intimate position. It's not surprising. But don't stress about it. We both know this reaction means nothing. Lukas will understand." He stood and yawned. "I'm dead tired."

She hoped Lukas would understand. She couldn't lose him. She sniffed and rubbed her nose. "I miss him."

"I know you do."

Blaire yawned as Dominic turned away to move the bag of food to the dresser.

He walked back to the bed and removed his robe, laying it over the foot of his bed before crawling beneath his own covers. "I'll have us money tomorrow, and then we can figure out where we're going to go from here. Right now, I'm lacking the brainpower to do anything but sleep." He turned out the lamp between the beds and darkness gave a curtain of privacy.

Alone with her thoughts, Blaire thought more deeply, wanting to parse the difference in these experiences. Aiden, Lukas, Dominic.

When she thought of Lukas, she wanted to be near him. To occupy the same air. Being next to Lukas comforted her differently than the others. With Dominic and Aiden, her mind wouldn't stop. With Lukas, she could turn it off and trust he would be there to keep everything at bay. She could fully let go and rely on him.

She and Lukas could sit in silence and enjoy the little things. A movie. Food. The smell of the flowers in the courtyard. They could be together without the awkward need to fill the tension—because there wasn't any.

She hadn't experienced that before. She always had to keep watch for what came next, friend or not. With every new person she met, her radar was always on the lookout.

Would she need to be mindful of the food on her plate? Standards and expectations must be adhered to, or she'd be criticized and rejected. In contrast, Lukas shared his food because he didn't care about her weight. He shared concerns when she lost so much weight during her kidnapping, but only in regard to her health, not because he thought she was too scrawny to be attractive.

She would worry about a gesture her friend made during a movie. She would chew on the nuance of everything, overthinking in circles, afraid of the consequence of the incorrect reaction. With Lukas, she could fall asleep while a movie played because she fully relaxed at his side.

The reassuring affection from Dominic while trapped together in the dungeons, and on the run, stood in such stark contrast to being trapped with the unhinged Vincent for two months, that Blaire struggled to see her connection to him for what it was when physical arousal was thrown into the mix.

Vincent hadn't been trapped by her. He forced her into that. *She* had been trapped by *him*. Dominic had been trapped *beside* her; he hadn't trapped her, and she hadn't trapped him. It had been so long since she had a friendly male presence—barring roughly a week between the two capture events—that the lines blurred.

The reminder of her previous attraction to Aiden sat heavy in her mind. Thinking back to the early weeks of their friendship revealed something new. The more he gave her the affection and protection she so desperately needed that her stepbrother denied her, the more she desired Aiden, but something remained missing that she found with Lukas. A pull remained between her and Aiden that went beyond attraction. It was easy to draw parallels, easy to see where she began associating his brand of emotional support with sexual arousal. With Vincent trapping her in another abusive situation she couldn't escape, under the guise of love like Caleb had, she latched onto the first positive and gentle affection from the opposite sex presented to her after her escape from him, and more recently, from the dungeon—Dominic. The same thing happened when she got away from Caleb and met Aiden. Even her boss at the diner had been confrontational and made her crave acceptance.

Why did kissing, cuddling, and all the rest with Lukas hit different? What did she find with him that was missing with Aiden, with Dominic, with…anyone?

She tugged the covers up to cover her shoulders and sighed.

Lukas being so hot and cold, and aggressively so in both directions, might be exactly what she needed to satisfy her longing for an equal partner. She wanted to laugh at the absurd idea, but it held merit.

By his not bombarding her with affection and constant positivity, she didn't blindly fall for him or mistake her need for emotional support as anything more than that. She saw the reality of him, and the back and forth allowed her to stay grounded—to discover the things missing with someone else that she needed to feel safe in a long-term relationship. Even if the positive aspects of his strengths had equally negative aspects that drove her nuts.

Professor Sinclair would have a field day with that theory. She didn't know what would happen with the light of a new day. If Dominic had contacted whoever sent him to Blackthorn Academy, maybe they would help them relocate. Somewhere she could hide from the Order. She had no idea how Lukas would fit into this, and she didn't want to leave her friends behind. But if the Order sacrificed her, that would happen regardless.

The only lingering worry as she stared at the ceiling of the dark motel room was why Dominic remained unaffected by her blood. It hadn't taken Vincent long to spiral into crazytown. Was he a unique case? Lukas seemed fine, but he was her Korrena, and they theorized that with their bond came immunity to the maddening effects of her blood.

Blaire didn't bother asking Dominic—he was asleep already anyway. He wouldn't know. Likely wouldn't understand. Vasirian didn't feed directly from human bodies. It was against their laws—except in her unique case with Lukas. Not because human blood was dangerous; they drank it all the time from blood bags. So, it definitely stood to reason that whatever made her different—made her blood different—was the reason Vincent had been adversely affected.

She only hoped Dominic wouldn't have a delayed reaction.

28

Apprehended

When Blaire woke the next morning, Dominic wasn't in his bed. She rolled onto her back and looked up at the ceiling. She didn't want to move. Her muscles still protested the fact she was awake, but the clock said nine in the morning, and they would either have to check out soon or pay for another night.

The toilet flushed. She rolled her head over on the pillow as Dominic stepped out to the sink and washed his hands.

"Morning, Sunshine."

Blaire huffed a small laugh. "Does it have to be?"

"Afraid so."

They could pretend it wasn't morning. The blackout curtains above the two-seater table blocked any sunlight from the other side.

Dominic came around the foot of her bed and sat on the edge as she scooted up to sit against the headboard. He handed her a cold bottle of citrus green tea.

She took the bottle, and her brows furrowed. "Where'd you get this?"

"Vending machine down the hall. I remember that woman guard bringing you tea and what you said about pop."

"Pop?"

"Soda. Soda pop. You don't like it, right?"

"I don't. Upsets my stomach."

He nodded and stretched his arms high above his head, then twisted side to side, popping his back. "I have to go pick up the wire transfer. A convenience store nearby accepts it. I'll grab something good to eat while I'm there from the restaurant next door. Do you like Chinese food?"

Blaire's stomach chose that moment to growl loudly. "You have no idea."

Dominic laughed, and his face split into a wide smile. "The receptionist gave me a menu." He nodded to the takeout menu on the nightstand next to the phone. "Pick out what you want, and I'll get going. Get as much as you want. I'll probably get way more money than we need."

Blaire leaned over and snagged the menu, opening it, and scanning the various dishes. "Want me to call it in?"

"Nah. I have no idea how long the wire transfer process will take, so I'll order it when I get there." He stood and opened the nightstand drawer, pulling out a small notepad with the motel's logo on the top and a pen with the same branding. "Just write what you want on this." He moved to his bed, sitting down, and putting on his shoes.

She jotted down her order of Mongolian beef, fried cheese wontons, and a small house lo mein. She lamented the fact they didn't serve crab rangoon, but fried cheese wontons were the next best thing. "Close enough," she mumbled and tore the page out of the notebook, setting it on the bed for Dominic.

"Will you be alright while I'm gone?"

"Yeah, of course. How are you getting there? You said it's nearby, but..."

"It's walking distance."

Blaire shook her head. Just the mention of walking again made her shudder. If she could, she'd stay in bed for the next week.

Dominic stood and walked to the door, key card in hand. "Once I take care of this, I'll walk back here from there. Don't open the door for anyone."

She rolled her eyes and folded her arms over the blanket covering her stomach as Dominic left the room, the lock engaging. Blaire wasn't ready to give up the sweet embrace of her cushy bed, so she rolled over in favor of additional shuteye.

Fragrant garlic and other delicious scents stirred her awake. The clock's red numbers showed noon.

"Shouldn't we already be kicked out by now?"

"Got us a second night. Just in case."

Dominic stood at the two-seater table in front of the window, unpacking their lunch-slash-breakfast. His movements were slow, and he set the containers down gently. She assumed he didn't want to wake her, but her quick nap turned into something much longer. She needed to get up.

"How'd it go?" She cleared her throat and reached for the bottle of citrus green tea she'd left on the nightstand to ease her dry mouth and scratchy throat.

Dominic turned when Blaire sat up in bed to drink. "As expected." He held up a prepaid Visa card. "We have enough to make plans. I'm thinking clothes first?"

"Nope." She reached over the bed and grabbed her dirty jeans from the floor, throwing the cover off her lap and shimmying them up her hips. "Food first."

Dominic averted his eyes and chuckled. "Naturally. But after, new clothes."

"What about blood?"

"I can pick some up while we're out."

"Yeah, but you can't drink it while we're clothes shopping."

This wasn't Blackthorn Academy, or the home of someone who knew his secret. She didn't think a man walking around Walmart drinking blood from an actual medical-grade blood packet would go over so well. She wouldn't overlook it. Of course, there was an entire website dedicated to the weirdos of Walmart, so maybe it wouldn't be so alien to see. Still, she didn't think they should draw unnecessary attention to themselves.

"I think you should go get that first, come back here and drink in peace, and then we'll go clothes shopping. Why don't you have a little before you go? I don't want you ill or, you know, craving."

Dominic sat in one of the chairs and tilted his head. "I suppose you're right." He held out his hand.

Blaire blinked. "Um… What?"

"Give me your arm."

"But my neck—"

"Is bruised after last night. Your wrist, not so much."

Even in this situation, Dominic still considered her physical condition. He was a good guy. Lukas couldn't be angry at someone like that. She hoped.

"Besides, I told you I wouldn't do it there again. It's better for us both not to be in such a compromising position."

Blaire placed her hand in his, her cheeks warm at the reminder of that hot illicit kiss. He turned her arm over, bringing it up toward his face. His breath wafted over her skin before she felt the sharp sting of fangs breaking her flesh. He only took enough blood to satisfy his need, licking away the lingering blood from the wound until it stopped bleeding, and then released her to eat.

Blaire opened the lid on her Mongolian beef and breathed in the pleasant scent of garlic and scallions. She glared when Dominic stole a cheese wonton from the smaller box. "Mine." She pulled the box toward her and mantled it.

Dominic paused with the fried wonton in front of his mouth, his lips parted to take a bite. He sputtered, "But I…" He grinned. "I went out and got it. I think I've earned a cheese wonton or three."

"Shoulda got your own."

"You're being selfish."

"No. I'm being hungry."

"You're serious?" He huffed, amused. "We can't share?"

"I told you. I never joke about food."

Dominic snorted a laugh and shook his head in disbelief. "You're really going to ice me out of a few pieces of food. Unbelievable. After all that walking I did so the princess could stay in bed." He chuckled again.

He wasn't upset. Softening, Blaire wouldn't deny him the food.

Sliding the box to the middle of the table again, she sighed. "Fine. I suppose I can share some with you, since you're going to cry about it."

"Oh, how magnanimous of you."

She smirked. "I try."

Her heart felt lighter. Happier. Being out from under the Order allowed her to let down her guard. It had been months since she could let go, and she felt like joking around and being playful with someone. Dominic had the right personality to engage in verbal sparring in jest.

She missed this kind of fun with Riley, and watching Riley and Seth bicker, but she wasn't sure when she'd see her friends again.

They ate the rest of their meal in companionable silence. Occasionally they commented on the flavor, avoiding the topic of what came next after they got clothing and not allowing complete silence. Blaire wasn't sure where she could go. Dominic could easily go back to whoever sent him to Georgia. Especially if that person resided across the border in Canada.

When she sat back and patted her food baby, Dominic cleared the table of their trash, putting it in the takeout bag and dropping it in the room's small trashcan beside the dresser.

"I'm going to get the receptionist to order me an Uber, and then I'll visit a local medical clinic. I'll be back as quickly as possible, then we can either stop by Walmart, or this store called Citi Trends the receptionist mentioned carried a better selection. Not designer or anything, but apparently 'trendy.'"

His expression showed that wasn't his choice of words. Blaire doubted Dominic thought about trends when he chose his fashion. He didn't seem like the type. While he looked polished and refined when she'd first seen him in the dungeon, he marched to his own beat. She doubted his casual style would be like every other guy around town. His eyebrow piercing and the spiked stud and dangling cross on his left ear gave hint to a more alternative style.

Alternative fashion wasn't a local phenomenon. People in the South snubbed it in favor of clothes better suited to a golf course, country and western chic, or the colors and logos of their favorite teams or university. Rosebrook Valley was no different, which made a few of her newfound friends stand out like sore thumbs—more so than they already did as Blackthorn Academy students.

Dominic stood in front of the door, once again ready to leave her in the room. He frowned. "Are you sure you're okay to wait here for me? I know you slept last time, but I don't think you'll get any more sleep."

"Go. I'm fine. I'll just find something on TV."

He nodded. "I'll be as quick as I can."

Blaire waved him off as he exited the room, and sighed heavily into the silence of the room when it was empty. She didn't dislike solitude, but she'd be lying if she said it appealed to her right now. Being alone made her think of Lukas, her friends, and if she'd ever see them again. She wished she knew their phone numbers, or at least had her planner with her. She cursed herself for not using some of the allowance Blackthorn Academy provided her to get a basic cell phone plan.

She reluctantly got up from the chair, grabbed the remote, and turned on the large flatscreen. Blaire didn't watch TV much except to catch a movie with her friends or watch Aiden and Seth play video games. Sometimes Lukas joined in. Sometimes they asked her to play a round of something. She wasn't the gaming type; that was Charlotte's wheelhouse.

Her eyes rolled at the Valentine's Day commercial. It was early January, and already jewelry stores were pushing the "every woman loves diamonds" shtick. Aside from the jewelry her father had given her mother that she inherited, Blaire owned few genuine diamonds. She liked to look nice, but they could never afford things like that. When her mother married into the Wilcox family, Blaire didn't ask for shiny baubles. She had perfectly fine cubic zirconia earrings, especially since she didn't wear them often, so they didn't dull quickly. She gravitated toward colorful gemstones, anyway.

Flipping through the channels, she stopped on a channel that played music videos, and settled back into her chair by the window, peeking out the thick curtains.

The sun was bright overhead, and the warmth reached her face, but the glass felt cool to the touch. She closed the curtain. Leaving them open and exposing herself to the outside world when they didn't know if the Order was tracking them seemed foolish.

Blaire sat listening to music, trying to keep her brain from betraying her and wandering into territories she didn't want to be in. Had she never noticed how the lyrics of every song related to a love relationship? The one currently playing hit too close. After several minutes, she stood and padded barefoot across the scratchy motel carpet to the sink.

Squeezing toothpaste onto a corner of a washcloth over the sink, she scrubbed her teeth and tongue until the sweater on her teeth and the chalkiness on her tongue disappeared. She cupped her hands in the running water to rinse out her mouth and wash her face.

She'd have to explain things to Lukas. He'd understand. Probably after a fit of jealousy, which she couldn't blame him for. The situation hadn't been ideal. But this was life or death. The dopamine reaction invoked by being fed upon, the stupid hangups around someone caring for her… He'd understand. He'd have to.

Keep telling yourself that enough times, and it might come true.

Dominic caging her in his arms, his mouth hot on hers, tongues laced together. That noise he made as she kissed him back…

She slumped forward and put her hands on the counter. *Who are you kidding, Blaire? You've betrayed Lukas. He's going to…* She took a shaky breath. Just the thought that Lukas might leave her made panic claw at her throat.

She turned from the sink and surveyed her surroundings, trying to find something else to focus on to keep the panic at bay until Dominic could return. When even the music videos couldn't shake her out of her mental funk, she closed herself into the bathroom. She hadn't been in there long when she heard movement outside the bathroom door. Had it been long enough for Dominic to do his tasks? It hadn't felt like long enough, but she wasn't watching the clock.

Finishing up her business, she opened the door to wash her hands, but froze one step outside the door. Angelo, Tobias, and seven members of Blackthorn Security were searching the room, going through her backpack, the food bags, and the dresser. A twisted smile crossed Angelo's face when their gazes connected.

She darted back inside the bathroom and threw the door closed, locking it as heavy pounding followed her, rattling the door. In the other room, the music increased in volume. She pressed her shoulder against the door and held the handle tightly as someone tried to twist it. Each slam against the door jolted her. But she held tight, wedging her foot against the bathtub for leverage.

The Order had found her.

Where was Dominic?

Had they already caught him?

The wood splintered and cracked where it latched in the door frame before it all stopped. No banging or rattling of the handle. She still didn't trust they'd left, so she held the handle tightly. Locked or not, she didn't trust the cheap door. She held her breath as Angelo's thick Italian accent breeched the door, contempt in his tone.

"Miss Wilcox, please do us all a favor and be the smart girl we know you are and come out. Hiding in a tiny bathroom when we know you are there is foolish. Don't insult our intelligence like this."

"I'm not going back." She was proud of how strong her voice sounded. Her eyes darted around the bathroom, and she cursed the tiny rectangular window at the edge of the ceiling over the back of the shower. It didn't open, and only a toddler would be able to squeeze through it—if they could even reach it.

"Oh, but you are. You are too special to let get away. I hope you understand. You can make this easy and come peacefully, or—"

"You're going to kill me!"

He sighed. "What makes you believe that?"

"I heard it!" Her voice cracked. "You're… I'm not going to let you sacrifice me to some bullshit false god!"

"Oh my, how crass. I didn't know she spoke so vulgarly. I simply don't know what they see in you." She didn't ask who he meant, but he provided the answer anyway. "Those meddling children have been a thorn in our side when you *agreed* to these experiments."

Had her friends tried to intervene? Had Lukas? She wasn't surprised, but what happened to them when they tried?

"I didn't agree to die. You told me you wouldn't kill me."

"Girl," he snarled, dropping the guise of the pleasant leader. "We're not going to kill you."

"What?" Her voice shook and her grip loosened on the handle.

"We wish to perform one last experiment instead of the sacrifice. A ritual. Should you survive, then no harm is done."

"Should I…" Blaire stared at the door in disbelief. They honestly thought she would submit and come with them on the off chance she would survive whatever they planned to do? *Nope. Not happening.* She rubbed sweaty palms on her pants then reinforced her hold on the door. "Find another human experiment. I'm done," she snapped.

"There's none quite like you. So unfortunately, we're stuck with each other." He sniffed and shuffled on the other side of the door. "Looks like you've made your choice."

After a few beats of silence, the door splintered in the middle as a burly security guard barreled his way through the cheap material. The force knocked Blaire back, and she hit her head on the bathtub. It wasn't enough to knock her out, but the pain disoriented her.

She looked up as the meaty arm of the security guard reached through the hole he'd made and unlocked the door. Two guards stepped inside and hoisted her from the floor. The sudden movements didn't help her dizziness.

"She's bleeding," Tobias said from where he stood in front of the TV that still played music videos. The music likely drowned out the commotion, preventing neighboring rooms from hearing what was happening. Besides, if she screamed for help, she risked other humans. It didn't sit well on her conscience.

Angelo looked at Blaire, his nose wrinkling. "And?"

"And if you kill her before you do whatever you're planning, all this becomes a useless endeavor."

Angelo sighed in resignation. "This is why you're my right hand, Tobias." He snapped his fingers. "Gregory, Samuel, get Miss Wilcox a wet washcloth and tend to her wound so we can leave and not have the human's blood all over my newly upholstered leather seats. They cost too much to make a mess of."

Blaire twisted in the grip of the guards holding her. "I'm not going anywhere with you!"

"You are, and you'll keep quiet while doing it. Do not make us use other methods to gain your cooperation."

She stiffened in the guard's hold. Tobias's brows rose at her capitulation. Angelo smirked, like he'd finally obtained her obedience. It wasn't obedience driving her reaction. The flood of memories of the days Vincent kept her in a drug-addled state to keep her compliant assaulted her mind, and she trembled. She couldn't go through that again. So, when a bald guard with a thick copper beard and bushy eyebrows approached and began cleaning the blood from her face, she didn't fight him.

After he finished tending to the wound, a taller guard with thick chestnut brown hair applied a butterfly bandage to her forehead. His eyes glowed a bright malachite, and she tensed, afraid.

Angelo snarled, "Samuel. Step down."

The guard—Samuel—stared at her, growling under his breath, until the bald guard pulled him away. "Sorry about that," the bald one said with a lilting accent. "Sammy here is sensitive to human blood."

"Fuck off, Greg." Samuel jerked out of Gregory's grasp and stalked across the room, leaning on the wall with his arms folded over his broad chest. "Let's get the hell out of here before someone shows up."

Her eyes met Tobias's, and once again, hesitation shone in his aquamarine eyes, but he wouldn't save her, not in direct defiance of Angelo. She glanced over at the foot of her bed where her dirty hoodie lay. Dominic would know she wouldn't leave the room without it for warmth. She promised not to leave the room.

Blaire didn't dare ask where Dominic was, in case they didn't know he'd escaped with her, but with both of them missing from the dungeon, it wasn't hard to connect the two of them together.

She could only hope they hadn't already gotten him, too.

29

Telephone

Halfway into January, the warm front promised by the weather anchor finally settled across Rosebrook Valley, suggesting a possible early spring. The school still had on the heating in the classrooms, and depending on the body count, it got stifling in certain classes. Lukas supposed he could be thankful there were fewer students than usual in his classes of late.

He unbuttoned the sleeves of his uniform shirt and rolled them up his forearms, loosening his tie and undoing the top button. If the professor had a problem with it, they could turn the heat down, but he doubted Professor Montague cared. She was too preoccupied addressing the concerns of the group of parents surrounding her desk to notice he wasn't styled prim and proper.

"I didn't send my child here to be in danger," one parent at the front of the room snapped, adjusting her purse on her shoulder.

The man next to her nodded. "Cora told me that *human* you allowed into the academy got involved with the Order and is causing them all sorts of trouble. What do you intend to do about it?"

Lukas glared at the man, instantly pissed off at how the father said "human" using all the disgust he would show if he found dog feces on the bottom of his shoe. Lukas tapped his pen on the top of his desk as he tuned them out, glancing around at the students conversing around him. Layla's attention was focused on their Literature of Western Europe textbook, and with how her brow was furrowed in concentration, he decided not to disturb her. His attention settled on a conversation to his right between the guy next to him and the two girls behind them, though he moved his eyes back to the book in front of him.

"—she wasn't sick."

The guy scoffed. "I never thought she was sick. They tried to say she had an illness, but she was gone for months! Now where is she?"

"Gone again," one girl behind him confirmed.

The girl next to her lowered her voice. "I heard the Order was involved, and her Korrena attacked an upperclassman."

Lukas tensed. He could feel eyes on him, but he didn't make a move to acknowledge them.

"I heard that too," another guy said from nearby. Lukas didn't dare look to see who it was. "But I heard it was a TA, and he had a secret relationship with the human."

One of the girls said, "She cheated on her Korrena?"

"Sounds like it."

Lukas's grip tightened on his pen to keep from objecting to the guy's words and making a scene. Blaire would never do something like that.

"Her Korrena was jealous?"

"Yup."

Lukas gritted his teeth.

"Where is she now?"

"Jessica told Gabriela that Meghan told her Adam said the human ran away with the TA. They're both missing."

The guy lowered his voice. "Do you think he killed them? I heard some things..."

A couple students who'd also overheard the gossiping turned in their seats to give Lukas wary glances. *Great.*

The guy continued, "He was locked up for it, but I don't know why they let him go free."

Apparently, the students of the academy were playing a game of telephone, and Lukas was losing.

"That's not what I heard," a girl in front of Lukas said, glancing back at him warily. He clenched his fists on his desk. He would not hurt anyone in the classroom, but their judgmental stares—as if they were expecting him to go feral at any moment—set him on edge. The girl's eyes held sympathy. She kept her voice steady as she shifted her attention to the gossiping students. "I heard the TA attacked her. That he was crazy. I don't know where she is now, but I heard he got in trouble with the Order."

All eyes moved to Lukas for confirmation, and he sighed and scrubbed a hand over his face. Either he could end this telephone game, or let them continue with the rumors. Maybe if he said something, they would stop dragging Blaire's name through the mud.

He grated his words through clenched teeth. "Vincent Brandt attacked my pair. Tortured my Korrena for months." He glared at the ones who'd spoken of jealousy and cheating. "I did nothing more than defend her. She never betrayed me."

One girl gasped, and the guy next to him scrunched his face in confusion. "Where is she now, then?"

Lukas swallowed the lump in his throat. "I don't know."

"What? How can you not know?"

"She—you know what? I can't do this." He stood from his seat and the commotion at the front of the classroom stopped. Two sets of parents and his professor settled their attention on him. Layla lifted her head from her book, finally taking note of the situation.

"Him!" The woman with the purse pointed. "That boy is the reason for this. If he hadn't brought that stupid girl into the academy, we wouldn't have to be having this conversation."

Lukas froze, glancing around the classroom as all eyes settled on him. His neck grew hot under his collar at the increased scrutiny.

"Now, Mrs. Robertson. You know as well as I do that we can't control who the gods choose as our Korrena pair."

The parent glared at Lukas. "He could have left the academy with her. Instead, you all allow him to attend classes after being incarcerated for the gods only knows what! He's a threat to the students here!" She looked at a girl sitting in the front row. "Heather, collect your things from your dorm. Until they sort their business here at Blackthorn, I'm not spending another dime for you to attend."

Heather—one of the girls who had bullied Layla previously—rose from her seat and grabbed her books as the other parents called for their children to do the same. Seven students with their parents filed out of the classroom to the sounds of arguing and whispering gossip in the classroom.

One parent remained, standing next to the desk two rows over, glaring at him as her son gathered his things. "Collin, I hope you're not friends with that criminal."

Lukas gritted his teeth and looked away, unable to make his feet move.

"Your future in the Senate depends on staying far away from the degenerates of society. He'll never be anything in our world if he is on Blackthorn's shit list." The woman turned and headed for the door after her rant, her son following her in awkward silence.

Several students looked at Lukas, and his body tensed.

Despite the students of Blackthorn Academy being of adult age, many remained closely linked to their families. Something Lukas never understood. While humans typically separated from their parents around the age of eighteen and moved on into the big world, as far as Lukas believed, Vasirian stayed connected with their parents into their mid-twenties while they attended Blackthorn Academy locations. They paid for tuition, after all.

Lukas stood stock still in the middle of the classroom, willing his feet to carry him out of the middle of the gossiping students.

When another student made a snipe at Blaire's situation, he grabbed his things and rushed from the classroom. He couldn't deal with it anymore. He barely registered Crystal making a snarky remark to Layla about her failing in a relationship with Lukas before it even began.

"Are you okay?" Riley asked, looking up at Lukas as he dropped into his seat at the cafeteria table in the corner near the floor-to-ceiling windows that overlooked the forest.

He sighed long and loud. "Do I even need to ask what you mean?" He didn't think he did. The stares as he made his way through the floors to the cafeteria spoke volumes. Blaire was once again the hot topic of conversation. The fact that some students gave him a wide berth didn't help his mood. He wasn't dangerous.

"They're all talking about it, man." Aiden slipped a straw into a tear in the blood packet he held. "The rumors are ridiculous. Did you know people actually believe you tried to turn Blaire and killed her instead?"

Lukas slumped lower in his chair. He laid his head back, staring at the arcing roof of the modern cafeteria that differed in architectural style from the main floor of the academy's central building. The entire lower floor reminded him more of cathedrals and castles from Europe. It was strange the small things his mind latched onto when searching for distractions from his thoughts. Thoughts that tormented him with the fact he almost *did* kill Blaire when he tried to turn her. If only the students knew how close to the truth they were with that one.

Seth stacked tomato, lettuce, and onion onto his burger. "The TA in one of my creative writing classes was talking with a student and didn't think we could hear, but they said the reason parents are coming into the academy and pulling their kids is because it's gotten around that Blaire and Angelo's daughter got into a fight, and Clarissa got seriously injured. Rumor has it the Order is involved in Blaire's disappearance this time."

"They are," Riley said, snatching a fry from Seth's plate.

He glared at her.

Aiden sighed. "While it's true, they're also speculating they've been involved in whatever happened to Blaire before, and why she's covered in bruises."

Lukas looked at Aiden. "Different story in my class." He didn't elaborate on the twisted rumors the students indulged in, and the parents' nasty opinions. "I sort of set the record straight, but it probably won't matter. Never does with gossip."

"Layla's mom is talking about pulling her from the academy," Riley said.

Aiden set his crumpled blood packet on his tray. "A lot of parents pulled their kids out. They don't want their children caught up in whatever is happening with the Order. The corruption rumor is spreading like wildfire." Sighing, he looked at Riley. "Mom asked if I wanted to come home until it blows over, since she knows we're friends with Blaire, but I told her no."

Riley frowned. "I'm not gonna leave. What if Blaire gets done with the testing and comes back to find us all gone?"

Lukas tried to ignore the covert glances students sent his way as he drank his blood packet. He wasn't going to leave the academy. Blaire needed him here. But did he consider dropping a class or two? The thought crossed his mind a few times, especially given the new rumors surrounding his incarceration and potential danger to the students. But Layla was in most of his classes for their major, and so were her bullies. He didn't feel comfortable leaving her to face them alone. If for no other reason than it gave him something to focus on. Plus, having someone on his side in class who didn't buy into the rumor mill made it a little easier.

"Speaking of…" Seth muttered around a wry smirk.

"Riley, honey!"

Lukas would recognize Aiden and Riley's mother anywhere. A short woman, she had jet black hair cut into a stacked bob style. As usual, her voice preceded her arrival; she was more boisterous than her daughter. She hurried toward their table with her hands outstretched.

Riley stood and hugged her mother, and Lukas almost chuckled. Riley's mother was only five feet tall, so seeing Riley taller than someone was comical.

"Hey, Mama."

Mrs. Easton put her hands on Riley's cheeks and smooshed her face, giving Riley duck lips. "How are you? I've heard so many awful things 'bout what happened with that friend of yours. I'm so sorry, baby."

Riley wiggled out of her mother's grasp and rubbed her cheeks, glaring at Seth as he tried his best to restrain himself from laughing. "I'm fine, Mama. And half the rumors aren't even true." Her voice carried a more pronounced accent than usual. Riley always slipped into a looser dialect when her mother was around. The woman had a heavy accent, and her dialect screamed sassy Georgia peach. Both Aiden and Riley had been born in Atlanta, and Lukas learned early that their parents grew up in rural Georgia.

"Oh, I know. Buncha blabbin' punks. If you say she's a good egg, then I believe it." Mrs. Easton fluffed the stacked layers of her hair that were teased within an inch of their life and turned toward Aiden, her bright blue eyes sparkling with love as she looked down at him. "My boy," she said softly. She pinched his cheek when he didn't get up.

"Hi, Mom."

"No hug?"

Aiden chuckled and put the fry he held down on the tray and stood, pulling his tiny mother into a hug.

"That's better."

They looked like a normal mother and son—passable to humans—with Mrs. Easton appearing only forty-five to fifty years old. The reality was she was well on her way to one hundred and twenty years old. She'd found her Korrena only thirty-seven years ago. It had given both Aiden and Lukas hope that their Korrena pairs were out there, but neither of them relished the idea of going a century before their pair came along. Lukas was glad to no longer be waiting.

Aiden released his mother and grabbed a chair from the table behind him, pulling it over for his mother to sit down.

"Such a sweet boy." She tapped his cheek with her hand, the charm bracelet on her wrist tinkling. "So, tell me," she said as she took her seat. "Do y'all want to come home n' stay with me and your daddy?"

"No!" Riley shouted, and then dropped her gaze as her mother turned wide eyes on her. "I mean, no ma'am. I don't want to leave Blaire."

"Honey…"

"No, Mama, I'm serious. She's gonna need us."

"I know that, baby, but it's dangerous 'round here right now." Her gaze cautiously drifted over to the exit where a few professors had gathered. She lowered her voice. "There's been some talkin' 'bout that dag blame Order gettin' involved in some really nasty things." She snorted derisively. "Never did trust that bunch of ne'er-do-wells."

Mrs. Easton's gaze landed on Lukas, and her features softened. "I bet you're just goin' crazy, ain't ya, sweetheart?"

Lukas shifted uncomfortably in his seat.

"Mom," Aiden hedged, and she shifted her attention to him.

"What? This whole mess stinks like your Aunt Rachel's meatloaf."

Seth huffed a laugh, snagging her scrutiny.

"Seth Emerson," she chastised in her sternest mom voice. "How come you're hidin' there? Come here and give me some sugar."

"Mama!"

"What?"

"Seth doesn't need to kiss you."

"Now, Riley. That boy has been givin' me sugar since he was knee high to a grasshopper."

"He's a grown man." Riley turned her eyes on Seth, and he looked back at her with a shrug.

"I don't mind." He stood and rounded the table, placing a gentle kiss on Mrs. Easton's cheek. "How are you, Mrs. E?"

Normally, Lukas would be under the crosshairs of her kissing and hugging barrage, but she was likely taking pity on him and the situation. Mrs. Easton's love language was touch.

"Better now." She patted Seth's arm as he retreated. "I don't know what's gotten into that girl."

"Probably jealousy," Aiden said with a chuckle, and Riley narrowed her eyes at him.

"Jealous? What you jealous about, baby?"

"Nothing." Riley slumped and sucked blood through her straw.

When Mrs. Easton turned her eyes on Aiden for an answer, Lukas knew what was coming.

"Probably wishes some of that sugar was aimed her way."

Riley spluttered, blood splattering across her tray and the table in front of her. "Aiden!"

And there it is…

Aiden lost it. He put his forehead on the table, bursting into a belly laugh Lukas hadn't heard from him in a long time. Maybe being around his mother calmed his stress.

Riley quickly wiped her mouth and looked between Seth, who sat staring at her with an obvious question on his face, and her mother.

Mrs. Easton's wide eyes glittered. She was an overly emotional woman. "Riley, are you and Seth—"

"No!" Riley objected too quickly as Aiden tried to recover from his laughing fit, but succumbed to another bout of laughing at Riley's protest.

"Oh, honey." Mrs. Easton placed her hand over Riley's. "If you're finally datin' someone, you can tell me. And if it's Seth, then I'm beyond thrilled." She looked over at Seth, who looked like he'd seen a ghost. "You've always been part of this family."

"While I'm happy to be welcomed in the Easton clan, I'm afraid it's true. We're not together." Seth looked down at his phone, his jaw ticking. "If you'll excuse me."

Seth stood quickly from the table, picked up his tray, and turned away from the table, leaving them all staring after him.

"What a shame. He's such a nice boy."

"Mama!"

The entire back and forth with Mrs. Easton helped lift Lukas's mood and shift his attention from the rumors and stares that followed him the rest of the day. Mrs. Easton let him know if things got bad enough, he could come stay with her and Mr. Easton. She understood Lukas was alone.

But as much as she'd tried over the years to play a surrogate mother figure when he came around, it never quite fit for him.

30

Fear

An entire week passed since the hotel incident with no word from the Order or Dominic. An entire week where Blaire stewed in her misery and only interacted with others when Rue—escorted by Blackthorn Security—came to feed her or take her to the lab for daily showers. They hadn't experimented further on her, and made no mention of the supposed experiment Angelo spoke of back at the motel.

The isolation started getting to her, and she missed Dominic's presence, which made her first stint in the dungeons tolerable. Especially with Rue under constant watch. When Marcus was briefly distracted, she slipped Blaire a note that, after reading it later, Blaire flushed down the toilet. The note said her role in the escape remained a secret, but Blaire noticed the guards stayed hypervigilant of every move, and word, Rue said.

If it weren't for Rue's daily visits—even if they couldn't interact much—Blaire would have already gone crazy. Still, she couldn't stand the silence. Putting a pillow over her face, she screamed into the plush material until her lungs burned.

"Cathartic, isn't it?"

Blaire sucked in a startled breath and threw the pillow to the side, sitting up on the bed. Her eyes locked on a pair of inquisitive blue eyes the shade of light aquamarine gemstones.

Tobias.

"*You,*" she breathed. "Tell me what you've done with him!"

"Whatever do you mean?"

Blaire jumped from the bed and approached the front of the cell, grabbing hold of the bars, glaring daggers at Tobias as he stood before her, hands tucked casually in the pockets of pressed black slacks. With the black button-down shirt and black belt with tungsten buckle, he looked prepared for a funeral. Maybe hers.

"Dominic. Where is he?"

He tilted his head, his artfully styled pale strands of hair swaying with the movement. "Isn't that interesting? You didn't seem too concerned about your dungeon mate back at the motel. What changed?"

Perceptive bastard.

Blaire looked off to the side at the floor. "You know him." She took a shallow breath. "I didn't know if security knew he was with me."

"Ah, I see." He scratched his chin. "What gives you that impression?"

"You were in his cell."

"That's the only reason?"

"Yep," she said, popping the p, calling on one of Riley's habits for strength. She turned her attention back to him. She wasn't about to reveal her hand to the enemy.

"If I did know him, why would acknowledging that fact change anything?"

She gripped the bars tightly, her knuckles turning white. "Because you won't hurt him."

"Won't I?"

They stared at one another, neither backing down or admitting their truths. It seemed Tobias would not be someone she could shift to her side. She expected as much, but if she could only find out what happened to Dominic, she'd feel better. Minutes passed before Tobias sighed in surrender.

"You are as stubborn as they say."

Blaire arched an eyebrow expectantly.

"Dom is still out there. We never found him."

Blaire dropped her head forward and exhaled heavily in relief. She didn't miss Tobias's slip-up with Dominic's name. Knowing Dominic was still out there and could get her help, or at least find his own freedom, eased some of the tension knotting the back of her neck.

"What's going to happen to me?"

Tobias stepped over to peer into Dominic's old cell and paced back in front of her, delaying answering her question, much to her frustration. He stopped and looked over at her bed as he spoke. "Angelo lied to you."

"Surprise, surprise."

His intense blue gaze turned on her. "The experiment he wants to perform… it's what you expected. A sacrifice. His words played on a loophole. The ritual doesn't require death, but no human could survive what is required."

"What's required?"

He turned away from her.

"Tell me!"

Tobias sighed and glanced over his shoulder. "I shouldn't even be here."

"Then why are you?"

"I haven't figured that out yet."

With those parting words, he left Blaire standing alone. Her hands slid down the bars as she sank to her knees, reality crashing in on her.

She was going to die.

"Blaire?" Rue ran toward the front of her cell and dropped in front of her, reaching through the bars and grabbing Blaire's arm.

She looked up at Rue with tears in her eyes and whispered, "I don't want to die."

"Oh, Blaire…" Rue squeezed her arm.

Marcus approached Rue from behind, having the decency to look uncomfortable, but not having enough fortitude to set Blaire free. "We have to go."

"Can't you see she's upset?"

"You're not supposed to be down here right now. I'm only letting you come down here because… well, it doesn't matter. Just finish your business and hurry up." He looked toward the end of the hall.

"Fine." Rue let go of Blaire's arm and stood. Her voice softened. "I'll be back later with lunch."

Blaire watched them disappear down the hall and slowly pulled herself up, dragging her feet across the worn stone floor where she collapsed on her bed face down, burying her face in the pillow. The faint scent of coconut teased her senses.

She lay there for what felt like hours before a strange sensation filled her chest. She turned her head on her pillow, too mentally drained to even care to move her body.

For the last week, strange pangs of emotion she didn't recognize as her own bubbled through her awareness. Mostly melancholy feelings, but occasionally, a happy emotion would pass through her. In the silence, the sensation grew to a point where she recognized the flavor. An angry sadness. Something uniquely Lukas. Anger often bled into his sadness, as if he got angry at the idea of allowing himself to hurt. She cracked a smile at the memory of him. But she wasn't happy he felt that way.

Even that little wave of emotion from her Korrena satisfied her need for affection more than the physically intimate moments she shared with Dominic. She took a deep breath and blinked away her blurry vision.

She wasn't sure how she could feel Lukas, but she closed her eyes and let his emotions wash through their empathic link, attempting to push her own emotions to him. She had no idea if such projection was possible. But what else could she do? Lie here and rot? She could at least think of her Korrena hard and hope her feelings reached him. She needed him to know she loved him and missed him, so she focused on those feelings. Focused on feelings of reassurance in an effort to soothe the tendrils of loneliness trickling through their connection.

Unfortunately, she couldn't mask her fear of what was to come; if he could sense what she felt in this moment, he would know she was afraid for her life.

The courtyard buzzed with life as students from different years of their university studies quickly moved about the courtyard, several accompanied by their parents.

Lukas watched another high-end sedan with tinted windows pass along the road between where they sat in the tree grove and the hedge maze on the other side of the road leading to the gates of Blackthorn

Academy. The heavy perfume from the yellow blossoms of cascading winter jasmine wafted down from the side of the road along the edge of the hedge maze.

Riley sighed. "Do you think they'll postpone classes?"

Lukas looked over to where she and Layla sat next to a cluster of shrubs on a blanket beneath a flowering apricot tree with large pink blooms, sorting through an assortment of snacks and drinks. Several petals scattered the blanket and grass around them. If he didn't feel so terrible, he might have appreciated the aesthetic of the scene more, but the tension at the academy had become oppressive.

As the week stretched on, parents pulled more students from the academy, and it felt like a ghost town in their classes.

Seth took a seat next to Riley on the blanket and snatched a packet of sour worm candy from in front of her. "I think the administration needs to make an announcement. We all know they're full of it, but they aren't even trying to address the truth or the spread of misinformation."

"Are they so caught up in this thing with your Korrena that they don't see what's happening?" Layla asked, lines creasing her forehead. "My aunt says she hasn't heard anything, but the staff building is buzzing with the same rumors."

Lukas shook his head. "I don't think they see it as a big deal."

"If they want to pull students, they have to go through administration. They have to be aware of it," Aiden said, leaning against the same tree Lukas rested against.

"Is your mom going to pull you out?" Riley turned to Layla.

She shook her head. "No, but my aunt is keeping a sharp eye on me. I can't leave the academy grounds."

"Seriously?" Seth shook his head in disbelief. "You're old enough to decide for yourself."

Layla sighed and looked at Seth. "You don't understand. I have to follow what my parents want if I want them to support my choice of degree. They didn't want me to be a journalist, but I really like the idea of traveling the world and seeking out all the fascinating new things that are happening with humankind."

Riley asked, "So that's why you're in the Modern Languages and Cultural Studies major with Lukas?"

"Yup! Next year I'll go into a focus on languages and get my concentration route there."

"And none of that happens if you don't follow their rules?" Seth popped a sour worm into his mouth.

"Pretty much." She shrugged lightly. "I don't mind. It's not like they keep me under lock and key. They mostly let me do what I want, but stuff like this? I can't really blame them for interfering, since they don't know the whole situation. The rumors are pretty dark."

"I'm ready for this shit to be over. I want—" Lukas paused as a chill ran down his spine.

"What is it?" Seth said, studying Lukas intently.

Aiden pushed himself off the tree to crouch in front of Lukas. "Hey, man. What just happened?"

Aiden reaching out and touching Lukas's leather jacket snapped him out of the brain fog he'd been in suddenly. He raked a hand through his long hair and took a deep breath, shaking the terrible sensation. "It's nothing. I'm fine."

Aiden's brows pinched, but he didn't question further. When he stood, the same sensation rushed through Lukas again and stole his breath.

Fear. A crippling, all-consuming fear raced through his veins, lighting him up from the inside.

Blaire.

He leapt up from the ground and looked around frantically.

Layla and Riley paused their laughing and conversation, looking up at him, startled. Seth rose to his feet, and Aiden looked around for whatever threat Lukas sensed.

"What's going on?" Riley asked.

"It's Blaire."

"Where?" Riley's voice pitched high as she started looking around, rising on her knees to see over the shrubs. "I don't see her."

"She's not *here* here."

"What?"

"I *feel* her."

Aiden crossed his arms and frowned. "I thought you couldn't feel her out here anymore."

"I haven't been able to feel much for two weeks, and nothing at all for several days at one point. But…" He shivered as the feeling intensified and made the hairs on his arms prickle beneath his clothes. "She's terrified."

"What? What's going on?" Riley stood from the blanket and approached Lukas.

"I don't know. I can't read her thoughts or anything like that. I just feel her fear, and her sadness. Whatever she's afraid of, she's also sad about it. There's this…" He rubbed his brow as he squinted, focusing everything he had on his Korrena. "Acceptance, but she doesn't want it."

"What are they doing to her?"

"I don't know that either, okay?" Lukas snapped.

Riley's hands went up in surrender, and Seth stepped up behind her. "Alright, alright. Calm down."

Lukas tightened his fists and released the tension in them repeatedly in an effort to relax, but the harrowing feelings of anguish and panic banged around in his chest, threatening to pull him under with them.

"We need to—"

Professor Velastra interrupted Aiden's words. "I suspected I would find you all here. I need you to come to my office." She glanced at the administration building. "Immediately."

A dark tendril of trepidation ran down Lukas's spine and settled deep within. His own panic mingled with Blaire's fright, their fears feeding off one another and multiplying inside of him until he could crawl out of his own skin.

Could she feel his anxiety?

The scent of vanilla and jasmine hung thick in the air inside Professor Velastra's office when they entered. Lukas glanced around, and his eyes landed on the small potted plant on the professor's desk with tiny white blooms. He sighed. Blaire was everywhere he went, and he wondered how many small things like this he passed without notice before she came along.

He settled into the black leather chair in front of Professor Velastra's desk, and Riley plopped down into the seat next to him. Aiden took a side chair in front of the bookshelf on the left wall, and Seth casually leaned against the back of Riley's chair, arms over his chest. When Layla entered to take the chair across from Aiden, Professor Velastra paused.

"She knows everything," Riley said, turning in her chair. "She's cool."

Professor Velastra gave a quiet nod and moved around her desk with her usual grace. She adjusted the opal pendant at the end of a long chain she wore, untangling it from the large bow hanging loosely from the collar of her silken crimson blouse like a scarf. Nothing about her body language matched the urgency in her tone out in the tree grove, and Lukas almost snapped at her to get on with it, but refrained. After smoothing her black pencil skirt, she lowered herself into the plush leather chair behind her desk and slid forward, clasping her hands on top of one another as she fixed her gaze on Lukas.

"We have a problem."

Seth rolled his eyes. "What else is new? The question is… What's the problem now?"

Professor Velastra slid her gaze over to Seth briefly before settling back on Lukas. "The Order has changed tactics. One of their hired scientists who conducted research on Blaire's blood came to me to provide a warning."

Riley slid forward in her chair. "Warning?"

"Yes." The professor's gaze hadn't left Lukas, and he started getting the feeling he would not like whatever was about to come out of her mouth. "While they wouldn't tell me why, and what they found, the results, and lack of further developments, have driven Angelo to dark and dangerous paths."

"Just tell us already," Lukas finally snapped, unable to handle the vagueness.

"Angelo has obtained old texts and plans to take Blaire to a long-abandoned temple deep underground below the academy for a ritualistic sacrifice. The last documented use of this location was hundreds of years ago, and nothing good ever happened there. Very little documentation remains, as it is with many of the texts lost from Rosendo Blackthorn's reign. That being said, the purpose of taking Blaire there is grave, indeed."

Lukas stopped breathing.

The muffled words ringing in his ears didn't connect, and he hadn't clearly heard the words the professor spoke after "sacrifice." An eerie stillness settled over him, like sitting at the bottom of a dark lake. Suffocating pressure surrounded him on all sides, and his head throbbed from lack of oxygen. The rushing blood, combined with the pounding of his heart echoing in his ears, didn't sound normal. Everything grew disjointed, and the colors and lighting in the room blurred and fragmented around the edges of his vision like a kaleidoscope. When blackness crept into the edges of the visual auras, a hand on his shoulder startled him out of fully caving into the drowning sensation.

Everyone stared at him with varying degrees of concern, the room eerily silent.

"What do you think?" Professor Velastra finally asked.

"Think about what?" His voice sounded foreign to his own ears.

"Hang on," Aiden said, as he moved around the chair to crouch in front of Lukas. "Talk to me. What's happening?"

Lukas stared down at his best friend; not sure he could formulate words.

"I think he's having a panic attack," Riley said so softly he almost missed it. "I've seen Blaire have them, and she kinda zones out like this too sometimes."

At the mention of Blaire, Lukas bolted up in the chair, snapping out of it, making Aiden stand abruptly to avoid being knocked over. "We have to find her!"

"There he is," Seth said.

"We know where she is," Professor Velastra said. "I had asked if you thought we should wait until they move her to the temple—if we can find the location first—or if we should try to break into the dungeon and rescue her before they make their move. I believe the latter is the best solution, but I wanted all of your input on something like this."

Lukas had heard none of that.

"We need to get her out of there now. I'm not taking the chance they'll start whatever twisted shit they have planned before we can get to her."

"Unfortunately, 'now' isn't going to happen."

"Why the fuck not?"

Professor Velastra sat back in her chair and tapped her slender fingers against the armrest. "She escaped."

"What?" Riley and Aiden asked at the same time. Aiden moved to stand behind Lukas's chair.

Layla's mouth opened in surprise. "She escaped the dungeons? Why didn't she go to her Korrena?"

"I don't know the details, but somehow, she got out of the dungeons and fled the academy through an underground tunnel system I didn't know existed. I don't know how she discovered it, but I've learned it has been there as long as the temple has existed. It leads to a forest outside of Swainsboro."

Layla's face fell, and she lowered her head, murmuring, "She couldn't get to him. How sad."

That explained why Lukas could no longer feel Blaire in the tree grove. Before, it came in small fragments, but for a brief period it had ceased entirely. Was she on the run those few days?

"Swainsboro? That's almost a hundred miles from here! How did she get that far on foot?"

"I don't know. I don't know how long it took or how she survived without water or food. But she did. However, from what intel I've gathered, the next day after her emergence from the tunnel system, Blackthorn Security apprehended her and brought her back to the academy. She's been under heavy surveillance ever since."

"So, if we try to get her now, we'll run into opposition," Aiden surmised.

"Precisely."

"So, what are we supposed to do? Sit around and wait?"

"For the interim." When Lukas glared, Professor Velastra added, "I won't just be sitting and twiddling my thumbs, Lukas. I have further intel to gather. While my source didn't outright say it, I have a suspicion, based on certain things shared with me, that Blaire had assistance in her escape."

Riley's head tilted. "From who?"

"I don't know. I don't even know if it's true. But something seems off. I plan to spend the next few days trying to sort that out. From my understanding, they won't be making a move for another week. They've stopped experimenting with her blood and have left her alone to wait in the dungeons. She's safe there for now."

Like the Oracle said.

Seth shook his head. "What do you want us to do in the meantime?"

"Nothing. Continue with your classes, pretend like you're still waiting on Blaire's return. Take no action to arouse suspicion." She turned her gaze on Lukas. "And stop antagonizing the guards and the Order. I heard about the incident where you tried to get into the administration building. That does not do you any favors."

"Might get me back with Blaire."

Professor Velastra smacked her hand on the desk in a surprisingly bold move. "Or it might get you shipped off to Cresbel Asylum, since you've already been in the dungeons once. Do you want to be half a world away from your Korrena? Think, Lukas. This is bigger than your bond. This is Blaire's life we're now dealing with."

Lukas put his elbow on the arm of the chair, resting his head on his palm as he gripped his hair in his hand in agitation. Professor

Velastra was right. He couldn't argue her point. Even if he fully didn't feel like he deserved Blaire, he still wanted to get to her; but if it was the choice between her life and seeing her sooner, he could be patient. He didn't have to be happy about it.

"I've also made discoveries about your other missing friend," the professor said, pulling him from his thoughts.

What now?

When no one said anything, Professor Velastra motioned with her hand toward the window behind her desk, where they had an unobstructed view of the administration building. "Rueanna Wainwright is the niece of none other than one of the Order's council members, Nathaniel Wainwright. Her father is his younger brother—much younger, in fact."

Riley nodded. "We know."

Professor Velastra arched a finely groomed eyebrow.

"Yep. Liam told us. But they aren't close."

"No, I don't think they are either. In fact, Nathaniel and Rueanna's father have been at odds for many years."

Aiden leaned back against Lukas's chair. "Do you think they have something to do with Rue's disappearance, then? Because of her dad?"

"It couldn't hurt to follow that lead."

"We should tell Liam," Riley said.

Lukas shook his head. "No. We shouldn't."

"Why not?"

"Because if we give him even the smallest thread to indicate where she's at, he's going to charge right into that building and get himself hurt."

Seth chuckled. "You'd know all about that feeling, wouldn't you?"

"Fuck you." He said the words with a laugh, but Seth still seemed to take them more menacing than he intended, raising his hands in surrender.

"Hey, man. I was just joking. Chill out."

"Sorry." Lukas sighed. "I wasn't serious. Yeah, I know the feeling. I feel it now. It's hard not to storm right into the lion's den when you think your Korrena is in there." What he didn't say was that by knowing for sure his Korrena was there, the need was infinitely stronger.

Professor Velastra clapped her hands. "Like I said before, I want you all to proceed as normal." She turned her attention to Lukas. "Stay out of the administration building. In fact, try not to even walk near the place. Security has increased around the building, and seeing you loitering will set off alarm bells. They might relocate Blaire."

Lukas ground his teeth.

Layla asked, "Is there anything we can do to help with getting that information you're looking for?"

"No. I can't reveal my sources and put them at risk. The scientist already placed themselves in grave danger by even giving me the information they did. Should the Order discover I have students investigating them, they'll remove me from Blackthorn Academy and likely banish me to Cresbel Asylum."

"Then you'll be no good to any of us," Seth muttered.

"Correct."

Aiden nodded. "Lying low is for all of our sake, then."

31

Distraction

"Lukas, you can't." Aiden's hand tightened around Lukas's arm.

They stood next to the fountain in the main courtyard, looking up at the large clock face on the administration building. Lukas's body vibrated with the need to get in there. Every time he got near the tree grove this week, Blaire's fear over the twisted delusions of old men who let power go to their heads, and her growing resignation toward the fate they dictated, infuriated him.

Blaire was stronger than that. She had to be strong to put up with his shit.

He huffed a self-deprecating laugh and sat on the edge of the fountain. Pink and yellow petals skittered over the cobblestone in front of him from the flowering apricot trees and winter jasmine lining the courtyard like delicate snow.

Aiden took the space beside him and nudged his shoulder. "We'll get her. We did before. At least we know she's safe for now."

Lukas stared at the front of the main building of the school, his eyes drifting over the red, burgundy, and black stained-glass windows in elegant arches along the front of the building framed by dripping ivy from the rooftop. But counting the tiny lines across the windowpanes didn't provide the distraction he needed.

They met with Professor Velastra three days ago, but heard nothing but radio silence since then.

At the fountain, he was close enough to wherever Blaire was underground to feel her. For reasons he couldn't understand, her feelings reached him solidly again. He didn't know what happened in the last week, but after the connection between them faded for a long time, only to disappear, it came roaring back. Their empathic link almost seemed to reach for each other.

Lukas focused on her more in an effort to let her feel him. To let her know he was here. He hadn't forgotten her, or moved on, like she believed when she'd been with Vincent. Maybe she was attempting to reach out to him too, and that was the key to strengthening their empathic connection again.

"I need to get out of here before I do something I'll regret." He turned to Aiden, who stared at him with that brotherly concern he always carried. Even if Lukas didn't admit it out loud, he needed it now more than ever.

"Alright. Where to?"

Just like that. His best friend was on board with whatever Lukas needed that didn't involve getting thrown in the dungeons or shipped off to a distant land. Though he had to wonder if Aiden wouldn't back him up with that. Riley would probably bring a shovel.

"Fuck if I know." Lukas smirked and rubbed his hands together between his knees.

"Hungry?"

"Not really."

"Want to go to the movies?"

Lukas sat forward and put his elbows on his knees, hanging his head forward with a sigh. "I don't know if I could focus."

Aiden scratched his jawline, and Lukas wondered if the light stubble of black hair was a fashion choice or if he too had been stressed out this week to the point of missing the simple things. Lukas finally shaved his face when the itching became too much. He hated facial hair.

"Want to get drunk?"

Lukas tilted his head as he turned his gaze on Aiden. "Drunk? You?" Not that he was one for getting drunk, either. His best friend was running out of ideas.

Aiden shrugged. "Figured we could go to Haven."

"Veto."

"What? Why?"

"The last time I was there, Blaire and I had a fight. Don't need the memories."

Aiden cursed and speared his fingers through his inky black hair. "I wasn't thinking, man. I'm sorry."

"You know what? I think I am hungry." Lukas stood and rubbed his hands over the front of his thighs, straightening his black jeans. "Sushi?"

"I could go for a California roll."

Lukas snorted. "That's not real sushi."

"Oh, don't act like a sushi purist. Blaire is rubbing off on you with that foodie shit." Aiden grimaced. "Sorry."

Lukas shrugged. "She's everywhere." He cleared his throat, pushing down the emotion that raked its way up his esophagus, threatening to come out in ways he didn't enjoy. "Call Riley and Seth. I think Layla said she had dinner plans with her parents tonight.

I heard her talking to Riley about it."

"Too bad Mera and Kai aren't around. They'd be able to distract you."

"How you figure?"

"Studying."

Lukas rolled his eyes. "No, thank you." He needed distraction, not torture.

Aiden pulled out his cell phone and tapped his screen while Lukas scanned the courtyard. Hardly anyone ventured outside, despite the warmer temperatures as January approached its end. An announcement that morning informed students and staff that despite a modest percentage of the student body being pulled out, they weren't postponing classes. He later learned that with the generous "donations" pumped into the school by the families of those who'd withdrawn temporarily, their precious babies' academic records wouldn't suffer adverse effects from their absence. Bribery was one way to keep the school's bottom line in the black with the outflux of students. The more he learned about the Order, the less Lukas was surprised to learn of under-the-table methods accepted by administration.

The walk from Blackthorn Academy to Sakura Hanami tested his patience. Riley kept asking him questions about Blaire, and he half wished Layla had been able to come to distract her. The warm and friendly girl hadn't fully fit into their circle, but she made pleasant company. At some point, Seth recognized the tension in Lukas and started pestering Riley in only ways Seth could.

Lukas hadn't visited the sushi restaurant Riley suggested on the west side of Valley Center Plaza. The brand new leather seating in the waiting area and pristine decor evidenced the newness of the place.

An indoor koi pond surrounded by dark branching shrubs with white blooms greeted them in the foyer. The babbling fountain churning in the middle of the pond added to the ambiance.

"How are you not freezing?" Aiden asked Riley as they entered the foyer. Despite the warm front, a chill hung in the air, so they all wore jackets except Riley, who wore an oversized black sweater.

Riley shrugged. "I'm used to it."

Lukas didn't know how she could wear her normal style in the winter. The ripped black stockings she paired with a short black skirt couldn't do much for warmth. Maybe her knee-high boots helped, but the rest of her short legs were exposed. Even in his black jeans and leather jacket, the cold sank into his skin.

Divider walls made of paper that Riley called shoji screens accented the different sections of the restaurant they passed as the server took them to their seats. A large tree stood in the middle of the room caged in by the back of several booths. Branches of pink blossoms stretched out along the ceiling over the tables, creating a serene setting.

After the server led them to their table, she asked if anyone had food allergies and took their drink order. Lukas tried to ignore the other table of Blackthorn Academy students who stared at him and whispered.

Riley grabbed a tablet that looked like an iPad from a metal stand on the table. "So, you've never been to a place like this, right?"

"Nope," Seth said while Lukas shook his head.

"Aiden and I went to this one place with Mama when Dad had this work thing in California." She walked around the table to position herself between Lukas and Seth, pointing at the several categories and small photos of various sushi pieces on the screen.

Seth slid his chair over to make room for her, and she paused, leaning over to sniff him.

"Why do you smell like sugar cookies?"

Seth raised a brow. "I don't know."

"I thought it was just Christmas in the air, but since December all I ever smell around you is this sugary vanilla scent."

He lifted the sleeve of his shirt and smelled himself.

She laughed. "You don't stink. I just wondered if you changed body wash or shampoo. I can smell your usual stuff if I'm close enough, but the sweet vanilla is stronger."

"Nope."

Riley looked at him for a moment longer and shrugged, returning her attention to the tablet in her hands.

"So, this is an all-you-can-eat deal, where you pick a category and click on the pictures to select how many of whatever item you want." Riley spent the next several minutes pointing out the various categories and different food options, adding a few things to the cart for herself. Once she finished explaining, she stood from her bent position and returned to her seat on the other side of Seth, smoothing her skirt beneath her before sitting. She punched in the remaining items she wanted and sent her order off to the kitchen before passing the tablet to Aiden.

By the time everyone placed their orders, and the server brought them drinks, another server was bringing the first round of small dishes. Riley received her sashimi, Aiden was handed a small tray with an assortment of maki roll sushi, Seth received a bowl of udon noodle soup and a small plate of steamed dumplings, and Lukas took his plate of chicken cutlet and a few pieces of nigiri sushi.

They spent several minutes eating in silence, the server bringing more delicious dishes to their table, before Riley spoke up.

"Have you talked to your parents?" She brought a tiny bowl of miso soup to her mouth and sipped the broth.

Lukas shook his head. "Nope."

He wasn't getting into the details about his apprehension around that. He'd made a concentrated effort to push away his guilt. Facing his parents would not only expose him their disappointment for failing as a Korrena, but also as a son because he withheld information from them.

Seth pinched a steamed pork dumpling using his chopsticks only to have it spin out of his weak grasp and plop back onto the plate. He cursed, slamming the two pieces of bamboo on the table. "I don't see how you can eat with these."

Riley laughed. "Like this." She made a big show of slowly grabbing one of Seth's dumplings with her chopsticks and holding it up to him to bite. He glared at her the entire time, but he took a bite. Once he finished the dumpling, she set down her chopsticks.

"Here. I'll help."

"I don't need help."

"Oh, stop being a stubborn ass."

"I don't—"

"Okay, you don't *need* help. I'm forcing you to accept my help. You're accepting it under duress."

Seth smirked. "That so?"

"That's so. Now let me show you before I knock you into the next zip code."

Aiden laughed. "I'd pay to see that."

Riley took Seth's chopsticks and positioned his hands. He watched her with furrowed brows, his jaw tightening with each adjustment she made of his hold on the chopsticks and teasing remark out of her mouth.

Lukas took a sip of his water before picking up a piece of salmon nigiri with his fingers, dipping the fish in soy sauce and stuffing the entire piece into his mouth. The rice was warm and soft, melting on his tongue.

Aiden's gaze caught on something. "That waitress is making eyes at you, Seth."

Seth paused and looked up. Sure enough, a petite girl with cropped black hair and big blue eyes stood watching him near the server station.

Riley tensed as the waitress sauntered over and placed a piece of paper in front of Seth. She gave a flirty smile before walking away swaying her hips.

Seth looked down at the paper and crumpled it, putting it on his plate.

"Not pretty enough for you?"

Seth raised his brow at Riley's cutting remark.

"No." He cleared his throat. "She's exactly my type." He turned away, saying nothing else, when Riley asked why he ditched the number if that was the case.

If she couldn't make the connection on her own, then it wasn't good to force the information. Seth wouldn't appreciate it, and Lukas wasn't sure how it would go down.

Seth sighed and looked at her. "Are you gonna finish helping me or not?"

Flushing, Riley resumed her strict education on the way of the chopstick.

Lukas chuckled when Riley slapped Seth's hand and he growled in response.

It had been a good idea to come out. Good food. Good friends. Distractions from torments he'd need to face eventually but couldn't do anything about. He wanted to get to Blaire, but that would be the stupidest thing he could do for her right now.

Riley left Seth to his own devices when he stabbed a dumpling with a single chopstick like a child and took a bite, challenging her with a gimlet eye.

She turned to Lukas. "So, I hate to bring up a sore subject, but I heard something when I was passing the administration building on my way to deliver papers to the staff building."

"How'd you get back there if you were going to the staff building?"

Riley shrugged. "Went the long way around."

Lukas had a feeling she was trying to gather information. "What did you hear?"

Riley tore pieces of her napkin and looked at the table.

"Riley?" Aiden asked, setting down his chopsticks.

She sighed. "There were like seven members of Blackthorn Security standing around at the bottom of the stairs, which isn't normal, right?" When Aiden nodded, she continued. "So, these two men were talking about how they hadn't found the guy Blaire escaped with."

Seth swallowed his dumpling. "So someone did help her escape."

"Yeah, but it sounds like he was also a captive in the dungeons." She looked at Lukas with uncertainty shining in her eyes. "What if he's dangerous?"

Aiden shook his head. "Blaire is back in the dungeons. If whoever this guy was had ill intentions toward her, he would have already hurt her in those tunnels Professor Velastra mentioned."

"True, but..." Riley sighed. "Where is this guy now? If Blaire is back in the dungeon and he's not... Did he set her up?"

"Why help her escape only to set her up to be captured again? That doesn't make any sense."

Riley looked at Seth and tapped her black nails on the table anxiously. "I guess not, I'm just… Something is weird about there being another person down there with her."

"I haven't heard anyone mention the Order having anyone in custody," Aiden said.

Riley pointed her chopsticks at Aiden. "Have you ever heard about the people brought in for trial or transfer to Cresbel, though?"

Aiden rubbed his jaw in thought and shook his head.

"Exactly. He could be a rogue."

Lukas didn't think rogues were a major problem. On rare occasions, a rogue Vasirian who'd succumbed to sanguis manie went mad, needing to be neutralized. Other times, a rogue who didn't like whatever the current leadership ordered, or new rules put in place, would stir things within the Vasirian community to the point the Order needed to intervene.

Was this just another rumor, or had Blaire gotten herself connected with someone who could possibly help her? If they escaped together, and only Blaire got caught, had the man abandoned her? This revelation only revealed more questions and made Lukas's head hurt.

32

Survival

Blue fireflies blinked among the thick brush in front of Blaire as she made her way through the forest. The leafy understory vegetation came to mid-calf. Large toadstool mushrooms and smaller, glowing yellow and blue mushrooms grew in bunches along the path. Glittering stamen in several bushes of flowering plants cast their own light. Tiny orbs of light floated through the air, so small she couldn't discern if they were something magical or actual living creatures. Fluttering insects left their own trails of glowing dust. The various things lighting her way through the forest ensured she would not get lost.

The sun rose high in the sky, but only faint traces of it breached the canopy overhead.

The blue fireflies disappeared through a gap in the trees, and when she stepped through, Ciro sat in a clearing by himself surrounded by dozens of small purple and red flowers. Butterflies of various shades fluttered in pairs over the tiny blooms.

When those intelligent eyes found hers, his tail wagged. She smiled, amused by the response; there was more to Ciro than the average wolf.

"Hey, you." She stopped a few feet away. "The Oracle not joining us this time?"

Ciro pawed the ground, and Blaire pressed her lips together, brow scrunching. She didn't know what that meant.

"Will I get to see the other you this time?"

He pawed the ground again and huffed.

"You don't want to show me?"

He huffed again and whined long and low.

Blaire laughed and shook her head. "We're not going to get anywhere like this." She took a breath. "Okay. One paw for yes, two paws for no. Got it?"

Ciro pawed the grass once.

"Good. Now, will the Oracle be joining us?"

Two paws.

"Will I get to see you—all of you?"

Two paws and a whine.

"You don't want me to see you?"

He pawed the ground twice, roughly.

"No, you do want me to see you, or no, you don't want me to see you?" When Ciro whined, she realized she hadn't asked a yes or no question. She hummed in thought. "Do you think you'll scare me?"

One paw and a whimper.

"I won't be afraid. I promise. Please show me. I want to see who's been there all these years. All of them."

Ciro stood and padded through the grass toward Blaire, circling her and sniffing her legs before whining low again.

"Please trust me. How can I trust you if you won't trust me?"

Ciro growled and nudged her with his nose before darting off into the trees.

She stared after him for so long she worried she might need to chase after him, but rustling in the foliage caught her attention. She sucked in a sharp breath as not a wolf, but a man with pale skin, perhaps in his late thirties, emerged from the forest barefoot, dressed in loose lounge pants and a plain t-shirt that showcased broad shoulders.

The man stood at the edge of the trees watching her, his head downcast, his medium-length brown hair pulled back in a low ponytail at his nape. He looked tall, but she wasn't sure how tall from twenty feet away. He tilted his head up enough to show his eyes, confirming her suspicions. Those bold blue eyes told her the man before her was none other than Ciro, the wolf.

"So, this is what you really look like?"

His eyes widened a fraction, and thinner lips parted on a reply he didn't deliver. She wondered if it surprised him that she wasn't afraid. She didn't see a reason to be afraid of someone essentially inside her head. Yes, the Oracle said this place and Ciro existed, but right now, she could only visit them in her mind. Maybe if they were in the waking world, she'd feel different standing at the heart of a large forest alone with a man she didn't know.

"Wolf got your tongue?" she joked, hoping to get a response.

Ciro's scant breath as he exhaled through his nose—from the crinkles at the corners of his eyes, she took this to mean amusement—came before his words. "All these years, and you still surprise me." His voice was deep, and his cadence smooth.

"*I* surprise *you*? I'm not the one who can shapeshift."

He gave a throaty chuckle. He stepped toward her slowly, watching her intently as if she might bolt at any minute, until he stood a few feet in front of her, the same distance she had stopped before wolf Ciro.

A breeze moved through the clearing from behind him, wafting the aromatic scent of coconut.

She squinted. "It's you."

"What's me?"

"It's always been you, hasn't it? The coconut."

Ciro's head tilted from side to side, studying her, before nodding. "I've been told I smell like that." He sniffed his arm. "I don't smell it." His brows puckered. "Do you hate it?"

"No! It's…" She bit her lower lip, trying to think of how to explain without coming across as a creeper. Sighing, she said, "It's comforting. I have candles with the scent. I've always kept coconut scented things because it calmed me. When I was little, I used to smell it all the time, and I started getting items that reminded me of that smell when I was old enough."

Ciro inclined his head but kept his eyes trained on her.

"Not a man… wolf… of many words, are you?"

"No. And you can call me man. I'm both. My wolf lives within me."

"In you? Like another being?" That reminded her of what Lukas described about the Vasirian part of himself feeling like a separate entity, but he and she both knew that was hyperbole. Was Ciro actually two beings?

"In a sense. The spirit of my wolf is there, but I have the most conscious control in both forms—unless I relinquish control to my wolf."

"Does your wolf have a name?"

"Ciro."

Blaire laughed. "No, I mean, does your wolf have his own name? His spirit."

Ciro looked confused, and he glanced around the clearing before returning those startling blue eyes to her again. "I don't think there is a reason for the spirit to have a name. He doesn't want another name."

"How do you know?"

"He told me."

"Told… you."

"Yes."

"Wait a minute. You can talk with it?"

"Yes."

"And it talks back?"

"Yes, he does."

Blaire groaned and rubbed her eyebrow. "This is wild. I can't even imagine having another being inside of me. Spirit or not."

Though, sometimes the empathic connection felt that way when Lukas's emotions contrasted her own.

"It's all I've ever known."

She dropped her hand and looked up at Ciro. He stood at least a half foot taller than her or more. "You're born this way?"

"Everyone of my kind is born with the spirit of their wolf. Communication becomes easier as we age."

Exhaling a breath, she crossed her arms. "So, why am I here?"

"What?"

"Every time I wake up in this place, there's a reason. A message for me or something."

Ciro crossed his arm over his chest, resting his other elbow on his hand, and balled his fist in front of his mouth, thumb tucked beneath his chin as he contemplated. After a few moments, he dropped his arms. "I remember."

"Remember what?"

"I'm supposed to take you somewhere."

Blaire blinked.

"Come with me."

Blaire followed Ciro back through the forest, back the way she came, until they emerged at the edge of a drop-off. She peered over the edge. Five feet below them lay a crystal-clear pond. Fish with glimmering scales of various colors lit the depths. Golden flecks of something glittered and swirled in the water.

"Why are we here?"

"To help wake you up."

"I don't follow."

Ciro crossed his arms and sighed. "It has been a long time since I have been in this form. I'm finding speaking more difficult than before."

"You should change more often."

A smile crossed his face—the first she'd seen since he changed forms. She could always tell when wolf Ciro smiled. "Perhaps you're right. Something bad is about to happen to you."

Blaire tensed. "I know," she whispered and looked at her feet. "I'm not ready to die."

"I'm not ready to let you die." He touched the top of her head with one hand and left it there. "But I cannot cross to where you are. I can only help your mind through the ordeal. It is going to take what is inside of you to survive. But it is possible."

The more Ciro spoke, the clearer his words and diction became. His insight gave her hope of getting through whatever the Order planned with the sacrificial ritual.

"What do I need to do? I don't know what's inside of me."

"It should have surfaced with time, but time isn't on your side, and I'm not above moving fate's hand."

"Is that why the Oracle isn't here?"

"If the Celestial Conclave punishes me for this, then so be it."

"Punishes you for what?"

He still hadn't told her what hidden ability inside her would help. If an unknown trait or skill would get her through the next part of her journey in this world, she was all ears. Her brows furrowed when he slipped his hand from her head and rested it on the center of her sternum. She looked up at him.

"For this."

He shoved Blaire over the edge of the drop-off into the water below. She didn't have time to take a breath, so she sank like a stone toward the bottom of the pond, fighting the impulse to inhale. The fish, casting soft bioluminescent light in the water, moved around her as if dancing. Golden glitter settled against her skin. The water pressed against her as viscous as syrup; she couldn't right herself to kick for the surface. Before everything went black, Ciro's words echoed in her mind.

"The magic of these waters will resonate with your own. You must wake up. I need you to survive."

Blaire jackknifed up in the bed and took a gasping breath, clutching her chest as she struggled against the invisible water that drowned her. Chuckling at the edge of her awareness brought her crashing back to reality. She slowly turned her head to find Angelo watching her from the front of her cell with an amused smirk on his face.

"Bad dream? I suppose a dungeon will do that."

"What the hell do you want?"

"Must you be vulgar?"

"Normally, I'm not. You're a special case."

Blaire gave Angelo sass, fed up with his holier-than-thou ways.

So, what if she was human? She wasn't beneath him or his stuck-up hellspawn. She had no courtesy to give him.

"I'm flattered." He sighed as if his next words brought him pain. "It is a shame to lose you."

"Yeah, I know what you're going to do."

"Oh, but do you?"

"Kill me, right?"

When he chuckled, she shot him a death glare and turned on her bed, throwing her legs over the side. She needed to go to the bathroom, but she would not go into that small space with him right there. If he came in while she was trapped in that glorified porta-potty, she didn't know who would die first. Her, if he came in to hurt her while she did her business, or him, when she shanked him with the toilet roll holder—if she could rip it from the wall.

"You're special, and you have something I need."

"Oh, lucky me."

Angelo growled low. Blaire's mouth was going to get her into the fire if she didn't stop, but what did she have to lose at this point?

"You know, your little friend wasn't as mouthy as you," he said.

"Huh?"

"Rueanna, Nathaniel's niece." Angelo smiled, pleased to have Blaire's attention. It was obvious he enjoyed having the upper hand. "You should show your appreciation and cease acting so uncultured." His gaze trailed over her arms that only held faint traces of the Order's experimentation. The bruises from her time with Vincent were long gone. "She wasn't as mouthy as you, yet she was the one beaten, and you sit here unmarred."

Blaire rushed to the cell wall and grasped the bars. Her eyes burned, but she wouldn't give the psychopath in front of her the satisfaction of seeing her cry. "What did you do to her?" she shouted.

"Why?"

Angelo adjusted his ruby cuff link on his crisp white button-down. "Because she facilitated your escape." His gaze briefly flicked to the adjoining cell. "And his."

"No, she didn't!"

"Do *not* lie to me!" Angelo shouted, his eyes flashing a brilliant amber.

Blaire staggered back at the rage in his features. He snarled at her, his fangs glistening in the dim light from his saliva.

She hyperventilated, backing all the way to the back wall of the cell to put as much distance between her and the enraged Vasirian in front of her. No Vasirian looked as vicious, and truly terrifying, as Angelo did in that moment. She choked on the air, sliding down the wall to sit on the cold stone floor, wrapping her arms around her shins, pulling her knees to her chest, and jamming one heel against herself to avoid wetting her pants. He growled low at her. She looked away as tears burned a path down her face. If he killed her now, she wouldn't have to be sacrificed.

After she got her breathing under control, she hedged a glance at the madman.

While his fangs remained descended, his features weren't as twisted in fury as before. His eyes were closed. He was obviously trying to get control of himself.

"I… abhor liars, little human." He slowly opened his eyes to look at her huddled on the floor. His eyes still glowed dimly, and a growl underscored the words he spoke. "You would do well to remember that lest you face something worse than death."

Angelo gave her no time for rebuttal, turning away from her and leaving her alone in the cold dungeon.

She clambered to her feet and rushed into the bathroom, having almost lost control of her bladder in her horror. How could a Vasirian scare her so badly when she'd been through so much with Vincent, and seen other Vasirian give in to their beasts? Was that the power of the old Vasirian? She didn't dare question what would have happened had the bars not been between them when she lied to Angelo.

Her stomach sank.

Lukas was out there. She felt him. Doubting him struck her as foolish; he'd come through for her before, but the closer they came toward the sacrifice—she still hadn't been told when it would happen—the more she feared he had no way to save her this time.

She tried to escape before, and that backfired in a blaze of glory.

Surely her friends were searching for an answer. By now, they would know this was more than experiments. Maybe Dominic had reached them.

She hoped when they found her, it wouldn't be too late.

33

Loneliness

Heavy rock music filled his ears from earbuds as Lukas lay on his bed with his eyes closed, hoping to forego more nightmares. Yesterday afternoon in the tree grove, the waning fear from Blaire ramped to a suffocating crescendo. Convinced something happened to her, he called Aiden and Seth, and they had to stop him from charging into the administration building. It wouldn't have been the smartest move, despite every nerve sparking with the need to steamroll the guards and take his Korrena back.

He wasn't an idiot. Blackthorn Security wouldn't let him get past the steps.

The Order knew what they were doing by increasing their guard around the administration building. They'd seen the anger of a tested Korrena pair, and this entire ordeal definitely tested his patience.

Professor Velastra said to wait a week, but a week and a handful of days had passed, and she had nothing new for them. He looked at his phone and sighed. February first. Blaire had been in the Order's grasp for a month and a half. Of course, she escaped for a brief period, but that was a mere blip in time. He didn't want to go months without her again. This time, he knew where she was and still couldn't do anything.

Hard knocking on his door pulled his attention away from his thoughts and the music. He pulled his earbuds out, tapping his phone screen to silence the music, and set them both on his bed. Standing, he straightened his t-shirt and went to the door and pulled it open. His heart dropped to his feet. His mother stood on the other side of the door smiling up at him, her bright green eyes shining.

"Mom?"

"*Poika!*" She stepped forward and put her small hands on his cheeks, looking him over. Her perfectly arched, dark blonde eyebrows furrowed. "You have raccoon eyes. I'm so sorry."

Lukas pulled from his mother's hold. "I'm fine." He didn't know what she had to be sorry about. He stepped back to let her into the room. His father trailed behind her, giving Lukas a nod as he passed, his face schooled and impassive—which wasn't what Lukas was used to seeing the rare times he saw his father. "What are you two doing here?"

Christmas already passed; they hadn't visited him during the holidays this year because his father had some sort of business dealing to attend to. They never gave details, but the same business acquaintance had them cut their trip short the previous Christmas. He was growing used to their absence even more. His jaw ticked.

Lukas tried to focus on the changes in his parents to distract himself from his rioting thoughts. His father's light brown hair had grown longer, slicked back off his face, dusting the collar of his gray button-down. He wore black slacks and onyx cufflinks. He must have come from work. Normally, his father wore casual jeans and a pullover for his visits, or a button-down for nicer occasions.

His mother scanned the dorm room, while his father sat in one of the two desk chairs. When her eyes zeroed in on the framed photograph of Blaire and her mother on the nightstand, Lukas tensed. When she picked it up, and her features softened further as she studied the photo, his heart felt like someone wrapped it in a garrote.

"So, this is our girl." She sighed and shook her head. "She is truly beautiful. Jyrki, look." She stepped beside her husband and extended the photo for him to see.

"Lovely. I hope to meet her one day."

Lukas couldn't move. He didn't even think he could breathe. But the fact he stood there staring at his mother in horror, instead of lying on the floor dead, said he still breathed. When Lukas didn't reply, they both looked up from the framed photograph.

"Lukas?" His father's baritone timbre broke through his internal maelstrom of anxiety and loathing.

Lukas sat down heavily on the edge of his bed, pushing his hair back on his head, gripping the top as he bent his head forward. "She's… gone." He finally said the words. Words he struggled to admit to them, even back when Vincent kidnapped Blaire. He braced for the disappointed looks and reprimands.

His mother placed the photograph back in its spot on the nightstand and moved to stand in front of Lukas. "We know. That is why we're here, *poikani*."

His head snapped up to stare at his parents with wide eyes. Did he hear them correctly?

"Professor Velastra reached out to us a few days ago and told us everything," his father said. "We would have arrived sooner if there were flights available. This morning was the earliest we could land in Atlanta, and the drive here in the rental took longer than expected.

Traffic on the highways near the city…" He shook his head. Eyes a similar pale green to Lukas's connected with his and a half smile hooked his father's mouth. "But we're here."

Lukas's mother sat beside him and brushed a few strands of his hair from his face with her slender fingers. "Why didn't you call?"

Lukas clenched his jaw tight, grinding his molars.

"Lukas?" She tilted her head, and he looked over at her. "Talk to me."

How was he supposed to explain the guilt that ravaged his mind? How was he to tell them he almost killed his Korrena pair when he was meant to protect her? His muscles wound tighter as he prepared for their judgment. He couldn't say with certainty they didn't care, either. With him finally bonding with someone, they seemed more interested in him. He wasn't a disappointment anymore. Wasn't a lost Vasirian. But he couldn't do the most important thing—keep her. In fact, he'd lost Blaire twice now.

Lukas stood abruptly from the bed and paced the room, finally throwing words at them he knew were the wrong ones as soon as he unleashed them. "What do you care?" he snapped. He groaned, stopping, and squeezing his eyes shut as he lay his head back. "That's not what I meant."

"What did you mean, son? We do care."

Lukas whipped his gaze to his father. Anger and sadness fought for dominance beneath the surface, and he didn't know what to do with them. Reasoning he never used to possess kept his instinctive reactions at bay. While it burned within him to lash out and blame them for all the years of loneliness—to blame them for why he felt emotionally stunted—he couldn't do it. It wasn't their fault. They worked hard to ensure he had a future. Blackthorn Academy wasn't cheap.

"Why?" he finally croaked, even that single word sounding broken.

"What do you mean?" His mother wrung her hands in front of her, and she looked ready to get off the bed, but he didn't know why. Did she want to leave already?

Lukas looked away from his mother and sighed. "Why do you care? You've never been here."

His words settled in the room with a heaviness that made him nauseous. He'd always been the quiet son who didn't complain. Never protested when his parents had to leave for the holidays. Never cried when they called the student liaison and informed the school—not him—that they wouldn't be able to visit for a year. Now, with his Korrena gone, he chose to rip off the bandage?

If I'm going to lose everything, may as well do it all at once and avoid prolonging the pain.

Even in his own mind, he couldn't stop lying to himself. He was floundering, grasping for the one lifeline he always wanted.

"What are you talking about? We visit you every year." His father sighed. "I know we don't make every Christmas with my work, but that doesn't mean we don't care about you, son."

Lukas leaned on his desk and crossed his arms. "Do you honestly think a two- or three-day visit once a year where you spend a portion of it on the phone at the hotel is enough?" Since he was a child, he told himself it was enough. Told himself not to complain or he would lose that little time with them. He cherished every moment he could get.

His parents looked at each other with varying degrees of apprehension, a silent communication passing between them as they stared at one another.

"Lukas, my work—"

"I don't even know what you do!"

His father's brows rose to his hairline, his eyes widening at the outburst. "I… you don't know what I do?"

"I don't know what you do for a living, no." Lukas scrubbed at his eye with his fingers until spots of light flashed behind his eyelids. "You've never told me."

"I work in international trade. Specifically, as a cultural advisor."

His mother smiled softly. "Why do you think it thrilled us to hear you are pursuing a degree in linguistics?"

Lukas shook his head. "You never said anything."

"We didn't?"

"No," Lukas said bitterly, not able to look at his mother. "I didn't tell you my concentration." It was probably yet another piece of information they obtained through the student liaison and not through communicating with him.

"Oh, Jyrki. How have we missed so much?"

Jyrki slowly shook his head and raked a hand through his hair. Lukas's eyes tracked the movement. Did he get the habit from his father? Lukas tried to stop the habit after Blaire pointed it out. She joked once about how he'd start losing his hair if he kept pulling on it. He sighed as her face entered his mind. His heart hurt to think of her.

"I'm sorry my work has kept me so busy. The companies that hire me have worked with me for many years and trust me to communicate with those they can't speak with. There are others with my position, but not with the trust I've accumulated."

Lukas bit the inside of his cheek.

His father's reasoning made logical sense, but at the same time, his father prioritized the trust and repertoire he'd built with his company over his own son. Did that make him a spoiled child? He didn't think so, but it didn't stop him from feeling like one. He never made waves with his parents.

Only when the copper taste of his blood hit his tongue did he loosen his bite. It tasted bitter. Bitter, like his feelings.

"That's more than enough," Lukas's mother said with a frown. "Lukas does not need excuses. We have failed him." She swallowed and looked at Lukas. "We never meant to make you feel less important than anything. Have you always felt this way?"

Lukas sighed, putting his hands on the desk on either side of him, gripping tightly. This wasn't even close to how he expected this conversation to go. He never thought he'd pour out fifteen years of bitterness like this, and he expected more disappointment than they gave.

"Helena, I wasn't—" Jyrki paused, and he shook his head. "No, you're right. There is no excuse. I'm sorry, Lukas." His brows knotted. "I wish we had this conversation sooner, so we could have corrected this sooner."

"You don't have to do anything. It's fine."

"No!" Helena said loudly, surprising him. "It is *not* fine. This is why we did not know you suffered so. You must tell us when you feel things like this. Give us the chance to fix it for you."

Lukas's forehead tightened as his brows pulled together, his lips slightly twisted. He fixed things for himself.

"We love you, *poikani*."

"Your mother is right. It's our job to be there for you, but if we don't know—" Jyrki paused again. "No, I suppose we should know." He looked at Helena and sighed. "I'm not good at this."

Helena laughed softly. "It would seem you boys have something in common. Communication is important. But right now, we need to focus on the bigger picture, yes?"

"Yes, my dear, you're right." Jyrki's eyes crinkled as he smiled at his wife. He looked at Lukas. "Your Korrena—"

"About that," Lukas interrupted. *Here goes…* "The bond… it's broken."

"Did you not reclaim her after her rescue?"

Lukas looked at Jyrki and flattened his lips, dragging his lower lip over the top as he released them, the sharp pain distracting him briefly. He took a breath, readying himself. "I messed up. When we…" He waved a hand and his father chuckled. "I tried to kill her."

His mother gasped and covered her mouth.

"Not intentionally!" He held a hand out to stop his parents from saying anything. "But I had this thing riding me. Pushing me to turn her. Telling me she was fragile, so if she would become like us, she'd be safe. I didn't stop fast enough when I drank from her. She almost died." Lukas released a long breath as he laid everything out at their feet. He awaited their judgment.

Jyrki smirked, and Lukas blinked. That was not the response he expected, and it stunned him so much he didn't react.

"Well, that isn't surprising." Jyrki cleared his throat and schooled his expression. "I'm not laughing at you or what happened. Believe me, I know this is a serious situation; however, I was waiting on this."

"Waiting on me to almost kill my Korrena?" Lukas asked incredulously, his voice rising.

"Waiting on you to stake your claim."

"She's not an object to claim." Blaire and his friends drilled this into his head constantly because of his possessive behavior.

"You're correct. But, Lukas,"—Jyrki stood and pushed his index finger and middle finger in the center of Lukas's chest—"this in here? It wants to own her. It doesn't care you're in love with her, or what her feelings are."

Lukas looked up at his father with wide eyes. He couldn't believe what he was hearing. This wasn't what they taught in Blackthorn growing up.

"If you don't get control of it, it will destroy both of you."

"What are you saying? I didn't think there was another part of me—we're not two parts, right?"

"That's correct. But when a Vasirian is newly discovering their bond with their Korrena, everything is different. Something chemically changes inside, and it feels like a split personality. I sometimes wonder if it isn't. Something we must tame in order not to lose what the gods have blessed us with." He sighed. "The younger you are, the worse it is. And the fact that your Korrena is a human?" He shook his head. "You're facing a triple threat."

When his father stepped back, Helena patted the bed for Lukas to join her. He sat next to her, and she put her hand on top of his. "Your father is missing an important detail." She squeezed his hand. "The part of yourself you must tame is a dominant part of your actual personality." Her eyes moved to Jyrki. "He forgets all Vasirian are possessive, but they can be reasoned with."

Jyrki raised an eyebrow. "Well, of course."

"What he does not acknowledge is you two are similar. He had to conquer a stronger need to possess as well. Jyrki's grandfather passed away when Jyrki was a baby, and his grandmother struggled to express her love after losing her Korrena. Jyrki was so afraid of losing me that he acted like a heathen."

Jyrki scoffed. "Was I that bad? You know what, don't answer that. I remember."

Helena laughed and turned her attention back to Lukas. "I think this disconnect you have had with us created a hole the most primal part of yourself is desperate to protect and heal."

Lukas ran his hands over his face and collapsed back on the bed, hands dragging over his mouth as he looked up at the ceiling. The entire problem fell back on something he could have prevented? If he only told his parents how he felt? Things weren't that simple. He couldn't have known they cared more than he thought. They couldn't have expected a child to just ask, right?

The root of a Vasirian in a Korrena bond was strong possessiveness, and even stronger love. But if the Vasirian's dominant personality influenced how they developed a bond with a Korrena, did that mean he could overcome it simply by changing himself? He thought he had done that.

Not enough. Never enough.

"Son, you shouldn't blame yourself for this. How did your Korrena feel about what happened?"

Lukas rolled his head to the side to look at his father. "She said she didn't trust me."

His mother grimaced and shook her head. "She does not trust you? From what I heard from Professor Velastra, she put on quite the show at that awful man's trial, and she is currently sitting in a dungeon because she traded herself for you. I would say trust and love reign strongly in that girl's heart."

"I just… I feel so guilty."

Helena asked gently, "Why?"

He closed his eyes. "Because I did the one thing she feared the most. The one thing I promised her I could do for her above all else. I let her down." His eyes burned behind his eyelids, and he pushed down the emotion bubbling up in his chest.

"Trying to turn her?"

Lukas looked at his father. "No. Stopping. She was afraid of dying. Afraid I couldn't stop. She says she's fine, but… I can't forgive myself for that betrayal of her trust."

"Then you are being a foolish boy, *poika*."

His eyebrows slammed down at his mother's words. "What?"

"That girl gave herself for you. Do you think she would do that for another?"

"No."

"Do you think if she did not trust you, she would have bailed you out of the dungeons at the expense of herself?"

"No."

"Then get your head out of the sand. You made a mistake, and she forgives you."

Jyrki nudged Lukas's leg with his knee, and Lukas looked up at him. "The best thing you can do to honor and respect the trust given to you is get out of this pit of self-pity and angst and save your Korrena. I still want to meet her, after all."

"I don't know how." Lukas covered his face again.

"That is why we have come. We want to meet with Professor Velastra and help. This has gone on long enough."

34

Consequences

Lukas trailed his parents through the courtyard as the sun set, casting the skies in beautiful shades of rich orange and red. They made their way to the side of the administration building where several high-class sedans used for guests of Blackthorn Academy were parked. Other students stared and whispered when they left the dorms. It was impossible to ignore the way students avoided him. When they climbed in the car, and he got into the backseat, he could finally breathe normally.

His mother shrugged off her coat, adjusting the collar of her emerald blouse, and looked back at him. "We will talk about it at dinner."

"What's there to talk about?"

"Son," his father said, looking in the rearview mirror. "We know some of these kids look at you like—"

"Like I killed my pair?"

"*Poika.*"

"No, Mom. That's what they're saying. They're saying I killed Blaire. They're saying a whole lot of other shit, too." Lukas put his head back on the seat and shut his eyes. "Let's just get out of here. Please."

Jyrki reversed the car, and when they finally passed through the iron gates of Blackthorn Academy, heading into the Valley, he finally spoke. "We know the rumors, Lukas. People will talk. They'll always have something to say about things they don't understand. The secret is to learn what ends to nip in the bud, and what gossip to let roll away like water off a duck's back."

The car turned onto the highway, heading toward Savannah as twilight fell.

"Okay, so which ones are worth doing something about? I've tried to set the record straight, but more rumors circulate, and the story keeps changing. I wanted to drop out of class, but—"

"Absolutely not." His mother looked back at him with a sharp frown. "Dropping out will do more harm than good."

"I know." Lukas's head rolled to the side, and he stared at the cars on the highway. "Where are we going? Why'd I have to dress like this?" His parents asked him to wear slacks and a button-down dress shirt. His mother requested a tie as well, but he couldn't bring himself to go that far.

"Your father has reservations in Savannah for dinner for the three of us. More importantly, you need to understand something." She reached across the console, and Jyrki took her hand.

He squeezed her hand and said, "Your Korrena needs you to be strong. If you run away, you make yourself look guilty, and she will bear the brunt of the rumors when she returns."

Blaire wasn't the only one who needed him. He didn't want to leave Layla to deal with her bullies alone. Now that they had additional ammunition to levy against her about him, he was sure their taunting would escalate.

They continued to drive in silence for a short time before the lights of Savannah came into view. The streets turned to cobblestone, and they drove along the Savannah River. When they pulled up in front of a warehouse on the river and a valet approached, they exited the car, and his father passed the keys to the waiting young woman. Inside, they were led to the back of the restaurant to a table in front of a window with a clear view of the Savannah River and the Georgia Queen, the famous riverboat docked and waiting for the next load of tourists. Its bright lights glittered on the rippling waters.

"Hungry?"

Lukas shrugged. "Haven't had a huge appetite in a long time."

"Not surprised. But, son, we're going to take care of this. Tonight, I want you to relax and enjoy your dinner with us now that we've had a breakthrough of sorts." His father's casual smile relaxed him.

After ordering water to drink, he opened his menu, looking over his options as his parents ordered their meals and drinks. He still wasn't sure about eating too much. Anxiety kept his stomach in knots, and indigestion wasn't a welcome thought. Finally ordering the pan-seared salmon with parmesan risotto and grilled asparagus, he turned to his mother.

"Mom."

Helena handed their menus to the server and looked at Lukas. "What is it, *poikani*?"

"I know Dad said he wanted to relax and have dinner, but"—he tugged at the collar of his dress shirt—"it's hard, you know?"

Bringing up his insecurities with his parents wasn't something he thought he'd ever do. But if he didn't at least try to meet them halfway, they never would be able to prove themselves like they asked for the chance to do.

"I miss Blaire. I remember when she came… I didn't want her at the academy. I didn't want a human Korrena. But then I got to know her. I got to experience her fierce loyalty to her friends, her understanding, her quirks, and mannerisms that make me happy to be able to wake up with her." He sighed. "At least what little time I've had with her in the last several months. She's been through hell, and she had to convince me things would be okay. She's stronger than me. I underestimated her because of her humanity, and I don't want to do that again. I want to be her support, not the weight that drags her down." He looked at his father. "I've screwed up, and now I'm worried about being the man she needs when this is all over."

Jyrki set his wineglass down and loosened his tie. "What happened between you two when you felt that need to turn her—"

"No, Dad. That's not what I mean."

"Then what?"

"I overheard something I haven't been able to get out of my head." He cleared his throat, leaning in and lowering his voice. "Being locked up… What does this mean for the future? This isn't like human jail." His jaw worked. "The Order runs everything in our world. How am I ever going to get a job? How will I hide my age in the future if I can't get cooperation from our kind? How can I take care of Blaire if no one trusts me because I have it on my record that the Order had me locked up?"

Helena looked down at the tiny plate in front of her where a lone bread roll sat untouched.

"I've been thinking about it." Jyrki reached over and put his hand on Helena's on the table. "*We've* been talking about it."

Lukas looked up at his parents.

"Your father and I plan to go to Europe after we handle things with Professor Velastra to try to clear your name with the Blackthorn Clan."

His eyebrows knotted. "How? Don't you have to go through the Order before you can get an audience with the monarchy?"

"Usually. But your father's connections with his work allows him access to people in a direct line with the king's security. He has called in a few favors, and we believe we can get your charges expunged from your record."

"Why? On what grounds?"

"You didn't get a fair trial."

"Actually, Jyrki, he did not get a trial at all."

The server approached and set their meals in front of them. Lukas didn't know what to say. The Order had security take him away and lock him up with no trial or defense. Vincent received better treatment than him, and he was a verified monster who kidnapped and tortured a human—his Korrena. A growl rumbled in his chest, and he pushed it down before diners nearby could hear.

Jyrki spooned cream sauce over his chicken as he continued his explanation. "Helena is correct. It can't be considered a gross miscarriage of justice because you weren't tried." He cut into the meat and took a bite.

"You are also a student," his mother started.

"I'm not a minor, though."

His father set his fork down. "No, but you're a student still learning of a new Korrena bond—even though they do not teach of the bond in university. That means something. The pressure that comes with exams, papers, school life. Coupled with being late in life finding your pair, and acclimating to that while under that pressure, has to account for something. Especially when that pair is a human—something not understood by our kind."

It surprised Lukas to know his parents thought that far ahead. That his parents thought of him at all meant the world to him. Just how much had they done for him over the years that he didn't know about? Had he been so wrong about them?

"Do not stress it, *poikani*. Let us take care of you so you may take care of your pair when she comes home to you. Now, eat your fish before it grows cold. Fish tastes terrible cold."

The conversation turned casual as they finished dinner together, followed by a short walk along the river. It was too cold to stay outside long, so they wrapped up their night, and before he knew it, Lukas was back in his empty dorm surrounded by things that reminded him of Blaire. Only this time, he didn't feel the crushing weight of loneliness and pain that accompanied the empty space.

Something shifted since his parents arrived, and he wasn't sure what it was. So many things about his perception of life changed with their presence. He felt cared about by more than his small circle of friends. Protected. Things he'd never experienced before. He wasn't alone anymore. Not only did he have his parents in his life again, but when Blaire came home, his family would be whole.

Because that's who she was. Family.

If his parents could get him out of his legal trouble without trial, he would have the opportunity to protect Blaire and provide a future for her. No matter how short it might be.

35

PROTECTION

When Lukas walked into Professor Velastra's office with his parents the next evening, Aiden sat up in his seat with brows raised. Lukas shook his head and sat across from him on one of the new leather chairs in front of the bookshelves. He would explain things to his best friend later. After his parents left for their hotel last night, he didn't have the energy to reach out to any of his friends and explain the revelations.

The information his parents provided—from dominant personalities, to his guilt, and even their own relationship with him—set his entire world on its axis.

Riley stood from the chair in front of Professor Velastra's desk. "You can sit here, Mrs. Virtanen."

"Sweet Riley. Such a beautiful child." Helena smiled and touched Riley's cheek. "I have always loved your pretty pink hair. But call me Helena."

"Yes, ma'am."

"Aiden, it has been too long. You look more handsome than last I saw you. You are growing wonderfully."

Aiden chuckled and gave a small shake of his head. "I don't think I look too different from a couple years ago, but thank you, Helena." They didn't age that quickly. The only difference between then and now was the light stubble on Aiden's face.

Seth shook Jyrki's hand and turned to Helena. "Mrs. Vir—" He cut himself off when Lukas's mother raised her dark blonde eyebrow in challenge. He cleared his throat. "Helena."

"Seth. You look handsome. What is this?" Her gaze trailed over Seth's exposed forearms, his uniform sleeves rolled up. "Tattoos?" She looked up into his eyes.

"Yeah, I've got a few." He shrugged. "How are you?"

Lukas flattened his lips to keep from commenting. "A few" was an understatement. Seth's tattoos covered one arm, a few places on his torso, and he'd started his sleeve on the other arm around Christmas when they thought Blaire wasn't in trouble.

"I have been better. This week has been stressful." She glanced at Lukas with a smile. "But we are repairing."

"Let's get this taken care of, dear." Jyrki put a hand on Helena's elbow, guiding her to the empty chairs in front of Professor Velastra's desk.

Helena took the seat Riley offered. Jyrki took the one on her other side. Riley stood beside Seth against the bookshelves behind Aiden.

"So, tell me Professor Velastra," Jyrki said, resting his hands on each arm of the chair, leveling a stern gaze at her. "You informed us on the phone that our son's Korrena is currently in captivity. This is still the situation?"

Professor Velastra inclined her head once, but before she could speak, Jyrki spoke again.

"And am I to understand this is the second time in less than six months you've allowed this to happen on academy grounds?"

"Circumstances—"

"And am I to also understand that in response to my son defending his Korrena, he was locked away from her, and she had to trade herself for his freedom?"

Professor Velastra didn't respond, allowing Lukas's father to speak his piece. Lukas didn't know his father had this protective side to him, but everyone had fallen silent at his commanding tone. His mother shifted in her chair and her facial features pinched in echo. Whatever his father felt in that moment, his mother likely felt through their empathic link.

"Do you not screen students before you put them in authoritative positions? In what world did you find it appropriate to allow a human girl to offer herself for experimentation to a group who has allegedly been behind several attacks on her? I want to know what kind of academy we're paying for our son to attend."

Professor Velastra sat up straighter, her body tight.

Helena folded her hands on her lap, took a breath through her nose slowly, then looked at her husband. "Jyrki. Enough." The words came out calm and low, but Jyrki snapped his gaze to hers, and his body deflated on a sigh. Lukas wondered if they were responding to each other on an emotional level.

Professor Velastra smoothed her hands over the front of her dark green chiffon blouse, tugging at the hem of her black pencil skirt. "Mr. Virtanen, I can assure you the decision Blaire made to trade herself for experimentation was purely her own."

"And you *allowed*—"

"Jyrki."

He huffed, a hand going into his hair, and Lukas bit back a laugh at his father's reaction. Was this his future?

"If you knew Blaire the way we all do"—Professor Velastra waved a hand toward Lukas, Seth, Riley, and Aiden—"you would understand if Blaire wants to do something, no one will stop her. She is… stubborn, to put it lightly. Furthermore, if I had known this would lead to what it has, I would never have 'allowed' it, even if it brought on negative consequences."

"We know you have done the best you could," Helena said calmly. "Please understand our son is in peril, and his Korrena is in danger. We want nothing more than to rectify this situation."

"Yes, I'm aware. This is my desire as well. To answer your question about our TA acceptance protocol…" Professor Velastra sighed. "Until now, we have had no such screening process beyond educational merits and qualifications. Never have we needed to consider a personality screening. Going forward, I plan to propose a screening system through our Psychology department before we promote students into these roles."

Jyrki nodded. "It would go a long way to ease the minds of parents."

"As for the rest? Mr. and Mrs. Virtanen, while we knew the Order was not acting appropriately, never did I think they would stoop to the level of human sacrifice."

Lukas tensed.

"Human sacrifice?" Jyrki shouted, leaping to his feet.

Helena spun in her chair, her eyes meeting Lukas's. Whatever she saw there made her face crumple from shock to despair. Her eyes filled with tears, and Lukas's knee bobbed rapidly as his anxiety spiked.

"Wait. You don't know?" Aiden asked, and Jyrki twisted to face him.

"Know what?" He looked back at the professor. "What information have you kept from us?"

Professor Velastra sighed. “Mr. Virtanen, please sit down.” When he sat, appearing calm, but his body rigid, the professor continued. “I wanted you both to be here to hear this in person. This information I do not wish to be leaked, and I don’t trust the lines of communication. The Order doesn’t know I have obtained information about their intentions with Blaire, so we have the element of surprise.”

“We are here now. Tell us.”

Lukas didn’t know how his mother could sound so calm when the walls were closing in. Riley stepped around the chairs to sit on the arm of Lukas’s chair. She leaned against his shoulder, putting her weight against him. When his shaking abated from her nearness, he finally understood why she did that.

“I have already informed your son and his friends that after Blaire escaped the dungeon after the experimentation wrapped up and they failed to release her—which I have now confirmed was in response to the threat on her life—they have increased security. We can’t get to her.”

“But what is this about a sacrifice?”

“Mrs. Virtanen, the corruption with the Order, and Angelo Moretti, runs deeper than I imagined. I don’t know all the details, despite my attempts to obtain information. My efforts to reach the Blackthorn Clan came with the threat of banishment.” She took a scant breath through her nose. “Angelo has taken tomes from our archives and plans to take Blaire into the abandoned temple beneath our school for a ritualistic sacrifice.”

Seth held his fist tight in front of his mouth, one arm crossed over his chest. Aiden sat on the edge of his chair, elbows on his knees. Both appeared tense. They wanted to go to the administration building as badly as Lukas did, but they couldn’t.

Jyrki tapped his fingers on the armrest. “What kind of ritual?

The last ritual—the only ritual—I know of, is the blood ritual that stole my son's bond from him."

"The only information I discovered since I gained this knowledge, is the ritual is related to magic and the gods."

Helena's brows pulled together, and her lips parted for a moment before she spoke. "Magic? Why is fiction in the archives? What does this have to do with what they plan to do with my son's pair?"

"I can fill in the blanks here, Professor."

Everyone turned their attention to the Oracle standing in the open doorway, her hands clasped in front of her. She wore a simple, hooded black robe with no baubles or markers to expose her identity if she pulled her hood up. Her hair was pulled into a tight, sleek bun at the nape of her neck.

Professor Velastra stood abruptly from her chair and straightened her skirt. "Oracle."

The Oracle smiled warmly, casting her gaze around the room.

"We have much to discuss. Truths to reveal. But it is not safe here." When Jyrki opened his mouth to speak, she raised her hand. "Come."

The main building at this time of night was void of life outside of their small group, and the occasional security guard on patrol they avoided. Most of Blackthorn Security had congregated around the administration building.

Lukas rolled his eyes when Riley observed, "This is creepy," as they descended the narrow, spiraling stone steps the Oracle revealed behind bookshelves in the far back corner of the main building's library.

Considering few people accessed the geographical section, it wouldn't be easy to find the hidden chamber. Further, it required pulling several books out in a specific order to activate the sliding mechanism to get the shelves to move.

They had their phones out, using their flashlights to guide their way. Metal torch holders along the walls held unlit torches, but they had no access to fire.

The Oracle led the way. Professor Velastra and Lukas's parents followed close behind. Riley and Seth followed next, and Lukas and Aiden took up the rear to keep watch for anyone who might follow.

Riley squealed and ducked, losing her footing, but Seth caught her, pulling her up against him from behind. She put a hand over her chest, puffing heavy breaths. She aimed her phone's flashlight at the broken webbing dangling in front of them. Seth swiped the offending, dust-covered cobwebs out of the way and released her. "After you," he said with a chuckle.

Riley pulled away from Seth and started down the stairs again.

The temperature dropped at the bottom of the stairs, and the musty smell of old books suffused the air. The Oracle clicked a wall switch. Hand-wrought iron chandeliers hanging from the ceiling illuminated the entire room. The French Gothic chandeliers carried four top spiral finials on a hollow center structure. Whoever did the maintenance on the archival room updated the chandeliers with porcelain sockets and faux candles that flickered with an amber glow, modernizing them instead of utilizing wax candles. The amber glow wasn't as bright as modern lighting, but they placed enough chandeliers around the room to cast enough light to see.

The Oracle led them through an arching hallway between rows of dark oak bookshelves covered in dust. Cobwebs filled the corners of the bookshelves and they hung from the carved, scrolling designs Lukas couldn't see clearly in the low lighting.

Dark burgundy carpet with a black filigree border along the edges ran down the hallway beneath their feet, surprisingly clean despite the condition of the bookshelves. The dark hardwood down each aisle of the bookshelves shined beneath the amber light from fresh polish. Had maintenance not gotten to the shelves, or were the old books too fragile to touch to maintain the shelves as easily as the rest of the room?

Approaching the end of the hallway, the Oracle stopped. She motioned for Jyrki to open the plain dark oak door in front of them. The only decorative feature was the rectangular brass escutcheon carved with floral swirls in relief and the ornate doorknob with a medallion symbol in the center. The door was easily overlooked in a room containing so many beautiful antique accents.

Jyrki twisted the handle and pulled the door open, allowing the Oracle, Professor Velastra, and Helena to pass in front of him. Riley and Seth followed. Before Lukas could approach, Aiden put a hand on his shoulder.

"Is everything alright with your parents?"

While Lukas wanted to go inside, Aiden would worry if he didn't explain. He looked at his father waiting at the door. "Go inside. We'll be just a sec."

Jyrki nodded and stepped into the room, closing the door.

Lukas flashed a quick smile. "I didn't know they were coming."

"Who called them?"

"Professor Velastra."

Aiden looked at the door. "Why?"

Lukas shrugged. "I haven't asked her. I should have called them already, but I couldn't bring myself to do it. I'm glad she did."

Aiden turned to look at him. "You're glad?" He scratched the stubble on his cheek. "Huh."

"What?"

"You always seem so unhappy whenever they come around—*if* they come around."

Sighing, Lukas shook his head. "Because I wanted them here, but it felt like they weren't. You've had it lucky. Your mom and dad smother you both with attention, but my parents, and my dad's business…" He shrugged. "You know how it is."

Aiden hummed in confirmation.

"But I've had it all wrong." He huffed a laugh that held no humor and looked down at his boots. "They had no idea how I felt. No idea how lonely I felt."

"I could have told them that."

Lukas looked up at Aiden, meeting his eyes.

"It's not obvious to everyone, but you're my best friend," Aiden said. "I've known you since you were five. Blaire might be your Korrena, but I can read you, too." He lightly punched Lukas's arm. "I tried to be there. Tried to pull you into my family, but nothing beats the real thing, I know." He took a deep breath. "So, you were able to sort things out?"

"Yeah, I think things might be different going forward."

"Good. You deserve happiness, man."

Lukas was grateful Aiden didn't push further for information about what transpired with Lukas's parents. He protected Lukas without being overbearing. One thing that made their friendship so strong, is they both knew when to push the other, and when to back off.

Aiden looked at the door where everyone waited on the other side. "Come on. Let's get the rest of your happiness back."

36

Searching the Past

Silence settled as Lukas and Aiden stepped inside a large room with a table in the center. An empty fireplace took up a considerable amount of one wall and a large mirror bordered in gilded floral scrollwork hung above it. Antique vases, and stone figurines of dragons, wolves, and other fantastical creatures, lined the mantle alongside candles of various heights in brass holders.

The other walls displayed paintings of dragons in flight, wolf packs in the forest, and fields of flowers, all in similar framing to the mirror. A large Persian area rug took up most of the space beneath their feet in shades of green, accented in black and gold. Overhead, a chandelier like the ones in the archival room cast a soft light over the space.

Candles in hurricane globes cast rings of amber light on the polished wooden table. Riley and Seth sat on the right side of the table on a green, diamond-tufted leather sofa, while Professor Velastra sat in a plush armchair with the same diamond-tufting in front of the door on one end of the table. Jyrki and Helena sat on a larger sofa of similar design across from Seth and Riley, and the Oracle stood across from the armchair. A side table holding a small candelabra sat against the wall beneath a large dragon painting behind her.

Lukas stood behind Professor Velastra, arms crossed tightly over his chest, too restless to sit. Aiden moved to his side in silent support.

Jyrki was the first to speak. "Tell me why we're to trust this woman who is associated with the Order?" He looked at the Oracle. "I understand you are my elder, but you will have to forgive my mistrust, all things considered."

The Oracle inclined her head and offered a warm smile despite the situation. "Your unease is warranted, but I assure you, I am for the betterment of our kind, and I believe the choices the Order has made will not bring prosperity to Vasirian on a grand scale."

"You expect us to believe your words with no proof?"

The Oracle looked at Helena, but Professor Velastra spoke before she responded. "Mrs. Virtanen, the Oracle has guided our students through the trials they have faced since Blaire came along. Albeit, in obscure and often frustrating methods we realize are to circumvent altering our future."

Jyrki arched a brow and looked at Lukas.

He shrugged. "She's helped. Honestly, it's the only reason I'm not in Cresbel now. If I didn't know Blaire was safe in the dungeon, I'd have already broken in."

"Relatively, safe," Riley amended. "Experimentation can't be danger-free for someone like Blaire, right?"

The Oracle nodded. "Her inability to heal like we do, and her unique medical condition, makes it difficult to avoid all pain. That said, what could have happened if she were free, and they forced themselves upon her like they did before? It would likely have brought her death."

"She's at risk of death now!" Jyrki slapped his hand on the arm of the sofa.

Watching his father—hearing him say words Lukas restrained himself from also shouting—gave the impression they were more alike than he knew.

Helena placed her hand over her husband's clenched fist at his side.

"This much is true. I have tried to guide her. Prepare her. But there is only so much I can reveal without disrupting the fragile balance gradually mending."

Lukas stepped forward, his arms falling to his sides. "You've seen her?"

"Not on this plane of existence."

"What does that even mean?" he snapped. His patience with the way the Oracle communicated wasn't strong to start with, but considering the love of his life dangled in the balance between life and death, he had zero patience for cryptic phrasing.

The Oracle hooked her fingers together in front of her, looking down at her hands. "In her dreams, I have maintained an infrequent connection with her. In that place between sleep and wakefulness, I try to give her what I can to see her through her trials, but more trials are to come."

Lukas recalled the dream Blaire told him about. The deer with the large rack, and the woman with the visage of her mother.

"She is alright?" Professor Velastra asked.

"As much as one can be in her situation."

"Why are we here? Why go through all the effort to bring us to a secret archive I wasn't even aware existed, only to take us to a room like this?"

The Oracle met Professor Velastra's stoic gaze. "Because what I am to reveal to you this night cannot reach a living soul beyond these walls, or the consequences could be dire. Do not trust your conversations to be private on Blackthorn Academy grounds outside of this room. The walls themselves have eyes and ears not normally seen."

As she let those ominous words settle over the room's occupants, Lukas's mind rioted with all the potential meaning behind what she didn't say. There was always more to the statements she made. What consequences? Maybe this time there wasn't a hidden meaning.

"The school is bugged?" Seth asked incredulously. "That's an invasion of our privacy."

Riley looked at Seth. "Do you really think they care? I mean, after everything they've done, administration isn't exactly known for fair play."

"Kai once mentioned in passing he thought he saw a camera near the study cubicles in the library, but by the time we returned to check it out, nothing was there," Aiden said, finally taking a seat on Riley's other side. "If they also bugged the place for voice, they might have known we were going to check it out."

"How would they know?"

"Kai called me from there to talk about dinner plans. Told me about the camera he spotted, and when I said I wanted to see it, he said he'd meet me outside the library." He smirked and rubbed a hand over his mouth. "They must have a team monitoring things because it couldn't have been ten minutes between the call and our arrival."

The Oracle stood silently watching Seth, Riley, and Aiden speculate about the spying in the academy. They'd figured out the hidden meaning of her words, and while Lukas could appreciate the clever way she fed them information without forcing action, he also wanted to bang his head against the wall. The contrast in appreciation and frustration was startling.

Jyrki sneered. "Something needs to change with the leadership in this school. This is ridiculous."

Professor Velastra did what she did best—bring the conversation back on track. "So, our words and actions aren't safe. I suspected as much. What do you have to tell us that requires such secrecy?"

The Oracle looked at Lukas. "Sit down, child."

Ice cold dread ran down his spine at the look on her face. He couldn't move for a moment. Something in him screamed whatever the Oracle had to say was going to shake everything out of balance. She hadn't even spoken, and he already felt off-kilter.

"*Poika.*"

Lukas's gaze snapped to his mother's eyes.

Her hand was outstretched. "Come sit with me."

His already heavy boots became lead as he crossed to sit with his mother and father on the couch. Collapsing beside them, he leaned back against the plush leather and shut his eyes, trying to calm his nerves. His mother's steady hand gripping his kept him grounded.

"My memories from a time long ago have opened to me in my time with Blaire. With the return of these memories, the hold on what I can share has lessened. You need to know what you're fighting against and why Angelo Moretti wishes to sink his claws deep in Blaire Wilcox and not let go. It starts with the prophecy of blood."

Riley sat up. "Prophecy of blood?"

"Yes. A prophecy revealed to me at the time of the Blood War. A time no longer documented because of the destruction—which I'm sure you are all aware of—of the royal archives relating to Rosendo Blackthorn's earlier reign and the time before that."

"There was a war?"

The Oracle gazed in Aiden's direction. "Long ago. A war stemmed from fear, greed, and a lust for power. A time where many humans knew of our existence. This war, the lock put on my memories by Rosendo—"

"Wait. How could he lock your memories?"

The Oracle looked sadly at Riley. "By using the powers of one he would later kill."

A silence settled over the room as the Oracle spoke.

"From the beginning of our existence, we have found our Korrena pair bond in both Vasirian and humans alike." She looked at Lukas. "Blaire is not the first human Korrena, and if the balance is restored, she will not be the last."

Lukas's stomach tightened from the uncertainty moving through him. If she wasn't the first, and she was the key to restoring whatever this balance thing was—which they've repeatedly been told was the case—if she died… "If she dies, future Vasirian may miss their bond." He whispered his words, but everyone heard them. They stared at him long enough he squirmed beneath their scrutiny.

"That is correct." Everyone looked at the Oracle again, and Lukas deflated, finally able to breathe normally. "Blaire is the key to restoring an ancient balance thrown into disarray by the Blood War. Should she fail—by choice, or death—then many connections will be severed for Vasirian long before their birth."

"That's too much to put on one girl," Helena said with a shake of her head.

"It is as it was foretold."

Jyrki asked, "Why only her? Why not another human—or several?"

"Because their blood lies dormant. There are many Korrena roaming this planet who are not awakened, many past the age of maturity. Blaire is the last surviving human descendant of the Blood War. Other humans from that time period are alive, of course. Otherwise, mankind would cease to exist. But Blaire is different. Her blood is special."

"We keep hearing this, but *how* is it special?" Seth muttered, unable to mask his frustration.

"She is the only human alive with the ancient magic from centuries past flowing through her veins. One of the great grandchildren of the original pairing."

A constant debate had raged about why Blaire had special blood since she arrived at Blackthorn Academy. Everyone knew her blood held something special, but Lukas never would have guessed magic was the answer. It didn't sound real.

He broke the silence that descended on the room at the Oracle's revelation. "So, what does that mean exactly?" Even if she had magic, it explained nothing about her situation, or why they were facing what they were. It didn't explain how she was his Korrena and why magic connected humans to Vasirian.

"In the time before the Blood War, there were many special humans like Blaire. Witches and warlocks who wielded magic for the betterment of our world. Other humans were not aware of this secret they carried, but Vasirian knew. These special humans and Vasirian shared a connection now lost. The magic that ran through their veins used to allow them to awaken with the same energy that stirs the Korrena within Vasirian."

The Oracle clasped her hands tightly and looked at Lukas.

"The bond between a Vasirian and a human is the strongest of all Korrena pairings as a result of this ancient magic. The blood of a human witch or warlock is unlike anything a Vasirian will ever taste. It can drive a weak Vasirian mad. It is one of the most addicting and

The Oracle gazed in Aiden's direction. "Long ago. A war stemmed from fear, greed, and a lust for power. A time where many humans knew of our existence. This war, the lock put on my memories by Rosendo—"

"Wait. How could he lock your memories?"

The Oracle looked sadly at Riley. "By using the powers of one he would later kill."

A silence settled over the room as the Oracle spoke.

"From the beginning of our existence, we have found our Korrena pair bond in both Vasirian and humans alike." She looked at Lukas. "Blaire is not the first human Korrena, and if the balance is restored, she will not be the last."

Lukas's stomach tightened from the uncertainty moving through him. If she wasn't the first, and she was the key to restoring whatever this balance thing was—which they've repeatedly been told was the case—if she died… "If she dies, future Vasirian may miss their bond." He whispered his words, but everyone heard them. They stared at him long enough he squirmed beneath their scrutiny.

"That is correct." Everyone looked at the Oracle again, and Lukas deflated, finally able to breathe normally. "Blaire is the key to restoring an ancient balance thrown into disarray by the Blood War. Should she fail—by choice, or death—then many connections will be severed for Vasirian long before their birth."

"That's too much to put on one girl," Helena said with a shake of her head.

"It is as it was foretold."

Jyrki asked, "Why only her? Why not another human—or several?"

"Because their blood lies dormant. There are many Korrena roaming this planet who are not awakened, many past the age of maturity. Blaire is the last surviving human descendant of the Blood War. Other humans from that time period are alive, of course. Otherwise, mankind would cease to exist. But Blaire is different. Her blood is special."

"We keep hearing this, but *how* is it special?" Seth muttered, unable to mask his frustration.

"She is the only human alive with the ancient magic from centuries past flowing through her veins. One of the great grandchildren of the original pairing."

A constant debate had raged about why Blaire had special blood since she arrived at Blackthorn Academy. Everyone knew her blood held something special, but Lukas never would have guessed magic was the answer. It didn't sound real.

He broke the silence that descended on the room at the Oracle's revelation. "So, what does that mean exactly?" Even if she had magic, it explained nothing about her situation, or why they were facing what they were. It didn't explain how she was his Korrena and why magic connected humans to Vasirian.

"In the time before the Blood War, there were many special humans like Blaire. Witches and warlocks who wielded magic for the betterment of our world. Other humans were not aware of this secret they carried, but Vasirian knew. These special humans and Vasirian shared a connection now lost. The magic that ran through their veins used to allow them to awaken with the same energy that stirs the Korrena within Vasirian."

The Oracle clasped her hands tightly and looked at Lukas.

"The bond between a Vasirian and a human is the strongest of all Korrena pairings as a result of this ancient magic. The blood of a human witch or warlock is unlike anything a Vasirian will ever taste. It can drive a weak Vasirian mad. It is one of the most addicting and sexually stimulating blood there is to our kind."

Lukas looked around the room as he swallowed the tightness in his throat. Riley's mouth gaped open, and both Seth and Aiden held looks of concern. If they were thinking what he was, then the looks made perfect sense. Vincent had gone mad off Blaire's blood. He couldn't handle it.

Jyrki leaned forward, asking, "Does this mean my son is strong, or is it the result of being the human's Korrena?"

"Lukas is a strong Vasirian, but he holds nothing preternatural that I am aware of. His connection as Blaire's Korrena pair is the reason he can consume her blood without losing his mind the way another did."

"Well, that explains the raging hormonal whiplash," Riley grumbled.

"A bit." When Riley looked at the Oracle, she elaborated. "Lukas not only had to contend with the powerful blood, and the euphoric thrill it presented, but he also faced the natural evolution of a Korrena bond and the already potent effects a Korrena's blood provides."

"Korrena blood is already sexually potent," Professor Velastra added, glancing at Riley. "This apparently adds gasoline to the fire."

The Oracle nodded.

A deep wrinkle formed between Aiden's brows. "So, what was so wrong with it? If the magical humans were good for Vasirian, what happened to them?"

"Well, you see, the children of these pairings also became powerful, but it was unpredictable if they would be born human or Vasirian."

Lukas sat upright. "Humans and Vasirian can reproduce?" His voice cracked.

"They can."

His jaw ticked. A few times he and Blaire lost themselves to passion and didn't use protection, sometimes failing to stop in time. They had been playing with fire the entire time. Neither was ready to become parents.

"The children of a human-turned-Vasirian and another Vasirian are the most powerful beings to walk this planet, followed by children of those not turned who have magical blood and a Vasirian, and then the descendants who are not in direct line to the original pairs—those who currently walk with dormant blood. After that, the children of Korrena-born pairs are stronger than those of compatible pairs—which everyone is aware of but believes are the only two options."

When Lukas slumped back into his seat, the Oracle continued. "No Vasirian I am aware of during those times had been born with magical affinities—only humans—but that didn't quell the fear that rose in the current king's grandfather. Rosendo feared the power that would come if a Vasirian came into existence with the same magical powers as these Korrena-bonded humans. While he had a right to question the power they would have—combining the power of a Vasirian with magic—his fear, and desire to remain at the top of the power chain, drove him to commit one of the darkest acts in our history."

"What happened?" Riley whispered.

"Rosendo Blackthorn ordered all existing witches, warlocks, and Vasirian pregnant by human warlocks to be executed to stop the bloodline from growing. To erase the potential life of a being too powerful for the Blackthorn Clan to control."

"By the gods!" Professor Velastra exclaimed, her hand covering her mouth.

Riley gasped, and Helena sucked in a breath as Jyrki growled. Seth's brows were at his hairline and Aiden's mouth gaped. Lukas felt sick, and his mother squeezed his hand tightly.

A king obsessed with keeping power took it upon himself to commit genocide—no wonder they called it the Blood War.

"If the people knew about this..."

Professor Velastra's words hung heavy in the air.

If all Vasirian knew what happened so long ago, how would they react to the Blackthorn Clan? Would they hold respect for Adrian Blackthorn like they did now? From Lukas's understanding, Adrian Blackthorn was stern and feared, but not because he was cruel. If Vasirian from modern days knew he came from such bloodstained hands, would they accept him as their king?

"The Blackthorn Clan did not approve of Rosendo's decision," the Oracle said, alleviating Lukas's worries. "The discord that arose in the monarchy served as fuel to back the push for the bloody war that followed. Without a subset of people disrupting their balance, peace could return. It was a weak argument at best, one Rosendo didn't need in order to command his followers to fulfill his wishes.

"The king's order was final. As it is today. But unlike before, the previous king strived to put laws in place to protect humans. His son, Adrian, has upheld these laws and does not tolerate those who break them. That is why the Blackthorn Clan banished Vincent Brandt to Cresbel Asylum. With the revelation of our sordid history, I now understand why Luciano did such a thing. There were no laws to protect humans before the Blood War."

When the Oracle finished speaking, and silence once again descended on the room, Lukas scrubbed his hands down his face, balling his fists in his lap. His skin itched. So, he now knew what made Blaire special, and the history, but it still didn't answer the many questions that burned his throat.

He watched the flickering flame of a candle on the table. "Why is

Angelo Moretti planning to sacrifice Blaire?"

"Did they figure out her secret?" Helena added.

"No. They are unaware of the Blood War and our history. They simply discovered that her blood holds magic, and in the same desire for power that Rosendo Blackthorn held, Angelo wants to seize the opportunity to extract that power from her through a ritual believed to commune with an ancient deity of magic. The tomes he reads from are pure fiction, but his lust for power blinds him, and his need to reign over all consumes him."

Aiden scoffed. "He thinks killing Blaire will give him magical powers?"

"The ritual does not call for the complete death of the 'sacrifice,' but more a sacrifice of her blood. However, no human could survive the ritual. The amount of blood required over a long period is too great for the human body to replenish."

Lukas was vaguely aware of his mother beginning to cry, her hand gripping his again. Apparently, she needed it more than he did. He focused on the candle. Everything that was happening in his and Blaire's life centered on greedy men who couldn't be content with what they had. Men who turned their lives upside down in a grab for power. He wanted to take Blaire and run away. Go some place far away from Blackthorn Academy. Far away from the expectations of his kind.

"I cannot see what future is in store for our kind should Blaire not be saved beyond the loss of the base magic. I suspect it will weaken our species when the magic flickers out, resulting in the children born with magical blood ceasing to exist. Of course, we don't have those children now, so I'm not sure if much will change at all for our kind than the course we're already on."

If nothing much changed, then why wouldn't the Oracle tell

everyone to leave Blaire alone? Why was restoring the magical balance necessary if nothing would change? More was not being said.

"Though, the Vasirian who have destined Korrenas with dormant blood will never find them. Nor will future pairs of that kind be born. How large of a population of our kind will go without finding their Korrena, I'm unsure."

Helena shook her head. "So many wait for their fated one. Some refuse to take a compatible pair. They will die without bringing life into this world."

Another strained silence settled on the room as the implications of those words hung in the air. Lukas itched to go find Blaire, unable to handle the quiet.

The Oracle finally spoke again. "The blood prophecy that came to me at the end of the war I held secret until Rosendo's passing. I delivered a message to Luciano that there would be children born with dormant magical blood. One of these children, a descendant of a woman who somehow survived through the war by hiding underground with her Korrena, would find her own Korrena"—her gaze fell on Lukas—"after certain events happened, setting the wheels in motion for the restoration of the balance between the two species."

Professor Velastra's lips thinned. "What events?"

"The death of Luciano Blackthorn, and the rise to power of Adrian Blackthorn."

"Lukas met Blaire two months after Adrian Blackthorn's ascension to the throne." The professor's gaze slipped to Lukas. "We need to find Blaire. When is this ritual to take place?"

"February third, when the Centaurid meteor shower approaches."

Lukas jumped to his feet. "That's tomorrow night!"

Seth's gaze narrowed. "Don't you think it would have been better to let us know this piece of information *before* now?"

The Oracle inclined her head. "If I had known, of course. However, I did not. I am not with the Order for every meeting and decision they make, and I suspect much of the facts surrounding the choice to perform a sacrificial ritual on a human student wasn't carried out in an official council meeting." When her eyes met Seth's, he sat back and sucked his teeth.

"What are we going to do?" Riley asked, her gaze darting frantically around the room.

"In preparation for the ritual, Angelo has ordered Blackthorn Security to take the night off. He doesn't want interference."

Jyrki's lips curled in derision. "The man knows they wouldn't agree to kill a human like this. Not everyone is anti-human. We must stop him before it begins."

"Tomorrow night, they will lock the administration building tight, but I will unlock the doors at seven o'clock. Once inside, you must hurry down to sublevel four, where at the end of a narrow hallway, you will take an elevator down two more floors. Once you exit, you'll find yourself in a labyrinth of halls. These halls are in place to protect the temple at the heart of the labyrinth. I will provide your professor here with a guide on how to navigate this maze. Once you reach the temple, it is on you how you wish to proceed. Any further interference from me will disrupt the natural order."

"We'll save her, son."

Lukas looked at his father, the same green eyes as his own staring back at him. The same determination and resolve burning beneath the surface. Never in his life was he as happy his parents were with him than in that moment.

37

RITUAL

The marble surface Blaire lay on made her lower back and sacrum ache, but she couldn't move. Her arms lay outstretched from her body, her legs tight together. Heavy metal cuffs around her wrists and ankles, attached to chains, bound her to iron poles protruding from the ground at the sides and bottom of the marble altar. She appeared posed for a crucifixion on her back.

Around the base of the altar, if she turned her head far enough, she could see grooves in the floor that led away from the altar, down the sides of a set of marble stairs, and out to the center of the room in two long lines. The grooves circled left and right around a sunken platform, with four places branching off into smaller grooves that ran into the pit. The four smaller grooves led in straight lines to the center, feeding into a strange symbol in the middle surrounded by six circles carved into the floor. She'd been tied up here long enough to count all this and was growing cold from the marble acting as a heat sink.

It wasn't hard to imagine the purpose of the grooves. How many people had died down here?

Several bodies in black robes circled the pit in silence, each taking up a position around the center of the room, away from the pit. There had to be at least twenty people here.

The room itself was massive and reminded Blaire of cathedrals in Europe without the rows of pews. Vaulted ceilings extended high overhead, arching around the room, with large chandeliers hanging in various places, dripping in crystals that reflected the amber glow of their light. The room appeared bathed in blood with the dark amber light reflecting off the stones, glass along the walls, and crimson accents. The walls were covered in scrolling relief, and the decorative, carved stonework of the tracery encased similar stained glass to the main building of Blackthorn Academy. It seemed strange to have stained glass windows deep underground.

Two hooded figures began lighting the dozens of candles of various sizes surrounding the grooved ducts around the altar. The candles spread around the upper dais where the altar sat, and melted wax coated the floors around the base of candelabras and tiered steps around the altar.

Blaire wanted to scream at them to release her, but her throat was raw from the screaming she already did as they brought her down into the temple while she fought with everything she had. All her fighting and screaming did was exhaust her and make her barely able to speak. None of the robed figures who brought her down into the temple reacted in the slightest to her protests, tears, or begging. No one heard her cries for help, despite how loudly they echoed. They were far beneath the Earth's surface.

If someone had told her a year ago she'd be chained to an altar wearing a white gown like a sacrificial virgin from a cheesy eighties horror movie, she'd have laughed in their face and told them to lay off the bath salts. Part of her wanted to laugh at the ridiculousness of it anyway, but there was no humor in the situation.

Groaning, Blaire blinked. Dehydration was getting to her after her boisterous protests. She stared up at the black fabric dripping from the arching vaults above her. The gossamer fabric looked like wraiths moving about whenever a draft from the halls branching from the temple's main chamber moved across them.

A door opening echoed into the chamber. Blaire lifted her head. Six hooded figures in burgundy and black robes filed into the room. The Order. Five of them took positions around the symbol on the circles marked into the floor of the pit at the center of the room, completing the core of the tiered circular formation the other bodies started. Where was the seventh member of the Order?

The sixth robed figure, wearing robes different from the others with extra gaudy details only Angelo Moretti could appreciate, approached the altar, climbing the marble steps. He pulled his hood back and smiled serenely down at Blaire. "It has been a pleasure making your acquaintance, human, but I'm afraid our time has come to an end."

Blaire spit at Angelo's face. "I wish I could say the same, but my experience wasn't pleasurable in the slightest, asshole." Her voice was raspy, but she made her point. She no longer had a reason to be cordial or to cooperate with him. Their deal was off. He wasn't going to return her to Lukas, so she wasn't going to play his game any longer. Too bad he had the upper hand.

Angelo's eyes flashed, and he wiped his cheek with the sleeve of his robe. "Disgusting to the bitter end." He turned away from the altar as Blaire glowered at his back, lifting his arms to draw attention to himself. "For years we have been in the dark about our history! And while we still long to know where we come from, how we have the unique abilities that set us apart from humans, and our purpose in this world, we have discovered one secret in this world that can set us above other species indefinitely!"

Low chanting started from the robed figures around the room surrounding the Order members. Blaire couldn't make out what they were saying, or even what language they were using. But she didn't like the chill of apprehension that raced up her spine.

"This human"—Angelo waved a hand in Blaire's direction—"has blood unlike anything we've ever encountered. Blood with untold power waiting to be tapped and harnessed for the greater good of Vasirian kind!"

He really is a madman.

Did he honestly believe taking her blood would grant him some kind of power? Did these people truly believe if it did, Angelo would use it to take care of anyone other than himself?

Blaire's eyes moved over the five members of the Order around the grooved symbol on the floor at the center of the temple. None of the bodies resembled the tall and lithe physique of Tobias. Was he with Dominic? Was Dominic alright? Maybe Tobias was here, and she was confused. She hadn't eaten, or had a drop of water, since Angelo informed her yesterday of what was to come tonight. Dehydration didn't help her keep a clear head.

Several more figures dressed in black robes filed into the room carrying boxes, placing them around the altar. What Blaire saw when one of the robed figures opened a box made her nauseous.

Blood. So many vials of blood.

The same vials the researchers used, and some she recognized from her time with Vincent. She heard they were destroyed. Hadn't the researchers used all of them? Was this why they took so much? Saving it for this moment? Did they intend to do this to her all along?

She had already calculated there was no way to get enough blood from her body in one go to fill the channels leading from the altar down to the area below.

Her breathing quickened when a robed figure moved to stand next to the altar. They held in their palms a large dagger with a jeweled hilt. Another came to the other side of the altar holding a worn black tome opened to pages so stained they appeared bronze.

The scent of coconut filled her nose, and her heart rate slowed. Ciro. She wasn't alone. While she wanted Lukas here—wanted to see him one last time—it comforted her that Ciro wasn't going to let her face the afterlife alone.

She hadn't had another dream of the Oracle in a long time, and the last dream she had of that fantastical place, and Ciro, occurred a few nights ago. If only she could stay in that place. She didn't even get the opportunity to get to know the spirit guarding her since she was a toddler. The Guardian her father sent to protect her. His last wish. A tear rolled down her temple and into her hair.

Angelo faced the altar, standing at the foot of the marble surface, looking down at Blaire with hate-filled eyes, while the robed figures began pouring the blood into the grooves around the altar, allowing the crimson liquid to move slowly downward toward the symbol at the bottom of the stairs.

He said, "I don't know what you are, or where you come from, but you will grant me what I seek."

Blaire's brows furrowed in confusion. She tried to cooperate before. Everything she did was to appease their curiosity so she could return to Lukas as quickly as possible. She didn't fight it, thinking the more she cooperated, the more likely she could return sooner than later. Until she learned about this sadistic ritual, she had every intention of seeing the experiments through, no matter how much they hurt and dragged on beyond what she felt was reasonable.

"Magical bloodlines date back to the dawn of time amongst the stories of your kind. Witchcraft is a thing existing from the days of the garden of Eden. Perhaps there is truth to these works of fiction that fill libraries across the world."

He retrieved the tome from the robed figure at his side and held it in front of him, reading. "The old blood of the lamb mingles with the fresh blood of the slaughter." He nodded to the robed figure on his left, who began cutting down the length of Blaire's inner arms. She wailed in agony as her skin was sliced open. Angelo spoke louder over her screams of pain. "With the joining of that which is old, and the spark of life in the new, we beseech thee, Xilanith."

The chanting grew louder, but Blaire could barely hear them over her own cries. She struggled against her bonds, but as her blood spilled from the deep cuts, her strength waned quickly. She squeezed her eyes shut and opened them, trying to focus but failing as her vision grew fuzzy around the edges.

"Xilanith, harbinger of divinity, keeper of magic, I beseech thee to free me from this mortal bond. Infuse me with the power of generations old, and I shall serve at your feet for eternity!"

The sharp blade of the dagger dug into her leg, dragging downward. Her heart thumped in desperation; they were preparing to drain her of all her blood. There was no way they wouldn't hit an artery. Were there many arteries on the outside of her legs? The ones in her arms were at risk, but since her blood oozed out and didn't spurt out like in a bad horror movie, they hadn't hit them. She'd be dead fast if that happened.

The nurses from the health department and Mera had explained the difference between venous bleeding and arterial bleeding after her first near-death experience at the hands of the Order. But they never cut her like this before. Surviving these wounds wasn't a likelihood. Her head spun as she tried to call on the information. Now wasn't the time to overanalyze things. Her mind tried to hyper-fixate on anything but the excruciating pain radiating through her limbs.

How stupid she felt for arguing the need for her humanity, when it did nothing to save her now. A Vasirian could die from this, but they stood a better chance.

Her blood spilled over the altar into the grooves, blending with the red liquid they already added. Her head spun until two Angelos watched her with glowing eyes as he continued his inane ramblings. Was he seeking immortality?

She drifted her gaze around the room; a faint glow of different colored eyes peeped from beneath the hoods of several of the bodies around the room. Vasirian responding to her blood. If the dagger didn't kill her, she might become a meal instead.

Blaire never expected to leave Lukas so soon—if ever. She wished for the change, but it was too late. Lukas wasn't here to make it happen. Hot tears ran over her temples into her hairline.

Before the robed figure reached her other leg, blackness pulled her under, and she welcomed its quiet embrace. But she never would get to take that trip with Lukas.

38

Mole

Sneaking into the administration building seemed too easy a task. The Oracle said Blackthorn Security wouldn't be around, but that made little sense to Lukas. Why would an entire security team for a university filled with students who had to hide from the human world accept the night off? Maybe it was the stress of the situation, but the hairs on Lukas's arms stood on end. He couldn't shake the feeling something was terribly wrong, and they were going to be too late.

Professor Velastra led Lukas, Aiden, Seth, Riley, and Lukas's parents through the main chamber of the administration building. Moonlight spilled through the tall windows across the marble floor, casting the space in dappled crimson and an eerie purple hue where the blue moonlight passed through red glass. The chandeliers reflected the moonlight off their crystals, but otherwise cast no light. The only other lighting in the space came from candles in various ornate sconces.

As they made their way to the hallway leading to the descent into the sublevels, a voice behind them made the group halt their steps.

"I'd ask what you're doing here, but I would be wasting your time and mine."

Lukas's eyes narrowed on the man with alabaster skin from the Order council.

"Tobias," Professor Velastra said hesitantly, stepping around the group, standing in front of them protectively. "We were—"

"Do not treat me like a fool and make excuses for your presence in a building none of you have a place in." His intense gaze slid to Lukas. "You wish to save her."

Lukas couldn't contain the growl that rose in his chest.

A smile he couldn't interpret tilted one side of Tobias's mouth. "I have waited twenty years for this."

Tobias motioned to a side hallway. A tall woman with a light olive complexion, a man with a darker tan and deep brown, almost black hair, and another man with ghostly white skin and pale hair similar to Tobias, stepped from the shadows dressed in clothes that screamed money. Chiffon blouse, pressed suits with silken ties; the high quality of the fabrics was obvious even from where Lukas stood.

The woman's perfectly-styled dark brunette hair cascaded over her shoulders in loose curls. An amethyst-accented comb pulled a portion of her hair back to reveal teardrop diamond earrings. The pale man to her right wore a diamond stud in his left ear. They mirrored each other with their movements.

The woman was the first to speak; her accent was hard to place. It sounded like a mix between British and Spanish. "Which of you belongs to the human?" The woman's dark, sultry eyes scanned the group slowly until settling on Lukas. "It is you, isn't it?"

Aiden's dark green eyes cut to Lukas, filled with concern.

"How did you…" Riley started, but the woman lifted a hand, halting her.

"You vibrate with the song of hostility. Speak."

Lukas's face hardened at the commanding way the woman spoke. "We belong to each other," he ground out through clenched teeth.

"Such is the way of the Korrena." She turned to the pale-skinned man to her right. "Are the preparations in order for transport?"

Adjusting his deep purple tie, he flashed a brilliant white smile at the woman. "Of course, my love. Dimitri is with Blackthorn Security awaiting our call."

Jyrki stepped forward, and Helena tightened her hold on his hand. "What is happening here?" His voice held that same authoritative, protective parent edge he used when addressing Professor Velastra the day before.

The woman and man stopped speaking, turning their dark eyes on Lukas's father. The other man with them crossed his arms over his chest, parting his feet in an intimidating stance; but since he stood shorter than the others at his side, with a build even slighter than the woman, he didn't physically give the impression they should fear him. The confidence and inner strength he exuded gave that impression.

Tobias stepped around the three unknown Vasirian. "As much as I wish we could spend time discussing the ins-and-outs of a coup d'état with you, we do not have time. Blaire does not have time." He looked at Lukas. "We must go. I will explain as we walk."

Aiden and Lukas shared a look. Did the guy honestly expect them to trust him? The Order had made their lives a living hell for a year. To have one member show up and start trying to run things, with three complete strangers, while they were breaking into the administration building, struck Lukas as odd. Tobias didn't immediately make a summons for Blackthorn Security to come and apprehend them.

Instead, he'd mention Lukas's desire to save Blaire, and seemed attentive to the little time they had to execute that task.

Lukas glanced at his father. He nodded and motioned for Lukas to follow Tobias and the three strangers. Having his father at his back, and his friends close behind, made the long walk bearable. When they reached the stairs that descended to the sublevels, Tobias turned to the group.

"We take the stairs. The elevator is noisy and will arouse suspicion. No one should be in the upper floors at this hour."

They began the descent. The back stairs weren't as extravagant as the rest of the place. The risers were the same marble as the rest of the flooring, but the burgundy walls of the spiraling staircase lacked the portraits and oil paintings found throughout the main chamber and stairs leading to the council room. Only wrought-iron fixtures every few feet dangling round lights on chains lit their way. Occasionally, a sturdy door in an alcove on the outer wall indicated a new floor.

Tobias motioned to the woman. "This is Mariana Blackthorn." He nodded to the man with pale blond hair, and paler skin, walking alongside her. "And her husband, Felix Blackthorn." He extended his hand to the other man a few feet ahead "And that is Gabriel Blackthorn, her cousin."

"Blackthorn?" The professor stopped her descent, the tapping of her high heels ceasing their echo in the stairwell. They paused and looked back at her. "You are from the monarchy?"

The darker-skinned man—Gabriel—blew a breath of amusement. "There are only a handful of souls with the Blackthorn moniker, love." His accent sounded more British than his cousin Mariana's.

"What are you doing here?"

Gabriel's head tilted, and he glanced at his cousin, clearly deferring to her. It appeared she was the one calling the shots in this group.

Mariana motioned for them to continue walking. "We have watched the council overseeing the Americas for many years. We've had suspicions of corruption in the ranks dating back forty years, yet only twenty years ago could we make a move to do anything about it."

No one spoke, likely in an effort to not interrupt and lose out on the information one of the Blackthorn Clan members so freely provided.

"Twenty years ago, we planted a mole." She glanced at Tobias. "One of our own. My father believed by having my cousin infiltrate the Order, we would find the information we sought faster than a proper investigation. Much of the Clan agreed. It has only been since my father's death, and Adrian's ascension to the throne, that we have obtained damning enough evidence to take them out."

Lukas frowned, chewing on that information. Not only was the former king's daughter here with them, but Tobias was also part of the monarchy, and had been spying from the inside for twenty years.

Lukas studied Tobias's youthful face. "How old are you?" he blurted before thinking better of it. The men of the Order were older than dirt, but Tobias didn't look much older than he did. The numbers weren't adding up.

A wry grin cut across Tobias's face. "Caught that timeline, did you?" He chuckled, and it was an odd sound from someone who had seemed so imposing on the throne during Vincent's trial. "I'm forty-seven."

"Hold on. You joined the Order at twenty-seven?"

Tobias winked at Riley. "Youngest member ever to join rank, but I came highly recommended by King Blackthorn himself." He rolled his eyes. "Of course, Angelo would want to have someone at his side who came with such a connection to the Blackthorn Clan. A young, impressionable steppingstone for him to climb over in his quest for power." His lip curled, showing no love lost there even if they'd spent twenty years working together.

"So, why are you here now?"

Mariana looked at Aiden. "Tobias informed us of the human, and what has taken place with her, and what is to take place tonight. By order of King Adrian Blackthorn, we are here to stop this sadistic ritual and bring the Order to its knees." She looked at Professor Velastra as they reached the bottom of the stairs. "He told us how you, and another professor, tried to reach out to us and were met with threats. I am deeply sorry for any distress that may have caused. Know that your life and your livelihood are safe. They will answer for their crimes."

Professor Velastra nodded in acquiesce.

Tobias led them down a long corridor that opened into a spacious room with vaulted ceilings in dark wood and stone. Several hallways with high ceilings branched off in many directions. Had they come down here without Tobias, Lukas couldn't help but wonder if they'd have ever found their way out.

"Once we reach the temple, we must be quick. I don't know what all the ritual entails, but I have vague ideas." Tobias's gaze settled on Lukas. "You must get her out of there as quickly as possible. We will apprehend the council members and make the summons for their transport to Europe to stand trial." His jaw worked, and he looked at the rest of the group, who'd remained silent. "Do not be surprised when we arrive if there are many people and a lot of blood."

"What?" Jyrki's eyebrows slammed together. "These kids can't fight a hoard of people."

"No. You're right. Luckily for all of us, they are a bunch of nervous scientists who follow their master's command. If confronted, they'll tuck tail and run."

"What about the blood?" Riley said, glancing at Seth. "Whose blood?" Seth didn't handle freshly-spilled human blood well.

"Angelo isn't aware I know, but that lunatic has been hoarding vials of blood since Vincent Brandt was in the picture. The ritual requires a lot of the human's blood."

"Blaire," Lukas, Aiden, and Riley snapped at the same time.

Mariana's perfectly manicured brows rose, and Helena laughed.

Tobias cleared his throat. "The ritual requires a lot of *Blaire's* blood. Both old and fresh."

Seth shifted uneasily, and when Lukas gave him a concerned look, he shook his head. "I can handle it. She needs us."

"You sure?" Felix raised a blond brow skeptically. "You're not one to go feral, are you?"

Seth scoffed. "Hardly."

"We need to go," Gabriel said. "It is too late for the boy to back out now, anyway. Your Korrena doesn't have a lot of time."

Blaire was strong, but the mind could take only so much. The focus for a long time had been on how her body withstood everyday life because of her medical condition, how what the Order, Vincent, and even Lukas did to her body would heal physically. Even now, their concern was physical—rightfully so. Ensuring Blaire survived was the most important thing at that moment. Was her mind strong enough to handle this? Would this be the thing that pushed her over the edge and away from him?

Lukas took a breath and tried to steady his heart that beat too fast for his liking, as Tobias, and the three Blackthorn Clan members, led them into one of the many hallways.

No one had considered the impact on her mind, but it concerned Lukas. Seeing a counselor after arriving at Blackthorn Academy did wonders for Blaire, to cope with what she endured mentally before ever meeting him, and to adapt to his world. Everyone saw it. But the things the Order did to her, Clarissa and Vincent invading their lives, the trauma of being held in captivity—twice—while facing physical trauma at the same time, and the push and pull of their unstable bond… Blaire might not recover from this. With nothing guarding her mind, would Blaire end up more broken by his world than what her stepfamily put her through?

She told him her counselor tried to help her the week after her captivity; they met several times. Things might have gone worse if she hadn't seen Professor Sinclair. Blaire had friends. She had him. But would that be enough? Especially when his naivety at how to handle his primal side while adapting to their bond almost got her killed.

Lukas ground his teeth. He was supposed to be the one person above all she could trust to keep her safe.

Tobias said old and fresh blood. Lukas clenched his fists as worry coiled inside him. He hoped they wouldn't be too late, and fresh blood hadn't already spilled.

39

Acceptance

As they neared the end of yet another long hallway that seemed to go on forever, chanting reached them. The sound echoed into the hall and bounced around. If there wasn't only one direction to go aside from the way they came, he wouldn't know where to follow the sound to with how it reverberated around them.

"Remember thc plan," Tobias said, turning to Lukas as they walked. "When we get inside the temple's central chamber, your goal is to get Blaire out of there as quickly as possible. We'll handle the council members."

Lukas braced for the onslaught of anxiety and sickening dread that came when he thought of what was ahead, but it never came. Instead, he filled with an eerie sense of nothingness. Two hallways ago, he felt Blaire. Her fear spiked before an odd acceptance settled in his stomach. And love. Love so strong it choked him. He wished he could have sent it back to her, wished he could soothe her, but he couldn't. He asked about it when he felt Blaire's fear in the tree grove. His mother told him it wasn't possible.

Now he felt nothing. Were they too late? Had she told him goodbye? No. He wouldn't accept that. His footsteps quickened as they reached the end of the hall when the strong scent of Blaire's blood filled the air, making his heart pound.

Nothing could have prepared him for the sight that greeted him. He couldn't even focus on the opulent design of the room, or the rows of robed figures with hoods circling the center of the room. His gaze focused on the altar at the front of the room where his Korrena lay motionless in what might have been a white gown, had it not been saturated with so much blood. Chains and metal cuffs bound her ankles and wrists, holding her arms outstretched, revealing deep gashes along the length of her arms.

The sight of Blaire lying still overrode the discomfort in his gut at the overwhelming scent of her blood permeating the air.

Lukas couldn't move.

He tried to get his feet to work, but he stood frozen to the spot as chaos erupted around him.

As predicted, the robed figures around the outer edges of the circle began fleeing the room. They wouldn't get far. Mariana informed them that Blackthorn Security came down into the sublevels shortly after their descent. At the end of the labyrinth of halls, the entire force waited with her half-brother Dimitri.

"What is the meaning of this?" Angelo demanded from the bottom of the stairs at Blaire's feet. He held a worn tome in his hand. "Tobias, what are you—"

"Angelo Moretti," Mariana's commanding voice echoed in the chamber. "By order of King Adrian Blackthorn, you and the sitting council of the Order—with the exception of Tobias Nilsson—are hereby placed in our custody until such a time as a trial can begin in accordance with the provisions set forth by the late King Luciano Blackthorn."

Angelo's face twisted in outrage. His eyes flashing bright amber. "On what grounds?" he shouted. Did he honestly think he wasn't doing anything wrong?

Aiden gave Lukas's shoulder a push, his hand firmly gripping his long-sleeved pullover. "Focus."

Lukas looked away from the arguing members of the Blackthorn Clan to the altar, where his parents and Professor Velastra crowded around Blaire. Riley stood off to the side, pulling one of her arm warmers off and wrapping it around Seth's face, using a safety pin from her skirt to secure it behind his head like a face mask. His eyes were narrowed, and a subtle white glow encircled his steel-gray eyes. He wasn't a danger to Blaire; he was merely struggling with the smell.

The problem arose when Jyrki lifted a hand to touch Blaire.

Everything moved in slow motion.

The disconnect from everything happening around Lukas—to the point he felt numb, and like he wasn't taking part in the events unfolding, watching from above—faded. A sudden and violent need to protect his pair rose in him, and he cleared the space between himself, and his father, faster than he knew he was capable of. One minute Aiden was trying to get him to move, and the next, he had his father pressed against a pillar, snarling in his face.

"Don't. Touch. Her."

Jyrki slowly lifted both hands in a surrendering gesture. "Son," he said calmly, "this isn't you. Release me. I have no intentions of harming your pair. She is yours."

Lukas's hold loosened at the acknowledgment of who Blaire belonged to. Part of him felt sick at the way it framed her as an object to own. The twisted thing inside of him relished in the pleasure of hearing his father's declaration.

"She's dying, son."

Lukas released his father completely, coming to his senses. He choked on a breath and stuttered, "W-what?"

"Look at her."

Jyrki tilted his head forward, directing Lukas's gaze back to the altar. He could see Blaire clearly now. Not only did her arms have deep cuts down their length, but her legs were cut open in the same manner. Her lifeblood dripped from the marble surface of the altar, puddling beneath her body. Her skin was so pale she looked gray and ghastly. Lips tinted blue were parted and her eyes closed.

In that moment it hit him, and he wasn't prepared for the magnitude in which his emotions slammed back into him. His world shattered, and he walked—at least he thought he walked—to the altar and placed his hands in the pooling blood on either side of her hips, looking down into the face of the one thing that felt right in his life.

His eyes burned, but he refused to blink. Refused to look away from what his actions caused. The choices he made in the last few months set this in motion, and now Blaire was gone.

Lukas couldn't even cry. The pain that gripped him with blackened claws turned his heart to ice. It felt as if he had died with her. His soul ached to such a degree he couldn't muster the anger required to burn everything down. He felt none of the recklessness he normally did. Nothing remained inside but emptiness.

Slowly lowering his head, he barely brushed his lips against the cold, dry lips that felt so foreign to him in their current state.

Riley's words cut through the anguish gripping at his soul. "Is she dead?"

"She can't be!" Aiden shouted from somewhere behind Lukas.

But she is. I couldn't save her. Couldn't protect her.

Finally, the wet, fiery trail of a tear rolled down his cheek—but that was it. Everything froze inside of him.

"She's alive."

It took entirely too long for Professor Velastra's words to breech the thick miasma clouding his mind. Slowly, he looked up from Blaire's face to see the professor's fingers pressed against the side of Blaire's neck.

"Barely alive, but alive." Her stern gaze collided with Lukas's. "You must turn her. She won't make it out of here to receive medical treatment otherwise. The walk back is too long, and she's lost too much blood."

The metal chains hit the floor as Seth picked the locks of the cuffs binding Blaire to the table.

A commotion from behind him pulled his attention. Angelo struggled against the hold of Gabriel and Felix.

"You must not stop the ritual! It isn't complete! We must extract her magic! I must—" His words cut off when Gabriel did something to his neck. Angelo strained to say "traitor" as he looked up at Tobias before he crumpled into a heap of dead weight in Felix and Gabriel's hold.

"Lukas!"

He turned back to the altar where Professor Velastra's usual poker face held so many emotions Lukas couldn't read them.

It was too much to process. Blaire lived. But he had to turn her for her to survive.

He shook his head vehemently. The thing he wanted for so long lay within his grasp and he couldn't do it. "I can't," he rasped, finally finding his words.

"You must!"

Glaring at the professor, Lukas shook his head again, tightening his hands into fists on the altar. "There must be another way. Tell me another way!"

"Isn't that what you wanted?" Seth asked, standing away from the altar now, his hand over the face covering to give added protection.

"Not like this!"

Lukas would never again try to take the choice away from Blaire. It should be for her to decide—without his constant coercion. He'd been a fool. A boy playing at acting like an adult. Throwing around his ego and demanding things he had no right to demand.

If he had to lose Blaire to finally give her the freedom for once in her life, to not be forced into something she didn't want, he would let her go.

He would finally let her have peace.

"I'm so sorry. You don't have to fight anyone anymore." Lukas's chest tightened to the point he found breathing difficult as he put his forehead against Blaire's, closing his eyes and letting the truth of his pain drip onto her face from his cheeks.

"You're letting her die?" Riley shouted incredulously. "Don't do this!"

"I'm giving her a choice! No one gives her a choice! No one has ever given her a choice!" His voice cracked as he spat his words, never taking his eyes off Blaire.

He put his head against her chest and listened to her slow heartbeat until no sound reached his ears. His heart cracked in two. Words failed him, and he couldn't tell the others Blaire was already gone. He merely lay there on her chest, absorbing what little warmth remained on her chilly body before he had to let her go forever.

When Riley opened her mouth to say something more in protest, Aiden grabbed her arm. "Stop it. You know he's right. Gods knows it sucks, but it's the truth. She isn't capable of making a choice right now."

Riley glared at her brother. He was perceptive and knew how Lukas felt. Knew the guilt that warred inside him. Aiden knew the way Lukas's mind worked.

Helena sighed softly and looked at Riley. "If your friend wakes up a Vasirian—lives as we all wish her to—but discovers my son stole her choice after everything they went through… Do you think she would be happy? That she would stay?"

Riley's eyes glistened with liquid emotion. "I don't want to lose my best friend." Seth pulled her into a tight embrace, and she sobbed into his chest.

"None of us wish to lose her. I have not gotten the chance to know the girl who changed my son." Helena looked at Lukas, who couldn't lift his head, willing the silent heart beneath his ear to beat once more, whispering words of love no one else could hear. "And as much as it hurts, the choice to let her be free in the only way he can, is the right one."

Lukas didn't want to let Blaire die. He didn't feel like he gave up on her. A strong conviction in his gut said by not choosing for her, he set her free. Technically, allowing her to pass made a choice for her, but it was either force her into a lifetime of knowing she was bound to something she made clear she wasn't ready for, or let nature take its course. Both options pained him. All he wanted was to join her on the other side now.

"Lukas?" Professor Velastra's words sounded muffled, despite being so close.

"Son." His father stepped warily toward the altar. "What is it?"

"No," Aiden breathed. "Not yet."

Riley sobbed harder, her wailing echoing in the silent temple. The

Blackthorn Clan members, Tobias, and the Order had gone.

Helena turned and tucked her face into Jyrki's arm. His face pinched as he looked down at Lukas, who didn't have the strength to lift his head.

"No matter where you go after this life, I will find you. I'll never stop searching until I find you. I love you."

At Lukas's quiet declaration, his mother burst into tears. Even Professor Velastra couldn't hide the tears falling from her eyes.

He couldn't dwell on the reactions of those around him. In that moment, two things became apparent at once. One, the slow and increasingly steady beat of a heart beneath his ear, and two, the rise and fall of a chest that had been still for too long. He bolted upright and stared down at Blaire. She looked the same.

"Lukas? What is—" Professor Velastra sucked in a sharp breath as a faint golden glow surrounded Blaire like a second skin.

The hairs on Lukas's arms stood on end, but he couldn't move. Couldn't tear his eyes away from the warm light weaving around Blaire, coiling with a glowing red light that danced across her skin. Gaping wounds began closing themselves, leaving no scars to speak of. Bruises and bite marks that littered her arms and shoulders faded until only the smooth, creamy, porcelain skin he remembered remained. Even the scar from when the Order took a chunk of her skin last school year disappeared before his eyes. Everyone stared dumbfounded as blue lips turned petal pink, and pallid skin turned warm with the rush of fresh blood. The strong smell of coconut mingled with the sweet jasmine that spoke of life and Blaire.

As the red and gold lights faded, leaving behind faint embers of gold glittering magic that settled into her flesh, Blaire didn't move. She lay in the pool of blood on the altar, looking alive and well, but still, she didn't stir.

"Is she…" Riley pulled away from Seth and stepped forward. "What just happened?"

"Part of her has awakened."

Lukas whirled on the altar to look at the Oracle standing in the center of the circle at the base of the stairs leading up to the altar.

"The girl lives. Do not despair. The magic it took to restore her life force merely took everything out of her. She needs rest."

"How did—"

"How did it happen?" the Oracle finished for Jyrki. "I cannot begin to understand the power that lies within Blaire Wilcox, or how it stirred in the manner it did. Though I suspect outside interference." She looked as if she had scented the air. Curious. "But the catalyst that allowed it to happen was you." She settled her gaze on Lukas.

"What did I do?"

"You let go. You let go of the need to control and own."

Lukas looked down at Blaire. Never again, he promised silently. She knew what he wanted, and he would never make her feel as if she didn't have a say in the matter. Whatever this thing was inside him—a dominant side to his personality, another being entirely, a split personality—he didn't care. He would fight against it and prove to Blaire he was worth it.

A hush fell over the chamber for several long minutes before Riley spoke.

"What do we do now?"

"Take her home. She doesn't require a hospital or infirmary. Let her rest. She will awaken when her body replenishes itself." The Oracle looked down the hall, and a figure moved in the shadows. "I must go. I will travel with the others to Europe and give my testimony regarding the Order's actions. They may call upon you. Be ready."

With those last words, the Oracle turned and left them.

Blaire was alive. Sleeping. Lukas put trembling hands coated in blood on the sides of her face, stroking her cheek with his thumb. He would do whatever it took to help heal her mind.

They belonged together, and maybe with the Order gone, they could be together.

40

Reunited

A warm breeze stirred Blaire's long, blonde hair, and she pushed it from her face. Sitting on the edge of the fishbowl valley, staring at the stormy portal of the Shimmer Gates, she sighed. Looking over at Ciro, who quietly focused on the massive structure in the center of the valley, she recalled the last time she felt him. Recalled the smell of coconut at the ritual.

"You were with me."

"Yes."

"Am I dead now?"

Ciro made a strangled sound in his throat—he sounded pained. He shook his head as his lips pressed tight. Blue eyes met hers. "No."

"What happened?"

After she lost all that blood, and blackness took her, the smell of coconut occupied her full awareness for the longest time until Lukas flooded her senses. She could smell him—feel him. Even in the space she drifted between life and death, she heard his voice nearby.

But none of that could have been real.

She faced those madmen alone and didn't die, according to Ciro. So where was she outside of this place now? If she survived the ritual, had they moved her back to the dungeon? She could only imagine the scars once the wounds healed. No way would they properly stitch the gashes in her arms and legs.

Ciro sat beside her and looked at the sky, watching once again as a dragon emerged from a cloud bank and flapped its massive wings once before disappearing into the fluffy white clouds again.

"When I pushed you into the pond, you absorbed the golden life magic from the waters. It mingled with your own, and when you most needed it, your body called on it, saving your life."

"Much to the Celestial Conclave's surprise," the Oracle said.

Blaire pivoted her upper body to look at the Oracle emerging from the tree line. The crow companions that followed her everywhere landed next to Blaire.

"Surprise? I thought they were all knowing."

The Oracle smiled warmly. "Even they can miss a thing or two." She cocked an eyebrow at Ciro. "You interfered in ways that go beyond what you're allowed."

If Blaire hadn't looked at Ciro, she would have missed the subtle tightening of his shoulders.

"Is he in trouble?"

"I don't know, child."

"He saved my life! They can't punish him for that."

The Oracle gave her an indulgent smile and slowly lowered herself onto a log near them. "He wasn't the only one."

"I don't understand."

"Your Korrena finally understands."

Blaire's nose wrinkled, and her brows lowered. Her head hurt too much to try to make sense of the cryptic way the Oracle spoke. Why did her head hurt so much in a dream?

"You love him." It wasn't a question, but why did Ciro throw it down like a challenge?

"Of course, I love him."

"Why? I've sensed the distress he has caused you time and time again." His startling blue eyes bored into hers. "I was sent to protect you, but you've allowed him to hurt you. His personality can't be good if he hurts you."

It probably should bother her he knew so intimately what happened in her life, but if he only sensed emotion, and didn't have an actual window into seeing her private life, it wasn't so bad. If he could see them in bed, or her in the shower, she didn't think she could tolerate having a Guardian.

She smiled, thinking of Lukas. "Love is more than perfection. Genuine love sees beyond the best insecurity, beyond their flaws. When you love someone, you love them with your whole heart. You love all of them, not just the perfection. You take the bad traits with the good, and you grow together, building something bigger than you started with."

The surge of emotions stirring within her at her own words—her truth—clogged her throat. Lukas was a possessive control freak. He might never fully overcome that side of himself, but she accepted he wasn't perfect. As long as he tried, she wouldn't give up on him.

Ciro closed his eyes and crossed his arms over his chest. "I've never experienced it."

Maybe the day when she finally reached whatever point the Oracle mentioned before, Ciro could move on and meet his person. Did his kind have Korrena pairs?

"Um. Do wolves have Korrenas?"

"Shifters have mates, yes. But we don't call them Korrenas. Every species has a different name, but it is the same thing at its core."

"What do you call it?"

"*Notalme.*"

"What?"

"No. Tall. Mey," he enunciated slowly. "It's the same pair bond as you share with your Korrena. We just have a different title and a different way of sealing our bond."

"How?"

His gaze slid to hers, and the Oracle chuckled. "Everything is the same but the blood. We bite to mark our Notalme, and the wound never fades. There isn't a black symbol like the Vasirian have."

Blaire tilted her head. "Without the mark, how do you know? Lukas saw the mark on me."

"Our wolf knows. Senses it. Tells us."

What other species might be out there? What other shifters did Ciro refer to? What might they call their pairs, and how different was their bonding? Everything about this new world fascinated her. Would she ever explore it outside of her dreams?

"You won't be able to physically come here in your time."

Blaire looked at the Oracle. "Why not? If that whole balance thing works itself out, and I become a Vasirian at some point, why wouldn't I be able to come here?"

"Your place is in the realm where your waking body is. If you walk the path that restores things to their rightful place, your descendants will walk these lands."

Her descendants.

Did the Oracle mean Vasirian or human descendants? Her children or their children? Children with Lukas or with someone else? She shook her head quickly. No. There was no one for her other than Lukas. Even if she didn't want to be a mother so young, her entire being rejected the notion of having another man's child.

The Oracle's gentle eyes and soft smile said she read everything that crossed Blaire's mind.

If she survived the ritual, then she needed to escape and find Lukas. She didn't know how she would get out of the dungeon without Rue there to help, and Blackthorn Security didn't seem to want to interfere. Her chest tightened as panic filtered in. Would she ever escape?

Before she could ask the Oracle or question the confusion on her face, a sudden pull jerked her body forward without her control. She squeezed her eyes shut to ward off the dizziness, and when she opened them, she was staring at a mess of light brown hair with blond highlights.

Blaire blinked and blinked again. Lukas held her upright in bed in the tightest embrace she'd ever felt from him, his head tucked into her shoulder. He must not know she was awake, but why had he pulled her up?

Confused, she grew aware of their wider surroundings, the dimly-lit dorm room she hadn't seen in two months. She knew the room, but it was still unfamiliar to her. She'd been held captive by Vincent for two months and spent only a few days with Lukas in this new room before he was locked away in the dungeon for a week, leaving her alone. To lie in a comfortable bed soaked in scents that relaxed her body next to her pair after being apart from him for so long made it hard to believe this moment was real and not another dream.

She tried to speak, but her hoarse voice made a croaking noise.

Lukas lifted his head quickly and stared at her with wide eyes. The pale green of his irises stood out against the dark circles around his eyes. "Blaire," he whispered, placing a trembling hand against her cheek. He brushed her hair back from her face with his fingertips.

She tried to speak again, and managed a raspy, "Water."

Lukas reached to the nightstand, keeping his other arm around her, and grabbed a glass of water, which he lifted to her lips. She drank and received instant relief. The entire time, Lukas stroked her hair gently. He didn't stop touching her.

When he set the glass aside, she cleared her throat.

"What happened? Why am I—Why are you holding me?"

Lukas didn't let go, toying with her fingers with his free hand. "I didn't think you'd wake up." He looked up at her eyes. "Then I heard you mumbling, right before your panic hit me. I don't know what happened in your dream, but I needed to hold you."

Blaire tried to recall what made her panic in her dream. She was having a pleasant conversation with Ciro and the Oracle, and then…

"What is it?"

"Huh?"

"I feel you, Blaire. So strongly. Why are you scared?"

Blaire swallowed. "I was dreaming of that place again, but I didn't know I was free from the dungeons. Did you know they put me in the dungeons?"

He nodded slowly.

"I was thinking how if I survived their stupid ritual—Do you know about that?"

Another nod, and he squeezed her hand.

"I was thinking of how I would escape. How I needed to get to you."

"I'm here. You're safe. The Order is gone."

"Gone?"

Lukas tightened his hold on her hand and went into the entire story of how they found out about Blaire's escape, the ritual, and how

Tobias, of all people, assisted them with the help of the Blackthorn Clan to rescue her. He still looked like he held something back, and the uncomfortable feeling pouring from him that she couldn't identify made her nervous.

"Tell me."

He avoided her eyes.

"Lukas."

Was he crying?

Blaire took the hand not clasped in his and touched his face, pausing briefly to notice the bandage on top of her hand, before turning his face to her. His eyes were red, and his lashes were damp. His nose looked red around the nostrils.

"Talk to me."

Eyes clouded with emotion met hers, and he took a breath, nostrils flaring. "You died, Blaire." His voice cracked on the admission. He took a shuddering breath as he added, "And I… I let you go."

"I… What?" Her chest tightened at the sorrow radiating from him, from the memory that obviously came back to him as he got a distant and pained look on his face. "You're serious," she whispered.

His eyes turned sharp, and his brows lowered, his lips tilting down in a tight line. "I would never joke about something like that."

"Hey." She squeezed the fingers still interlaced with her own. "I'm not saying you're joking. I'm just surprised. I don't understand. What do you mean you let me go?"

Lukas looked away from her. "When it happened, they wanted me to change you. To make you one of us." He looked into her eyes. "You've lived your life being told what to do, forced into situations you didn't have a say in. Coerced into things that weren't fair to you. Blaire, I don't want you to be bound to me that way. I couldn't live with myself knowing I took that choice from you. Even if I had to spend the rest of my life without you, I wanted you to have at least one thing someone else didn't push on you."

"You let me die? I wasn't already dead when you found me?" His body stiffened, and she immediately grabbed his hand and added, "I'm not upset. I just want to understand. It doesn't change how I feel about it."

"How *do* you feel about it?"

"I didn't want to die. If I had been aware, I'd have asked you to do it." She resisted laughing at his shocked expression at her admission. "But like you said, without me being conscious, I wasn't able to make the choice. You didn't know. While I didn't *want* to die, it means so much that you considered my ability to choose as the most important thing."

"Riley wasn't happy about it."

Blaire laughed and shook her head. "I would hope no one would be happy about my death." She laughed harder when Lukas looked up, startled. "I know you weren't either. I just mean, I'm happy you understood me. Understood where I've come from, and what it would mean to me if you did that, even if I would never know you did that for me." She reached up and cupped his cheek with her free hand.

She didn't know Lukas was capable of such a selfless act. Sure, he was a caring guy who wasn't entirely selfish, or callous, but most people would choose to save their loved one without considering their feelings. Wouldn't they? She lowered her hand and looked at her lap as she considered that. She didn't know what she would do in the same situation. Most wouldn't understand his decision, but she saw it for what it was. At least, she thought she did. It wasn't that he didn't care. Right? It had to have taken a lot for him to let go of that need to possess and control everything, to watch her die without interfering. Maybe another person would be angry to be left to die, but she didn't view it that way. He didn't just leave her to die; he gave her rest.

Still, a part of her wasn't settled. She couldn't place why.

Lukas leaned in and put his forehead against hers, a charged moment where the powerful emotions passing over her spoke of his feelings for her. "I love you, Blaire." His lips brushed hers. "I'm glad you're home."

"I missed you," she whispered.

Another kiss. "It's been hell without you."

"I'm here now."

Their words were spoken so softly she was surprised they could hear one another. As if speaking above a whisper might upset the fragile connection growing with every word, every kiss. Too afraid of messing up after all the misunderstandings, inner turmoil, and external forces that tried to separate them.

They needed one another. No doubt of that fact lingered in her mind.

While others saw Lukas's need to control and possess as negative—and she wouldn't lie to herself and say it wasn't at times—it also made sense to her. The more he worked on reining it in and using it constructively, the more he gave her the stability she lacked. Her life had been turned upside down when her mother married into the Wilcox family. She never felt like she had control over her own life. Never felt protected, even from her own mother, once the Wilcox family sank their claws into their lives. Lukas gave her that protection. His unwavering devotion to her, and need to have her with him, gave her peace she didn't have before. That he released his need for control to allow her one last chance of control over her own life spoke volumes.

Lukas had grown up without a proper family; she knew familial love and understood the loneliness he carried. The same loneliness she suffered when her mother died. Few could understand the deep-rooted pain of abandonment if they'd never experienced it. While her mother didn't intentionally leave her, she was gone, and Blaire remained. So, while she could guide him through learning to accept care and affection like she experienced growing up, he would be her pillar for what she had lost. They were each other's family now.

Perhaps when Blaire first accepted their bond, and told Lukas she loved him, she rushed into the relationship. Relied too heavily on the Korrena connection she only understood after her time apart from Lukas.

One could argue she rushed into her love for him, but no one could control when, or if, he or she fell in love. Out of everything, Blaire was most certain about her feelings for Lukas.

Accepting the bond had felt right when they claimed one another, and she didn't regret it. She loved him then as she did now. But with all the uncertainty over the future, and Lukas's inability to let go of his need to control his surroundings because of his own fears, problems arose.

It wasn't surprising Vincent and Clarissa had manipulated them so easily.

Lukas pulled away. Disappointment settled in Blaire's belly. They needed to talk. There was so much she didn't know—like why she was in her dorm and not dead. And still the niggling, unclear thought lurked in the back of her mind regarding how he let her die. Something that grew louder the more she left it alone.

"When you… you know." Lukas sighed. "When your heart stopped, I don't know what happened, or what triggered it, but there was this bright red and gold light—magic—that covered your entire body." He perked up and looked at her with wide eyes. "Your wounds, the fresh ones and the old ones, they all closed! It was insane." He turned her arm over and she looked down at it. "Even the old scars are gone." True enough, the scar from the stitches after her run-in with the Order was gone.

"I think I know what happened."

"What?"

She didn't know how to tell him about her ancestry. About what she was. But she remembered the pool Ciro shoved her into with the gold light, and the explanation of why he did so. "You know those dreams I've had about the other world?" Lukas nodded, and she looked down, pulling at a hangnail on her thumb. "Well, there were these waters I fell into in my dream. Magical waters." She would tell him about Ciro later. "Apparently, my body called on them when I needed them most—they interacted with magic already inside me."

When Lukas said nothing—didn't freak out or act shocked—she looked up and found him sitting calmly.

Her brows lowered. "Why are you so calm?"

"Why wouldn't I be?"

"I just told you I was in magical water and the magic I absorbed mingled with my own. My magic, Lukas. As in, my blood is magical, or something like that."

"I know."

Her mouth fell open. How was he acting so nonchalant about it? "You *know*?"

"I do. The Oracle filled us in."

She slumped. At least she didn't have to go into the details about what the Oracle had revealed to her. The fact that magic saved her life was hard enough to believe, but after everything she'd seen in the dream world, it made this information easier to digest. Still, being allowed to die on an altar was a bitter pill to swallow.

Blaire's hands tightened in her lap as she considered her time in the dungeon and the clues she didn't catch from Tobias. The looks he'd given her during Vincent's trial and the day she traded herself for Lukas. Tobias had never wanted to hurt her like the other members of the Order. He was working against them. He was a part of the monarchy—a member of the Blackthorn Clan.

Brows furrowing, she recalled another piece of important information. Dominic called Tobias his cousin. Did that mean Dominic was also part of the Blackthorn Clan? That made little sense. Why would he be sneaking around and plundering archival vaults if another mole was already in their ranks? Blaire wondered what she should tell Lukas about Dominic. She didn't know what happened to him, and it worried her to think the Order caught him and either he was dead, or had his memory wiped. Had her blood finally hurt him in a delayed reaction? She looked at Lukas, who was studying her.

"There was someone locked away with me."

"I know."

"You do?"

"Riley overheard security mentioning a guy."

"Dominic."

Lukas frowned. Blaire couldn't read anything more in his expression, and his emotions weren't strong enough to reach her. He finally said, "Did he help you?"

"He did. But…." She looked away. "I had to help him, too. We were in that tunnel for so long, and it was, I dunno, like seventy hours or something before he could go get a packet… I had to help him." Her eyes found his when his grip tightened on her hand.

He looked conflicted. "Are you telling me what I think you're telling me?" His voice was calm, and he wasn't reaching her through their empathic connection, but the muscle jumping at the edge of his jaw betrayed his discomfort.

Blaire took a steadying breath that stuttered as she exhaled. "Yes. If he didn't drink blood, he could have killed me. You didn't see how much he was suffering. How long he put it off before…" She sighed.

"Did he force you?"

"No! Actually…" She laughed with little humor at the memory. "I called him a coward for refusing."

Lukas couldn't hide his surprise, and his brows rose, forehead wrinkling. "You called a manic Vasirian a coward?" He shook his head. "That sounds like a Riley move."

"Yeah, well, I did what I had to in order to survive."

It wasn't the only time she called on her little friend's strength.

Lukas sighed. "Did anything happen?"

Again, she knew what he was asking without having to say the words.

"He didn't hurt me, or make me do anything. I…" Her teeth sank into her lip as she tried to think of how to tell him her feelings without triggering his jealousy. She didn't think she could handle it. But he deserved to know. How did she tell him she felt sexual attraction to another man? Or *had* felt sexual attraction. She didn't want Dominic.

"Blaire?"

"Lukas, something happened when Dom drank my blood." She sighed. "I felt things. When Vincent touched me—when he took my blood—I hated it. I wanted him to take me, Lukas! I wanted him to take my body instead!" She lowered her head and grasped the hair on top of her head, squeezing hard enough pain spiked where she pulled the strands. "It would have been better if he raped me instead of drinking my blood. Knowing what it means to you…" She averted her gaze.

He pulled her face back by her chin gently. "Please don't say that. I would have hated if he did that."

"But Lukas… I know what it means to share blood."

"It only means that if you want it to mean that. Korrena pairs want that. To pairs, it's special. To me, your blood is. But because a monster took advantage and drank your blood doesn't discredit what we have. You can't help that he wanted more from you."

Blaire lowered her hands, and her eyes filled with tears. "I did something terrible."

"What are you talking about?"

She blinked, and the first stream of tears tracked down her cheeks. "I got excited."

"What?"

"When Dom drank my blood, I didn't feel those awful things I did with Vincent. It… shit. I can't do this. I can't do this. I can't…" She scooted off the bed, unable to handle the situation any longer.

"Hey, wait." Lukas reached out, but she was already off the bed. "Talk to me. What did you feel?"

Blaire lay her head back and stared at the ceiling. "I wanted him to… I wanted to…" She looked back at Lukas. "I wanted sex, Lukas." Her voice cracked on his name.

"Sex? Why?"

"I don't know!" She licked her lips, salty from her tears. "I don't know why it happened. He bit my neck, and we were close together, and it felt good. It didn't feel like what Vincent did."

He slid to the edge of the bed, watching her. She still couldn't get a read on him, and the silence was freaking her out even more.

"He told me about the chemicals. That I just responded to physical stimulus, but I shouldn't have." She wiped her cheeks. "I shouldn't have…"

"Chemicals?" Lukas squinted. "And what do you mean you shouldn't have responded to physical stimulus? You can't control that."

"I should have! He didn't even want me like that. He didn't even touch me inappropriately aside from a kiss, and that was only after I practically threw myself at him. He tried to explain my reaction, explained the dopamine reaction that happens when a human bite victim accepts a bite willingly, and even acknowledged my love for you." She crossed her arms. "I tried to picture you whenever it happened, to help me out, but it made me want more. I thought if I could put you in his place, it would change things… It didn't. God, I'm an awful person." Her lip trembled as she stared at him.

"You kissed each other?"

"Yes. I'm so sorry. Please don't hate me."

He stood from the bed and stepped forward. "I could never hate you, Blaire." His hands cupped both of her cheeks. "Look at me. Listen to me. I love you. I will never hate you."

"You should."

"No. You should explain to me what the hell you're talking about with this bite victim and chemicals mess."

"Dom told me he didn't know it was true before, but supposedly if you drink from a willing human, Vasirian release chemicals to make the process pleasurable for the person receiving the bite. If they don't accept it, the chemical reaction doesn't happen, and it hurts. He said that's probably why Vincent's bite hurt, and I didn't feel the same with him."

When Lukas didn't respond for a minute, she pulled away and took a few steps back. "Should I leave?" She resisted the urge to throw herself at him and beg him to keep her in a last-ditch, desperate attempt to hold onto the guy she loved.

"What? No!" He pulled her into his arms. "Blaire, no. Stop." He looked down at her. "You gave him your blood to fulfill the need for him to survive. To keep him from going mad and killing you. You saved both your lives. It wasn't because you wanted to have sex with him. I've never heard of the chemical stuff, but the likelihood it was mentioned in class is high—you know I didn't pay attention back in the Korrena education classes when I was younger."

"But what about the rest of it?" She buried her face in his chest.

He sighed. "Tell me about him."

"What?" She pulled back to meet his eyes.

"You said he didn't hurt you. You said he didn't force you. He helped you escape. So far, he doesn't sound like Vincent. So, what else? What else made him different?"

"Different?"

He gave her a gentle smile. "I don't think you would feel that way with someone you didn't trust, chemicals or not. So, I assume you trusted him."

"I did—I *do*."

"Why?"

"We spent a long time locked up together before escaping, and he made it tolerable. He comforted me when I couldn't take any more of their experiments. He made me laugh. He became my friend, Lukas."

Lukas inclined his head. "He took care of you." He kissed the top of her head. "I'm so glad he took care of you when I couldn't." He cupped her cheek. "But I understand this. Or at least I think I do."

"You do? Because I sure as hell don't."

He laughed, guiding her back to sit on the bed. "After what happened with Vincent, then having your trust shaken by me with everything that happened before I was locked away." He held a hand up when she started to protest. "I know you trust me now, but then you didn't. The thing is, when we did get together again, I didn't reassure you as much as I wish I could have. My guilt and lack of trust in myself didn't help our situation. So this guy…"

"Dominic."

"Dominic." Lukas nodded. "He was the first person in how long that you felt you could trust completely outside of Aiden? Someone who didn't make you doubt things, or didn't make you think they had an ulterior motive. I guess I'm not totally surprised to hear you formed a connection with him."

Blaire frowned.

"Then when an intimate act—one you've only associated with love and sex with me—happened, and there were actual chemicals involved which were designed to stimulate you, a human, of course you responded to it."

"How are you not mad at me?"

How could he sound so cavalier about it? It made little sense for him to be so calm. To be helping her through rationalizing the feelings. Why wasn't he throwing a fit?

"I'm not mad. I know it meant nothing. I know you."

Lukas had been so jealous of Vincent and Aiden, yet nothing with Dominic? She didn't understand. She admitted to wanting to have sex with Dominic. She hadn't with the other two.

Her expression must have given her confusion away because Lukas laughed softly and said, "I'm not happy about it. I don't like to know another man touched you." He trailed his fingers over her neck. "Drank from you." He dropped his hand. "But I'm not stupid. I know what it was. Other times when I acted like a tool, well, they wanted you. One of them you wanted, too." At her raised brow, he added, "Aiden. But I know it's not that way anymore. You said yourself this guy—Dominic—respected our love. Didn't try anything with you. He helped you escape, even if it didn't pan out."

"But we kissed. Aren't you angry about that?"

He had been so angry when Aiden kissed her.

"I admit it's hard to hear, but there is so much he did positive for you that I can't fault him if you were triggered by chemicals, and it stirred a reaction out of him. The important part is he didn't follow through. What happened to him?"

"I don't know. I'm worried. He went to get a blood packet, and while he was gone, the Order and Blackthorn Security broke into the hotel and took me back. I'm worried my blood might have hurt him."

"We need to tell Professor Velastra about him."

"Thank you for not exploding about it." Blaire sighed and looked down at her lap before snapping her gaze back to his face. "Rue!"

"What?"

"The Order has Rue. They forced her to bring me food and take care of me while they experimented on me. She's the niece of one of the assholes, and they've been keeping her in the diplomat wing where I was at before." She knotted her hands and swallowed hard. "I think she's in trouble. When they discovered she helped Dom and me escape, Angelo said something about a beating, and I haven't seen her since."

41

RESTORATION

"Calm down. We'll tell the professor about Rue. Right now, you need to rest. You've been through a lot."

Blaire yawned as if prompted by his words, and he smiled, running his fingers through her hair.

"Fourteen hours, yet you still look sleepy." Lukas couldn't help but laugh at the way Blaire's pretty green eyes widened and her mouth gaped. His thumb brushed gently over the top of her hand as he studied her face, her bedhead, and her flawless skin after the magic healed her. He shook his head and tried to rid himself of the image of Blaire laid on the altar like a sacrificial lamb.

"Fourteen hours?"

"The Oracle said you needed rest after what happened. You've been asleep, and for a while, the health department had you on an IV so you didn't get dehydrated."

It took effort to stay in control of his emotions, especially after hearing another Vasirian drank her blood, but she didn't need his intensity after what she went through. Rationally, he understood. He didn't lie when he accepted what happened, but that didn't mean he didn't feel jealousy and a need to wrap Blaire up and not let her out of his sight for an undetermined amount of time.

Blaire looked down at her hands, holding one up in front of her and twisting it around to study it in wonder.

"What is it?"

Lowering her hand, she sighed. "I'm still trying to process the magic thing, and why it saved me." She licked her lips. "My dreams have revealed a lot to me, but I'm still in the dark on why me, you know?"

"Did the Oracle not tell you?"

"Tell me what?"

"What you come from?"

The look of confusion on Blaire's face said it all. He couldn't feel her as strongly now that the situation was calm, and their bond was still in a tender place. But as he revealed the information the Oracle told them about the Blood War, witches and warlocks, Vasirian and human pair bonds of the past, and how Blaire was the only human remaining of that bloodline, her emotions peaked and broke through whatever barrier existed between them. He squeezed her hand.

"There's no one else?" she asked.

"She said something about dormant blood, but you're the catalyst to waking it up—whatever that means. Those people apparently aren't descendants, but have the qualities to be magical. Something like that."

Blaire let out a startled noise when Lukas pulled her into his arms again and held her tightly, whispering into her hair. "I've missed you. You have no idea. I'm so sorry I put you in that situation." He needed her to know how he felt. "I'll never make you choose. You're fine as you are. Human, Vasirian, it doesn't matter. Just don't leave me."

Her arms curled around his back, and as her slender fingers tightened into the fabric of his shirt, he finally relaxed for the first time in months. He almost didn't hear her whispered question.

"I still can't believe you didn't turn me. You've spent so long wanting me to be a Vasirian. The opportunity was right there."

"I told you," he mumbled into her hair. "I didn't want to let you die, but I wasn't going to force you into this life you weren't ready for." He wasn't even sure she could hear him, but he needed to tell her everything. "I wanted you to finally have the chance to not have someone else control your path." He lifted his head to look into her shining green eyes. "You ended up choosing your own path in the end. You overcame death itself in your choice for the life you want." Releasing a mirthless laugh on an exhale, he stroked her cheek, brushing away a stray tear. "You really are amazing."

Blaire sucked in a breath as he leaned in and brushed his lips across hers. Soft and warm, so different from the coldness from when they were in the temple.

He brushed his thumb across her lower lip, tugging it down as they stayed locked in each other's stare. Her love poured over him. He swallowed. "I want you. I *need* you. Please tell me you feel the same."

Blaire's lips parted, but instead of speaking, she leaned forward and kissed him, slow and soft, hesitant in the way her lips moved against his. But he could feel it. Feel her love, her forgiveness, her need. When she broke the kiss, she slowly pulled back to smile at him. "I told you before. I love you. That doesn't go away because things happened between us, or trust was broken. When you really love someone, it doesn't just go away. Not that easily." She looked up at him through her lashes. "I'll always need you. All six-foot-three inches of alpharoll you've got."

His brows pulled together. "Alpharoll?" He remembered her using the term alphahole, but this was new.

Her soft giggle warmed his heart. "Another book phrase. You're this bossy, possessive alpha type on the surface, but inside? Inside, you're a squishy cinnamon roll. Sweet and warm."

Lukas scowled, but there wasn't any bite to it. "That's not me."

"Oh yes, it is." She snorted at whatever she saw on his face, and warmth burned his cheeks and neck. "I like it. A lot."

They stared at each other in silence for a long time, peacefulness settling over them that hadn't been there before. Desperation, anger, confusion always lay beneath the surface as they struggled to reconcile the new situation they found themselves in. But now, the stillness gave him hope. The quiet of his mind encouraged him.

He placed his hand on her cheek. "Trust me?" He needed to know before he did anything more that he hadn't lost her trust completely. If even a crumb remained, he could work with that and build something stronger.

She leaned into his touch. "Longer than you've believed I did."

His heart pounded in his ears.

"I trusted you before they locked me up. You just didn't trust yourself."

A shuddering breath left him. He hadn't trusted himself to make love to Blaire that night. He tried, but he didn't trust himself not to hurt her again.

Guilt could be such a burden. All-consuming and destructive to the mind and heart. He let the guilt for not having control over something he didn't fully understand guide his actions until he didn't trust himself, and further pushed the rift that split their bond open. However, with the help of not only his friends, but his parents of all people, he realized that carrying such a massive burden wasn't for him to undertake. Blaire forgave him. Trusted him.

He had been prepared to let her go instead of forcing his desires on her when she was at her most vulnerable, knocking on death's door. He'd whispered his love straight to her non-beating heart, poured everything out to her, and swore he would find her again. She answered him in the most spectacular way possible.

A tortured, moaning whine left Blaire's mouth when their lips collided in a deep and ravenous kiss. He pushed her back on the bed, posting one hand above her head on the pillow and cupping her face with the other. His long hair framed her face as he ducked his head to devour her lips. He couldn't describe it any other way; he was hungry. He had been denied for so long he was starved for her kisses, starved for the sounds she made as he explored her mouth with his tongue. When they broke apart for air, her wet, swollen, parted lips and lust-glazed eyes made him dive back for more.

"Blaire." He sounded hoarse and needy, pressing his lips against Blaire's neck, mouthing, and nipping at the sensitive flesh. When she gasped at a bite that pricked her skin, he shuddered at the bead of crimson liquid that met his tongue. "I want you. I want you so much." His fangs dragged down the column of her throat while his hands parted her thighs, her t-shirt riding up to her hips.

Shaking hands made quick work of removing her t-shirt and panties, and as she lay there breathless, flushed, and staring up at him with such open trust, he ached inside. Ached with sorrow for the person he was less than a year ago before they met, for the angry, lonely boy he'd been. If he could go back and tell himself of Blaire, of what was to come, he would.

He pressed a chaste kiss to Blaire's lips before sitting up, pulling off his long-sleeved pullover, and tossing it aside.

Lukas lowered himself to spread hungry, wet kisses over Blaire's pale skin, pausing at her breasts to nibble and suck at the rosy buds peaking in the cool air of the room. He worshiped her skin with his tongue and teeth while making quick work of his belt, only pausing briefly to climb off the bed to rid himself of his jeans and boxers.

His full body shuddered at the undisguised desire that shined at him in Blaire's eyes when he turned back to the bed. She greedily drank in the sight of his naked body and unmistakable arousal. Her pupils were blown so wide he barely saw the green of her irises.

"Need you," she breathed, reaching for him.

Lukas stretched out over the top of her body and groaned at the sensation of their naked bodies pressing against one another. He didn't even have to be inside her to feel pleasure down to his toes.

But Blaire didn't let him revel in the satisfaction long. She pawed at him until he lifted his weight, and he hissed as she wrapped her fingers around his erection. It took him a few embarrassing seconds too long to realize what she was doing. When did she get her hands on the condom? He glanced at the open nightstand and then closed his eyes as a shiver passed over him when she rolled the condom down his length, her hand squeezing along the way.

When she removed her hand, he growled and crawled over her again, aligning himself with her center. He dragged his length down her soaked slit, making her lips part with a begging whine.

Fully lubricated, he lifted to his knees. She parted her legs for him with no provocation or guidance from him, completely compliant and eager. He placed a hand on her knee to steady himself. Lining his aching cock up with her entrance, he pushed in slowly, the muscles in his arms tightening with the effort not to slam home no matter how much he wanted to. When he bottomed out, Blaire's walls clenched around him. He cursed, his cock twitching and literally throbbing with need.

Heavy-lidded eyes met his. "I'm not made of glass." Her smile did strange things to his insides.

He groaned as he pulled out slowly and thrust back inside faster than he originally pushed in. Her answering moan spurred him on. His fingers pressed into the soft skin of her inner thighs as he held her legs spread apart, watching himself disappear inside the slick heat over and over again. The sight was intoxicating, and he felt drunk on the pleasure.

He set a steady rhythm, rolling his hips occasionally, and her answering mewls and whimpers pleased him.

"Harder," she said with a gasping breath.

With a grunt, Lukas fell forward and tucked his head against her neck, his hips snapping forward at a punishing pace that had Blaire crying out and hooking her ankles around his tense thighs. He took her at a fast and hard rhythm; the sounds of their sweat-slicked skin slapping together filling the room, joining the chorus of moans, grunts, and mattress squeaks.

Blaire's needy moans were heady. He always loved hearing his Korrena come undone, knowing he was the reason. That he could bring her such pleasure made the arousal much more potent. She looked dazed, her cheeks flushed pink, her chest rising and falling rapidly with her panting breaths. Wet, swollen lips called to him without words.

Lukas moved to her mouth, claiming it in a mess of lips, tongue, and teeth. He didn't care about finesse or technique. His thrusts grew wilder as he tasted her breath.

Her arms wrapped around his neck, one hand digging sharp nails into his shoulder while the other kept a painful grip on his hair at the nape of his neck.

I love you so fucking much.

Lukas couldn't say the words out loud, too caught up in kissing her. He'd die if he stopped.

He drove himself deeper and harder, bathing in the blissful sounds of her broken moans against his lips. He wanted to crawl inside her, bury himself deep for days, and it scared him how intense the need to be part of her was. But he knew she felt it too. Her emotions were washing over him, and he was drowning in them. He didn't want to swim.

When the familiar flutters began around his cock, he reluctantly broke the kiss, panting heavily.

He lifted himself and put his hands on each side of her head, staring down into her unfocused eyes, admiring the pink stain across her cheeks. His movements faltered when she ran a tongue over her lower lip, and the answering tightening of his balls let him know this wasn't going to go much longer. It had been too long.

He nearly came when Blaire tilted her head in silent invitation. His movements slowed to a near stop as he teased her with languid thrusts. She still wanted it. Still trusted him.

The demanding voice in his head remained silent; the beast was somehow satisfied.

His nostrils flared as he tore into his own wrist, knowing he would heal, and it would be fine. Her breath hitched.

Leaning down, he dragged the flat of his tongue over the front of her throat to the side of her neck, suckling the skin, and making her squirm on his cock.

Groaning, he positioned his arm beside her head on the pillow and sank his teeth into the perfect flesh of her neck, pulling her lifeblood into himself. The warm liquid, coupled with the sensation of her tongue running over his wrist, lit all his nerves at once.

When she tightened her legs around his hips and greedily sucked at his bloody wrist, he moaned against her neck and pumped into her at a punishing pace.

It didn't take long. Blaire broke her hold on his wrist, arching into him as her walls tightened and squeezed in a fluttering stranglehold when she reached her climax. The electric need raced down his spine and ripped through his belly. He mouthed the wound on her neck as he filled the condom, no longer drinking, struggling to breathe as white spots filled his vision from the force of his orgasm.

They stayed close together through the aftershocks, shuddering against one another, breathless and spent. When his mind was no longer in a haze, he kissed the two holes on her neck and used his tongue to seal them with his saliva. Smiling, he lifted his head, knowing he needed to feed her after sleeping for so long and drinking her blood. The IV didn't feel like enough nourishment to him.

He paused, staring down at her. Swallowing hard as emotion welled up in his throat, he slowly moved to meet Blaire's gaze.

Moving his sweat-damp hair aside, Lukas didn't speak. As tears filled Blaire's eyes and spilled over her temple into her hairline, he collapsed forward, wrapping his arms around her from beneath, and pulled her tightly to him. He didn't care that he was heavy and might squash her. He didn't care that he was crying. He didn't care that he hadn't removed the condom and it didn't fit as snugly as before.

All he cared about were the emotions flowing from her. Their mark was back. The bond repaired. He'd never let her go again. He never wanted her to let him go.

42

Family

The cafeteria was noisy for the middle of the night as Lukas led Blaire inside. Her eyes widened at the tables filled with students and adults she didn't recognize. Their usual table was empty.

"Blaire!"

Blaire *oof'd* as Riley collided with her and wrapped her in a punishing hug, sobbing uncontrollably.

"Can't... breathe." Blaire sucked in oxygen desperately when Riley let go. She'd forgotten how physically strong Vasirian could be if they tried or weren't paying attention. Tears rolled down Riley's face and her lips quivered, so Blaire pulled her back into her arms. "I missed you too," she whispered into the top of faded pink hair.

"You can't leave me like that!" Riley wailed and hiccupped against Blaire's hoodie.

Blaire looked up as Aiden approached. His jaw clenched and his piercing gaze burned into hers. When Riley released her, he stepped forward, and before Blaire could say anything, he pulled her into a tight embrace, burying his face in her hair.

She froze and looked at Lukas, whose lips turned down as he looked at his best friend. It wasn't a look of jealousy or anger. It was concern and sadness. Blaire felt it.

Slowly, she lifted her arms and put them around Aiden's tense back. His arms tightened around her as his body relaxed. After a few minutes, he finally released her, whispering as he pulled away, "You can't leave me, either." She looked up at him, and he leaned down and kissed her forehead.

Lukas stepped over, and he and Aiden hugged one another. Blaire rarely witnessed affection like this between them, but this entire ordeal shook everyone up more than she knew. Being unconscious or dead for most of it would do that to a person.

Aiden and Riley led them to a group of round tables on the other side of the cafeteria where Professor Velastra sat talking to a few other adults, Kai, Mera, and Seth.

"There she is," Seth said, and all heads swiveled in Blaire's direction. She wanted to squirm away from the scrutiny of eight pairs of eyes.

"Mama, Dad, this is Blaire!" Riley announced, still wiping smudged makeup from beneath her eyes as she pulled Blaire from Lukas's hold and dragged her to stand in front of a man with a muscular build much like Aiden's, dark brown hair, and familiar forest green eyes. He sat with his arm around an extremely short, curvy woman with a hairstyle that could only be described as big Southern hair. "Blaire, this is my mama and dad, Annie and Jack Easton."

Fluffing said layered hair, Annie's blue eyes lit up. "Oh, my goodness, gracious! She's stunnin'! Isn't she gorgeous, hon?"

Jack gave his wife an indulgent smile and chuckled. "She's pretty."

Blaire's eyes darted between Jack and Aiden.

"What?"

"You two could be twins."

Both father and son chuckled, and the uncanny valley sensation increased.

"Dad and Aiden do look a lot alike, and Dad is only sixty, so he doesn't look too much older than Aiden."

Blaire whispered, "How old is your mom?" She studied the woman who talked animatedly to her husband. She looked like a mother. She didn't look old, but she looked old enough to have a twenty-year-old son. Maybe forty-ish.

"One-hundred-eighteen."

Aiden took a seat next to his mother, and Riley took the empty seat next to Seth.

Blaire squirmed at the way a couple at the next table over watched her. When the woman caught her looking, she smiled warmly and tucked her short, dark blonde hair behind her ear. She was dressed in a sophisticated style; dress pants and a soft-looking, pale blue wrap-around blouse tied at the waist in a big, loose bow. Blaire looked away.

Lukas came up behind her and wrapped an arm around her waist, pulling her hair aside and dropping a light kiss on their mark. She sighed in contentment and melted against him.

"Wait. It's back?" Riley perked up in her seat. "But that means…"

Blaire flushed.

Riley shouted at Lukas, "Why didn't you tell me she was awake?"

"We were a little busy."

At Riley's death glare, he tucked his head into the side of Blaire's neck and laughed softly.

Blaire again caught the eyes of the couple sitting alone at the next table, and her brows furrowed at the way they stared at her with affectionate expressions.

Lukas lifted his head. "What's wrong?"

"Huh?" She looked up at him over her shoulder.

"You're uneasy."

Blaire laughed. She'd need to get used to that again. Her gaze slid back to the table where the woman and man were speaking to one another.

Lukas followed her line of sight and sighed. "Come on."

He led her to the couple. The man studying her with pale green eyes looked to be in his thirties, with longish brown hair swept back from his face and brushing the collar of his sweater. The woman smiled as they approached, reaching over, and clasping her hand over the man's. Her eyes were watery. Their expressions confused Blaire.

"Mom, Dad… this is my Korrena, Blaire."

Oh.

Lukas wrapped his arm around Blaire's lower back and pulled her close, likely sensing the spike of nervousness that shot through her. She thought he and his parents weren't close. She'd been told they only came for the holidays, if at all. As far as she knew, they hadn't been to visit since she'd met Lukas.

Smiling politely, she nodded at them. "Nice to meet you." It felt forced. She didn't like that she felt so uncomfortable, but knowing how lonely Lukas had been since he was five, and knowing they were the reason, fired within her an animosity she didn't want to feel.

When Lukas shot her a questioning look, she didn't know what to say, but she didn't have to say anything, because Professor Velastra stood and cleared her throat, clapping her hands to gather the attention of those around. Blaire had never been more thankful for that weird habit of the professor's until this moment.

They sat at the table with Lukas's parents. Blaire made a point of not looking at them or Lukas until she could get herself under control. She would talk to them, and she would tell Lukas her feelings, but she had to sort them out first. She owed him that much.

Professor Velastra stood where everyone could see her. "Not everyone is here tonight, but I wanted to at least make an informal announcement for the parents present regarding what occurred here on academy grounds." She swept her gaze across the cafeteria to the tables of students sitting with their parents. "Your children are safe here at Blackthorn Academy—"

"How can we be sure of that? I heard there was a raid recently, and before that, wasn't that human over there kidnapped?"

Blaire looked down and pulled her lips between her teeth as embarrassment curled around inside of her. Lukas turned in his seat to take her hand.

"You can rest assured we apprehended the culprits behind the situation during the raid in question."

Professor Velastra detailed how the current administration had gotten involved in some underhanded things, fending off complaints when parents weren't satisfied with her lack of details. It wasn't something she could openly discuss while an investigation was underway by the Blackthorn Clan. She explained she has been made the de facto administrator overseeing academy activity until further notice. She even fielded criticisms about Lukas being dangerous. Blaire hadn't known that was a concern. But her explanation about the administration's corruption seemed to go a long way in settling the negative opinions around Lukas. She didn't discuss Blaire, her death, the magic, or anything that didn't directly involve the other students of the academy.

Lukas told Blaire on the way here that Riley told Mera and Kai when they returned from their trip last night. Blaire suspected Riley let her parents know, which was okay. But she didn't want the entire town to know, so she was thankful Professor Velastra used discretion.

After handling the many questions parents and students presented until they left the cafeteria, the professor returned to her seat with a heavy sigh. Mera set a cup of dark coffee in front of her.

"Thank you, Mera. It's been a long night."

Mera sat beside Kai and looked at Blaire. "I'm glad you're okay."

Kai nodded. "You continue to surpass my expectations of you." His heavily-lined eyes assessed Blaire with a strange awe.

Blaire looked down, flushing.

Seth sat back in his chair and crossed his arms. "So, what happens to the Order?" He looked at Professor Velastra.

Mera nodded, tapping her black nails against the side of her bottle of water. "Someone needs to not only run the academy, but also oversee the Vasirian population in this part of the world."

It was reasonable for Professor Velastra to take over temporarily at the school, but she couldn't manage the political dealings for so many Vasirian alone. Did she even have a political background?

"When I spoke with Tobias, he informed me that for the time being, the Blackthorn Clan will take over and delegate business from Europe until the investigation is concluded, and either a new Order can be named, or something else."

"Something else?" Jack asked.

"I'm not sure what that something else is. They need to go through Angelo's files and determine what information is accurate and what loose ends remain." The professor released an exasperated sigh. "I assume they must also sort through years of corrupt actions."

"That man needs to get his come uppin's." Annie tsked, sucking her teeth. "His parents had the wrong idea naming him Angel. Nothing angelic 'bout that psycho." She tilted her head in consideration, pursing her lips and raising both brows. "Of course, these churches 'round here teach that Lucifer was also an angel, so…" She left her words to linger in the air as she sipped the sugar and milk drink that she claimed was coffee, but it looked so pale, Blaire had her doubts.

"Angel? Mama, his name is Angelo."

"Italian, honey. It means Angel."

Riley's face flushed.

"Or messenger," Kai added.

"Yeah, well, that man doesn't fit either ticket."

Kai chuckled.

Riley's brows furrowed, and she leaned forward in her seat, propping her arms on the table. "So, if Angelo is in trouble, what about Clarissa?"

Seth raised a brow at her. "I thought you hated her."

"Riley Abigail Easton."

Riley groaned. "Yes, Mama?"

"It's not nice to hate people."

"But she—"

Professor Velastra cleared her throat, interrupting the mother-daughter duo before they could get started. Blaire wondered if she'd dealt with them before. Riley's mother's personality loomed larger than life, just like her daughter's. Blaire hadn't thought much about Clarissa, but Riley's question stirred her curiosity, even if she also felt nothing but disdain for the girl.

"With Angelo's assets frozen until the Blackthorn Clan can ascertain what he garnered through legal means, Angelo's daughter has been removed from the Blackthorn Institute and now lives with her aunt in Florence, Italy."

"Blackthorn Institute?"

Professor Velastra looked at Blaire. "The European branch.

Mostly comprised of children of diplomats in the Vasirian world and our royalty. It is the pinnacle of what Blackthorn education offers."

Mera frowned. "Will Clarissa get to return to school after they settle Angelo's finances?"

"Doubtful. With the reports of what Clarissa did, Angelo's involvement, and the uncertainty of how much Clarissa was involved in the Order's plans, no one can say what problems might arise at the institute."

Jack crossed his arms. "At least the clan is thinking smart with that."

Professor Velastra looked down at her coffee cup. "There's also something else I debated on sharing, but to spare the guilt of thinking this is anyone's fault for her obsession, I feel it might be best to divulge the information." Her eyes met Lukas's.

Aiden crossed his arms. "What is it?"

"It hasn't been long, but she already found another target for her fixation after her arrival at the institute. Unlike here, she didn't have her father's influence to help her manipulate her way into what she wanted. Her roommate discovered her journal open with obsessive ramblings about one of the senior students—portions of it quite dark and legitimately threatening. She was set for an administrative review, but before that could happen, she attacked the poor boy when he rejected her advances. She was apprehended, and a trial was set to take place when word came about the situation here. The Blackthorn Clan stepped in, and with the additional information of her violence, they opted to not let her stay in the interim. It is unlikely they will let her attend again."

Blaire sat back and sighed. She thought Clarissa was merely a spoiled, overeager airhead with a superiority complex, but the truth was so much worse. The girl needed professional help. Help it didn't sound like she would get in Italy if she was sent to live with family and banned from academia. Her obsession with Lukas wasn't a one-off situation.

Had Lukas not had Aiden and the others, would Clarissa have hurt him in her desire to get what she thought belonged to her?

Riley and Mrs. Easton talked loudly for another hour. Then as most everyone filed out of the cafeteria, leaving only Blaire, Lukas, and his parents, Blaire watched them leave. Lukas worried at how she held herself rigid, wound tighter than a piano wire despite everything that happened between them. It didn't help that he could *feel* the discomfort seeping from her pores.

When she turned back to the table, she looked down at her hands clenched on its surface.

"It is wonderful to finally meet you, Blaire. I'm Helena, and this is Jyrki."

Startled, Blaire looked up, her beautiful green eyes wide. Lukas didn't like what he saw there. She didn't want to be here.

His father's eyes narrowed, and he leaned in, resting his arms on the table. "You're upset."

It surprised Lukas how perceptive his father was. He didn't share an empathic connection with Blaire, and other than the wide eyes, nothing about her posture overtly said "upset" to someone who didn't know her well.

"I—"

"Jyrki, do not make her uncomfortable."

Jyrki had the decency to look embarrassed, scratching the side of his neck. "Habit from work. When you're around many people who don't speak your language as their first language, you learn to read their body language. It helps with negotiations. Sometimes it seeps into my everyday life. I apologize."

Blaire's cheeks pinked, and she lowered her head. "It's fine."

Lukas gritted his teeth. He hated seeing her cowed. When she looked at him, he knew she sensed his agitation.

Helena frowned. "Is there something we can do?"

"Blaire, talk to me."

Blaire looked at Lukas again and sighed. "I don't know how to act." She looked at his parents. "I'm so sorry. I don't even know you, but…" She shook her head. "I'm making a terrible first impression."

"But what, dear?"

"You haven't made a terrible first impression. Seeing my son as happy as he was holding you over there"—Jyrki pointed to where Blaire and Lukas stood earlier—"says all I need to know about you. You make him happy."

Blaire bit her lip, and Lukas reached out to tug it free. She sighed. "It's hard to be cordial when I know you…" Her face scrunched and she shook her head, cutting herself off. Her brows lowered as she edited what she clearly wanted to say. "When he was alone… No, um." She looked at Lukas with pleading eyes.

Before Lukas could say anything to help her, his mother spoke.

"Alone?" Helena's puzzled expression faded as her eyes widened. "Oh… I get it."

"What?"

Helena looked at Lukas. "Just as you have to fight your dominant traits, so does she. We are a threat." She laughed softly.

Lukas snapped his gaze to Blaire. Never in a hundred years would he consider his parents a threat. What was his mother talking about? The puzzled look on Blaire's face backed his thoughts.

"You're not a threat. You wouldn't hurt me," Lukas said.

Jyrki inclined his head. "Not physically, no. But we've been emotionally hurting you for fifteen years without realizing it."

"Your Korrena is protective of you. Of your heart."

Lukas looked back at Blaire, who stared at the table, frowning.

"I'm sorry. I can't help it. I just…" Her gaze lifted to his parents. "You have no idea how lonely he feels. How he feels when his friends who are siblings are together. I saw it before I ever felt it through our bond. I couldn't name it until I *felt* it."

Her fists tightened on the table, and her eyes looked glassy as she said, "My parents are dead. But you two? You may as well be." She paused and grimaced. "Not that I wish that. But you force him to live a life as if you are. And it's so much worse to tease him with crumbs… I would give anything, *anything* to see my mom again, or my dad—who I can't even remember—if only for a holiday. But to know they lived, and that's all they would offer me?" She shook her head and the look of derision turned into unmasked pain. "I would rather them not come at all to remind me of what I can't have." She pushed from the table and stood. "I'm sorry. I can't sit here and be cordial. Lukas has me now. I'm his family. I'm not going anywhere."

Lukas sat in stunned silence. The hostility and love fighting for dominance in Blaire was overwhelming. His own emotions pushed hers to the back of his mind as the implications of her words hit him. She was his family. He already felt that way, but hearing her say it… She claimed him and challenged his parents. He rubbed at his solar plexus roughly as his heart beat faster.

Jyrki started laughing, and Helena smiled with tears in her eyes. His parents had lost the plot.

Blaire stiffened with indignation, her fists tight and shaking at her sides.

"You're absolutely perfect," Jyrki finally said after getting control of himself. “She’s perfect, son.”

Deep lines settled between Blaire’s eyebrows as confusion set in.

“Protective and rational. Perfect for you.” Helena looked up at Blaire. “We have made grave mistakes in the past and have talked to our son. We did not know the damage we inflicted.” She looked down. “We are ashamed of ourselves, and he is giving us the chance to make it right.”

“Won’t you?” Jyrki said, sitting back and dropping his arm over the back of Helena’s chair, stroking her arm with his thumb. “We love our son. We didn’t know the impact our absence had on him. We were foolish.” His jaw hardened. “Allow us to prove to him the truth of our feelings—to prove them to you.”

“You don’t need my permission,” Blaire said softly.

“We do. He is your Korrena. We won’t interfere. But we would like to support him as his family and as yours.”

Blaire blinked, startled. “What?”

Lukas looked at his parents as they both smiled at Blaire.

“We would like it if you saw us as family too,” Helena said.

Jyrki nodded. “Maybe not today, but at some point, when we have proven ourselves to you, we hope you’ll see us as family.”

Blaire swallowed audibly, slowly lowering herself into the seat. Lukas slid his chair over to her and pulled her into his arms, doing his best to reassure her. If she wanted him to walk away from his parents, he didn’t know if he could. He just got them back. But Blaire wouldn’t do that to him, not if his parents were trying.

“If you make him feel that way again…”

Jyrki chuckled at Blaire’s murmured threat. “She’s feisty.” His face turned serious. “You’re a strong Korrena. Good for my son. You have my word I will be the father I should have always been.”

Helena nodded.

For all his attempts to protect and come to Blaire's defense, Lukas never expected her to do the same for him. At least, not like this. Not that she didn't care, but he wasn't used to having someone stick up for him emotionally. Aiden and Seth always backed him in a physical fight, but no words were necessary, and certainly no feelings were involved.

Yet, this beautiful human being who worked her way under his skin noticed the loneliness and longing without him ever having to tell her. Without their bond revealing the pain he tried to hide from everyone. No one had seen it. At least, no one cared enough to say anything if they did. He suspected Aiden knew. Aiden always included Lukas in everything like a brother, but he didn't think Aiden understood on the level he needed.

Blaire did.

His hold tightened on her as she finally relaxed against him, talking to his parents while they tried to get to know her.

It would take time, but if his parents were serious about building a relationship with him, Lukas could finally have the family he thought he lost and the family he wanted to create.

43

Fallout

The atmosphere was peaceful in the tree grove. A perfect place for a picnic lunch. It was Riley's idea, and she encouraged both Mera and Layla to come along with them. While Lukas said his goodbyes to his parents, they spread the blanket and started unpacking lunch.

Blaire relaxed against the shade tree in the grove across from the hedge maze, listening to the birdsong overhead and chatter of students in the adjacent courtyard, many having just returned after their parents were assured of their safety.

Lukas had told Blaire how he felt her emotions strongly in this space, and she recalled her own senses connecting to him when he was locked away when she passed by the same grove. Both suspected the dungeons were beneath the grove, but they would never know for absolute certainty without a blueprint.

Blaire yawned and closed her eyes, listening to Layla talk excitedly about something her little brother said.

Layla had been shy at first—nervous to meet Blaire—but she warmed up quickly. Blaire hadn't thought a human could intimidate a Vasirian. Layla explained it away by saying she wasn't used to making friends with humans. Apparently, her parents kept her sheltered.

An azalea-scented breeze ruffled the tree grove, and Blaire sighed. The fuchsia, baby pink, and red blossoms bloomed a couple of weeks early this year; they usually graced the area with their presence from late February to March. The perfumed breeze, coupled with the delicate pink petals falling from the flowering apricot tree around them, and other early spring blooms, relaxed her. Fresh air and sunshine provided a much-needed change from dimly-lit dungeons and dirt tunnels.

Her mind drifted first to Dominic, then to Rue. When she told Professor Velastra about Rue, the professor expressed her shock and requested Blaire not share the information with anyone else, aside from their small group who already knew, until she could look into it properly. Thankfully, she hadn't seen Liam. She didn't think she could keep that a secret from him. She still needed to tell the professor about Dominic, but since he wasn't a student, she didn't know what could be done—or even if he'd get in trouble for breaking into the academy.

Lukas's lips, brushing hers, startled her out of her thoughts. She hadn't even noticed his return.

He smirked. "What has you distracted?"

"I was thinking about Professor Velastra."

"Rue?"

"Mm." Blaire popped the lid off the plastic container of chicken Caesar salad she got from the cafeteria. "I hope something gets sorted sooner rather than later. I'm worried about her."

"I'm sure she'll be fine."

Riley looked at Lukas. "I haven't seen Liam since the raid."

Lukas sighed and settled on the blanket, knees bent, feet apart flat on the fabric, and rested his forearms on his knees. His hands hung limply between them. "I haven't spoken to him in a while, all things considered. But we've never had much of a relationship. Not that I dislike the guy… I only ever really saw him with Rue, and that was with Blaire, and Blaire has been gone, sooo…"

Blaire pressed the back of her fist that held her fork against her mouth to avoid laughing. She always found it endearing when Lukas got awkward. It was one of the rare times he talked a great deal. She didn't think he was even aware of the habit.

"Where's Seth?" Riley asked Lukas, her cheeks flushing as she poked at her own salad absentmindedly.

"With Kai, distracting Aiden while I talk to you."

She looked up at him, small lines creasing her eyebrows. "Distracting?"

"Do Mr. and Mrs. Easton have any plans for Aiden's birthday this year? I know sometimes you visit Brandon in South Korea."

"Brandon?" Layla asked.

Riley looked at her. "Our older brother. He's got his own cooking show and several restaurants in Seoul."

"Wow. That's amazing."

"He does make a killer *daeji bulgogi*."

Layla's small nose scrunched. She looked like a kid when she did that, Blaire mused. She thought Layla was someone's freshmen sister from the high school branch until Riley introduced her as Lukas's classmate. "Isn't *daeji* pork?"

"Yeah."

"I prefer the beef kind."

"Don't knock it till you try it."

"I have. Mom and Dad took me to a restaurant in Seattle once that sold it."

"Ew. That's not authentic. When you've tried the real stuff, then you can complain."

Mera shook her head with a small smile on her face. "Not everyone has a chef for a brother."

"It is pretty awesome."

Blaire had no opinion whatsoever. She didn't know anything Korean aside from a few common words for family members she heard repeatedly in TV dramas she hadn't watched since early high school.

"Back on topic," Lukas said, reaching over and grabbing the blood packet Blaire had kept for him while he saw off his parents. "Aiden's birthday. Plans?"

"Not this year. Brandon is relocating one of his restaurants and can't take the time."

Layla closed her empty salad bowl. "When is his birthday?"

"Next week, the seventeenth. He'll be twenty."

"Milestone."

Riley shrugged, flicking at a buckle on her boots with her fingers. "Not really. He's not old enough to drink legally—which he's not a big drinker, anyway, and we always get drinks at Haven without ID." She laughed at Layla's expression of surprise. "What? Never been?"

"No."

"You're not missing a lot. Music, dancing, drinking." Mera turned an assessing eye on Layla. "Unless you're into that?"

Layla looked down at her lap, pulling on the hem of her plaid uniform skirt. "I wouldn't know."

Riley frowned. "Why do you say twenty is a milestone?"

"Well, my parents consider us adults at twenty. They finally stopped hovering over my older brother when he turned twenty and moved out with his Korrena."

"That explains a lot."

"What do you mean?"

"Your parents."

Layla shrugged. "I'm used to it."

Blaire took a sip of her peach tea and got an idea. "Maybe we could rent one of the back rooms at Haven for Aiden's birthday? Didn't you say they had private rooms for small gatherings?"

"For, like, ten or fifteen people."

Lukas waved a hand. "There's eight of us. Ten, if you count Rue and Liam, if that works out by then and she's okay. I doubt your parents will want to go to Haven."

"You underestimate how weird Mom is."

"What about Charlotte?" Blaire asked. "She enjoys hanging around with us, and she and Aiden get along. She'll be leaving for Athens soon."

Charlotte wasn't a Vasirian, and while Haven was a Vasirian-owned nightclub, and humans were allowed to go there, she wasn't sure if they would want to be on guard for Aiden's birthday. If the party lasted too long, they'd need to drink blood. She shuddered, remembering the early effects of sanguis manie.

Riley cocked her head to the side. "Why couldn't she come too?"

"Won't you need blood?"

Lukas twisted his lips in thought. "I don't see why we can't arrange a solution. I doubt we'd be there long enough to where it's a problem if we drink beforehand. We'll have to talk to her."

Charlotte was already annoyed with the school for keeping Blaire away so long for "testing." Which hadn't been a lie when they told her, according to Lukas, but now it was more than that. She only hoped Charlotte didn't ask more questions. Blaire wasn't in the mood to lie to her friend. She wouldn't.

Blaire put her things in her backpack. "I'm supposed to meet Professor Velastra after lunch." She looked at the clock on the administration building. "I'm going to be late if I don't go."

Lukas pushed to his feet. "I'm coming with."

"Not without me." Riley shoved her things into her messenger bag and stood, looping the strap over her petite frame to wear across her chest. "I wanna know what happened to Rue."

"I can clean up everything," Layla said.

Mera looked up. "I'll stay and help. I want to see Kai anyway when we're finished."

"I'm happy to see you're well and there haven't been lasting effects," Professor Velastra said, taking her seat in the large leather chair behind her desk.

Blaire sucked in a surprised breath when Lukas sat in the smaller leather chair in front of the desk and tugged her into his lap, encircling her waist with his arms, pulling her against him. She was used to his proprietary actions, but he usually reserved them for casual gatherings, not serious meetings. Not that she was complaining. His arms comforted her in ways she couldn't explain, but she didn't try to, melting into his support.

Aiden took the seat next to them and Riley sat on the arm of his chair, facing Blaire and Lukas.

"Any news?" Riley asked.

Professor Velastra nodded. "Rueanna Wainwright was discovered in the room next to where we found Blaire in the diplomat wing. She was dehydrated and suffering from a case of sanguis manie. From my understanding, only after Blackthorn Security got her stabilized could Rueanna reveal what happened to her."

Riley cocked her head sideways. "Which is what? Is she okay?"

"After the Order discovered her involvement in your escape,"—her gaze lifted to Blaire—"her uncle repeatedly beat her until she could barely move, only to have it done again once she healed." The grim look shadowing Professor Velastra's face turned something in Blaire's stomach. "During this time, and the time leading up to her rescue, they only gave her blood once every couple of days. Not even a full packet. Not enough to keep the madness at bay, but enough to keep her alive."

"That's sick," Aiden said. "Torture."

"It is, and for that reason, her parents have taken her from the academy. Liam has joined her, and I doubt she will return to classes anytime soon, if at all. The trauma of what she experienced has done significant damage to her psyche. While the physical wounds have healed, she has a long road ahead of her to heal those psychological wounds."

Blaire tightened her fists in her lap, staring at her hands. If only Vasirian healing worked on the mind as it did the body.

She felt a perverse gratefulness for the things she endured at the hands of her stepbrother and his grandparents, and at losing her parents young; these human losses built coping mechanisms and strength within her before coming to the academy. Having Ciro there, though she was unaware of his presence, had given her an advantage. In spite of everything she had gone through, she hadn't snapped and become a shell of herself. Therapy helped. Friends helped. Maybe the magic in her blood helped. But not many walked away from the things she'd endured unscathed. Rue's breakdown was a perfect example of that. Before the beatings and deprivation of blood, Blaire saw the cracks. Being separated from Liam, and forced to do what the Order wanted, set Rue up for a fall.

"I also wanted to mention," Professor Velastra said, resting her hands on her desk, "one of the guards seemed particularly concerned about your well-being when witness reports were made."

"What?" Blaire glanced over at Riley, then back to Lukas, before looking at the professor again. "Who?"

"Katie Dover. She informed me of the things she did while you were locked up, and she was concerned about what happened to you. I've assured her you are safe and well."

"Is she okay?"

"The only punishment she faced for her actions was reassignment. I believe Tobias had a hand in the lesser punishment, considering the way the rest of the Order would likely have acted."

Riley tilted her head. "What did this Katie do?"

"She looked out for me until she was caught. Brought me nice bedding, toilet paper, something to drink besides water, and food outside of the few times they brought meals. She was nice."

The knowledge that Katie was okay brought immense relief. The woman didn't deserve to suffer for her role in making the dungeon tolerable.

Blaire looked up at the professor. "There's one other person I'm worried about." When no one commented, she said, "A young man was locked away with me. He's the same age as Lukas, if I remember right, but he's not a student."

"The guy you escaped with?"

She looked at Riley and nodded. Lukas tensed beneath her, so she rubbed soothing circles over the top of his hand resting against her stomach.

"His name is Dominic. I don't know his last name. I think… I think Tobias knew him—was related to him, maybe a cousin. I caught them talking in his cell once when I woke up."

"I didn't hear anything in the reports from security, but I can investigate it. What happened?"

"When he went to get blood after our escape, the Order captured me. We got separated."

Professor Velastra's thin lips pressed into a stern line, and she nodded.

Lukas shifted and pulled Blaire closer when silence settled. "I told Blaire about what the Oracle said. About the witches and all that. It's obvious she knew about the magic in Blaire's blood at that point, but she had no idea about Blaire's family history."

Aiden looked at her. "Nothing strange ever happened that you know?"

"No. Dad died when I was a toddler, and I didn't know my family on either side. It was only Mom and Dad."

She debated mentioning what the Oracle told her about her father, and his plea for the Celestial Conclave to keep her safe. Mentioning that information, and Ciro, might mess things up more than they were if the Oracle's warnings about revealing too much information were to be believed. She would tell Lukas. But she didn't see how it applied to her family history. They knew the same information about magic in her bloodline that the Oracle shared with her. They had even found out more through the Oracle than she had.

"I really don't have any family that I know of, so it's a possibility something is different about my father's side."

Professor Velastra crossed her legs and gave her a cool, assessing stare. "Your father's? Why not your mother?"

Blaire's shoulders bunched.

"Blaire?"

She turned to look at Lukas. "I was going to wait to tell you."

"Tell me what?"

Blaire huffed. She hated the feeling of being muzzled. "I don't know how much I'm supposed to say or not, but at this point I don't care."

It took a while to fully describe her dreams. To tell them about the other world she kept dreaming of. She refused to lie about it, and for her to tell them only select parts, she'd have to lie about other parts or omit them, which would make her story confusing and unbelievable. It was already far-fetched. She told them about the Shimmer Gates, Ciro, and her father's request. What Ciro was.

Aiden looked confused. Riley bounced in place, more than excited. Lukas projected a mix of emotions. She'd told him about much of it, but not about the newest revelations from the dream world. Not the fact their world was separated from another, the gates, or Ciro. His confusion made sense. The flare of jealousy over Ciro made sense, so she reminded him Ciro was old enough to be her father. She didn't ask Ciro about shifters and aging. It was irrelevant. Maybe if they ever met again, she would.

Professor Velastra closed her eyes and exhaled heavily. "It is clear now that you're important to the survival of the ancient connection severed by Rosendo Blackthorn." She opened her eyes and looked at Blaire. "With your father's death, you became the sole descendant with the power to restore that balance."

"I don't know how."

"No, but in time that might become apparent, and the key to those answers lies in the messages you've already received."

Riley looked from Blaire to the professor. "Becoming a Vasirian?"

"Part of it, yes, but I think her magic has something to do with it as well. For now, though, we must keep this information quiet."

"Why?"

Professor Velastra glanced at Aiden, and then let her gaze move over each of them before speaking. "Because if it gets out in the Vasirian world how important Blaire is to our kind, she may find herself in more danger than she's ever known. The likelihood is high that Vasirian exist who would agree with Rosendo's stance on separation of human and Vasirian, and who fear the power that comes with their union—especially among those already prejudiced against humans."

Riley's nose scrunched. "Like Angelo and Clarissa Moretti?"

"Precisely. This information paints a massive target on Blaire's back."

Unease settled in Blaire's stomach, and she felt like throwing up. When Lukas pulled her in, tucking her head against his neck and placing a comforting hand on the back of her head to cradle her like a child, she didn't stop him. She soaked up the love and conviction to protect her coming through their bond, wrapping her in warmth.

She knew being part of this world wasn't going to be easy. That it would be dangerous. As much as she would like a reprieve from the insanity that had become her life, she could make it through. The people around her wouldn't let her give up, anyway.

"Now I have a question." Lukas tightened his arms around Blaire, and when the professor nodded for him to continue, he said, "What are these chemicals that make someone bitten feel pleasure?"

Aiden smirked. "I don't think the chemicals work with Korrenas. It's your bond. And your feelings for one another."

"But you know about the chemicals?" Blaire asked, lifting her head.

Aiden looked at Blaire. "Of course. We're all taught about them in middle school. If there's a willing—"

Lukas rubbed his face. "We know that part. I just wanted to see if what we heard was actually true."

Professor Velastra crossed her arms over her chest. "What's going on?"

Blaire looked down. Her chest, neck, and scalp prickled with heat. "I allowed Dom to drink my blood."

"Dom?" Aiden asked.

Riley jumped up. "You what?"

Blaire looked at Aiden. "His friends call him Dom. We spent a lot of time together." She shrugged and looked at Riley. "He was suffering from the early stages of *sanguis manie*. I was scared he would end up killing me down in the tunnel because we were only halfway through, and he was showing signs of aggression." She looked from Riley to Professor Velastra. "The problem came when I…" She looked at Aiden and frowned, her face heating more. Talking about sexual things in front of guys other than Lukas made her squirm.

"Go ahead, it'll be alright," Lukas mumbled into her hair as he pulled her close.

Blaire sighed. "When he bit me, it excited me."

Riley's mouth formed an O as if she finally understood.

Aiden shrugged. "That's normal."

Relieved to have it out in the open, Blaire's tongue loosened. "That's what he said. Lukas didn't know about it, though, so we weren't sure."

Professor Velastra nodded. "I understand your concern, especially with a stranger. But he's correct. If you offered your blood willingly, his body chemistry would naturally respond and feed you chemicals to make the process easier to experience."

"But that doesn't make any sense," Blaire said.

"What doesn't?"

"How can his body chemistry know I'm giving him my blood versus him just taking it from me against my will?"

"I'm sure there's a science to it, but it isn't something I'm well-versed in." Professor Velastra tapped her fingers on the arm of her chair. "I'd wager the one initiating the bite feels relaxed before feeding from a willing partner. If it were merely a situation of predator versus prey, stress hormones would be heightened, and the body might not act accordingly. At least, that sounds like the best plausible theory. And no, Korrena pairs don't require the same chemical to make sharing blood stress-free when there is such a strong connection between them."

The additional reassurance from the professor helped ease Blaire's mind. Not that she didn't trust Dominic, she just didn't understand. Part of her also wanted Lukas to hear from someone else besides her to give him reassurance and remove any possible doubt he may still feel, despite his telling her he was okay with everything.

"I'm worried about him though," she said.

"Why?" Riley asked.

Blaire looked at Riley. "When they captured me again, they didn't get him. I'm worried something may have happened to him... like my blood finally getting to him. He didn't go crazy the few days he fed from me, but what if the reaction is delayed?"

"I'll look into it," Professor Velastra said. "We'll find out what happened to him." The phone on her desk rang, and she lifted the receiver. "Soomin Velastra speaking."

The room fell silent. Professor Velastra stared at Blaire, lines tight around her eyes as she tried to maintain her poker face but failed.

"Yes, yes... Of course... I will prepare them... No... She will need a passport, yes... Right... The others are well traveled... No, he probably doesn't. One moment." Professor Velastra placed a hand over the receiver. "Lukas, do you have a passport?"

"I do. Mom always kept mine up to date, even though I've never used it."

She put the phone to her ear. "He has one… Yes, of course. I'll prepare them… You as well… Goodbye."

Blaire studied the professor, unsure what to make of the one-sided conversation.

The professor sat studying all of them, then said, "That was the head of affairs in the Blackthorn Clan's manor outside of London."

The seed of unease bloomed into curling vines of anxiety.

"We are officially summoned to the manor to stand before King Adrian Blackthorn to make our witness statements as to what occurred. Specially, he wants a detailed summary directly from Blaire of her experiences since joining the academy. He has conceded to having you do as you did for Vincent's trial, making a report he can study prior to meeting you, as it is a lot of information."

She looked at Aiden and Riley. "Your presence, as well as Seth's, is also requested for witness statements as to what you've experienced, and what happened when the Order was apprehended."

Aiden crossed his arms and shrugged. "Whatever is necessary. When?"

"Due to several events happening around the monarchy this month, we won't be able to gain audience until sometime in March, which gives you time over the next couple of weeks to get your statements together and prepare what you need for travel. You will be excused from classes and given time to make up what you miss. I advise having this done sooner rather than later, in case they summon us at the start of March."

Blaire twisted the edge of her skirt. "What about my passport? I've never had one of those."

"There's no way she can get one in two weeks," Lukas said.

Professor Velastra nodded her concession to Lukas. "Usually, no.

The liaison working with the Blackthorn Clan has agreed to speak to the appropriate authorities to expedite the process."

Aiden shook his head. "Pulling rank in human government to expedite a single passport is surprising."

"Apparently, King Blackthorn has been eager to close this case on Angelo Moretti, and the other members of the Order, for quite some time." She stood from her desk and looked out the window behind her. "I will speak to your other professors. Inform Seth, and speak of this to no one else."

"But Mera, Kai, and Layla are always with us. Can't we tell them? I mean, Charlotte we can't tell, but she's leaving soon for college, so it's easy to keep it secret there." Riley sighed and kicked her leg out, her boot buckles jangling as she pouted.

Professor Velastra arched a slender brow at the childlike behavior. "Your trusted inner social circle is different. Your human friend can simply believe you're taking a school sanctioned trip. It is imperative no one outside of that circle knows to prevent problems."

The idea of traveling to another country had always excited Blaire, but she thought she'd never have a chance. Faced with actually going out of the country, she twitched with nerves. Not for the traveling, but at the possibility of danger waiting for her. If Professor Velastra was serious, she now wore a target on her back. For something more than being a mere human.

She was the last of her kind from the old days.

The last witch.

At least until she found a way to wake those born with dormant blood.

Final Note from the Author

Thank you for picking up (or downloading) my book and completing it. I hope you loved it as much as I loved creating it. I appreciate every one of you.

If you enjoyed this book, and the others, please consider leaving a written review. Indie authors rely heavily on the reviews of their readers to make it in the self publishing world, and sites like Amazon, use those reviews to determine visibility.

Stay in Touch

Join Stephanie over on Facebook in Stephanie Denne's Book Sanctuary Facebook Group! It's a place to discuss current works, future works, and interact directly with Stephanie.

https://www.facebook.com/groups/743979797516659

Social Media

TikTok: https://www.tiktok.com/@stephaniedenneauthor

Facebook: https://www.facebook.com/stephaniedenneauthor

Instagram: https://www.instagram.com/stephaniedenneauthor/

Newsletter

Sign up for Stephanie's Newsletter to keep up to date on the latest news around the Blackthorn world and future series, and get special sneak peeks at the writing process and chapter previews for future books.

http://eepurl.com/h_N5uP

About the Author

Stephanie Denne is an author of Paranormal Romance and Dark Fantasy for new adults and adults. The Blackthorn Saga marked her debut in the literary world.

Inspired by art and music, she felt the need to give life to characters that had been rolling around in her mind for 12 years. Never having written anything before, when she sat down and started drafting, she discovered she had a passion for the craft and the story naturally grew into something much bigger than she could fit into one book—much less a few, or even one series!

Born in the United States of America in the Southeast, Stephanie has now called Ontario, Canada her home since 2011. When not writing, she can be found reading her favorite stories, playing video games with her husband, painting with watercolor, or cuddling with her two Golden Retrievers. But not the cat—the cat has her own agenda.

ACKNOWLEDGMENTS

To everyone who supported me through the creation of Sanguine Prophecy, I want to extend a huge thank you. Navigating the world of self publishing as a rookie writer isn't always easy but having a strong support system from not only my husband and friends, but readers who have reached out to me along the way after reading book one and two of the Blackthorn Saga has been an exciting journey.

Thank you to my wonderful editor Kelly for helping me build and grow the world of Blackthorn. Helping me expand and be a better writer without squashing my voice, while maintaining patience and keeping me on track, makes our partnership one I will never forget. Thank you so much.

www.ingramcontent.com/pod-product-compliance
Lightning Source LLC
Chambersburg PA
CBHW020522310726
48979CB00014B/2170/J

* 9 7 8 1 7 3 8 7 2 7 2 7 8 *